Wife
in the
Fast Lane

◄••••••••••••••••••••••••► A NOVEL

Karen Quinn

A TOUCHSTONE BOOK
PUBLISHED BY SIMON & SCHUSTER
LONDON NEW YORK TORONTO SYDNEY

TOUCHSTONE
Rockefeller Center
1230 Avenue of the Americas
New York, NY 10020

TOUCHSTONE and colophon are registered trademarks
of Simon & Schuster, Inc.

For information regarding special discounts for bulk purchases,
please contact Simon & Schuster Special Sales at 1-800-456-6798
or business@simonandschuster.com.

Designed by Sue Walsh

Manufactured in the United States of America

10   9   8   7   6   5   4   3   2   1

Library of Congress Cataloging-in-Publication Data
Quinn, Karen.
    Wife in the fast lane : a novel / Karen Quinn.
            p.   cm.
        1. Businesswomen—Fiction. 2. Parent and child—Fiction.
3. Women athletes–Fiction. 4. New York (N.Y.)—Fiction. I. Title.
    PS3617.U575 W54 2007
    813'.6—dc22   2006050076

ISBN-13: 978-0-7432-9396-9
ISBN-10:   0-7432-9396-7

To my husband and my children,
who keep me running in the fast lane,
and to my friend, Tan.

Acknowledgments

Trish Todd and Kate Lyall Grant, thank you so much for your editing advice and guidance throughout this project. Special gratitude also to Suzanne Baboneau, Sarah Nundy, Shari Smiley, Nigel Stoneman, Robin Straus, Sally Wilcox, and Stuart Calderwood. You are all brilliant at what you do, and I'm beyond lucky to work with you.

To my family: Mark, Sam, and Schuyler Quinn, I love you so much. Sam, now do you think it was worth it for me to work on weekends? To my first family, Shari and Sonny Nedler, Michael and Don Nedler, and Monica—Mwwwwah! That's me throwing you a big kiss. And to Beverly Knowles and Kathleen Stowers, you are goddesses in my eyes. What would I do without you?

There are so many other people to thank who made *The Ivy Chronicles* such a success, and who helped bring *Wife in the Fast Lane* to life. Writing a first book opened my eyes to how many friends and cheerleaders I have in the world. I will always remember the support and inspiration each of you offered along the way. Special *merci beaucoup*s to: Matt Autterson, Paula Bailey, Andrea Bardach, Carol Becker, Elizabeth Buchan, George and Betty Buckley, Nancy Bowling, Meris Blumstein, Ellen Bregman, Scott Bond, Rick Bruner,

Tiffany Cammarano, Alison Chase, Claire Chasnoff, Kevin Che, Jane Cleland, Jennifer Cohen, Vicki Conway, Stacy Creamer, Kelly and Michelle Curtis, Catherine Cusset, Robin Daas, Drew Davies, Jennifer Deare, Lisa Drapkin, Trish Duval, Randy Dwenger, Kathy Dwyer, Carole Fetner, Amanda Filipacchi, Judy Finnigan, Robyn Spizman Friedman, Brian Fun, Mark Goldberg, Victoria Goldman, Ken Gomez, Shelly Griffin, Rita Gunzelman, Kathy and Johnny Herman, Richard Hine, Phyllis Horowitz, Pat Hurlock, Ron Hogan, Carole Hyatt, Marla Isackson, Scottie Iverson, Tracey Jackson, Rachel Jones, Charles Jordy, Barbara Kantor, Janice Kaplan, Jill Kargman, Kathy Kaye, Holly Kylberg, Susan Kleinberg, Vicki Kline, Judith Levy, Pat Lipton, Lois London, Richard Madeley, Bonnie Marson, Murray Miller, Alexandra Morehouse, Kirsten Mullen, Cindy Ng, Eva Okada, Candice Olson, Allison Pearson, Victoria Pericon, Beth Phoenix, Amy Pizzarello, Chopin Rabin, Alessandro Ricciarelli, Nancy Salz, Ariel Sandberg, Michael Schneider, Leslie Schnur, Gail Schupak, Kathleen Smith, Linda Spector, Augusta Sterne, Sally Stitch, Brooke Stachyra, Kim Stroumbos, Marie Tambero, June Watson, Katharine Weber, Danna Weiping, George Wilman, Lynne, Vic, Wendy, Janet, and Ted Quinn, and Catherine Zeta-Jones.

PART 1

Working

Girl

We're in for a Rough Ride

L ook for Highway 380. That's our exit," Katherine said. "I'm looking, I'm looking. According to this map, we have a ways to go." Christy checked her watch again. It would be close. If they could keep up this speed and not get lost, they should make it with just enough time to change their clothes. *There it is! There it is!* Get in the right lane."

"Jesus, you said we had a ways to go." Katherine swerved and the Taurus careened across three lanes, miraculously avoiding at least five collisions and inspiring a cacophony of horn honking. "*Oh my God,*" Christy said as she covered her eyes and ducked. Katherine was silent, intent on getting them to Menlo Park before two. When their plane had landed in San Francisco, more than an hour late, they'd called the Steiner McClane office. The meeting couldn't be postponed. Mr. Roche was booked solid, then leaving for Europe on Monday.

"Good thing it stopped raining." Christy had the habit of pointing out the positive whenever things got tense. Katherine preferred working up a good head of steam.

"Oh no, *no*, NO," Katherine said, spying the traffic ahead. In seconds, they slowed to a complete stop. "How much time do we have?" she asked.

Christy checked her watch. "Thirty-two minutes," she reported, biting her lip.

"You know, Chris, maybe Baby G Sports wasn't meant to be. It could be a sign," Katherine said.

"It's *not* a sign. There's an accident ahead. See those flashing lights?" Christy climbed into the backseat and unzipped her garment bag. "I'm getting dressed. So *when* we make it, I can run in."

"Good idea. With this traffic, it could take us half an hour, maybe more."

Christy shook her head as she unbuttoned the Chanel jacket. "I still can't believe you made me spend five thousand dollars for this suit." The thought of the amount made her sick.

The cars started moving again. "Trust me, Chris. You have to dress like you don't *need* the money or you won't *get* any. Steiner wants to turn us down, just like those other firms did," Katherine said. She sounded like she knew what she was talking about.

"Do you really believe they're gonna decide based on our outfits? What if they think we're *wasting* money?"

Katherine locked eyes with Christy in the rearview mirror as she spoke. "Chris, very few women ever get seen by these guys. Our performance has to be perfect or it's over. Could you have won the Olympics in a pair of Hush Puppies? No. This is the same thing."

"*Watch out*," Christy shouted as Katherine barreled into the back bumper of a Cadillac changing lanes in front of them.

"*Shit!*" Katherine yelled. "*Did you see the way that asshole cut me off? He never signaled!*" She pulled over to the side of the road, behind the Cadillac, and stopped. A red-faced man leaped out of the luxury sedan and inspected the damage, then began screaming and raging, waving his hands in the air.

"Why didn't you slow down?" he ranted. "For Christ's sake, couldn't you *see* I was pulling over?"

Christy was overwhelmed by a sudden and profound sadness. Is this it? Is this how the story ends? In her mind, she saw her fledgling company's life flash before her eyes: the first meeting around the dining room table; the moment Sasha, queen of hip-hop, bounded onstage in a pair of Baby G's; herself and Katherine collapsing in laughter the next day as the orders poured in.

"I *did* signal, dammit," Katherine was saying. "*Look!* My light's still blinking."

As they argued, Christy came to a decision. She stuffed her laptop and a pair of heels into her backpack. She put on her running shoes and slipped out of the car.

"I'm outta here," she shouted.

Katherine checked her watch. "You have fourteen minutes."

Back on Track

ive minutes later, torrential rain slashed down against the asphalt highway. Then it grew lighter. Then it poured again. Christy kept moving. A little water can't slow me down, she thought, imagining herself at the Olympic Trials, her father cheering her on. Christy threw her whole body into the run, head high, chest out, legs burning, heart pounding. She picked up the pace, flying over wet gravel, broken glass, cigarette butts. From the Sandhill Road off-ramp she put on her finishing kick, sprinting the last four hundred meters to Steiner McClane headquarters. Soaked to the skin, she stopped to catch her breath under their arched entry. Her legs were trembling, not used to running hard anymore. She couldn't believe how winded she was and vowed to add interval work to her training regime. Okay, you look like hell. You feel like hell. But you're on time, she thought.

Walking inside with less than a minute to spare, Christy caught the eye of the receptionist. The woman was pretty, perky, and athletic, which seemed to be the prereq at these West Coast firms. She gave Christy a look of confused recognition.

"Hi, I'm Christy Hayes."

"Oh my goodness. The bathroom's in there," the receptionist said, pointing toward a door. "In case you want to, ah, freshen up."

"Thanks."

"Bill's running about ten minutes late, so take your time."

In the bathroom, Christy looked in the mirror. She pulled a brush out of her dripping bag. Doing what she could with her hair, she left it wet and loose. Using Kleenex, she wiped the mascara stains off her face. She blotted her suit with paper towels and changed into her heels.

Christy took a deep breath, and walked back to the reception area. She looked around for the first time. The place felt like a modern cathedral, all glass and soft cream carpets. Unlike companies housed in New York skyscrapers, this was all on one floor. In California, power could spread out instead of stacking up.

Two dozen trim men dressed in office casual took note of her arrival. As Katherine said, not many women made the grade to get a meeting with this legend of venture capital. And Christy was a girl you couldn't help but notice, even soaked through—a trim brunette, shoulder-length hair, long defined legs. So far, she hadn't met a man who could quite deal with her looks, her obsession with work, and her athletic notoriety. Everyone assumed that men were falling all over her, but in fact, the only ones she ever saw were her employees and accountants. A few weeks shy of her thirtieth birthday, though, she remained hopeful.

Christy was sure that her future husband wasn't among these timid gatekeepers. She had imagined venture capitalists as adventurers, but from what she had seen, they were more like sheep. Nobody wanted to say yes until the guy down the block did, and then they got into a competitive feeding frenzy. So far, no one was willing to take a chance on Baby G, and now it all came down to this last hour to make Steiner Mc-Clane believe in them. *Her.* She realized she would be alone today. No Katherine with her brilliant mind and intimate understanding of the numbers.

"Bill will be ready in five. Would you like something to drink?" The receptionist walked Christy over to an open kitchen full of yogurt, fruit, candy bars, and bottled iced teas with Zen-looking labels. Christy grabbed two bags of peanut M&M's—when nervous, she was helpless in the face of sugar. She hoped Bill's delay would give her time to scarf down both bags.

A tall, lanky redhead with brown eyes and a warm smile walked up and introduced himself. He didn't need to: Bill Roche, venture capitalist par excellence, one of the few who had achieved name-recognition status in the wider business world. He was thin and wiry in that healthy California way. He looked like someone she might actually like to get to know, not like the other bean counters she had met this week.

"Christy Hayes?" he said, shaking her hand. "Did you fall in a lake?"

Christy laughed, relieved that Bill had a sense of humor. "No, we were delayed flying in. Then I ended up running here when our car got stuck in traffic. Sorry I'm such a mess," she said, looking down, suddenly mortified.

"Not at all. I'm impressed that you ran to make it. Lucky for you we don't make investment decisions based on appearance," he laughed.

"Of course you don't," Christy said. "That would be nuts." She wished Katherine had heard him say that.

"I've been looking forward to meeting you, Christy. What you've accomplished is really something. Hopefully, we can help you take it further. Let's go to my office and talk."

Christy had the strongest surge of hope since leaving New York a week ago. She floated down the wide, cushiony breezeway to a large, open room, all tropical greenery outside the glass. Bill motioned for her to sit at his small conference table made of beautiful inlaid walnut. She switched on her laptop, which remained absolutely mute. Her panic rose as she tapped the keys. Nothing. She tapped harder. Water began to seep from the case onto the table. The black screen stared back at her. Usually she did the vision thing while Katherine presented the numbers and fielded those questions. Today she was on her own. No Katherine. No numbers. No safety net.

Slowly, Christy closed the laptop. Her panic was giving way to the same adrenaline she used to feel at the starting line of a race. Just as she was poised to take off, Bill said, "Stop! Let me call an associate in to join us. Then I want to hear your story, start to finish."

In walked a familiar face, and, sad to say, a familiar body. David Baum. He had been with an investment group Christy met with three years ago, just as Baby G was getting off the ground. Like the others they approached then, no one at David's firm would back a girl Olympian trying to break into the competitive world of athletic footwear, and Christy was treated dismissively at each meeting. But she and David had connected. A hot romance ensued. She had fallen hard for him, and it seemed mutual. They alternated between New York and San Francisco on weekends and became familiar faces on the red-eye. But in the end, Christy couldn't build a company and keep a bicoastal relationship going. She ended it badly, as she did many personal things in those early days of struggle, just for lack of the energy and time to do it right.

Now David and Christy looked at each other. She blushed,

and he, smooth as all bankers, moved to cover his emotions. *Dammit*, of all the pitch meetings in all the towns in all the world, he has to walk into mine, Christy thought miserably.

But she composed herself quickly and told Bill and David her story. How they had gotten started using Christy's commercial endorsement money to stake the company; their market victories; the opportunities for growth. Bill asked completely different kinds of questions than the other bankers they'd met. He wanted to know how Christy handled disappointments, to hear about the mistakes they had made, things they usually kept under wraps in these gigs. He asked about the toughest decision she'd had to make, and she told them about the time their fall line came in from the manufacturer with a small defect in the architecture of the sole of their flagship model. They decided to pull the shoes, even though it almost put them out of business. Christy felt that Bill understood what it was like to be an entrepreneur; to be lost much of the time, but to have the kind of grit that keeps you going anyway. Christy could feel she was in her zone. She was known for her power of persuasion—part passion, part looks, part vision. She hadn't felt it with the other venture sheep this week, but with Bill, this High Priest, she was soaring.

Just before the meeting ended, David pulled his lean, athletic frame up and excused himself for another presentation, suggesting to Bill that they talk later. Christy shot him a pleading look as he stood to leave. She could read nothing in his eyes, even though he was looking right at her.

Bill spent twenty more minutes with Christy, and she could tell he was going to say yes.

"Christy, it was great to meet you," he said. "I was *really* impressed with your presentation. I just want to get David's take. It's good that you two know each other. Personal references are everything with us."

Christy smiled weakly and swore herself to chastity for life, or at least to dating only gorgeous waiter-actors unlikely to show up when her entire future was on the line. She hoped with all her heart that David would act in the interest of the firm—and not hold their failed relationship against her.

Christy shook Bill's hand and headed for the exit. She grabbed a few more bags of M&M's as she passed the kitchen. She had kept Bill interested for over an hour. He was known for his short attention span. Anything over thirty minutes was considered a done deal.

When Christy finally emerged, Katherine was waiting outside the office in their rented Taurus, with its crushed left hood. As she got in, Katherine gave her a look that Christy instinctively understood. "Yeah, I think we have a real shot. I do." She gave Kath the blow-by-blow as they drove off toward San Francisco. "Bill was great; he was really excited about our business."

"Christy, what is it?"

"Well, um . . . there *was one thing* . . ."

A Lucky Game of Rock, Paper, Scissors

An hour later, they sat at the airport TGI Friday's, chowing down on Philly cheese steaks. Ever since they began their money-raising trek, they found themselves eating as much red meat as they could—steak sandwiches, bloody sirloin, prime rib. Gone were the dainty salads of watercress, red peppers, cucumbers, and carrots. They were warriors who needed meat.

After two beers, the women were still handicapping the outcome. Katherine was sure they were screwed. A proud alpha male like David Baum would never let pass a chance to even the score. Christy tried to be optimistic. Certainly we were all grown-ups here, able to separate love and money, she said.

"Oh, yeah," Katherine howled. As usual, she regaled Christy with three sordid stories proving her point. The Harvard professor who gave her a B on her business ethics exam because she'd said no to a blow job the night before. The senior partner of a major consulting firm who offered her a plum position, *if* she'd become his lover, which she did—but as soon as he tired of her, the firm gave her a promotion to their Korean office, which amounted to firing her. The jilted boyfriend who happened to be a client of the next consulting company Katherine joined. He refused to do business with them unless she was taken off the team.

Christy had heard such stories about Katherine from others in New York, but she ignored the gossip. Katherine was a loyal second in command who was excellent at her job. Wasn't that all that mattered? Until today, she couldn't imagine how Katherine's sex life could come back to haunt them. Now she wasn't so sure. Even her own tepid past might cost them everything.

✺

"There's just one seat left in first class," the ticket agent said, looking at her computer.

"I'll take it," Katherine volunteered.

"Kath, c'mon. That's not how we make decisions at Baby G," Christy said, wagging her finger and laughing despite total exhaustion.

"Fine," Katherine said. "Ready. Rock, paper, scissors says *shoot.*" Katherine beamed when she saw that her scissors beat Christy's paper. "I won!" She looked at Christy, who appeared to be at breaking point. "Take it, Christy. You deserve it."

"Thanks, Kath," Christy said, giving her a hug. "Okay, I'll see you in New York. They're boarding first class."

Christy's phone rang as she stood in line to take her up-graded seat. She jumped for the cell, accidentally elbowing the next traveler, a stoop-shouldered road warrior who looked even worse than she felt. Christy apologized, but he swore at her anyway.

She cupped the phone to her ear and tried to hear over the gate announcements. It was Bill Roche. The moment he started talking, she could tell it was "no." He was kind, but said that his firm was very collegial and any partner could veto a deal. Apparently David didn't feel comfortable. Bill said he was sorry, that he was sure they would find their money. Christy's face crumpled. She wanted to start begging, "No, no, you were our last chance, *pleeeaase . . ."*

She didn't know how she managed to get off with her dignity intact, but as soon as she clicked off the phone, tears began to splosh down her cheeks. It was over. Three years of her life, all her money, people who would have to be fired.

Christy was pissed off. But mostly she was humiliated. How could her sex life, which had seemed almost nonexistent, have hurt the company so badly? People she loved would lose their jobs because she had been too busy to end her relationship like a grown-up. It was unforgivable. Dear God, she prayed, if you could somehow find it in your heart to help me rescue my company, I promise I will never mix business and pleasure again. I'll devote my life to Baby G and all the employees who depend on me. I'll swear off men completely. Just please help me save what I worked so hard to build.

Taking her seat, Christy willed herself to stop crying after noticing the stares she was getting from fellow first-class travelers. The iPod-absorbed rapper wearing pounds of bling. The rumpled salesman rushing home for the weekend. The tanned matron with dramatic black hair who probably paid full price for her ticket. Christy felt the force of their collective sneaky glances. Turning to the passenger next to her, who looked like the fatherly type, she smiled bravely.

"Boyfriend troubles?" he asked kindly.

"No, worse. It's my company." Christy went on to tell the gray-headed stranger what happened. She had to talk to someone. And odds were, this elegantly dressed executive wearing a gold Rolex and traveling first class would appreciate her plight. "After all that work and sacrifice, it's come to this. I just . . . I refuse to believe it," she said.

"You did your best. Eight out of ten new businesses don't make it."

"That's what my board said when I presented our worse-case scenario. The fact that they accepted defeat so easily just made me try harder. I was so *sure* I could win this one."

"I've been in business a long time. You gotta know when to walk away. It sounds like you have great experience you can parlay into a job; don't worry."

"But that's the thing, I don't *want* a job. I've put everything into *this*." Her eyes started to well up again, but thankfully, a flight attendant came by and offered water, orange juice, and champagne. Christy helped herself to a glass of bubbly and slugged it down. By the time she turned back to her seatmate, she was in control.

"The frustrating thing is, we were *so* close. We would have been in the black in two years. The Olympic Committee is considering us for the official shoe of the Games. They're tired of the sports shoe giants who are always throwing their weight around; they want to give one of the little guys a chance. You know, send a message. It's a once-in-a-lifetime opportunity. We were gonna use the money we raised to pay the sponsorship fee."

"When was all this supposed to happen?"

"In the next month. The deal hasn't been approved for sure, but they said we're a *shoe-in*. Ha-ha." The champagne was starting to kick in.

"I see you've kept your sense of humor," the man said, smiling. "By the way, I'm Niles Raines."

"Niles Raines? Raines Partners?"

"That's the one. Tell you what, after we take off, why don't you give me your pitch? Our firm represents sophisticated high-net-worth clients who look for unusual investment opportunities. Maybe we can syndicate the deal for you."

If Christy had been Katherine, she would have offered the man a blow job right then and there.

           ∽

Ten days later, they presented to five of Raines Partners' clients, offering them two points in the company for every four-million-dollar unit purchased. The five investors committed to four million each, contingent on the Olympic opportunity coming through. They insisted on that point, believing that the sponsorship would ensure the company's success. Without it, they weren't willing to take the risk.

While Christy waited for word from the Olympic Committee, she ate chocolate. Lots of chocolate. She ran around the Central Park Reservoir three times every morning, then three more times in the evening. She turned her cell phone off so she wouldn't jump every time it rang. And when she spoke to the Olympic guys, she tried not to sound desperate.

Finally, she got a call from the sponsorship director. He was wavering. There was so much pressure to play it safe. They were worried about backing a company that might not be around in two more years. He said it might be better for everyone if they waited until next time, let Baby G build its track record.

Christy played it cool. If she let him know how much she needed this, it would prove his point. She managed to find out that it was his boss who was against it. Christy got on a plane the next day, determined to change the man's mind.

୧୨

On a Monday, two weeks later, she made an announcement to the whole company at once. They had to rent an indoor basketball court from a nearby high school in order to accommodate all three hundred employees. She'd decided to tell them the truth. Katherine felt that total candor was a mistake; that employees couldn't understand all the complexities of the business. Christy almost always took Katherine's advice, but on this, she knew she was right. The reason her people trusted her was because she always leveled with them.

The gym was set up with bleachers, three hundred chairs, and an old floor-stand mike. She stepped out in front of her people and began to talk.

"Well, we're still here, all of us. After so many close calls. This one was maybe the closest, guys, and I'm glad that now I can tell you about it." She talked about the events of the last month, the road trip, the Niles Raines meeting, the Olympic deal. She left out only the part about how a tall sexy banker almost cost all of them their jobs.

"When we started, we knew we were going up against the Big Boys, and everyone said we had no chance. There were lots of times I thought they were right, that I had led you all on a fool's mission.

"And at those times, you were the ones who still believed, and who kept me going. Well, today, the Big Boys have seen us do what we've known we could do all along. That we are the future, and that their best days are behind them." There were cheers as the group became rowdier.

"Now we're playing a new game. We aren't the company out on the fringe that no one worries about. Now we've taken a piece of their action. Now they'll come after us with everything they have.

"All of us will have to step up our game. And I'll be standing behind each of you as you do, so that we can create the next worldwide brand."

As she came to a close, no one made a sound. But then the whole crowd was on their feet, clapping and stomping and whooping. Christy looked around. Okay, that's it. My life belongs to Baby G now.

Fifth Avenue Freeze-out

*E*ight years later . . .

After Baby G went public, Katherine insisted that Christy shape up and live like a New York City power woman. Though Katherine never came out and said it, it was obvious she found Christy's early sense of style to be just short of tragic. First she led her to Bergdorf's for wardrobe, John Barrett for hair, and Mimi Amurri for makeup lessons. Then she introduced her to manicures, pedicures, facials, and wraps. She found her a personal shopper, a presentation coach, a publicist, and a therapist. Katherine helped Christy understand that success in Manhattan carried an obligation to look and live the part.

On a flight to Mexico to visit their manufacturing plant, Christy suggested that they share their new wealth with the employees, even the secretaries. "I'm thinking we give everyone in management two thousand dollars, and five hundred to support staff. That leaves a hundred thousand for each of us. Sounds fair, right?"

"More than fair," Katherine said. "It's so you to be generous like that, but maybe we should hold back just a little. What if next year isn't as profitable? Everyone will expect at least the same amount. That's three hundred thousand dollars. It might be more prudent to set the bar a little lower, give us time for some growth."

The pilot interrupted with an announcement. "Ah, ladies and gentlemen, the control tower has put us in a holding pattern due to weather. We're expecting some light chop, so I've put the seat-belt sign on. If everyone could please stay in their seats, we'd sure appreciate it."

"So you think a thousand for managers and two-fifty for the support staff would be about right?" Christy asked, tightening her belt.

"Better, definitely better," Katherine said. "Although, that leaves less than two hundred thousand for each of us. I don't think anyone would begrudge you and me taking a bit more than that. We've sacrificed for this company in ways no one else has. Think about what we've been through—the late nights, the road shows, my marriage breaking up. Geez, you haven't even had time to start a relationship. Maybe we should think about two twenty-five for each of us and split the last fifty among the staff. It's not like they're expecting a bonus. And they all got stock in the public offering."

"Well, that's true," Christy said, "but I think they deserve something now that we've come so far. They've worked hard, too."

"And I totally agree," Katherine said, gripping her armrest as the plane weathered the turbulence. "They've earned a reward. But at the same time, now that we're public, it's important to the company that you and I finally buy our own apartments. We need places to entertain and to show the world that we're part of the Manhattan power scene. Nothing says you've arrived like an apartment in the right building."

Christy sighed. "What do you have in mind?"

A flight attendant walked by, checking to see that everyone was wearing a seat belt.

"We're buckled," Katherine told her as she whizzed past. "I really think, and I mean this for the good of the company, that you and I should split the entire five-hundred-thousand-dollar bonus pool. If we each cash in five percent of our stock, we'd have enough for down payments on apartments. We can do something very generous for our people, like throw them a big party. They'd love that."

"You think it's *that* important for us to have our own apartments?" Christy asked. "More important than giving bonuses to our people?"

"It is, Chris," Katherine said. "Trust me on this. Personally, I couldn't care less about owning, but Wall Street notices senior management who live in rental buildings. And believe me, it's not helping our reputations."

"I'd like to do more for the staff than just give a party," Christy said.

"And we can," Katherine said. "In fact, why don't we give everyone an extra free pair of our shoes? They'd flip over that."

Christy thought about it for a moment. She had really looked forward to giving everyone their first bonus checks. But if Wall Street actually cared where she lived, she supposed she had better live in the right place. "All right," Christy said. "This year, we buy homes. Next year, everyone gets cash."

"Absolutely," Katherine said.

෨෬

"So, it says here that you're not married," said Mr. Gibbons, the board president. "Are you seeing anyone?" Mr. Gibbons resembled your basic Bowery bum. People were always shocked to learn that he lived on Fifth Avenue and employed a manservant named Pierre.

"Oh no," Christy said. "I live a quiet life. Between starting my company, taking it public, growing it the way we have, it's a wonder I have time to work out anymore." She took a sip of water to wet her parched throat.

"When you do work out, do you walk through your lobby in your exercise clothes?" Mrs. Rich asked in an accusing tone. She was the type of woman who believed nice girls shouldn't sweat.

"Of *course* not," Christy said, trying not to sound defensive, as Meris Blumstein, her real estate agent, had advised her. "I belong to a gym and I change there."

Christy was on the receiving end of one of Manhattan's most reviled rituals—the co-op board interview. She had told Meris to find her a condo so she could avoid this humiliation, but then an apartment at 830 Fifth Avenue came up. The place was exactly what she had been looking for, except that it was a co-op, which meant that she'd have to pass inspection by board members who probably couldn't get in themselves if they were applying today. Christy sat at the round walnut table in the building's airless boardroom. She couldn't have felt more exposed if she were lying on her gynecologist's examining table covered by a thin paper gown.

"It says here that you're only putting down fifty percent. Is there a reason you need to take out such a big mortgage?" Mr. Crackstone asked, squinting as he read Christy's board package. Manny Crackstone prided himself on his good head for numbers. *Feet in the stirrups, young lady. This instrument may feel a little cold.*

"Well, after my company went public, I sold a million dollars' worth of founder's shares. The money will be applied to this down payment. But the bank has no problem giving me the mortgage. I'm pledging my stock options as collateral."

"And what if your stock goes down?" Mr. Crackstone pressed. "*Then* how will you cover your mortgage payments? You don't have much in savings. We like to see three times the value of the apartment in the bank at a minimum." *I'll just be taking a few cells here for your Pap smear.*

"Well, as you can see on line six," Christy said, pointing her clammy finger at the financial statement he was holding, "I have a generous salary. And I'll be able to exercise more options in a year to bolster my liquidity." Christy would have liked to ask Mr. Crackstone if he had three times the value of *his* apartment in the bank.

"I don't kno-o-ow," Mrs. Rich said, clucking her tongue. "This seems risky to me." *Right now I'm just feeling for your ovaries. Try to relax.*

"Mrs. Rich, on paper, I'm worth almost twenty million dollars. That should give you some sense of security." Christy felt obnoxious saying those words aloud. But she had to defend herself.

Mrs. Rich raised her eyebrows. "Ms. Hayes, we're more interested in *real* worth. Paper worth means nothing to us." *Oh, did that hurt? Sorry about that.*

I'm screwed, Christy thought.

"Do you have any pets?" Mr. Gibbons asked.

"No, and I don't plan to have any."

"How about children?" Mrs. Rich asked. "Your biological clock is ticking. Tell me, are you the kind of woman who would have a child without a husband?"

"Mrs. Rich, I have no plans to marry *or* have a child. I work twelve, fourteen hours a day. You'll hardly notice I'm here."

Mr. Crackstone held up copies of sign-in sheets. "According to the doorman's records, you've been up to see apartment 9G eleven times. Is that true?" *Now I'll be giving you a rectal exam.*

Christy scratched her head. She had no idea. "Maybe. I don't remember. I did visit a lot because I needed to bring my architect up."

"*Reeeally,*" Mr. Gibbons said. "You're planning a renovation? There's nothing in your package about a renovation."

"Not now," Christy said. "I just wanted to know if someday I would be able to make the changes I'm thinking of."

"Sure," Mr. Gibbons said, nodding. *You can take your feet out of the stirrups now.*

"Wait, is it true that you don't like our lobby decor?" Mr. Crackstone asked.

"*What?* Why would you say such a thing?"

"Our doorman mentioned that you made a remark about the mirrored wall we just added," he said.

"He must have heard me wrong," Christy said, furious that the weasel wearing the fake Austrian color-guard uniform was, in truth, a spy for the board. "I love *everything* about this building, *especially* the mirrored wall in the lobby. It makes the room seem so much bigger. In fact, I'll probably mirror a wall in my apartment."

"That's not mentioned in your package," Mr. Gibbons said, leafing through his papers.

"It's another one of those 'someday' things," Christy said.

"Well, thank you, Ms. Hayes. We'll discuss your application and let you know." *Your test results will be available in about a week.*

"Thanks," Christy said, standing and shaking each board

member's hand. She shut the door behind her and walked into the small waiting room where she'd left her coat and packages. Thank God that's over, she thought. As she gathered her things, she overheard the discussion inside.

"Have you *ever?*" Mrs. Rich asked. "As if we'd approve a single girl with her profile."

"Well, we did approve Janette Jaffe. And she was single," Mr. Gibbons pointed out.

"Yes, but she was from a socially prominent family. Her father's president of Winged Foot Golf Club," Mr. Crackstone said. "This woman doesn't have enough in the bank for cushion. What kind of CEO spends all her money on a down payment while she doesn't have a pot to piss in?"

"Mr. Crackstone!" Mrs. Rich said. "*Language!*"

"Sorry."

"Well, we know she's a liar. Who are you going to believe about the mirrored wall? Bobby or *her?* And eleven visits! She may as well have worn a neon sign that she'll be a pain in our backsides," Mr. Gibbons added.

"She's just another wannabe who thinks she can improve her social standing by associating with people like us," Mrs. Rich sighed.

Screw them, Christy thought. What snobs. She swung open the boardroom door to face her detractors. "So I take it I'm rejected?" Christy said.

Mrs. Rich's face turned crimson. "Well, of course we haven't made a decision yet," she said. "You've interrupted our discussion."

Christy rolled her eyes. "Don't bother. I'm withdrawing my application." She turned and walked out, this time for good. There are other apartments in the city, she thought. I'll find something yet.

Guess Who's Coming to Davos

*C*hristy was paying bills in her new study when Maria brought in the fat creamy envelope addressed to her in elegant scroll.

"This just came," Maria said. "It looks like a wedding invitation." Maria Ruiz had been Christy's housekeeper for years. In truth, she was more than that. Part mother, part sister, part loyal friend, it was Maria who waited for Christy with a hot, home-cooked meal every night, who nursed her back to health after her knee operation, who comforted her over failed love affairs—not that there had been many men in the last few years. It was Maria who gave a damn about Christy's day, from the glamorous moments to the boring details.

"*Whoa!*" Christy said, her eyes wide. "I've been invited to Davos."

"What's that?" Maria asked.

"The World Economic Forum in Davos, Switzerland," she explained, "where the most important people in the world get together every year. Everyone who's anyone goes. Except I've never been."

"What do they do when they get there?" Maria asked.

"You know, wheel and deal, share ideas, alter the course of

world events, that sort of thing. I can't believe they even know who I am."

"Well, of course they do," Maria said. "You're a famous athlete. You built a big company. Plus, you're on all those billboards."

Christy googled World Economic Forum and saw picture after picture of the planet's movers and shakers. "Look at who goes," she said. "See, there's the Dalai Lama, the mayor, President Clinton."

"Hrrmph," Maria snorted. "You're just as important as they are. *More* important."

Christy giggled. "Right. Maria, you are the only person in the world who thinks I'm more important than the Dalai Lama, but I love you for that." She stood and gave her a hug. "Now let's go see what's for lunch."

〜

Three months later, Christy arrived in Zurich bleary-eyed, wearing toe-pinching high heels, and schlepping her over-stuffed tote. Even after two Olympics and plenty of business travel, Christy always felt slightly homesick when overseas. However, she never failed to be cheered by Golden Arches, and there they were before her. Grabbing some French fries for breakfast, she continued her trudge to baggage and the big red tour bus. She took a seat in the front, avoiding her fellow jet-lagged delegates. At six A.M., it was too early to face the world's Best and Brightest.

She wished Katherine was with her, but Katherine hadn't been invited. Christy felt bad about that and considered canceling, but she just couldn't. This was too important. It was a chance to raise her company's visibility and make relationships that could mean millions of dollars in profits. If she was honest with herself, there was one other draw. She hoped she might meet someone interesting, though she had been careful not to share this thought with anyone, not even Katherine. Over the last ten years, she had kept her vow and barely dated. Truth be told, working fourteen hours a day wasn't conducive to falling in love. Now, at thirty-nine, with each new level of success she felt a deepening sense of loneliness.

As the bus drove higher and higher into the Swiss Alps, they passed picturesque farms and small mountain villages. She cast a few furtive glances at her bus mates. They looked slightly nerdy, rumpled, and unassuming. Christy couldn't believe that these were the giants who could move markets, shake up governments, and define modern culture.

As she discovered the next day, they weren't. Jimmy Carter, at his Life After Leading session, made a joke that you could tell the big shots by the helicopters they rode in on. A man in the back of the room shouted, "Didn't I see *you* on the bus?" The former president responded with an ear-to-ear grin.

Christy's bus sped past the Royalton Hotel, where the A-list CEOs and heads of state stayed, giving them the advantage of only having to crawl upstairs after the evening drinkfest instead of braving icy streets at the far edge of town. Christy debarked at a hotel that looked like it should be called the Earth Shoe and Granola Lodge. She overheard a famous German Nobel Prize winner cursing his secretary under his breath for forgetting to register him early enough at a more impressive venue. Christy chuckled to herself as he tried to cover his less-than-remarkable status among the world-renowned attendees. Oh well, she thought, at least Davos made me feel important back home.

After checking in, Christy walked over to the conference center in the middle of town. It was a beautiful concrete-and-glass structure that seemed to have been dropped in the midst of old churches, elegant storefronts, and beautiful townhomes that looked like they belonged to the local aristocracy. Davos was centuries old, sitting quietly under a blanket of snow. On one side, the mountains hovered over the town. A gracious alpine valley stretched out below on the other side. Four college-age male snowboarders sporting various facial piercings walked by, giving Christy "the look." Okay, she thought. I haven't lost it yet. That's good news.

Ahead were the tightest security checkpoints she had ever seen. She realized that a person unhappy with the state of the world could wipe out half of its leadership during one coffee break here. As she approached the conference center, two hunky six-foot Swiss guards in full army gear moved together to slow her down. Actually stammering, she told them she was here to register for the World Forum and showed her papers. Wordlessly, they parted again. She had a fleeting image involving black military boots and ripped fishnet stockings. Okay, back to work. Maybe she had kept herself on a short leash a little too long.

Glancing around, she noticed swarms of new arrivals brandishing name badges and official shoulder bags as they darted in and out of small espresso bars, the bookstore where every single book was written by one of the participants, and the VIP section for special members. That was weird. She thought *everyone* here was special. She was fast learning that Davos was a very good imitation of life at her old high school. There were concentric layers of coolness so that only a couple of people in the world could enjoy being in the truly last inner circle with no one to envy or try to displace. They just had to worry about losing their place to the guys coming up the ranks.

At the registration counter, a petite Swiss beauty wearing a Prada-like uniform looked over Christy's choices for sessions, all the while clucking and shaking her head. "Sorry, all full. Sold out. And this, too—no space." She explained patiently, as though to a child, that *everyone* who knows Davos sends their assistants in a day early to register for the hot speakers. Christy had hoped to attend discussions on currency flows, international markets, manufacturing plants in Asia, but she would have to content herself with more esoteric fare.

Christy was directed to the next counter, which held a huge pile of BlackBerries. The young gentleman who was hosting the booth handed her one, and turned it on to demonstrate. He told her that if she wanted to meet any Davos participant, invite them to a party, or have an e-mail conversation, all she had to do was click on his picture. He suggested that she check her mailbox, as she probably had a slew of messages already. She checked. Empty. The ongoing humiliation of being the lowest of the high continued.

For the official opening-night party, she made the trek again, this time navigating the icy sidewalk in spiky heels and a classic black Chanel cocktail dress with a vintage lynx shrug. She thought she made a pretty cool entrance, only to find that none of the bigwigs whose last names need not be mentioned were there—no Warren, no Bill and Melinda, no Hillary. They were all at private parties with their fellow heavyweights.

Still, Christy had an enjoyable evening hobnobbing with first-year CEOs, inventors, musicians, and scientists. She learned something about molecular biology, contemplative strands of Islam, brain activity, and perpendicular data-recording technology. The evening was only slightly marred by the A-list whose absence sent an unspoken message to the party: *You may be important in your own little world, but here at Davos, you are toe jam.*

That's not to say things didn't improve. Christy had been invited to be a panelist during one of the lunch sessions, Building New Brands. She was asked to open with a five-minute talk about how she'd launched Baby G. She arrived an hour early to prepare and to calm her nerves, only to find people already lining up to get in. When she asked Rosemary, the forum organizer, why the crowd, she was surprised to hear the answer. Apparently the draw was the sexy new hotshot—her.

Between the sessions, there was informal talk over croissants and espresso. After her panel, Christy was sought out by bankers and other CEOs who could help her grow the company. On the personal front, she had the advantage of being one of the younger and prettier single women at the event. That, plus her athlete status, was enough of an aphrodisiac to the unattached men to create a mini-stir. On day two, her BlackBerry started vibrating with amazing regularity. "Would you like to have dinner?" the Russian president proposed. "Can I interest you in a sleigh ride and midnight picnic?" a notorious investment banker wondered. "Would you like to get sex in the bed with me?" a prince of suspicious lineage asked.

Christy accepted the invitation of Francis Rich, managing director of Cantor Farrar, who had attended her session. Coincidentally, he was the estranged husband of that ghastly woman on the co-op board at 830 Fifth Avenue. They'd recently broken up—Christy had read about it on the *Post's* Page Six. He invited Christy to tag along with him to the most interesting sessions, the coveted parties, and private conversations from which she'd earlier been excluded.

Christy felt like a junior in high school again, when, as a certified geek, she'd been unwelcome at, well, everything until she went out with Ty Schwab, the senior tight end. Then her status was temporarily elevated to low-grade popular.

Fran was as dapper as they came—the sort of blueblood who always wore elegant wing tips and hand-tailored suits with shirts showing the perfect amount of white cuff. Christy thought he was the most sophisticated man she'd ever met. She was so in awe of him that, by his side, she felt flustered and slightly tongue-tied. She didn't know the protocol of dating a Master of the Universe, but she didn't want to blow it.

Like Ty, Fran expected Christy to show her appreciation for the privilege of being on his arm. On the fourth night, he leaned over and suggested they blow off the after-dinner discussion of the day's highlights. He led her outside the hotel and into a waiting sleigh drawn by two huge horses, its backseat heaped with fur blankets. They left the town behind as they turned up a small mountain road past cottages with bright lights inside. Christy could see that Fran was a man with a plan and her job was to go along and be impressed. And she was. The sleigh came to a stop where the snowplow had finished. Beyond them were the towering peaks of the Alps, shimmering in a hazy moonlight. There was a little lamplight from an inn fifty yards away, and they could just hear the slightly drunken voices of delegates heading into eleven P.M. dinners. The driver turned around and nodded at Fran, then left them alone in the sleigh. Christy gulped.

Fran covered her with a warm fur blanket and asked if she wanted anything. Christy had no idea how she was supposed to answer that question, so she mumbled that she was fine, that it was all so beautiful. She was waiting for whatever came next. He traced a finger along her cheekbone and down her throat. Then he told her to take off her clothes.

Christy didn't know what to say, but she couldn't do what he asked. She sat frozen, staring at him.

"Christy, you are beautiful, sexy, smart. No man is going to spend time with you without wanting you. There's no reason to hold back. You deserve to let yourself go once in a while. Look, we're in the mountains, all alone, on a moonlit night. No one will miss us. Why don't you just let me take care of you? Tomorrow you can go back to being a CEO."

Christy prepared her comeback, but as she did, Fran ran his fingertips lightly down her thigh, slipped them between her legs, and began to massage her. She was startled by the wave of heat coming from his hand, and suddenly she wanted more. She took off her clothes, piece by piece, while Fran watched every move.

Later, she got dropped off at the Earth Shoe Lodge, where she sat up watching the sunrise, torn between hope and fear. He seems so interested, so solicitous. *Sure, until you gave him everything.* He said I was intelligent, attractive, and he was so gracious when he put me in a cab to my hotel. *Still, you should have waited* . . . and on and on until finally she pulled on her mukluks and went for a dawn walk through the empty streets, delighted to find a McDonald's sitting incongruously at the opposite end of town.

By Saturday night, Christy was feeling more confident. She'd come alone and done well. She had made dozens of valuable business contacts. Even really accomplished people seemed to find the story of her company notable—that any-one would have the balls to go up against the Nikes and Reeboks of the world. And she thought she had a real shot with Fran. It seemed important to make a memorable im-pression at the closing soiree, the only formal event at Davos.

She glided in gracefully in her black, wispy-as-a-breeze Versace. Even in the freezing Swiss air, the dress made Christy feel hot, with its tiers of sheer chiffon, its leg-revealing slit to the thigh, and its hand-embroidered leaves hiding the ties that held the backless outfit together. She could sense the heads turning, male and female, and realized almost shyly that her lean athletic body would always be one of her great assets, even at a gathering of the powerful and brainy. She just hoped Fran was watching.

Christy grabbed a red wine, then caught up with Fran, who was standing near a table with the Dalai Lama; Andreas Dracopoulos, the shipping magnate, and Galit Portal, the aggressive front-page reporter for the *Financial Journal*. This was the first time Christy had seen Galit in person, and she was spellbound. At six feet two, Galit seemed to tower above her colleagues, who ogled her like love-struck minions, leaning in and looking up in unison. She looked nothing like the stern and bespectacled journalist on the back of the biography she had written about Ian Malik. *Ravishing* was the word that came to Christy's mind. Her legs rose endlessly out of five-inch Lucite heels, sheathed in the sheerest seamed stockings. Above that were a black silk mini and a matching beaded cashmere that made even Christy want to reach out and touch Galit's voluptuous breasts. Her jet black hair fell almost to her waist, and her turquoise eyes seemed to promise intimacy. Galit was as famous for using her long legs and short skirts to gain access to media-shy CEOs as she was for having once been a member of Israel's most elite commando forces, the Sayeret Matkal.

Galit had Fran, Andreas, and the Dalai Lama enraptured and hanging on her every word like lovesick lap dogs. Meanwhile, Andreas's wife and the Dalai Lama's acolyte sat slumped in their seats at the far end of the table, both yawning. Christy wondered if she should call him Dalai, Mr. Lama, or Your Highness if they were introduced. She wasn't certain of the etiquette required in speaking to the Enlightened Being.

Christy gently put her hand on Fran's shoulder to let him know she was there. He ignored her touch, and Galit subtly turned her body about twenty degrees to shut Christy out. Christy rolled her eyes, wishing that Davos were more about business and less about reliving adolescence.

Galit finally stopped pontificating. Instead of introducing her, Fran took Christy by the arm and led her to the side of the room. "Listen," he said, "last night was fun, but I'm a married man with a reputation to protect. I think it would be better if we weren't seen together this evening. But if you want to come to my room later . . ."

"Wait," Christy whispered. "You said you were separated."

"No, the *Post* reported I was separated, but it wasn't true. Don't believe everything you read in the paper."

"Why didn't you tell me you were still with your wife?" Christy could barely breathe, she was so angry. "Is it because . . ."

"I wanted to fuck you?" he said with an amused smile. "What do *you* think? Admit it. You came here looking to get it on . . ."

"What? In your dreams, buddy." Jesus frickin' Christ, Christy thought. I came to Davos and did *this*! She wanted to kill Fran. But all she had was her glass. She flung the rest of her red wine in his face.

Since this was a public event, shots of Fran covered in red wine, and Christy turning on her heel, were captured on tape and replayed repeatedly back in the States on CNN and

CNBC. Even the *Post* got in on the action, running a front-page photo of Fran, looking wet, shocked, and confused. The headline read: BABY, GET LOST!

Hoping to avoid everyone, Christy fled to the empty hotel bar. She grabbed a seat and ordered a gin and tonic in a tall glass with extra lime. Give it up, Christy, just give it up, she thought. You did exactly what you said you'd never do again. You're the CEO of a public company. Love just isn't in the cards for you, sister. Get over it. Move on.

"Bartender, I'll have another," she said. She pulled a pen out of her evening bag and started sketching out a new PR campaign on a cocktail napkin. She had had enough of the world's movers and shakers. It was time to get back to work.

Hiding Out Is Hard to Do

As Christy diagrammed her ideas, the BlackBerry in her borrowed Judith Leiber bag went off. She pulled it out and checked the message. I'D LIKE TO BUY YOU A DRINK IF YOU WON'T THROW IT IN MY FACE. MICHAEL DRUMMOND.

Christy glanced at Michael, who was standing at the other end of the bar. He was a fit-looking man with a solid build that suggested strength. His eyes were dark, his hair was black with gray speckles, and the smile he was giving her was irresistibly lopsided. She'd read articles about him in *Forbes* and the *Wall Street Journal*. Michael was the contrarian who, after graduating from Harvard Business School, didn't want one of those investment-banking jobs his peers coveted. Instead, he took over the movie his roommate shot but couldn't afford to edit. Relying on his Visa-card line of credit for capital, he turned his friend's film into a critical failure but a box-office success. With the proceeds from that project, he bought and revived a flailing magazine venture. This led to the purchase of a book-publishing company, then a production operation, then cable stations. Twenty-five years later, Michael owned the largest privately held multimedia group in the country. And he'd accomplished all this without ever having to get a job. The man had a reputation for being clever, frank, and startlingly outspoken. Some found his directness refreshing; others called him rude. Attractive guy. Tough. Cute butt, too, she thought, sneaking another peek his way. Speaking of asses, don't make one of yourself again. Be polite, but no more.

"Is it safe to join you?" Michael asked as he took the bar stool next to Christy.

"Yeah, sure. My aggressions have been sated for the moment."

"I won't even ask why you did it. Knowing him, he deserved it."

She decided not to go there. "Why aren't you at the party?"

"I followed you out. I've wanted to meet you since that session on Teleportation."

". . . And Other Ways Quantum Physics Can Improve Your Life, right," Christy said, flattered in spite of herself to know that she'd made an impression on such an impressive guy. "That was mind-boggling."

"Not as mind-boggling as you winning the indoor 3k title while training for the marathon."

Christy almost spilled her drink. "Are you a big track fan?"

"Huge," Michael said. "I was the fastest quarter-miler at Andover. There were no black kids in the prep schools then, so I was unstoppable."

"No way."

"Way," he laughed. "Of course, when I got to college, I didn't even make the team. Now I'm one of those track groupies who goes to all the meets."

"*So do I*. Will you be at the Millrose Games next weekend?"

"I wouldn't miss it."

"Do you still run?" Christy asked. He seemed awfully normal for a Master of the Universe.

"Yeah. I'm competing in the Empire State Building Run-Up when we get back."

Christy and Michael talked about their passion for running and soon abandoned the hotel bar in favor of the Jacuzzi on Michael's terrace. Christy was grateful to have a place to hide.

To avoid any misunderstanding, Christy made her intentions clear. "You probably have women falling all over you, but I've sworn off romance for the second time this decade, so you don't have to worry about me . . ."

"Or me. I'm a harmless middle-aged workaholic," he said with a grin.

Since Christy didn't have a swimsuit, she kicked off her shoes, hiked up her gown, and dangled her legs in the bubbling hot water.

Michael changed into his trunks and got in. "This feels *so* good in the cold air. Let me give you one of my bathing suits," he offered.

"Kind of a half solution, don't you think?"

"I can lend you a shirt. They're in the closet."

"I'll be right back." Christy went into Michael's bathroom and took off her clothes. She put on one of his T-shirts, which came down to her thighs. Feeling safely unprovocative, she returned to the Jacuzzi and slipped into the water, sitting carefully on the bottom of his shirt.

The two spent the night drinking champagne and talking about everything. The pecking order at Davos. Their favorite cities. Foods they couldn't stand. Theater. Books. People they knew in common. Their worst fears. Their first loves. It was a relief to have romance off the table. Christy hadn't realized how much of a strain she'd been under, representing Baby G eighteen hours a day.

Michael talked about his childhood. "It was dull. We lived in Paris."

"Paris? *Dull?*" Christy said.

"Paris, *Texas*. Dad was a fireman and Mom a housewife. In high school, I was the only Texan at Andover, on scholarship of course. Summers, I earned my college tuition cooking Mexican food at La Fonda's in Frog Hop."

"Frog Hop?" Christy asked.

"The next town over. Couldn't get a girlfriend to save my life. I always smelled like enchiladas, no matter how often I bathed."

Christy laughed. She liked Michael's energy. He was warm and open. "I love Mexican food, especially Tex-Mex," she said.

"I can't even stand the smell of it anymore." Michael went on to tell Christy how he started his business after college. She knew the story, but wanted to hear every word again from him. Listening gave her a chance to take him in, his droopy eyelids, the laugh lines around his eyes, his messy hair. He was sitting with a kind of formidable grace, unaware of his own magnetism. Christy thought he was the kind of guy you'd instinctively want by your side if anyone tried to give you trouble. She liked that.

When he talked about his daughter, who was in junior high school, and his divorce, his tone changed. His body tensed up, his hands were clenched, and he sounded older, almost bitter. It was a different Michael. He was a little scary.

"Suzanna was a college girlfriend. Things were good. Then we had Ali, and everything changed."

Michael paused, looking away. "Suzanna became so possessive of her, never let Ali spend time with me. She seemed to be worried that I would somehow compete with her. Ali came to think of me as someone just to get money from. Suzanna threw herself into motherhood and society events."

"You don't strike me as a society-ball kind of guy."

"Yeah, it used to make Suzanna crazy. Whenever she'd drag me to a benefit, my hair would be a mess and my tuxedo shirt would look slept-in five minutes after I put it on. Couldn't help it. It just happens. Suzanna used to yell at me that she didn't spend thousands on gowns, jewels, hair, and makeup to be escorted by a guy who looks like the Unabomber in a tuxedo."

"I like your tousled look. It reminds me of Al Pacino," Christy said.

"Oh no, come on, *really?*"

Christy smiled. "Can I pour you another glass of champagne?"

"Absolutely," Michael said, holding out his glass. "So, do I remind you of Al in *The Godfather?*"

"Mmm, noooo . . . I'd have to say *Scarface.*"

He laughed, reached over, and touched her cheek. "You're funny, you know that? Anyway, the year Suzanna became PTA president, I was in a ski accident—almost died."

"I think I read about that."

"She used to visit me in the hospital, when it wasn't clear whether or not I'd make it. But once I was on the mend, she and Ali didn't stop by anymore. They were busy again with their own lives."

"Who took care of you?"

"She hired staff for that. As devoted as they were, a nurse, a chef, a maid, an assistant, and a massage therapist couldn't replace a wife. In fairness, I realized I had left them alone at times the same way when I was building my company. I wanted to start over, to make amends. But it was too late. They'd moved on. Suzanna served me with papers while I was still in the hospital."

"Ouch," Christy said.

"I'll say. After that, all I wanted was to build a relationship with my daughter. But things got worse. Suzanna turned Ali against me, even accused me of molesting her. She had me thrown in jail overnight, thinking I'd settle faster if it all hit the press."

Christy's eyes widened, and she gave Michael a studied look. Surely he couldn't have done anything like *that*. Could he? Maybe men this high-powered were all deranged. She moved away imperceptibly. All she said was "I can't imagine giving someone the ability to hurt me that much."

"Of course it wasn't *true*," Michael said, as though he was reading her mind. "That's a classic tactic in big-ticket divorces. It was awful." Michael looked embarrassed, like he regretted getting into all this.

"I love Ali so much. And to be accused of something so . . ." Michael drifted off. "Suzanna's publicist made sure the story hit the papers. I had to defend myself to my own board."

"Hearing stories like that makes me glad I decided to go it alone," Christy said, finishing her glass of champagne. Michael's experience freaked her out. The red-wine incident was just the tip of the iceberg of what could happen to her if she tried to take on a relationship.

"The judge threw the whole thing out. Anyway, we had a prenup. Before she pulled the child-molestation stunt, I'd offered her a lot more than we'd agreed to, but she wanted to keep Ali away from me. After she got my ass thrown in jail, I wouldn't give her a penny more than the prenup unless she'd let me share custody."

"And she wouldn't?"

"Nope. She finally settled for the contract amount, but grudgingly."

"And that wasn't enough?"

"That's what she said. But if a person can't make ends meet on twelve million dollars in cash plus eighteen thousand a month in alimony, that's just sad, don't you think?"

Christy's eyes widened. She couldn't imagine having that kind of money, let alone thinking it wasn't enough. She still counted every dollar.

"By the time the divorce came through, Ali wasn't speaking to me. We were supposed to have weekends together, but she wouldn't come. After the breakup, I focused on work; *then* my appearance *really* went to hell." He smiled innocently at Christy in an obvious play for sympathy.

She chuckled. To her, he was gorgeous, but she wasn't going to tell *him* that.

"I didn't care. The funny thing was, women *threw* themselves at me. For a former geek, it was nirvana. I dated beautiful girls who were half my age. Predictable, huh?" He laughed. There was that cute, lopsided grin again. As his tone lightened, his whole body uncoiled and he leaned back to extend his legs, looking like a jungle cat stretching after a fight.

"You're just a walking cliché," Christy agreed, shaking her head. She had never felt quite so much in the presence of a king of the hill, dominant even when he seemed vulnerable. Tough exterior. Soft inside. She felt safe. She realized that Fran had made her feel fumbling and inadequate.

"What about you? Tell me the real deal on the freshman who's rocking Davos," Michael said, his dark eyes fixed on Christy's.

She smiled, but the eye contact was making her feel shy.

"Well, I, uh . . . I grew up about a hundred miles south of Chicago. Middle of nowhere, really. Public school with four thousand kids. There was nothing much special about my life except my mom died when I was ten, and then my dad figured out I could run. He was the track coach at Glenbrook High."

"That was convenient," Michael said.

"Dad had never been an involved parent. When it became just him and me, I'd meet him after school and train with his team. I stayed with it when I got to high school."

"Did you love it?" Michael asked. He reached over her and turned the Jacuzzi switch. "The bubbles went off," he explained.

"Well, I loved Dad. Running track was a way to get him to love me back."

"There must have been more to your relationship than that," Michael said softly.

Christy shook her head. "No, there really wasn't. All we ever did together was train. Then we'd eat. Wyatt's Cafeteria every night, seven days a week. Dad's signature meal was chopped steak, green beans, fruit salad, and coconut pie. School. Train. Eat. Sleep. That was my life after Mom died."

"Jesus, how'd you come out of that in one piece?"

"Well, I'm not sure I did," Christy laughed, but Michael looked at her like he really wanted to know.

"Dad used to say that running was the thing that would save me," Christy said. She stopped, noticing how smooth the water felt against her skin. Michael moved closer. His shoulder was almost touching hers. She hoped he'd forgotten what she said about just wanting to be friends. You are so weak, she thought. *Who cares? He's adorable.* You swore off men, remember? *That was an hour ago.*

"Did it work?" Michael asked. He turned so that his shoulder rested against Christy's.

"Did what work?" Christy asked. She was flustered by his touch.

"Did running save you?"

"Oh, right." Pay attention, she thought.

Michael smiled. He seemed well aware of what was distracting her.

Christy acted like nothing was happening. "It taught me I would be fine as long as I won. Dad always told me that the world hates losers. He'd tell me that after every race I lost, even when I came in second. *Especially* when I came in second. And I missed a lot growing up that way. My strongest high school memory is running laps around that red tartan track."

"I'll bet you were popular."

"*Noooo*. My only friends were teammates, and we were pretty competitive."

"Are you and your dad close now?" Michael asked.

Christy looked away. "He died right after the ninety-two Olympics. Heart attack."

"I'm sorry," Michael said.

"Me, too," Christy said. "At least his dream came true, through me."

"You know, I'd heard a lot of your story, but I always wondered how you felt about track, whether you loved it or were pushed."

"I still lie awake a lot at night and feel scared I won't win, whatever that means."

"You know, I've followed you for years. But I was too shy to meet you."

"You, shy?"

"Yeah. I was a nerd in high school. It took years of therapy and financial success beyond my wildest dreams to get over it," Michael said with his lazy smile. He was making her crazy sitting this close. She sat on her hands to keep herself from reaching out to touch him.

"I was a misfit, too," Christy said. "In seventh grade, I was already five-eight, skinny, like a baby giraffe. In fact, that became my nickname in high school, and it stuck, do you remember?"

"Of course," Michael said. "I was in the Montjuic Stadium in ninety-two. We were all yelling 'B-G, B-G, B-G.'"

Christy chuckled. "Right. Baby Giraffe. That's why I named the company Baby G. But trust me, it was no fun being such a gangly kid. I would have liked to disappear, but that's hard when you tower over everyone." As Christy spoke, she watched Michael listen. His face betrayed a mixture of amusement and sympathy.

"Well, I'm gonna call you Beegee from now on," Michael declared. "I like to think of you in the glory days."

"That was a long time ago," Christy said as she started to get out of the water.

Michael watched Christy emerge in the wet T-shirt that clung to her body. She realized this might not have been the best idea.

A few minutes later, she came back onto the terrace wearing one of the hotel's plush robes. Her wet hair was brushed back, and she was carrying a bottle of lotion. Christy filled her champagne flute and his before settling into the chaise longue. She watched Michael drink the bubbly with obvious pleasure.

"I was at the Olympic marathon trials. I saw you qualify," he said.

Christy was startled. "You were? I guess you really are a serious fan. Do you remember how sick I was?"

"No, what was wrong?"

"I thought you might remember because there were all these rumors that I might drop out."

"*Wait.* You had diarrhea while you were running but you still won."

"Right." Christy was embarrassed. It was her moment of glory but humiliating as well. It was the day she realized how important winning was to *her*, not just her dad.

"Gutsy of you to run."

"My dad called it. No Trials, no shot at the Olympic team. But it wasn't only him. The Olympics were my only way out of Glenbrook."

"So why'd you stop running after Barcelona? You could have competed for at least four more years."

"Maybe," Christy said, smoothing her hair with her fingers. "But I got all those commercial deals after I won and they took a lot of energy. Two gold medals were plenty. I decided to go out on top."

"Hard to imagine you could give up all that glamour." Michael stepped out of the Jacuzzi and wrapped a towel around his waist. He sat down next to Christy, watching her.

"Running marathons is *not* glamorous. You must know that. I trained three, four hours a day—endurance work, speed work, drills, weights. When you compete at that level, you become completely one-dimensional. In the end, I wanted more. I thought I could build something lasting for myself. Something no one could take away from me. So I started the company. The funny thing is," Christy said, trying to seem oblivious to Michael's obvious attention, "when you become a CEO, there's no room for anything else, either. Only the most obsessed succeed. Don't you agree?"

"I do. That's partly why my marriage fell apart. But look at it this way—your athletic training prepared you to lead a company," he said.

"It did. It was my MBA," Christy said, smiling.

"You know, you're amazing, Christy. You're beautiful, charming, accomplished. Why do you push so hard?"

"Why do you?" she said, delighted that he thought she was amazing.

"I asked you first."

"I don't know. Ever since I started winning medals, I've had this terrible fear that someday I'll wake up and discover I'm ordinary. So I can't exactly stop and smell the roses, at least not yet. You?"

"I like making decisions, being the guy everyone can count on, especially when it's all on the line. Which is good, because I've never taken orders very well." Michael smiled in a sort of half-embarrassed, half-proud way.

Christy returned the smile. She couldn't reconcile Michael's hard-core reputation with the guy she was sitting with. Maybe it was those dimples. They were so disarming. Silently, she fumbled with the top to the lotion she had picked up in his bathroom.

"Let me help you with that," Michael said, taking the bottle, squeezing the cream into his palm, rubbing his hands together to warm it up. He positioned himself behind Christy, gently pulling her robe about halfway down her back. *Oh my God*, she thought, not quite sure what to do. Michael couldn't see how flushed her face had become.

Moving his hands in a circular motion, he applied the lotion, massaging the kinks out of her neck, working the knots above her shoulder blades. Slowly, gently, with just the right pressure, he moved his hands in parallel lines down Christy's spine, then up and out across her shoulders. He repeated the motion several times, his fingers conforming to the contours of Christy's muscles. She closed her eyes as he stroked her, wishing he would reach in front and caress her breasts. She felt his breath against her neck and waited for him to kiss her or lick her or bite her or suck her or anything he wanted to do. She suppressed a moan while his hands moved rhythmically against her skin. Then he spread his fingers, running them down her back like a rake. A shudder went down her spine, and she let out a helpless cry.

"You're ticklish," he said quietly. When she turned to face him, he had the look of a guy beating a hasty retreat. She wasn't sure what had happened.

Christy looked over and took in the gentle light. "Oh God," she said, "the sun's rising. We've been up all night." She pulled the back of her robe up.

"Do you want to take the gondola to the top of the mountain and watch it?" Michael whispered.

"No, I . . . I can't. I only have stiletto heels and a chiffon gown."

"I can lend you something."

Christy smiled at Michael, taking in those deep-set eyes. They were lovely. "I guess I'd better go. My flight's at one. Thanks for a wonderful night. You've restored my faith." Truth be told, Christy didn't want to leave. But her midwestern values kept her from saying yes to a man too easily, at least not twice in one week.

Michael shifted his weight and looked away, clearly uncomfortable. This is it, Christy thought. He's gonna ask me not to leave, to fly back with him on his jet. He's gonna say he's crazy about me.

"Christy, I'm happy we met. And I'm glad you want to keep this to a friendship, too. I've sworn off serious relationships. That's over for me. Been there, done that."

"Right," Christy said with a forced smile. "Of course."

"Maybe we can go to some track meets together," he said.

"Maybe," she said.

His chauffeur drove them back to her lodge. Michael walked her to the door. After kissing her on the cheek, he said good-bye. Watching him leave, Christy realized that she had fallen head over heels for a man who trusted her to ask nothing more from him than his friendship. Well, at least she hadn't made a fool of herself again.

Love Has No Pride

or God's sake, Christy, I've gotten calls from a dozen shareholders. I've had to defend you to all of them. But, frankly, I have the same question. Red wine? What were you thinking?"

Normally undone by criticism from Katherine, Christy just threw herself back into the work she loved while she waited for the phone to ring. The quarter was ending and there was plenty to do getting ready for the analyst's call and trying to close a few deals before the end of the period. She was spending a lot of time with Katherine on the numbers, which were looking good. For their young public company, every quarter mattered doubly now as they proved themselves in this new league.

A week went by. Two. Three. Four. Christy felt like she'd slammed against a brick wall. If Michael had felt even a tenth of the connection she had, he wouldn't be able to keep his vow of a friendship. So why hadn't he called?

On a Friday, Katherine took Christy out for a peace lunch. She couldn't stay mad at her friend for long, especially watching her slide into this state over Michael Drummond, a man who obviously didn't care for her. They headed for the Trattoria Dell'Arte, their favorite local bistro. They were deep in conversation about a key employee who had recently threatened to quit.

Suddenly, Christy felt Katherine tense up. She looked over to see Michael Drummond holding the door to the bistro for a lanky twenty-something brunette. Katherine gently took Christy's arm and led her away. They passed the restaurant staring straight ahead. Katherine kept saying, "Breathe."

Katherine stole a look back. Michael was staring at Christy's back as though willing her to turn around. His date leaned in to touch his face, but he didn't respond. He was watching Christy. He caught Katherine's eye for a split second, and then turned back to his date.

Christy and Katherine walked to Three Guys Coffee Shop a block away.

"Chris, you have to get a grip."

"There has to be a way to bring him 'round," she insisted.

"In my experience, even men who say they *want* to commit usually don't. I have *never* been warned off and had it not be real. The guy's been through one of those nasty society divorces. Trust me, Michael Drummond will spend the rest of his life with beautiful, young bimbos whom he'll dump the minute they ask for the order."

"But you have to understand, he wasn't like that in Davos."

"Christy, anyone can seem real for one perfect night in a quaint Swiss village."

"But . . ." Christy wondered for a minute if Katherine knew about Fran.

"Christy, bury it. You're the CEO, for God's sake. Move on. You're supposed to be our inspiration. The way you've been mooning around the office lately, you're not inspiring *anyone*."

Feeling guilty, Christy spent the afternoon visiting everyone's desk at Baby G, asking questions, being cheerful. She worked late on the end-of-the-quarter presentation and tried to decide how she could best position their successes.

That night, Maria was waiting for her with a bowl of hot soup and all the time in the world. Christy poured her heart out, telling her everything about Fran, Michael, the weeks of waiting, the Trattoria Dell'Arte. Maria held Christy for a long time, saying nothing. Finally Christy spoke again. "I know I need to listen to Katherine. She's always stood by me. Remember when she put her own savings into the company, when my endorsement money ran out and we couldn't make payroll? Katherine says he'll never call. I should listen to her, right? She's a pro when it comes to men."

Maria looked at her a long time, and then she spoke. "Honey, I know you love that woman, but there are times you can't pay attention to anyone else. I loved someone once, Renata's grandfather, and I let him get away by listening to other people telling me to be reasonable. I've never forgiven myself."

"You talk about him like it just happened. Wasn't that a long time ago?"

"It was, and it still haunts me. That's what I'm saying to you. Katherine may be a pro, but not at the real thing. If I hadn't listened to other people, maybe I could have gotten Juan to stay, to help me raise our daughter. If he'd been there, things might have been different; maybe she'd be alive today."

"It must be tough to live with regrets like that," Christy said.

"It is. I should have followed my heart back then. At least I have my granddaughter. She's all that's left of the two people I loved most in the world."

After two more weeks and still no word, Christy decided on a course of action that she shared with no one except Maria. She worked until six one night, then grabbed a cab across town. Entering a sleek modern office tower on Madison, she told the security guard she had a late meeting with Michael Drummond. The guard, who recognized Christy from her billboards, picked up the phone to announce her. Christy had to stop him.

"You know, Michael is a good friend, and I wanted to surprise him with a gift." She held up the coffee-table book—*Olympic Facts and Fables*—that she'd brought along. The guard, a tall, handsome black man in his fifties, looked her over carefully. He figured that she was a well-known person, probably not a stalker or a terrorist, too old to be one of Michael's girlfriends. So he let her up. Christy surprised him with a peck on the cheek.

When she reached the top floor, she stepped into a reception area as original as Michael. It was an open room with a huge aquarium in the middle, filled with quirky, colorful fish. There were bowls of snacks on a counter, including packs of M&M's, which Christy took as a sign. She grabbed a bag and ripped into it to calm her nerves. The receptionist, who was young and hip-looking, gave Christy a smile of recognition. For once, she was glad to be well known. When she asked for Michael, the girl looked quizzical.

"Is he expecting you?"

"Not really," Christy said. "I'm surprising him."

"I don't think you want to do that," she whispered.

"Is he in a meeting?"

"No, not quite," she hesitated, waiting for Christy to catch on.

"Oh, you mean he's *with* someone."

The receptionist was already dialing and giving Michael her name. It was too late to bolt. About three minutes later, a willowy brunette, a younger version of herself, charged out the door of his office suite, her lips tight, her eyes narrow. She gave Christy the once-over, then turned on the heel of one of her knee-high boots and disappeared into the elevator.

Michael stood at the door, red-faced and flustered. "Hi, Christy. Long time no see." Christy wanted to kill him. All the emotions she had been feeling since their first meeting rose to the surface. She could easily have collapsed into tears, but she refused. She held herself together and managed only to look Michael in the eyes without saying a word. He stared back at her in waiting silence. It was nothing like the reunion Christy had envisioned. Michael finally led her into his office, then closed the door behind them, gathered her into his arms, and hugged her tightly.

Christy broke away from his embrace. She had to face this man who was making her so crazy. "Michael, I know I . . . I promised to be your friend," she started. "But I can't do it. I'm thirty-nine years old and I've never . . . I mean *never* . . . felt this way about anyone. I can't . . . can't eat, I can't focus on my work, I can't even run . . ."

Michael started to say something, but she motioned for him not to interrupt. Christy had the courage to do this only once, right this minute, and she was determined to get the words out.

"The thing is, I can't believe you don't feel the same way. It doesn't seem possible that this is a one-sided connection. We're perfect for each other. I'm sure of it. And despite your disappearance since we met, *you* know it, too." She looked at him with defiance, daring him to deny it.

Michael regarded her closely for what seemed, to Christy, like an eternity. She stood tall, her hands on her hips, boldly meeting his eyes, the picture of sweet, unbridled determination. Michael lowered his eyes and then spoke.

"I'm not going to say I don't have feelings for you, Christy. I do. But I can't act on them. I wasted fifteen years of my life in a marriage, and most of it was a nightmare. I can't . . . no, I *won't* put anyone in a position to hurt me like that again. Not even you. I'm sorry."

Christy felt like she'd been slapped. Until now, she believed that if she could get up the nerve to bare her soul to him, he would open his heart and do the same. She felt her emotions slam shut, as they always did when she lost. "Fine," she said. "Fine. If that's how you want it." She turned around and walked out. He didn't stop her.

&

Christy began the task of trying to forget Michael in earnest. A week later, she started to sleep somewhat normally again. She got up at five A.M. to go over the daily sales reports. She ran miles and miles every morning, attempting to dull the pain she felt. Two weeks later, just as she was getting the smallest bit of traction on the rest of her life, she received a delivery at her apartment. She opened the package without thinking, and inside was a pair of old running shoes. She fumbled for the note, which read:

> Beegee, I can marry you or never see you again, but I can't go on a second date. I really don't want a prenup because if you ever leave me I will jump off my building. I have only a few needs: take my calls, even if you're in a meeting with half of Wall Street, visit me if I'm ever in the hospital, and no kids. Just you and me to the end.
> Love
> Michael

Christy jumped into the air and screamed. She knew it. She knew he was The One and now they were going to be together. She threw on a pair of sweats and ran to his office. This time she didn't even wait for security. She leaped over the turnstile before anyone could say a word.

Renata the Great

In a studio apartment in the Flushing section of Queens, eleven-year-old Renata Ruiz prepared dinner in a tiny kitchen for her grandmother Maria. She took the chicken out of the fridge, rinsed off the salmonella, and sprayed the pan with Pam. After carefully placing the chicken breasts into the preheated oven, Renata chopped up two tomatoes and an onion. Then she combed through the cabinet, looking for the Ortega taco kit. Renata loved making chicken taco casserole. The recipe was so complicated that she felt like one of those professional chefs on the Cooking Channel when it was all done. I am such a good chef, Renata thought. I can make macaroni and cheese, Shake 'n Bake chicken or pork, Chef Boyardee spaghetti. Vegetables were a cinch. She and Grandma preferred the frozen kind, and those just needed heating up in a saucepan.

Renata was in charge of making dinner for the family, which consisted of herself and Grandma. She had no memories of her mama, who had lived with them until Renata was three. Then she died of drugs. Daddy, well, people didn't talk about him. Nobody told her this, but Renata was sure Mama drove him away. She liked to imagine that he went on to a big career in television.

Renata had no other family in the United States. Grandma's parents passed on when she was little. Her brother was a carpenter and her sister a goatherd. Both lived deep in the Mexican jungle. They hadn't spoken in years. Not having relatives is the price you pay to live in the land of opportunity. That's what Grandma always said. She intended for her granddaughter to go to a fine Ivy League college so that someday Renata could buy the two of them a house on Long Island. She planned to raise Renata right, not like she did with Mama. Grandma was stricter this time around. She insisted on chores, good grades, and no back talk.

When Renata came home from school, she spent her first hour visiting with the old people who sat in their lawn chairs in front of the building. They fawned over Renata, and on Thursdays, Mrs. Alvarez made her Rice Krispie treats. If it was cold or rainy and her friends weren't outside, she'd do her assignments right away. After homework, Renata did housework. Monday was laundry and sheet changing. Tuesday was vacuuming. Wednesday was grocery shopping. Thursday was bathroom cleaning. Friday was dusting and polishing. Making dinner came after the daily job. They lived in a studio apartment in subsidized housing. Grandma could afford a bigger place, but she was putting money away for a down payment on a house. With such a small space, no task was ever too hard. Renata liked doing chores. They made her feel important. After all her work was done, she watched TV and waited for Grandma.

Grandma took care of a much grander apartment that belonged to Christy Hayes, the sports lady who was on all the billboards. When Grandma first went to work for her, she did everything—the cooking, cleaning, and shopping. Last year, after Christy married Michael, Grandma was promoted to be the boss of all the other cleaners and cooks at their Fifth Avenue apartment. The place had more rooms than Uncle Bill's penthouse on *Family Affair*. That was one of Renata's favorite shows on TV Land, the best channel on cable because it showed all the great sitcoms from the olden days. On school holidays, Renata usually stayed home alone and read or watched old shows and the Cooking Channel or Home Shopping Network. Sometimes, Grandma took Renata to work with her. A few times, Christy was there. She was a pretty lady and would always ask Renata questions about herself, which made sense to Renata because naturally Christy would want to get to know such a likable and gifted child. Christy always sent Renata presents for Christmas and birthdays, really big ones like an iPod and a computer. She even funded her college account because she didn't want Grandma to worry about saving for higher education. The reason Christy could afford to do all that was because she was working real hard at the kind of job Grandma aspired for Renata to have someday. Not a domestic job, a *professional* job.

After she'd finished changing the sheets, Renata sat on the couch and wrote in her diary, as she did every day:

DEAR DIARY,

ITS AFTER 8 AND GRANDMA'S NOT BACK YET. IT MUST BE BECAUSE MICHAEL AND CHRISTY ARE SLOBS. THEY HAVE GRANDMA PLUS A BUNCH OF OTHER SERVANTS AT THEIR HOUSE AND GRANDMA NEVER GETS HOME BEFORE 9. I BET MICHAEL THROWS HIS CLOTHS ON THE FLOOR WHEN HE GETS UNDRESSED. HE PROBABLY SPLASHES WATER OVER THE EDGE OF THE TUB AND EATS WITH HIS FINGERS. I BET CHRISTY HAS A MAID JUST TO WIPE HER BUTT JUST LIKE THE QUEEN DOES. REALLY, THERE IS SUCH A JOB AS A BUTT WIPER, WHICH

IS WHY I'M GOING TO COLLAGE SO I'LL NEVER HAVE TO BE
ONE. GRANDMA SAYS SHE HAS TO TAKE SPESHAL CARE OF
CHRISTY BECAUSE SHE'S ALL ALONE IN THE WORLD. I TAKE
CARE OF GRANDMA BECAUSE SHE HAS HIGH BLOOD PRESURE.
NO ONE TAKES CARE OF ME, BUT THATS OKAY BECAUSE I'M A
ROLLING STONE.
      YOURS VERY TRULY,
      RENATA RUIZ

Renata's favorite book was *Harriet the Spy*. It was Harriet
who had inspired her to watch, listen, observe, and keep
notes about things. So far, she had filled three journals. Renata wasn't as daring as Harriet, who would actually break
into people's houses to spy on them. In the projects, that
could get a girl killed.

The buzzer went off and Renata took the chicken out of
the oven. "First, I must chop the chicken into small pieces,
like so," she said, chopping for the imaginary home audience. Renata often practiced having her own show on the
Cooking Channel when no one was looking. She would set
Grandma's vanity mirror on the kitchen counter and look
into it like it was a camera. Placing the chicken, chopped
tomatoes, and onion into a glass dish, she continued. "Now
I'll add the Ortega salsa, diced green chilies, and seasoning
mix. I prefer the Ortega medium-spicy-style salsa because I
think it has the perfect level of hotness, but you may want to
use a hotter or less-spicy style. Then, I'll mix the broken taco
shells in like so, pat the whole thing down, and sprinkle
Cheddar cheese on top. Aaaand VWA-LAH! Here's what
your casserole will look like before it's cooked." She held the
dish up to the camera, then slipped the mixture into the
oven. "For those of you tuning in tomorrow, I'll be making

Kraft macaroni and cheese with hot dog slices, so you *may* want to pick up the ingredients and cook along with me."

Renata heard the key turn in the door, so she stopped talking. Not that there was anything wrong with pretending to have her own cooking show. It just wasn't something she felt like publicizing.

Grandma took off her coat and laid it over the chair. She was carrying a heavy shopping bag.

"Anybody ho-ome?" Grandma always said that when she came in. It was an inside joke between them, given the meager size of their apartment. Last summer, they painted the walls yellow because it is such an uplifting color. Their floor used to be bare parquet, but then they bought an orange rug from the neighbor down the hall who moved to a different building with better wheelchair access. Grandma slept on the flowery foldout bed she had rescued from a Park Avenue Dumpster. Renata couldn't imagine why anyone would throw away such a beautiful piece of furniture. Grandma explained that it was because crazy New Yorkers were always redecorating. As the rich gave face-lifts to their already fabulous co-ops, doormen, maids, and supers upgraded their own homes with the valuable cast-offs that magically and regularly appeared in trash rooms throughout the city.

"Casserole's just about ready." Renata went to Grandma, gave her a kiss, and took the package. "What's in the bag?"

"Christy had a party tonight, so they sent me home with food. But your dinner smells delicious. Let's eat this tomorrow."

Renata took the containers and placed them in the fridge while Grandma changed into her pink satin robe from Macy's. It had been a special present from Renata last Mother's Day. Grandma always wore it after a hard day because it made her feel comfortable and pretty at the same time. Renata pulled out a kitchen chair. "Sit, Mommy, you look tired." Renata and Grandma called each other "Mommy."

"I am. It was a busy day getting ready for all that company. I'm pooped."

Renata stood behind Grandma and rubbed her neck so hard that her fingers got sore. Grandma's shoulders were thick with knotty muscles underneath. Lots of kids at school didn't get along with their parents, but Renata loved Grandma. She was glad her mama didn't raise her. Her mama had been mixed up with trouble. Renata wouldn't have known what to do with a mama who was mixed up with trouble. Last year, Grandma gave Renata a snapshot of Mama in her white confirmation dress. Renata stuck it under her mattress that night. Later, Grandma bought her a wooden frame from Hallmark with red hearts just for that picture, but Renata placed one of her and Grandma in it instead.

"Thank you, Mommy," Grandma said. She looked at her granddaughter with so much love that Renata lowered her eyes. The child walked back to the kitchen, pulled the casserole dish out of the oven, and fixed two plates.

"This looks delicious," Grandma said. "You are a better cook than I am, Mommy."

Renata beamed at the compliment. "No, I'm not. Anyway, you taught me how to make this. Mommy, guess what?"

"What?"

"We're having a concert at school two weeks from today, and me and Andrew Gutierrez are singing solos. Can you come?"

"I'll do my best, Mommy. If Christy can spare me." Grandma was rubbing her forehead absentmindedly.

"Tired?"

"No, headache."

"Maybe you better go to the doctor."

"No, I'll lie down. A doctor can't do nothing for me."

Grandma finished eating, then opened up the couch and climbed into bed. Renata was glad today was Monday because Grandma had clean sheets. Quiet as a mouse, she rinsed the dishes and snuck back to her alcove, pulling the curtains closed and curling up with her journal beneath her Mary-Kate and Ashley quilt. Soon Grandma was snoring lightly. Renata got up and locked the door and the dead bolt, and gave Grandma a kiss. To Renata, being with Grandma in their cozy apartment was about the safest feeling in the world.

~

DEAR DIARY,

ITS STILL MONDAY BUT I'M WRITING AGAIN BECUASE GRANDMA'S SLEEPING SO I CAN'T WATCH TV. TODAY MRS. GERMER CHOSE ME AND ANDREW TO SING SOLOS IN THE CONCERT. YAY ME (AND ANDREW TOO)!!!! WE HAVE TO LEARN THREE SONGS IN SPANISH. EDDIE GOMEZ SAYS THERES GOING TO BE A TALANT SCOUT FROM NICKALODEON IN THE AUDI- ENCE. EVERYONE IN MY CLASS THINKS I SING AS GOOD AS JENNIFER LOPEZ SO THERES A BIG CHANCE THEY WILL PICK ME TO STAR IN A SHOW. AND HERES MORE GOOD NEWS!!! GRANDMA'S COMING TO THE CONCERT IF CHRISTY GIVES HER THE DAY OFF WHICH OF COURSE SHE WILL. BREAKING NEWS ON THE ROMANCE FRONT! EDDIE GOMEZ LOVES ME. I MEAN *LOVES ME* LOVES ME. HE CHASES ME IN P.E. ALMOST EVERY DAY AND WHEN HE CATCHES ME HE SITS ON MY CHEST. IF HE CALLS I WILL HANG UP ON HIM.

SINCERELY YOURS,
RENATA RUIZ

A Rich Brownie

*C*hristy couldn't believe what a difference a year could make. She felt she could almost reach out and touch the meringue caps of the treeless peaks on either side of her as the helicopter floated noisily up the valley toward Davos. It was her first copter ride. She could hardly fathom that she was arriving with one of the major players of Davos and that he was her very own. Never again would she have to worry about being in the freshman class. Or alone. Her life as a solo player had finally come to an end—to a fairy-tale ending, in fact. She smiled at her husband, and he squeezed her hand.

When their helicopter landed in Davos, a chauffeur met and drove them to their suite at the Royalton. They were considered, in Davos parlance, a "power couple." Michael's assistant had enrolled them in their sessions the day before, and Michael was leading one of the hottest panels.

Michael began sorting through invites to private parties. "Ha, ha! Your friend Fran Rich and his wife Brownie . . . what kind of a name is that . . . cordially invite us to a reception tonight honoring Jimmy Carter, the two George Bushes, and Bill Clinton. You interested?"

"No way," Christy said, shuddering at the memory of that

arrogant asshole and his snobby wife. "What do you say we go for a run, then hail a sleigh, drink champagne, and make out?"

"Mmm. That sounds perfect, Beegee," Michael said, kissing his bride and unbuttoning her sweater.

On Wednesday, Christy and Michael attended sessions together. That evening they were invited to the power-couple dinner at the Luhof Castle in the next village. As they drove up, Christy felt like she was in a movie. They entered through a thirty-foot stone arch lit with candles, and uniformed guards stood at arms. The castle had been converted into one of the finest restaurants in Switzerland. Once inside the cozy room with candles flickering against the ancient walls, a maître d' led them to their table.

Christy was mortified when they were seated with Fran Rich and his wife, Bronwen "Brownie" Rich. Brownie had a pleasant face, but her body was as squat and soft as Christy remembered from the co-op interview. If you didn't know that her maiden name was Biltmore, you might wonder what a man like Fran ever saw in her. When Francis Rich, banker, met Bronwen Biltmore, heiress, sparks flew. Brownie found Fran to be handsome and brilliant. Fran found Brownie to be loaded and connected. A merger was struck, and two daughters later, Brownie was Parent Association president at the Colby School, secretary of the co-op board at 830 Fifth Avenue, and founder of the Golden Latchkey Foundation. Brownie's hands were far too full to stand by her husband's side as he entertained clients and networked about town, not that Fran seemed to mind. This time, however, Brownie had decided to accompany Fran to Davos.

"I'm Brownie Rich, and this is my husband, Fran. I'm sure you remember Fran," Brownie said in a formal, clipped tone.

"Hi, I'm Christy, and this is Michael. I guess you don't re-member me. I applied for an apartment in your building once."

"I'm sorry. I don't remember. We get so many applicants," Brownie said, avoiding Christy's eyes.

"Right," Christy said, looking at Fran, who winked at her like they shared a secret. Michael caught the eye signal, and she felt him stiffen.

"We missed you both at our reception last night. Did you have something more important to do?" Brownie asked.

"We had some personal business that couldn't wait," Michael said, instinctively claiming his territory, putting his arm around his wife. Christy adored how romantic he was. Brownie looked scandalized. Fran eyed Christy up and down as if he was trying to remember what she looked like naked.

"So, are you enjoying married life?" Brownie asked, seem-ingly oblivious to the testosterone dance going on under her nose.

"It's wonderful. We're so happy," Christy said, trying to make reassuring eye contact with Brownie and find out how much she knew.

"I suppose you'll be quitting your company soon," Brownie sighed knowingly. "Being the CEO's wife is a full-time job what with the entertaining you have to do, the running of the house, maintaining your looks, being the brains behind the man."

Christy decided Brownie didn't know about her and Fran.

"I'd never want Christy to give up work," Michael said, reaching under the table, taking her hand. "I find it exciting to be married to a woman who puts herself out in the world instead of one living through her children. Been there. Done that. No offense, Mrs. Rich."

"Well, I *love* having a wife like that," Fran said, giving Brownie a peck on her thin, chapped lips. He was a man who could not help but compete.

"For God's sake, Francis, I've told you a hundred times not to do that in public. It's inappropriate for someone of your station," Brownie snorted. But she looked a little surprised and pleased.

"I can't keep my hands off her," Fran said.

"I don't blame you," Michael said, barely suppressing a grin.

"Brownie, I think the choice you've made is admirable," Christy added, trying to smooth over her husband's blunt honesty, one of the qualities she found most appealing about him.

"Well, if you ever have children, you'll change your mind," Brownie declared.

"That's not in the cards for us. Done that, too. I love my daughter, but raising a family is something I would only attempt once," Michael said.

"And your bride feels the same?" Brownie asked.

"Absolutely," Christy said. And she meant it. She couldn't imagine how life could be sweeter. For the first time, she had a protector *and* a playmate who could not only keep up with her but could actually inspire awe in her.

Brownie pressed on. "Yes, but if *you* knew what it felt like to raise a child, to educate her, to give your heart and soul toward the betterment of her school, you would *never* say that."

Michael spoke softly. "Mrs. Rich, I think it's great that enriching the lives of your kids and volunteering at their school gives your life meaning. I just think a lot of these rich kids are spoiled brats. I worry more about the ones who have never had a shot."

"But that's just Michael's opinion. Neither of you is wrong," Christy added, wondering what ever happened to small talk.

Brownie pursed her lips and said nothing. To everyone's relief, a waiter arrived to take orders. Christy and Michael asked for fish, knowing they would be facing many rich courses. Brownie and Fran went for beef. The lights dimmed, signaling the start of the entertainment. In keeping with the power-couple theme, Diana Krall and Elvis Costello were performing. Christy looked around the room at the half-dozen tables decked out in Continental finery, the couples dining in the rich glowing light, the centuries-old tapestries on the walls, and the golden candle sconces and chandeliers poised over everything. This is all so glamorous, she thought: my wonderful husband, this amazing life. She could hardly fathom how she had made the journey from Glenbrook to Davos, and to this remarkable man with his slightly possessive hand on hers.

୦୦

"Can you pour me some coffee?" Christy asked.

"My pleasure," Michael said, refilling her cup. Christy and Michael were being lazy. Instead of getting up at the crack of dawn to hear the much-anticipated speech on Shifting U.S.–Asian Alliances, the newlyweds got caught up in their own romantic alliance. Michael was an amorous spouse, and Christy was delighted by his need for her. They were cuddling in bed over breakfast, sharing the papers that had been delivered on a silver tray.

"You know," Michael said, buttering his croissant, "seeing Fran and Brownie last night made me so glad I gave up that life, not that I ever cheated on Suzanne."

Christy stiffened. She had never told him about herself and Fran. When she and Michael were first married, they decided not to drag each other through blow-by-blows of their pasts. "I guess he has a reputation for running around, huh?" Christy said.

"He does. Maybe you can't blame him. It's obvious he and Brownie don't care for each other. I was willing to settle for that once. After Suzanna, I promised myself I wouldn't date anyone I cared about and wouldn't care about anyone I dated. But now that I have you, I see how wrong I was."

Christy smiled and nuzzled closer to Michael. "I love you so much," she said.

"Me, too, Beegee," Michael said. "I just want to make you happy."

"You do," Christy said with a sexy smile. "In fact, after breakfast, maybe you can make me happy again."

Michael laughed. "I'll give you the front page for the Finance section." They exchanged papers and read quietly for a few minutes.

"Oh my God!" Christy said, spilling coffee on the bed. "Look. How could you miss this article?" She handed Michael the paper and pointed furiously at the headline:

CHRISTY HAYES'S LEADERSHIP LAPSE

by Galit Portal

In the fifteen years since Christy Hayes founded Baby G Sports, the company has expanded from three employees to four thousand, with profits of $50 million. Three years ago she led the company to a hugely successful public offering underwritten by Goldman Sachs. Still, inside sources report that last week, Baby G's board of directors issued an ultimatum to Ms. Hayes: Run the company under the supervision of Hamish Cohen, Managing Partner of Bain Consulting, or step down and allow a more seasoned CEO to take over. Sources say board members believe the company has become too complex to be managed by a leader who hails from the athletic world and who does not have an MBA. In setting this condition, the board cited the stock's lackluster performance in the last two years, which has dropped from $42/share the day of the public offering to $26/share. This is an average percentile loss for businesses in the sector, which has suffered an industry-wide downturn. For Ms. Hayes, this event represents the stiffest challenge yet to a career that was launched on the coattails of two Olympic gold medals. While this reporter tried to reach Ms. Hayes, she is out of the country at a conference and unavailable for comment . . .

Christy felt sick to her stomach. "Michael, *none of this is true*. I met with the board before we left. Everything was fine. The stock's down, yes, but sales and profits are up. How can they print something like this without verifying it?"

"Are you sure they didn't decide it after you left? Could they be planning to issue an ultimatum when you get back?" Michael was as surprised as Christy, but he'd learned to expect the worst.

"I can't imagine. We talked about *increasing* my incentive package. Why would they consider *that* if they were questioning my leadership? Look who wrote it—Galit Portal. Isn't she at the conference?"

"I haven't seen her. She didn't write a bestseller this year. Maybe she didn't make the list."

"They *do* that? They cut people off the list?"

"Sure. I heard Teddy Bartlett wasn't invited the year they indicted him." Michael grabbed his Davos BlackBerry and scanned for Galit's photo. "Wait, no, she's here," he said.

"Oh God, last year, Galit snubbed me at the closing party. I don't know what I did to offend her."

"Christy, just stay here and relax. Let me go find out why she wrote the story. Then I'll beat her up, okay?"

"No, you can't fight my battles." Secretly, she wished he could. "I'll track her down."

"We'll go together," Michael said.

Meet Galit

Michael and Christy decided to catch Galit by surprise. They walked over to the conference center and took the escalator down to the hospitality area where delegates gathered between sessions. Christy's face burned as she felt all eyes upon her. There were stacks of free *Financial Journals* throughout the building. Everyone knew. It was humiliating to be the subject of such damaging press in front of *this* of all groups. Michael put his arm around her as if to dare anyone to say anything. She glanced at him. He looked more disheveled than usual. His hair was wild, completely negating his finely tailored suit. His shirt looked like it had spent all night on the bathroom floor. That always happened when he was under stress. She found it endearing.

"I love you," she said.

"Love you more." He smiled.

They spotted Galit at the same time. There was no missing her. That long black hair topping the oh-so-perfect size-two body. She was wearing the same Marc Jacobs leather miniskirt that Christy owned. How does she afford to dress like that on a reporter's salary? Christy wondered. As usual, Galit was holding court, surrounded by a gaggle of Forbes 50 billionaires.

"I'll take it from here," Christy told Michael.

"You sure? You don't want me for moral support?"

I do! More than anything in the whole wide world. Don't make me face this mean lady alone, Christy thought. "No, this is something *I* have to do." She knew she'd appear weak if she confronted Galit with Michael at her side. Tapping the reporter on the shoulder, Christy interrupted Galit's diatribe on the so-called Leftist conspiracy to control the media.

"Can I help you?" Galit said. She had no clue who Christy was, at least that's the way it seemed.

"I'm Christy Hayes. You published an article about me today."

The tycoons surrounding Galit shifted uncomfortably and made excuses about why they had to leave.

"Oh, right. I didn't realize you were here."

"If you'd checked with my office, they would have told you. The thing is, your article's full of lies. My board didn't issue an ultimatum."

"That's not what I heard," Galit said.

"You heard wrong," Christy countered.

"I stand behind my story."

"How can you? It's not true."

"I beg to differ," Galit said. "Maybe *I* know something you don't."

Christy was worried but kept her face neutral. "You think *you* know more about what's happening at Baby G than *I* do?"

Galit lowered her voice. "Christy, I can't reveal my source. But if I were you, I'd get my ass back to my office to protect what's mine. That's all I'm going to say. Now if you'll excuse me." Galit executed a perfect pivot on a pointy croc-leather boot and walked away, leaving Christy standing alone with her mouth agape.

As if by magic, Michael materialized at his wife's side. "Honey, close your mouth. You look shell-shocked. C'mon, let's go back to the hotel."

Brownie approached the couple just as they left the conference center. She flashed her stricken expression, the one she reserved for funerals. "Christy, how *are* you? Fran showed me the article in the *Journal*. How very *terrible* for you."

"We're kind of in a hurry, Brownie," Michael said. Christy just smiled like she had taken one too many Valiums.

"Don't let the press rattle you. You've done *really* well for a girl who didn't go to grad school," Brownie added, patting Christy's hand.

Blowing past Brownie and avoiding eye contact with everyone else, they walked back to the hotel in silence. As soon as they returned to their room, Christy collected herself. "Honey, I have to go back to the States."

"Absolutely. I'll call for the jet and we'll leave as soon as we pack," Michael offered.

"Michael, you don't have to go."

"Of course I do. First of all, I have no interest in being at Davos without you. And second, you may need me when you get back. I want to be there for you."

"Thanks," Christy said, feeling a sense of relief she had never experienced. For the first time in her life, she had someone to lean on. So much for Xena, the Corporate Warrior.

Katherine Confidential

*C*hristy rifled through her papers as she waited for Katherine. Where could she *be*? Christy wondered. It had been well after midnight when she and Michael landed at Teterboro, the city's private airport. Katherine left a voice mail saying she'd be over first thing. Christy didn't want to do anything without talking to her. She must have dropped Alexandra at school, Christy thought. Katherine had recently broken up with her second husband, Alex's father, and he used to make the morning school run. Now that Christy was married, she couldn't imagine how Katherine managed to be a loving single mother to Alex, a formidable divorce opponent to Malcolm, and a good COO to Baby G, all at the same time. It was a lot to juggle.

After all these years, Katherine was still the person Christy turned to for advice about running Baby G. There was so much about the tough world of New York business that Christy had yet to master. But it came naturally to Katherine, who had the quiet confidence born into eastern girls whose ancestors hark back to the *Mayflower*. The only daughter of George Winslow, an older, wealthy financier and Claire Garcia, a former showgirl turned scion of horsey high society, Katherine grew up with multiple homes, each with an important portrait of Claire Garcia Winslow displayed at the top of a grand stairway. Pale-skinned and green-eyed, with her carrot-colored hair brushed straight back behind a black velvet headband, Katherine went to Miss Porter's School, became a debutante and famous party girl, and then confounded everyone by applying to Harvard Business School.

When Christy started Baby G, Katherine was one of six people who answered an ad for CFO. The two became best friends immediately. Through the years, Christy and Katherine had worked as a team to build the company. In recognition of her contribution, Christy named her COO. The board was against it because they didn't think the company needed anyone in that position. But Christy fought hard and won the promotion for her.

Maria escorted Katherine into the library. Christy hadn't even heard the doorbell. "I'll bring breakfast right away," Maria said.

"How *are* you?" Katherine asked, hugging her. "I've been so worried about you. What a nightmare."

"I'm okay. Upset. Confused. Pissed off. Did you have any luck finding out where the *Journal* got their story?"

"I called Galit in Davos, but she wouldn't disclose her source."

"Did you tell her it wasn't true?"

"Of course. Then I went to her editor on behalf of the board. The guy offered to print a retraction, but Slotnik recommended against it. He said it would just bring the story out again and it's better to let it die quietly." Rick Slotnik was the VP of public relations for Baby G. He had years of experience and both women trusted him implicitly.

"It makes me so mad. Who would tell such a lie?" Christy said. "Do you think I should hire a detective?"

"A detective?"

"Yeah. To find out who's leaking misinformation to the press. If it's someone internal, they need to be fired," Christy said.

"How can it be anyone internal? Everyone worships you. Oh, except . . . what about Chris Kelly? He went ballistic when you fired him."

"The guy was stealing."

"If he'd steal, he'd lie to the press," Katherine said.

"True," Christy mused. "What did the board say?"

Maria brought in a cart of coffee, orange juice, pastries, and fruit. She served and then discreetly disappeared.

"They're a hundred percent behind you. They'd never recommend that Bain supervise you. It's ludicrous."

"Rick Slotnik left me a message. He wants to do damage control. There's a reporter from *Wall Street Week* who's been itching to write an article on me and he's recommending I do it. What do you think?" Christy asked.

"Sounds like a good idea. Is the reporter friendly? Will the story be positive?"

"Rick thinks so. Michael says I should do it, but I'm not sure."

"What's your hesitation?"

"His angle is personal. You know, what makes Christy Hayes tick. From my midwestern roots to the Olympics to Baby G to Prince Charming."

"So what's the problem?"

"There's stuff I'd rather not publicize. My schooling, or lack thereof. My love life before Michael. Do you want a cinnamon bun? Some coffee?"

"Thanks. I'll pour it myself." Katherine made herself a cup, then took half a bun. She was always dieting. "You know," she said chewing daintily, "they can spin the education into a positive. Seriously, you could be an inspiration to kids who don't love academics. You know, don't worry if you struggle in school. You can still start a company and become fabulously successful. It makes great copy. And who's to criticize your love life? You weren't married," Katherine said.

"Katherine"—Christy lowered her voice even though she was in her own house—"remember last year when I was photographed with Fran Rich, that investment banker from Farrar? *I slept with him.*"

"Fran Rich?"

"Yeah. I thought he was separated from his wife at the time, but he wasn't."

"And you didn't tell me? How could you keep something like this a secret from *moi*?" Katherine giggled. "Was *that* why you threw wine in his face?"

"How'd you guess? I wasn't proud of myself, so I didn't talk about it. Never told Michael, either. You don't think the reporter could find out?"

"Not unless you or Fran admit it. And there's no danger of that." Katherine thought for a moment. "Christy, I think Rick's right. Let them do the profile. It'll repair your image and give shareholders more confidence. The risk is minimal. Just have Rick manage the story closely."

Christy sighed as she took the other half of Katherine's cinnamon bun. "Did you ever think, when we started our tiny company, we'd have to deal with crap like this? It used to be so much fun, didn't it?"

"Christy, you're totally romanticizing the start-up. Remember that tiny office? No money. No publicity. We shared a computer. Schlepping around the country, begging investors to fund us. Remember when we tried to make that *Times* reporter think we were so cost-conscious that we took the subway everywhere?" Katherine laughed.

"Yeah, we took him with us to the agency and got on the wrong train. I seem to recall that we ended up in the Bronx instead of Union Square. So embarrassing."

"And he *had* to mention it in his article, commandeered by the bimbos. The first of many mean-spirited pieces," Katherine pointed out.

"Not as mean as this one," Christy said.

"It'll be okay," Katherine said. "Why don't you invite the executive committee for lunch? Let Rick present his recommendations. Make them comfortable with the way you're handling this. Now that I'm on the committee, I'll be there. You'll be in a room full of supporters."

"You're right, as always. It's a plan," Christy said, hugging her friend. "How's Alex doing? She okay?"

"She's great. Did I tell you we moved her to Colby?" Katherine said. "The boys at Dalton were too much of a distraction. She was caught skipping school with a senior last April. But now that she's at Colby, her grades are better and she's more confident. They just elected her to student council, and it's only her first year. The teenage years are tough. Let's hope I survive them," Katherine said.

"I don't envy you."

"I just got her one of those Nextel phones with the satellite tracking device, the kind we have at the office."

"Our phones have tracking devices?" Christy asked, pouring herself another cup of coffee.

"You didn't know? Yeah, they connect to a satellite. You just go to their website, type in the number, and a map comes up showing the phone's location. It's a safety thing so you can find a child if she's in trouble. But I use it every day to make sure Alex isn't lying to me about where she's going and what she's doing."

"Smart," Christy said. "And if she gets kidnapped, that'll just be a bonus."

"Exactly."

A Morning Canoodle

Christy cuddled against Michael's back, engaged in a bit of postcoital neck nibbling. There was nothing she enjoyed more than making love with Michael. Morning, noon, night—it didn't matter. He made her feel safe and adored.

"That tickles," he laughed.

"Mmm-hmm," she teased. "Should I stop?"

"No, that's okay," he said, as Christy took a playful bite.

"Do you really have to go today?" Christy whispered into his ear. She had been single for so many years. Now that she had Michael, she hated it when he left.

"I do, but I wish I didn't. I'd rather stay here with you."

"Call your office and tell them you're laid up."

"You are so hilarious," he said, turning to his wife. "You should think about doing stand-up."

Christy punched him in the arm playfully. Then she settled into his shoulder, pulling the covers up. The bed was warm from the heat of their bodies and she was as relaxed as a cat napping in the sun.

"I hate it when you go," she said with a sigh.

"Me, too. But I'm only going to Denver. I'll be back soon enough." He kissed her again. "Phil's supposed to drop off the blueprints later. Can you have Eve FedEx them to me?" Eve was their personal assistant.

"Okay," Christy said, yawning. Christy and Michael were embarking on a gut renovation—a New Yorker's worst nightmare. They'd been living in Michael's penthouse, which sat high above the city but was decorated in that wealthy-caveman style so favored by recently divorced Manhattan alpha males. Lots of marble and glass, clean lines, and no soft spaces. The one exception was a dark-blue velvet reading chair, the only piece of furniture that Christy took when her father died. It stuck out like a bad accident in Michael's grand master bedroom, but to Christy it was a cozy refuge. She hadn't noticed how shabby it looked until Michael gently pointed it out, but he assured her it had a home with them as long as she wanted it. She'd been too busy with work to take on a decorating project, but now she was going to try.

"Oh, and also, Orrick Herrington's messengering over a bunch of papers for me to sign. Would you ask Eve to put those in the package?"

"Sure, what are they?"

"Well, now that Suzanna's remarried, I'm petitioning to cut off her alimony."

"She's not gonna liiiiiike that," Christy said.

"I know, but I think it's time that her Argentinean polo-playing husband supports her. We'll save eighteen thousand a month."

"Sounds like monopoly money to me. Want to go for a run?" Christy asked.

Michael glanced at the clock by their bed. "I can't. I'm getting picked up in forty-five minutes. Are you nervous about your board meeting today?" he asked.

Christy stiffened. "Ugh, don't remind me."

"Don't worry. Just walk them through your response to the story," Michael said. "They'll be satisfied. What else do you have going on?"

"Wednesday I'm flying to Mexico City to meet with the Olympic Committee. If I have time, I'll visit our factories outside town."

"When'll you be back?"

"Friday night, like you."

"Want to go to Aspen this weekend? A little helicopter skiing to make you forget your troubles?" Michael proposed.

"Sure. That sounds so glamorous!"

"That's what I love about you, Beegee. You're not jaded." Michael gave Christy one last kiss before getting out of bed and heading for the bathroom. "Don't fly back to New York; just go to Aspen. I'll meet you at the house."

"You got it, sweetheart," Christy said, throwing the covers over her head to postpone the inevitable for a few more minutes. Denial is such a good defense mechanism, she thought. She heard the water turn on in the bathroom and decided to get up and go for a quick run. As she reached for her shorts, Michael started singing "Hey Jude" in the shower. He is so damn cute, she thought. I can't stand it. Giggling, Christy ditched the shorts and joined her husband in the shower.

Staying Alive

Christy jumped into the backseat of her car and directed Steven to take her to the John Barrett Salon. While there, she outlined her presentation on all the good news in the business to offset this *Financial Journal* mess.

While Christy was out, Maria would make sure that preparations for the lunch meeting went off without a hitch. Christy felt guilty over not insisting that Maria take the day off to go to Renata's concert. There was other staff who could handle the luncheon. But Maria knew that her boss felt stronger knowing she was hovering in the background. And today of all days, she understood that Christy needed her there. She wouldn't hear of taking the day off, but it nagged at Christy just the same.

With her presentation, hair, and makeup as perfect as possible, she got back into the car. Steven headed for home.

"You look very nice, Christy," Steven said, giving her the once-over in the rearview mirror. "Important meeting?"

"Yeah, with the board." Christy studied her presentation quietly as Steven drove.

"Whoops, look. Can't stop in front," Steven pointed out. An ambulance blocked the way.

"That's okay. Just pull up beside it. I'll bet it's Mrs. De Mille," Christy said.

"Gotta be," Steven said, shaking his head. "And she just celebrated her ninety-fifth last weekend. What a damn shame. You know, she's been in the building since it opened."

"At least she lived a good life," Christy said sadly. "She had her faculties to the end. She walked to the reservoir and back every day. We should all be blessed with a long life like that. Can you see if there's anything we can do to help? Find out where the services are. I'll send some flowers. Well, wish me luck."

"Luck," Steven shouted, as Christy barely dodged a kamikaze pizza-delivery guy on a bike that swerved between the ambulance and her Mercedes. They seemed to be the only remaining entity in New York that bowed to no law, wreaking havoc on the well-ordered world of Fifth Avenue.

Christy made a mental note to call Michael as soon as her meeting ended. More than once, he'd mentioned wanting to make a bid for Mrs. De Mille's apartment after she died. Michael's penthouse was small and they were desperate for more room. Combining Mrs. De Mille's space with theirs would make a fabulous duplex. Christy felt terrible about acquiring it this way. But if she and Michael didn't act now, the woman's next-door neighbors certainly would. *Someone* would buy it. It was this kind of thing that made Christy uncomfortable about living in New York. You had to be tougher than everyone around you or you'd lose.

When Christy arrived upstairs, her front door was open. Walking inside, she spotted three uniformed people hovering over someone lying on the floor. Christy couldn't see the face, but she saw the shoes. They were Maria's navy blue Easy Spirit pumps. Yok Wah, the cook, and Cynthia, the maid, stood in the corner looking stricken.

"What happened?" Christy screamed.

"Stroke," the female attendant said quickly.

One of the paramedics was on the phone conferring with the hospital. The other was injecting some kind of medicine into a bag that was hooked to a tube connected to Maria's hand. The man on the phone said "thrombolysis," but Christy had no idea what that meant. She approached Maria and peered over the heads of paramedics. The right side of Maria's face drooped. "Is she . . ."

"She's stable, but we need to get her to the hospital," the woman whispered as the two men scooted Maria onto a gurney.

Christy took Maria's hand and squeezed it. Maria opened her eyes, looking terrified. Christy felt the same but tried not to show it.

"It's okay, Maria. You'll be fine."

Maria tried to speak but no words came. The attendants rolled the gurney into the hall and then the waiting elevator.

"Can I ride with her?" Christy asked, stepping inside with the medics and elevator man. She clenched Maria's free hand, which was cold and shaking.

"Sure," the female attendant said. "Is there family to call?" she asked.

"A granddaughter," Christy answered. "I'll do it. I think she needs more covers."

The paramedics pushed the gurney to the front of the building and into the ambulance. Christy climbed in with the others. "Where are we going?"

"Lenox Hill." The ambulance took off, and Christy could hear sirens blaring outside. The hospital was only blocks from the apartment. None of it seemed real.

A young dark-haired paramedic put another blanket over Maria, whose eyes were closed. Christy took her hand once more. "I'm *here*, Maria. We're going to Lenox Hill. You'll have the best doctors. I promise."

Maria opened her eyes slightly and tried to talk. "R— . . . R— . . ."

"Renata will be fine, I promise. I'll take care of her. Don't worry." You *have* to get better, Christy thought.

The ambulance stopped, and the doors sprang open. In a flurry of activity, hospital attendants wearing scrubs evacuated the rolling bed from the vehicle. Christy's stomach dropped when she saw the lost expression on Maria's face. "R . . . Re . . ." she slurred again. Christy caught up with the gurney. She knew Maria was thinking the unthinkable. She tried to pretend she wasn't more frightened than she'd ever been.

"Of course I'll raise Renata if anything happens. You know I promised you that, Maria. But you're gonna be fine." That's right, she thought, Maria will be fine. She just needs rest. When she gets out of the hospital, I'll send her on a tropical vacation. A sunny place where she can sleep and get her strength back.

Maria visibly relaxed. She closed her eyes and Christy could see that her lashes were wet with tears. The attendants told Christy to wait outside. They were taking Maria to a restricted area. In an instant, she was gone. Christy stood there, staring, as the door slammed in her face. She wanted to call Michael, but he wouldn't be landing for another two hours. She felt utterly and completely alone.

ര

Christy found her way to an empty orange plastic chair in the waiting room, brushed away a candy wrapper, and sat down to think. How could this be happening? Was there time to run home, handle the luncheon, and then get back to the hospital? *Maybe she should skip the board meeting.* No, she had to be there. Maria may be dying. *No, that's impossible.* Of course it's possible. People die every day. *Renata.* She had to find the child and bring her to the hospital. Christy called Katherine on her cell but got voice mail. She explained the situation and asked her to cover the lunch. She promised to call back in a half hour to brief her on what she'd planned to say. It'll be okay, Christy thought. Katherine has presented to the board before.

Christy called Steven and asked him to pick her up at Lenox Hill as soon as possible. Walking outside to Seventy-seventh Street, she realized she had no idea where the kid went to school. She knew it was in Queens, but that was all.

Steven pulled up and Christy hopped into the back. "Steven, you don't happen to know where Maria's granddaughter goes to school?" Christy was virtually sure that he didn't, but she asked anyway.

"I don't know the name of it, but I think I can find it. I drove Maria there in December for some Christmas show."

"Thank you. God bless you," she said. "Drive as fast as you can." Christy sat back, closed her eyes, and tried to steady her hands. Her head felt like it would explode. Keep it together, keep it together, she told herself. She couldn't show up at Renata's school acting hysterical. Traffic was a nightmare. Christy cursed the big trucks that were double-parked leaving only two lanes open for traffic. She pulled out her phone and called the Lenox Hill emergency room.

"Hello. It's Christy Hayes, and I was just there with Maria Ruiz. They said she had a stroke. I'm on my way to pick up her granddaughter. Do you have an update on her condition?"

Christy held long enough to hear "I Will Always Love You," "Uptown Girl," and the beginning of "Your Song" before the nurse came back. The music helped calm her. That was smart, she thought, playing lite FM on an emergency room's hold line. Christy listened to the nurse's update, then thanked her. She snapped her cell phone closed and stuck it into her purse. She found an unexpected pack of Big Red gum in the bag. She took a piece and offered one to Steven. Cinnamon gum is definitely the best kind, she thought. Maria is dead. Christy said these words to herself, but she couldn't really take them in. Today is Thursday. The sky is blue. Maria is dead. Words, just words. So many things she'd never said to Maria. She just felt there would always be time.

Renata's Big Day

*P*ublic School 223 was housed in a square, tan brick building with iron bars on the windows. After trying every door to the place, Christy found the only one that was open. She entered, passed through a metal detector, and approached the policeman on the other side. He made her show two forms of ID and sign in before he would direct her to the office.

Making two rights as the cop instructed, Christy found the place. Other than a jeans-clad woman answering phones at the PTA desk, the office was deserted.

"Can I help you?" the lady asked.

"I'm looking for Renata Ruiz. I think she's in fifth grade. Her grandmother, who's also her caretaker, just, uhm, *passed away*." Christy whispered the words *passed away*. There was an enormous lump in her throat, and she could hardly speak.

The woman looked up at Christy sympathetically. "I'm *so* sorry. And you are?"

"I'm her grandmother's employer. I mean I was."

"And I'm Jenny, Cecelia Moreno's mom," she said, extending her hand. "Ce Ce's in Renata's grade. Everyone's at the concert. Come. I'll take you."

Jenny accompanied Christy down the hall and up some

stairs. Inside, the place was like every school Christy had ever attended. Wide halls, white-painted cinderblock walls, Formica floors, children's artwork on display, that faint sweaty-gym-sock smell. Christy shivered. The place gave her the willies. School was never her strong suit.

The two women entered the auditorium. A group of students were onstage, arranged as a chorus, singing a medley of Broadway songs in Spanish. A girl and boy were featured soloists, backed by their classmates. Both kids had soprano voices.

"The girl performing is Renata," Jenny whispered. "You stay here. I'll get the principal."

Christy stood in the back, staring at the child who was singing a duet of "Sunrise, Sunset." "*Sol se suba, sol se baia.*" It had been at least a year since she'd seen Renata. She remembered her as a chubby little imp. Now she was a head taller than the boy she was singing with and had the face of an Hispanic princess. Her lashes were so long that Christy could make them out from across the darkened auditorium. Her black curly hair was pulled up into the same French knot that Maria always wore when Christy had formal parties. Corkscrew tendrils fell lightly onto the child's face. Christy let out a sob as she pictured Maria spending her last morning on earth styling Renata's hair for the concert she would not be able to attend. Christy would never forgive herself for this. *Never.* She watched Renata's full lips move purposefully as she sang. There was a cleft in her chin, and she imagined there might be dimples when the girl smiled. She wondered what her mother had looked like to produce such an exquisite daughter. Or maybe it was her father? She didn't resemble Maria, who had been plain and dumpy in the most comforting way.

Christy was struck with a wave of grief for the child. Her world was about to fall apart, and she didn't have a clue. Nothing would be the same after today. As Renata performed "Memories," Christy wept quietly for the child and Maria. *"Memoria, solo en la claro de luna."* An older woman tapped Christy on the shoulder and motioned that she accompany her outside. It was the principal, who introduced herself as Enid Greene.

Christy explained the circumstances of Maria's death and asked if she could take Renata to the hospital to say good-bye.

The principal clucked her tongue and shook her head. "Does she have family? Should I call social services?"

"No, no. I'm taking her. Maria always put me and my assistant down as her emergency contacts. And I'm Renata's godmother."

"Why don't you go back to my office? I'll bring her to you when her class finishes singing."

Christy agreed. She took a last peek at Renata, who was singing "Tomorrow" along with the rest of the chorus. *"Mañana. Mañana. Te amo. Mañana."* The child sang more enthusiastically than before, probably relieved that her soloing was over. In a fog, Christy walked back to the main office. Stopping in the bathroom to splash water on her face, she thought about the day her own mother died. There had been no chance to say good-bye because the crash happened right after she dropped Christy off at school. Mom kissed her, said she'd pick her up at three, and that was it. She never saw her again. Just like Renata. Christy knew what the girl was about to feel. There would be a hole in her heart that would never be filled. A feeling that something was amiss every morning when she opened her eyes. Christy looked in the mirror and for a moment saw Maria's face instead of her own. Tears spilled from her eyes, so she stepped into one of the stalls for privacy. Sitting with her head in her hands, she let out a wail. Then the sobs began, coming in waves and spasms. They were loud, plaintive, sorrowful cries between gasps for air. They were the cries of a child weeping for her mother and her beloved Maria, both of whom left the world way too soon.

What's Love Got to Do with It?

*C*hristy met Michael in Aspen on Friday as planned. She heard the telltale crunch of gravel as his Range Rover made its way up their driveway. Peeking out the window, she was momentarily blinded by the vehicle's brights, which Michael always forgot to turn off after he navigated the steep part of the road. It was starting to snow.

Christy put down her mug of hot chocolate, threw a cashmere blanket around her shoulders, and curled up in an armchair. There was so much warmth in this home. Michael had bought the place as a wedding present for Christy so he could share his favorite spot in the world with her. He chose a house that wasn't too big and grand—he knew Christy yearned for a simpler life than Manhattan and a more casual space than his penthouse. He had it decorated for her in a traditional American folk-art style. Christy loved it. From her spot in the living room, she could see mountains lit by moonlight in every direction out the windows.

Her stomach turned over in anticipation of Michael's reaction to her news. She knew he wouldn't welcome it. It wasn't that he didn't love kids; he clearly adored his daughter. But she had broken his heart. Every month, he wrote to her, telling her how much he missed her, asking to get together. The letter was always returned unopened. He gave Ali a Mac PowerBook for her birthday. It was sent back to his office. She refused to accept the new hiking boots he offered, even though Michael had heard she needed a pair. Michael would not want to make himself vulnerable to another little girl.

Christy knew she had to tell him in person. Under the best of circumstances, this wasn't the kind of news you could casually drop over the phone. "Oh, by the way, honey, we have an eleven-year-old daughter now. Isn't that super!" No, this was a conversation to have *mano-a-mano*. Eve, their assistant, would stay with Renata for the weekend. Christy felt awful leaving her alone just one day after they buried Maria, but getting Michael on board was critical. Christy had waited a lifetime to find this man, and she could not risk her marriage over someone else's child. But she had also made a promise to Maria. She couldn't renege on that, either. She wouldn't even have Michael if Maria hadn't given her the courage to go after him.

The front door opened. Michael walked inside and smiled. Christy's stomach still dropped at the sight of him, after even a short absence. She was blind to his imperfections, amazed that he had chosen her.

"Come sit by the fire, babe. It's freezing out there," Christy said. She had a cup of spiked cocoa waiting for him. I'm a CEO, a new mother, and a damn good wife, she thought, pumping herself up for the pitch. See, a girl *can* do it all.

Michael wasn't interested in hot cocoa. He pulled Christy passionately to him, kissing her as though they had been apart for four years, not four days. Christy finally pulled away, burying her face in the hollow between his shoulder and neck. She worried that her husband would whisk her straight to the bedroom. Then what would she do? If she waited until after sex to tell him about Renata, he'd think he was being manipulated. Christy didn't want that. Her relationship with Michael had always been honest; they'd never played games. But if she told him about Renata now, before they made love, it would ruin his mood for the rest of the trip. Oh, screw it. It didn't matter when she told him. This was a mood breaker if ever there was one.

"I brought you something, Beegee," Michael said.

"Honey, I told you to stop buying me gifts. You're spoiling me."

"You don't want to deprive me of that pleasure, do you?" Michael said, making his sad-puppy-dog face. His employees and competitors would be shocked to see this side of him. Reaching into his coat pocket, he pulled out a small, exquisitely wrapped package. "Here."

Christy sat on the sofa to open it. Michael stood by the fire, watching her. The gift was from Sonny's, a Denver jewelry store that was Michael's favorite. Inside was a necklace made entirely of diamonds. Christy had never touched anything this beautiful. It looked like something a movie star would wear to the Academy Awards. "Wow," she said. "Wow."

"I saw it in Denver and couldn't resist," Michael said. "I wanted to cheer you up. Here, let's see how it looks." Michael put the necklace on her and then locked the clasp.

"I . . . I don't know what to say," Christy said, feeling nervous.

"Don't you like it?" Michael asked.

"I love it. I love you for wanting to give it to me. I just . . ." Christy pulled back. "Michael, there's something I have to tell you." She couldn't put this off any longer.

"You look serious. Is it about that article?"

"No, it's not that." Christy had been too preoccupied to think about that. Luckily, Katherine and Rick had handled the board at Monday's luncheon, making them feel comfortable with their plan to repair the damage caused by Galit's story. It felt like a year had passed since then. It had been four days.

"Maria died."

"*Our* Maria?"

"Yes."

Michael came and sat next to Christy, rubbing her shoulder. "I'm sorry. I know how much she meant to you. When?"

"Monday. And she did mean a lot to me. I loved her so much. But that's not even the biggest part of the news." Christy hesitated, wondering if her perfect world was about to implode. "Did you know she had a granddaughter she cared for?"

"I think I heard her mention that."

"Yes, her name's Renata. She's eleven."

"That's a damn shame. Who's gonna take her now?"

"I am Renata's godmother."

"*What?*"

Christy visibly gulped.

"You're not thinking of *taking her*, are you?" Michael looked like he could hardly breathe.

Christy gave Michael her desperate, pleading face. The one that was usually irresistible.

"NO. NO. NO. There's *got* to be another family, Christy. There's *no way* we can take a child, not with our responsibilities and lifestyle. You promised me, Christy. This is the only thing I really asked you for."

"Michael, there's no other family. Why else would Maria have asked me to do this? Renata's eleven; we just have to get through seven years."

"Christy, parenthood doesn't end at eighteen. It *never* ends. Why the hell didn't you tell me you had a goddaughter before we were married?" She had never seen Michael angry like this.

"Would it have made a difference?" Christy could see that no matter what the outcome, she had already laid everything on the line. She wished she could take it all back.

"I don't know, but you should have said something." Michael looked at Christy with such fury that she recoiled.

"I forgot. I mean, who expects to take a child in when they agree to be a godparent? Maria seemed so healthy. I never thought I'd actually be called to duty on this. Michael, please don't be upset at me. Don't you have godchildren you haven't told me about?"

"Yeah, but they're in college. Not much danger of having to raise them."

Michael sat down and put his head in his hands. He ran his hands through his hair as he thought about what to do. That's what he did when he was upset. Instantly, he looked like he hadn't slept for three days. He wiped his forehead with a handkerchief. Then he stood and began to pace.

"I'm sorry. We're *not* taking the child. You *have* to find another place for her, *for her sake*. I was a total failure at this." Christy saw tears in Michael's eyes.

"Michael, honey, that's not true. You were never given a chance. Things will be different this time. Besides, if *we* don't take her, social services will."

"You can't lay this at my doorstep, Christy. This is the one thing I cannot do. Please *believe* me." Michael's face was practically purple.

"Honey . . ."

"DON'T. 'HONEY.' ME. We'll figure out an alternative. We'll find her a family, someone who can give her what she needs."

"Michael, please, at least consider it," Christy pleaded.

"I married you because I trusted that you actually meant what you said when you told me you didn't want children." Michael grabbed his coat and walked out of the house. Christy watched him through the window and saw the Range Rover's lights go on. She heard the engine grinding and wheels spinning in gravel. He gunned the SUV, backed out, and sped down the hill. Silently, she begged him to slow down.

Should she wait? Go after him? Christy didn't know how to fix this. She knew one thing, though. If she was forced to choose between Renata and Michael, she would have to choose Michael. That is, if he'd even take her back after this.

∽

Christy awoke with a start. Light spilled through the cracks in the curtains. She looked over: Michael's side of the bed was empty. The clock read nine thirty-four. Instinctively, she touched her throat. The diamond necklace was digging into her skin. She reached behind her and unlatched it, then dropped it on the nightstand. *Where* was Michael? She ran downstairs, hoping she would find him asleep on the couch. He was sitting in the kitchen drinking a beer.

He looked at her with an expression that told her he felt completely desolate. "That was our first argument," he said sadly.

"It was a doozy," Christy added. She sat down beside him and found his hand.

Michael stroked Christy's hair gently. "What do you want me to say? That it's okay to take the kid? That wasn't our deal."

"I know, and I'm sorry. But I feel such an obligation. It's

Maria's granddaughter." She hesitated, then spoke. "Tell me. What would we do if something happened to Suzanna? Would we take Ali in?"

Michael sat up. "Of course. I'm her father, her *real* father. But this is different. Renata's not your child. And we had a specific agreement that we wouldn't have children together. You want to go back on a promise that was fundamental to our getting married in the first place."

"Michael, *please*," she said. "Just give it a try. You'll see. *Nothing* will change. I'll keep Renata separated from you. You can pretend she's not in the house."

He looked at Christy. "I *can't* do that. How can I not interact with her if she lives with us? Next thing you know, we'll have a relationship. I'll be involved."

"And that would be a problem why?"

"Because I don't *want* another child in my life. I already have a daughter who won't speak to me. Christy, if I can't live with my own child, how can I live with someone else's?"

"Michael, I'm sorry you don't have a better relationship with Ali. But Renata's exactly the kind of kid you always say you *want* to help. Not spoiled, never had a break, and she's a straight-A student."

Michael ran his hands through his hair as he considered this. "Tell you what. I'll take her if we can send her to boarding school. How about that?"

Christy shook her head. "Please, *only* as a last resort, *if* she becomes a burden. She just lost her grandmother, who was like her mother, who died when she was three. Don't you think she needs someone to nurture her, someone like me?"

Michael looked at Christy and sighed. "Beegee, you don't have a clue what you're getting into. People like you and me make terrible parents. We have too many other obligations. I was a complete failure at it. I don't want you to get your heart broken like I did."

"But Michael, let *me* take the risk. I feel like this is happening for a reason. It's like I'm being given the chance to pay back a cosmic debt for all the good things that have happened to me, like you."

"You're too generous for your own good." There was an edge of sarcasm in his voice, but the wall was coming down. Christy could see that she hadn't lost him completely. She took his comments as a yes and didn't mention Renata for the rest of the weekend. She was smart enough to know when to stop negotiating.

Michael, for his part, thought of nothing else.

Renata the Refugee

DEAR DIARY,

   THAT MEAN SELFISH BICH CHRISTY HAYES KILLED GRANDMA.
GRANDMA WAS SO UPSET ABOUT MISSING MY CONCERT THAT
SHE HAD A STROKE. IF CHRISTY HAD LET GRANDMA COME IT
NEVER WOULD HAVE HAPPENED. CHRISTY DENIED IT BUT ITS
TRUE. I TOLD HER SHE HAS GRANDMA'S BLOOD ON HER
HANDS.

   AFTER THE FUNERAL CHRISTY LEFT ME WITH HER
ASISTENT EVE SO SHE COULD GO SKIING IN ASPEN. THAT'S
JUST ONE MORE EXAMPLE OF HER SELFISHNESS. EVE IS NICE.
WHILE CHRISTY WAS HAVING FUN, WE WENT TO BURGER KING. I
HAD A DOUBLE WHOPPER WITH CHEESE. EVE HAD AN ANGUS
STEAK BURGER. THEN WE WENT TO BLOCKBUSTER AND RENTED
THE STEPDOG WIVES. IT WAS BORING BUT I PRETENDED I LIKED
IT. WHY? I DON'T KNOW. I'M VERY CONFUSED RIGHT NOW.

         YOUR SAD, SAD FRIEND,
         RENATA

                    ∾

'So, what do you think of your room?" Christy asked, sitting on
the edge of the bed. It was her first day back after Aspen, and
when she learned Renata had been sleeping in the tiny maid's

room behind the kitchen, she moved her into the guest room. It was at the opposite end of the apartment from the master, so contact between Michael and Renata would be minimized.

"Can't I stay near the kitchen? I like it there. Yok Wah is nice. She shows me how to cook things. And it's warm and cozy. Plus it smells good."

"Renata, we need to keep that open for staff when they stay over. And your new room is so much bigger. Look, you have your own sitting area and TV."

Renata looked around. Her eyes welled. She didn't say anything.

"What?" Christy asked. "Tell me what's bothering you."

Renata gestured to the room around her. "It's just that, it's all so scratchy and shiny. It's way too big for me." She got quiet and looked down. "You wouldn't understand."

"Try me," Christy said.

"No, it's fine. Don't worry about it. It's a good room. I'm lucky to have it," Renata said flatly.

Christy walked over to the child, who was sitting stiffly in the reading chair. She knelt down and took the girl's hands in hers. "Renata, I was just a little younger than you when I had to go live with my father's sister for a few months after my mom died. I remember how I hated sleeping in a new room. It felt so strange even though it was nicer than my own bedroom. And my aunt who took me in, I hated her at first. I kept comparing her to my mom, who was gone, and, well, she couldn't win. You have to give this time, okay? Give us a chance? Please?"

Renata turned her head away from Christy and fought back tears. She stood up abruptly. "I have to go to take a shower—will you excuse me?" Then she ran to the bathroom and slammed the door behind her.

∽

"The best part about Renata's Lemon Soap with bleach is that it's specially formulated so you can use it to wash your hair, your hands, your body, and even moldy bathroom tiles. Let me demonstrate how Renata's Lemon Soap with bleach cleans this grimy sink." Renata held the soap bottle up to her face and smiled at the imaginary camera. "I'll just pour a smidge into the sink like so. A little goes a long way. Now watch me add a touch of water and TA-DAA!! Look how shiny my sink is." Renata smelled the soap and let out a satisfied "Ahhhhh" for the camera. "It smells like a summer day. And now, for the next five minutes only, you can buy two bottles of Renata's Lemon Soap for the price of one."

"What are you doing?" Christy asked. She was standing at the bathroom door, having appeared out of nowhere.

Hasn't this woman ever heard of knocking? Renata wondered. "Nothing," she said. Christy didn't need to know that she was practicing for the Home Shopping Network.

"I see," Christy said. "Okay, well, I just wanted to tell you that your new nanny will be starting on Monday."

"I don't need a nanny," Renata said, putting her soap into the cabinet.

Christy stood at the door. "Of course you do, sweetheart. Michael and I work all the time. You're eleven. You have to have adult supervision."

"Christy," Renata said (she wasn't comfortable calling her "mom" yet, not that Christy had even asked), "I've gone to and from school by myself since I was six. I do homework and make A's without nobody's help. I cook my *own* dinner and clean my *own* house. *Really*, I *don't* need a nanny."

"Renata," Christy said, "you live on the Upper East Side of

Manhattan now. Every kid has a nanny. It's the law up here. And you don't need to cook and clean anymore. We have staff that does that."

"Like Grandma, right? Why don't you just treat me like who I am, the maid's kid?"

Christy's eyes grew large. Her neck and cheeks got splotchy. Renata couldn't tell if she was mad or hurt, but she was pleased with herself for getting a reaction. She wasn't sure why.

"Renata," Christy said evenly, "I loved Maria. She was like a second mother to me."

"If you loved her so much, you wouldn't have made her work instead of come to my concert."

Christy bit her lower lip. "Renata, doesn't the fact that I took you in to live with me tell you that I loved your grandmother? Why else would I do that?"

"That's okay. I don't need your charity." But secretly, Renata *wanted* to be in Christy and Michael's family. She was already imagining them eating together, going on vacation, celebrating holidays—family things. But she wanted those things only if *they* wanted *her*. This was all very confusing.

"You don't need my charity? Is that what you think this is? What, would you rather live in the attic and scrub our toilets?"

"That'd be okay."

Christy looked crushed. "For God's sake, Renata, can't you see that I want to do the right thing here? At least meet me halfway. Do you know how hard I worked to get all this? You'll never have to clean another toilet or wash another dish. Most people would be *very happy* about that."

"I like washing dishes," Renata said primly.

"Aaargh. You're making me crazy," Christy said, leaving in a huff.

꩜

DEAR DIARY,

I HATE IT HERE. IT'S THE COLDEST, MOST LONELIEST HOUSE EVER. I WISH I COULD TALK TO GRANDMA ONE MORE TIME. BUT I KNOW SHE'D JUST TELL ME TO LOOK AT THE BRIGHT SIDE, LIKE CHIRSTY DOES, ONLY SHE'D SAY IT BETTER. THE ONLY BRIGHT SIDE IS THAT I GET TO LIVE WITH MR. DRUMMOND. I JUST HOPE HE WILL LOVE ME THE WAY UNCLE BILL LOVED BUFFY AND JODY ON FAMILY AFFAIR. BUT I'LL NEVER LOVE OR EVEN LIKE CHRISTY (THE MURDERER).

LAST NIGHT, I TOLD HER A SECRET THAT I MADE HER PROMISE NOT TO TELL. I TOLD HER HOW THE DOORMEN MAKE ME USE THE SERVICE ELAVATOR. BUT I EXPLAINED THAT I DIDN'T MIND BECAUSE THE MAIDS AND BUTLERS ARE MY PEOPLE. THEN CHRISTY (THE LIAR) BROKE HER WORD AND MADE ME GO DOWNSTAIRS WITH HER WHILE SHE BALLED OUT ANTONIO THE DOORMAN.

I WAS SO IMBARASED. TONY SAID IT WAS AN HONEST MIS-TAKE. CHRISTY'S WHITE AND I'M BROWN. WHAT WAS HE SUP-POSED TO THINK? THAT MADE CHRISTY EVEN MADDER. NOW THE DOORMEN WILL HATE ME FOREVER.

I'M STUCK IN A FANCY GUEST ROOM WITH HARD PILLOWS AND NOT ONE STUFFED ANIMAL. CHRISTY SAYS I HAVE TO GET A NANNY EVEN THOUGH I DON'T NEED ONE. MAKING IT ALL WORSE, THEY ONLY EAT HEALTHY ASHIAN FOOD HERE. THERE'S NO FROOT LOOPS, NO MACARONI AND CHEESE, NO SHAKE AND BAKE AND NO FROZEN VEGETABLES. I WILL <u>NEVER</u> NEVER NEVER LIKE FRESH VEGETABLES NO MATTER HOW LONG I LIVE.

    YOURS FOREVER,
    RENATA E. RUIZ

Thanks for the Memories

On Tuesday morning, Renata stepped inside her old apartment for the first time since the night she and Christy picked out Grandma's burial outfit. Christy had voted for her green church suit, but Renata insisted on the pink satin robe from Macy's. "It's what Grandma would have wanted to wear," she said. So Maria Ruiz was laid to rest in her pajamas and robe, covered by her granddaughter's Mary-Kate and Ashley quilt. At the church, Renata slipped her fifth-grade picture into the casket.

Renata scurried over to the kitchen as soon as they walked inside. She turned on the water and started washing dishes.

"Renata, what are you doing?" Christy asked.

"Dishes," she said. "This house is a mess."

"Renata, we're here so you can pack your things and show me what you want to take. Someone else'll clean up." Christy looked at her watch. "I only have an hour." Then she looked at Renata and softened. "Tell you what, I'll pack your clothes. Why don't you put a yellow sticky on anything you want to keep. Here, take these."

Silently, Renata took the Post-its. She hated the way Christy always acted like she was trying to be helpful. That was all it was—acting. And always in a hurry. Like she was the most im-

portant person in the whole world. She took the pad of stickies
and glanced around. The entire apartment was tinier than her
new bedroom. Funny, it didn't used to be this small. Grandma's
reading glasses were sitting on top of a two-week-old *Star* on the
brown table next to the couch. Renata picked them up and
stuffed them in her pocket. She opened Grandma's sweater
drawer and touched her cranberry cardigan. Renata brought it
to her face and took a deep breath, smelling Grandma in the
sweater. She put it on. Looking around the room, she tried to
commit the place to memory. On top of the bookshelf was the
picture of Grandma and her in the wooden frame with hearts.
Renata picked that up. She walked to the bed, reached under
her mattress, and rescued the picture of her mother wearing the
white confirmation dress. Then she snatched her pillow. She
hadn't been sleeping since she moved to Christy's. Maybe this
would help. The last thing Renata took was Maria's vanity mirror, the one she used as a camera when she practiced being on
television.

As Christy packed Renata's clothes into a torn plaid suitcase, she glanced around the apartment. Her eyes welled and
she repositioned herself to face the wall.

"I'm done," Renata said.

Christy glanced up and saw Renata standing in front of
her, wearing a big sweater, holding a pillow, a mirror, and a
framed picture. "That's it? That's all you want?"

"It'd be nice to have the couch if that's not asking too
much."

"It won't match anything in your room," Christy said.

"Yes, but it's very useful. It folds out into a bed. Guests can
sleep in it," Renata explained. "It was Grandma's."

"Ah," Christy said. "So it reminds you of Maria. You know,
I have a chair in my room that used to belong to my dad.

Even though it's old-fashioned and worn-out, I'd never give it up because it makes me think of him when I sit in it."

Renata stared at the couch, showing no emotion. If Christy thinks she can make me like her just because we're both partial to the furniture of the dead people we loved, she's barking up the wrong street, she thought. It'll take *way* more than that.

"Sure, bring it," Christy said.

Renata walked over and placed a yellow sticky on the piece. It fell right off. She put it on again, this time on the arm, where it stayed put. "If you want, I'll let you put it in the living room," she said.

"I think you should keep it, honey. We'll have someone pick it up later," Christy promised. "C'mon, we'd better go. Your new nanny's coming to meet you."

"I don't need a nanny."

Christy ignored the comment as they walked out of the apartment. Turning off the light, she gave the place one last look. " 'Bye, Maria," she said.

Renata ran ahead and jumped into the car.

"That was fast," Steven said.

"Christy's in a hurry. *As usual*," she mumbled.

"Do you want some music?" he asked.

"Sure," Renata said. Steven turned the radio to a station that played really bad grown-up music. There was no accounting for taste, that's what Grandma used to say. Still, Renata liked Steven. He brought Toll House cookies that his wife baked especially for her. He drove her to school every day. Soon, Renata and her nanny would have their own driver, Christy explained. But for now, she could be with Steven. Christy's maid had put Renata's hair up for the funeral last week. Her masseuse gave Renata a massage because of all the toxins in her system after Grandma's death. Everyone at Christy and Michael's was being real nice. Secretly Renata was grateful for their kindness, but she acted quiet about it so there would be no misunderstanding that she was happy about any of this.

Raising Renata

Renata set her vanity mirror up on the dresser and talked earnestly into it. "I'm not sure about that Christy Hayes," she said. "First she acts like nothing scares her. But then, did you see the way she was when she had to pose with that snake? She completely freaked out. I think her being afraid of performing with a boa constrictor around her neck will ruin her chances. I really don't think Christy Hayes is cut out to be America's *next . . . top . . . model.*"

Renata heard a knock at the door and she stopped talking. "Come in," she said, turning away from the mirror-camera.

Eve poked her head through the doorway. "Christy's waiting for you in the library with your new nanny. Better get going."

"Sure," Renata said, irritated that her segment of *America's Next Top Model* was interrupted for *this*. She tramped through the apartment, determined that everyone in her path should know her feelings about getting a nanny.

She peeked into Michael's library looking for Christy and this nanny person. The library was the only room in the whole apartment that she liked, because it was full of books and folk art—none of that hard glass or marble stuff. Queen

Latifah was standing next to the computer desk deep in conversation with Christy. Renata was speechless. Would Christy hire someone *that* famous just to take care of *her*? Maybe Christy *did* want her. Then she realized that a star as big as Queen Latifah wouldn't want to be a nanny, not even part time. It must be Queen Latifah's sister.

"That's all right. I'm just sorry I couldn't be here Friday like Eve asked," the nanny was saying. "I had sad business in Montgomery. I been nursing my sister through breast cancer for the last year. She died two weeks ago, and there was odds and ends to take care of, more than I thought."

"Queen Latifah?" Renata asked, shocked.

Both women turned and saw Renata standing in the doorway.

"Who?" the nanny asked.

"Your sister. Queen Latifah?" Renata said.

"No, Ambrosia Freedom. Two weeks shy of fifty-seven years old, and the Lord saw fit to take her, mmm-mmm-mmm. By the way, I'm Nectar Freedom. What's your name?"

"I'm Renata Ruiz." Renata walked in and shook Nectar's hand. "Sorry you lost your sister."

Nectar looked deeply into the little girl's eyes. "Thank you, dumplin'. And I want you to know how terrible I feel that you lost your grandma. Eve told me all about it, mmm-mmm-mmm, you poor child." The way Nectar said it, it sounded like "you po chall."

Renata soaked in the sympathy. She felt like crawling in between Nectar's humongous bosoms, curling up into a little ball, and crying herself dry. "Thank you," she mumbled. "Have you ever been a nanny before?"

"I have. I took care of J. R. Collins for ten years and then Marissa Ethridge till she was thirteen."

"The singer?"

"No, the child."

"I'm self-independent," Renata said. "I *don't* need a nanny."

"Well, that makes my job easier," Nectar said. "I can catch up on my reading while you're taking care of yourself."

Renata turned to Christy. "Do you have any questions?"

"I think you're doing a fine job on your own," Christy said, smiling.

"How old are you?" Renata asked Nectar.

"That's not a legal question to ask me, dumplin'. But I'll tell you anyway 'cause I like you. I'm fifty-nine years young."

Renata giggled; then she became solemn. "My grandma was fifty-nine when she passed."

"And that's *too* young to go. Course, 'he that cuts off twenty years of life cuts off so many years of fearing death.' That's a direct quote from Mr. William Shakespeare," Nectar said.

"Is that who you used to work for?" Renata asked.

"No, no," Nectar said, smiling. "Shakespeare was a famous writer from about four hundred years ago."

"Is it okay if I go to my room? I'm tired."

"Sure," Christy said. Renata said good-bye and ran to her bedroom.

∽

Christy shook her head as she watched Renata disappear. "She spends way too much time alone."

"Doesn't she have friends?" Nectar asked.

"Not around here. Not yet, anyway," Christy said. She looked into Nectar's friendly eyes and imagined how painful the last year of caring for her dying sister must have been.

She sensed that Nectar somehow needed them as much as they needed her. "Did Eve tell you the circumstances of our getting Renata? Did she mention that my husband and I travel a lot for business?"

"Eve told me everything."

"You'll be working plenty of overtime, I'd guess. Of course, you'll have Eve's full support for anything you need. And there's a maid, a chef, a driver. And I'm looking for a psychiatrist so Renata'll have someone to talk to. This has *got* to be hard for her."

"Even with all that help, I believe I can do as much for Renata as I can for you."

"I know you can," Christy said, giving Nectar a hug. Nectar reminded her of Maria—warm and loving, but formidable at the same time. "Now, I *must* get to the office. I haven't been there in weeks, and I'm dying to get back in the saddle."

" 'To business that we love we rise betime and go to it with delight,' " Nectar quoted.

"Shakespeare?" Christy asked.

"Yes, *Antony and Cleopatra*. I just love that William Shakespeare," Nectar said, chuckling. "He had such a way with words."

"Maybe you can teach Renata to love him, too."

"It'd be *my* pleasure."

"Eve'll be here in a few minutes to show you the drill. Are you sure you'll be okay?"

"Don't you worry about Nectar Freedom, darlin'. You just scoot. Go to work. And don't give Renata a second thought."

Don't give Renata a second thought. Those were the most beautiful words Christy had heard in a long time. But five seconds after the wave of relief came the pang of guilt about feeling relieved.

～

DEAR DIARY,

I JUST MET MY NANNY, NECTER, WHO SEEMS OK IF
I HAVE TO BE BABYSAT. CHRISTY'S ANSWER TO ANY PROBLEM
(SUCH AS ME) IS TO GET ANOTHER SERVANT. WHY DOES SHE
NEED SO MANY, DEAR DIARY? NO ONE'S EVER HOME TO MESS
ANYTHING UP. THE PEOPLE WHO LIVE IN CHRISTY'S BUILDING
ARE MEAN. THERE ARE NO KIDS. NOBODY SMILES. THE ONLY
GOOD PERSON SO FAR IS MRS. DAMILL. SHE'S OLD AND SHE
SITS IN THE LOBBY EVERY DAY WEARING GLOVES AND A
CHURCH HAT LIKE SHE'S WAITING FOR COMPANY. BUT NO ONE
COMES SO I SIT WITH HER AND WE TALK ABOUT TV SHOWS
AND OUR DEEPEST FEELINGS. I TOLD HER ABOUT GRANDMA.
SHE TOLD ME ABOUT BIRDY. HE WAS THE LOVE OF HER LIFE
AND THEY MET WHEN SHE WAS 88 BUT HE DIED THE NEXT YEAR.
CAN YOU BELIEVE HOW TRAJIC THAT IS?

MR. DRUMMOND IS NEVER AROUND. WHEN HE DOES COME
HOME, HE GOES TO HIS LIBRARY OR BEDROOM WHERE KIDS
(SUCH AS ME) ARE NOT ALLOWED. HE AND CHRISTY EAT DINNER
BY THEMSELVES EVERY NIGHT. I EAT IN THE KITCHEN WITH YOK
WAH. I WISH MR. DRUMMOND WOULD SAY HI JUST ONCE. HOW
DOES HE EXPECT TO BE A GOOD FATHER IF HE NEVER TALKS
TO ME?

YOUR LONELY FRIEND,
RENATA RUIZ

She Works Hard for the Money

When Christy arrived at Baby G's tenth-floor offices, her first urge was to kiss the ground, but instead she planted a big smacker right on the receptionist's forehead. It had been almost three weeks since she'd set foot in the place. First, she had gone to Madrid to work through a retailing deal with Déjà Blue, the new chain that was sweeping the youth market all over Europe. That was followed by the aborted trip to Davos. Then, Maria's death and all it had entailed. At this moment, in the safety of her office, among people who had worked for her from the beginning, Christy felt she was home. Here, she knew what she was doing. She was in control. Her apartment was no longer the safe haven it used to be.

As she walked through the sea of desks in the communal workspace, employees looked up and smiled. A few came over to greet Christy and welcome her back. She felt like hugging every last one of them. They fed her soul. Christy walked into her office, which would more appropriately be called a suite, though it was hardly elegant. To her surprise, there was Katherine, sitting at her desk and surrounded by the agency team. "Am I interrupting something?" Christy asked.

Katherine jumped. "Oh God! She's ba-ack." Katherine ran over and gave Christy a big hug. "We didn't expect you so soon."

"Hey, what can I say? I escaped. What are you guys meeting about?"

"One second. Let me introduce you to Skip Heller. He'll be writing that article about you for Wall Street Week. He was shadowing me today to get oriented."

Skip walked over to Christy and shook her hand. His grasp was firm, but his palm was so clammy that Christy unconsciously wiped her hand off on her skirt. Dressed in jeans, Skip was a short, compact guy who obviously spent his off hours in the gym. He wore a Yankees cap to cover his thinning hair. He had on Nike running shoes, which irritated Christy to no end. Would he follow the president of Pepsi around while sipping a can of Coke? She thought not.

"Great to meet you," he said. "Didn't expect to have the pleasure so soon. You don't mind if I sit in?"

"No, of course not." Christy walked over to Katherine and the agency people. "Looks like I'm just in time. What's going on?"

"We're reviewing the new campaign," Katherine said.

"We're doing a new campaign? Since when?"

"Why don't you tell her, Jack?" Jack Malone was Ogilvy's SVP on the account. He showed up only for high-level discussions and major presentations when someone with his keen strategic mind and $500-per-hour billing rate was warranted. Christy was surprised to see him meeting with Katherine, who focused mostly on operations and finance, not marketing. She wondered why Spencer White, her VP of advertising, wasn't there.

"Here, here, sit," Katherine said, gesturing to Christy's chair and taking a seat on the other side of the desk. "We think it's time to retire the old campaign. It's been thirteen years since you ran in the Olympics, and our younger audience doesn't know who you are."

Christy felt the bottom of her stomach fall out. Before she had time to think, she spoke. "*Everyone* knows who I am. I'm like Frank Perdue. He's chicken, I'm sports. *I'm* the brand. *I'm* Baby G."

"Yes, but they *retired* Frank Perdue," Katherine said. "And then he died, poor soul." She gave Christy a pleading look. "At least take a look at this. Consider it."

Jack continued. "Christy, you've always encouraged us to be straight with you. So we aren't going to sugarcoat what we learned. The new research shows that consumers *do* identify you with the brand, but most don't connect your athletic and business achievements. And for those who do, you're not relevant anymore."

"Not as an athlete, anyway," Katherine interjected.

"She's right," Jack said. "Eight focus groups can't be wrong. They see you as so thirteen years ago, if you don't mind my saying, nothing personal of course. So, we're recommending a *new* approach. Let's lock up the seven American athletes most likely to bring home gold next summer. We can get them now for a song. But after they win, we won't be able to touch them. We'll hire a photographer to photograph the athletes' perfect bodies, their faces in shadow—someone like Annie Leibovitz. The tag line will read "Body by Baby G." Everyone'll want to know who inhabits each mind-blowing bod. Only at the end of the campaign will we reveal. If the advertising moves the meter as we expect, we'll choose seven more athletes to represent us as the year progresses. The photographs will be breathtaking; kids everywhere will hang them on their walls. Dieters will post them on their refrigerators for motivation. They'll decorate every gym in America. Consumers will associate perfect physiques with *everything* Baby G sells."

"The focus groups loved it, especially the women, and they're eighty-three percent of our market," Katherine added.

"I know what our female market share is," Christy said.

"I think it's worth a test," Katherine added. "If it doesn't deliver, we'll consider it a short-term campaign and go back to our old imagery." The agency people nodded their heads in perfect choreographed agreement.

"You guys have certainly been busy while I was away. I'm impressed," Christy said evenly. "When did you field the new research, Jack?"

"It's been several months. You were on your honeymoon, I think."

"I told you about it," Katherine said.

"I don't remember," Christy replied.

"You must have been distracted by Michael. Anyway, do you like it?" Katherine asked.

"What'll it cost?"

"About two million all in. We have to secure the athletes and the photographer. Media expenses will be the same as they otherwise would have been."

"And you're certain this will deliver more than two million in contribution?"

"We'll set up comparative test markets and measure," Jack explained. "You can decide whether to roll it out permanently based on quantitative results."

"What does Spencer think of the campaign? He *is* the VP of advertising," Christy asked.

"I decided not to involve him yet. This was such an important decision that I wanted your input first."

"You guys have thought of everything. Let me consider it."

You Gotta Have Friends

*K*atherine returned after walking the agency team out. She sat across from Christy. Skip Heller, the reporter, quietly made himself at home on the couch, trying to blend in with the upholstery. "Gee, Katherine, I wish you'd given me some warning about this. I had no idea you wanted to be so involved in marketing."

"I was planning to tell you as soon as you came in. No one expected you today."

"Well, my nanny started, so I was able to get away."

"Really? Where'd you find her?"

"Eve put an ad in the *Irish Echo*."

"You should have used an agency. They screen for you," Katherine said.

"Well, Nectar seems terrific. I'm happy with her."

"Yes, but what do you *really* know about her? You'd better get a nanny-cam. That's what I use."

"Alex is a teenager. Wouldn't she tell you if her nanny was mistreating her?"

"Christy, Christy, Christy," Katherine said, shaking her head. "My naïve friend. Nannies steal *all* the time. In fact, I'm going to *give* you my nanny-cam. Blondell's been with me for five years so I don't need it anymore. I'll drop it off at your house this weekend and teach you how to use it."

"I don't think so, Katherine. What if she catches me taping her? I'm just not comfortable—"

"The camera's hidden in a clock radio. She'll *never* know. *Every* new mother does this, Christy." Katherine looked over at Skip Heller, who was taking notes. "She's a new mother; she needs my guidance, as you can see."

"Okay, okay, fine, whatever," Christy said, changing the subject. "So tell me again *why* you're so involved in the marketing campaign?"

"The agency brought this to us proactively. I babysat the project while you were away. You have no idea how happy I am to give it back." She did seem relieved that Christy had returned.

"I'm not sure how I feel about stepping down as spokesperson," Christy said, knowing exactly how she felt about it. But how could she say so in front of Skip?

"I'm not sure how I feel about it, either. But the numbers will tell us if it's time to retire the old campaign. You gotta check your ego at the door on this one." Katherine flashed her most sympathetic girlfriend smile.

"I guess." At least Katherine understood how hard this was. Christy hadn't realized how much it meant to her to be a well-known face. She knew that wasn't enough of a reason to ignore a good idea.

"Let's talk about something more important. How do you like being a mother?" Katherine asked.

"*Oh my God.* It's such a challenge. What do *I* know about being a mother, especially an Upper East Side mom? They're like from another planet. You know where I could really use your help?"

"Where?"

"We have to get Renata into a private school. Steven is driving her an hour each way to her old school in Queens. I'd feel better if she was in the neighborhood. Plus, she needs to make friends in Manhattan. What was that girls' school Alex is going to?"

"Colby."

"Would it be hard to get Renata in?"

"You mean *now*? You want to transfer her *now*?"

"If possible."

"What grade is she in?"

"Fifth."

"No way. It's impossible to get a kid in midyear, unless someone moved and there just happens to be an extra space. And Colby is the most in-demand girls' school in the city. I'll call the head of admissions, but don't get your hopes up. Does the kid have good grades?"

"Renata. Her name's Renata. She has straight A's. *That* won't be an issue."

Katherine's eyes widened, and her mouth formed a wise and knowing O. "*Are* there issues?"

"Only insofar as her grandmother just died, she's adjusting to a new family, Michael has mixed feelings about her, and her prepubescent hormones are starting to rage."

"You better get her into therapy."

"I was gonna ask about that. Can you recommend someone?"

"Alex's therapist is excellent. *This is off the record*," Katherine yelled to Skip Heller, who took down every word.

Christy froze. She kept forgetting that damned reporter was in the room. Then she tried to relax when she saw how casual Katherine was with the guy. She had obviously decided he was okay.

"She's Hispanic, right?" Katherine asked.

"Yes."

"Colby'll like that. Would you be willing to make a big donation? Head a major committee?"

"I'll do whatever it takes."

"I'm surprised you didn't ask Brownie Rich to help you. Her girls are at Colby."

"*KAAAATHERINE!*" Christy threw a yellow pad at her friend and laughed like she was goofing on her. There was a reporter in the room, for God's sake. "Skip, would you excuse us for a minute?" Christy asked.

"Who, me?" he said.

"Yes, I just need a minute with Katherine one-on-one. You understand?"

"Oh, sure," he said, sauntering out in his Nikes.

When Skip was safely out of earshot, Christy spoke. "Katherine, you have to be more careful with that guy listening. What are you thinking? Anything you say can end up in the article!"

"Okay, okay," Katherine said. "But he insisted on watching you operate in your real life. They won't do the article if all we give them is access to a bunch of photo ops."

"I understand. But there's real and there's *real*. He doesn't need to know I'm asking you to pull strings to get Renata into school."

"You're right. I'll be more circumspect. In fact, I'll call Colby *after* he leaves. Lucky for you they love me. I just made a six-figure pledge."

"*SIX FIGURES?*"

"This is the time. I need them to get Alex into a good college. After I pledged, they assigned her their best college counselor. Coincidence? I think not."

Christy couldn't get over how complicated parenthood was. The nanny. The driver. Clothes. School. Donations. Decorator. Camp. Therapy. And this was just the beginning. There was bound to be more. She wondered how Maria always managed to make it seem like raising Renata was no trouble at all.

Renata the Spy

DEAR DIARY,

YESTERDAY, WHILE NO ONE WAS HOME AS USUAL, I TOOK NECTER ON A TOUR OF THE APARTMENT. BUT SECRETLY, I WAS STAKING OUT HIDING PLACES. NOBODY TELLS ME ANYTHING AROUND HERE SO MY ONLY CHOICE IS TO SPY. THE BEST PLACE I FOUND WAS BETWEEN THE LIBRARY AND CHRISTY AND MICHAEL'S BEDROOM. THEY SHARE A CLOSET THAT YOU CAN GET INTO FROM EITHER ROOM. YOU CAN HEAR EVERYTHING IF YOU STICK YOUR EAR UNDER THE DOOR TO WHATEVER ROOM WHERE PEOPLE ARE TALKING. AND YOU CAN HEAR EVEN BETTER WHEN YOU USE A GLASS. THIS COULD BE A GOLD MIND!!!!

AFTER NECTER LEFT YESTERDAY, I VISITED MRS. DAMILL DE MILLE IN HER APARTMENT. GUESS WHAT? SHE IS RUSSIAN PRINCESS ANASTASHA, DECENDED FROM ZARR NICHOLAS. HER BIGGEST REGRET IN LIFE IS THAT SHE CAN'T GO BACK AND RECLAIM THE RUSSIAN THRONE. WE PLAYED WITH HER CAT AND I TALKED ABOUT GRANDMA. SHE TOLD ME THAT EVERYONE SHE'S EVER LOVED HAS DIED. MRS. DE MILLE IS THE ONLY PERSON WHO UNDERSTANDS MY PAIN.

THANKS FOR LISTENING!
RENATA

Coveting Colby

ou two are *super*lucky," Mrs. Hitchcock said. "Demi pulled Rumor, Scout, and Tallulah out last month so we just happen to have three extra spots. Very unusual. Demi was heartbroken about leaving, but she's making a movie in California and doesn't want to be separated from the girls."

"Demi's *such* a good mother," Christy said. "Not that I know her, but from everything I've read."

If Michael could have rolled his eyes at that moment, he would have. Christy kicked him under the table. He wasn't sure how to respond to that. "I hear Bruce is a great father, too," Michael added.

"So, Michael, it is *truly* admirable of you to adopt Renata. What concerns did you have about taking in an eleven-year-old Hispanic orphan?"

"I wasn't concerned at all. Renata's a great kid. Very special. I'm looking forward to being the father she never had."

"That's *sooooo* generous of you," Mrs. Hitchcock trilled. "At Colby, we specifically look for involved fathers. That's the number-one predictor of a girl's success in life."

"My dad was a huge factor in my life. He introduced me to running and pushed me to win," Christy said.

"Case in point," Mrs. Hitchcock said. "And Michael, you seem like a wonderful father. Renata is lucky to have you."

Michael grimaced. Christy reached over and squeezed his hand.

"So, Christy, Katherine told me you were interested in heading a major committee at the school. She suggested we put you in charge of fifth-grade graduation. We always celebrate the girls moving on to middle school. It's such an important rite of passage, don't you think?"

"I do, and that's a wonderful idea. I've never chaired a graduation before, but how hard can it be?" Christy said.

"Well, let's see, there's the ceremony itself, the speaker, and soliciting donations for the class gift. With all the volunteers we have, it'll practically organize itself. Everyone will be thrilled to have a chairwoman with the kind of connections you have," Mrs. Hitchcock said. "We'll be looking for a famous woman to make the commencement address. Someone who's a role model for young girls."

"Then this must be kismet," Michael said, smiling at his wife. "I'll bet Christy could get LaShaun Mason."

"*Reee-ally,*" Mrs. Hitchcock said, fascinated.

"No problem," Christy said. I'm sure the number-one-ranked tennis player in the world would love to speak at a fifth grade graduation right before Wimbledon, she thought.

Everyone smiled like they thought that was a super idea.

Mrs. Hitchcock wrote something on a piece of paper and handed it to Christy. Here's the number of our PTA president, Brownie Rich. She'll supervise you on the graduation."

"Honey, isn't that great? You *know* her," Michael said.

"You're friends?" Mrs. Hitchcock said. "How wonderful. Tell you what. Brownie's daughter, Stephanie, will be in Renata's class. She can be her big sister, you know, take her around and show her the ropes. I'll call Brownie myself to arrange it."

"Thanks," Christy said in a voice that was half an octave short of hysterical.

Soon Christy and Michael were at Mrs. Hitchcock's door, practically genuflecting as they bid her adieu.

In the car heading back down Park Avenue, Michael wasted no time launching into his tirade. "I pay Ali's tuition bill every year, and it's only twenty-eight thousand plus a ten-thousand-dollar annual-fund donation. I thought *that* was extreme. I can't believe I let that development guy get two hundred thousand out of me. And how could you let them rope you into running that graduation extravaganza? Believe me, Christy, I've headed enough Manhattan events to know how thankless it is to mobilize a pack of terminally privileged volunteers in a public gesture of goodwill."

Christy tried to protest, but she couldn't get a word in.

"You have no clue what you're getting yourself into," Michael said. Suddenly, he stopped himself. "You know, Beegee. I keep forgetting. You're an Olympic champion. You started your own company. I should never underestimate you."

"Right, and I landed *you*, too!" Christy said. "Don't forget that."

"And you talked me into taking Renata," Michael added. Then he smiled. "Colby won't know what hit them."

Fifth Avenue Fracas

*C*hristy and Michael were having their late candlelit dinner, a ritual that began soon after they met. It gave them time to relax and talk freely. Renata had been fed earlier in the kitchen by Yok Wah, who fussed over her and convinced her to eat soba noodles and seaweed despite the child's insistence that she was allergic. Renata would not be joining them. Christy was determined to show Michael that nothing would change with a child in the house. They would still have their special dinners. Tonight they were eating on the terrace, where warming lights surrounded the table. They had views of Central Park and Fifth Avenue. Yok Wah padded out and served the first course, shrimp in lobster sauce.

"Thank you for what you did today," Christy said to Michael.

"I did it for you," he said.

"Not for Renata? Not even a little bit?"

Michael focused on his shrimp.

"So you didn't mean what you said today, about being the father she never had?"

Michael topped off Christy's wine and poured some for himself. "Not really, Beegee."

Christy's face twitched ever so slightly.

"Honey, I told you how I felt from the beginning. I'm not letting myself get close to her. I'll be there when *you* need me, though."

"Thanks for all your help getting her into Colby."

"You're welcome. But . . ."

"Hmm?"

"Don't depend on me to be there for her. I don't think I can do that."

"I won't, I know." Christy went over and kissed Michael. "I love you."

"Love you, too."

Christy decided to change the subject. "God, it feels good to be back at the office. I never appreciated my job the way I do now that we . . . I . . . have Renata. I used to be able to focus on the company. Now, I have to worry about her care, too."

"Children are a lot of work," Michael said. "There's no way around that."

"I know, and I'm off-loading as much as I can. Everything's being outsourced. Nanny, driver, cook, decorator, therapist. They're reporting to Eve. I made her president of the Renata division."

"What about you? Weren't *you* supposed to nurture her? Isn't that why we didn't send her to boarding school?"

"Nectar's the primary nurturer, but I do my share. Eve schedules bonding activities into my calendar. I think Renata's feeling secure. We'll know for sure after she meets with Dr. Perlmutter, the psychiatrist Katherine recommended."

Michael nodded thoughtfully. "Whoever heard of raising a kid this way? Reminds me of how Suzanna managed my hospital stay. But you'll figure it out, you always do." He pushed his chair back, then leaned over and gave Christy a kiss, conversation closed. "I'll be in the library going over the contracts on seven-seven-seven." Michael was referring to 777 Madison, his new corporate headquarters.

"I can't believe you're closing tomorrow. I've been so busy I lost track of the days."

"We took your advice and hired Tai Beck Long for the design. It was a great recommendation, Beeg."

"Glad I could help. They're amazing." Christy gave Michael a long, tender kiss. "Marla will be here at eight-thirty. Don't forget." Marla had been Christy's masseuse for more than ten years. Since then, she had garnered clients like Ron Perlman and Michael Bloomberg, and had even been flown to an island off the coast of Africa by Georgio Armani. Christy joked with her that if she hadn't married Michael she might not have continued to make the cut. Marla always laughed, but Christy wondered. All the support people she knew in Manhattan seemed to rank themselves on their clientele. And there were so many big shots in the city; it was tough to keep your place on the list. In the old days, Marla would screen boyfriends for Christy. She had a mean deep massage, and if a guy wimped out, Marla let Christy know he hadn't passed the test. Marla discounted a few of them on basic grounds of aura. With Michael, Christy didn't even need to ask.

Back in the library, Michael was muttering to himself as he read through the documents for the next day's meeting. "I should have gone to law school," he said as he tried to digest the dense legalese.

"Mr. Drummond, Mr. Drummond, come quickly, hurry!"

Michael put his papers down and turned his attention to Renata, who was jumping up and down in the library doorway. She appeared to be having some kind of fit. "Renata, you're really not supposed to be in this part of the house."

"I know, *but this is an emergency!*" she yelled.

"What's the problem?" he asked calmly.

"Come now, *NOW.* It's life or death," she said.

"Is it Christy?"

"No, it's Mr. Ng. He's kidnapped Mrs. De Mille's cat, *you know*, Mr. Koodles. He's threatening to kill him. Mrs. De Mille is *crying*."

"Of course," Michael said. "Mr. Koodles."

"Come on, Mrs. De Mille *needs* you."

"Can't you get Christy or Neck . . . Necklace, Necktie, Nectar? I'm working here . . ."

"Mr. Drummond, we need a *MAN*," Renata said. "This is a kidnapping. *HURRY.*"

Michael stood up and languished behind the child as she dashed through the apartment, her long black curls trailing behind. He looked around for Christy, but she had disappeared.

They took the stairs down one floor. Mrs. De Mille stood outside of Mr. Ng's apartment in a thin blue cotton housecoat, the kind ladies wore in 1955. Her salmon-colored hair was up in pink sponge rollers. There was a bald spot on the top of her head that looked like a peach-colored yarmulke with liver spots. Mr. Ng's door was open, chain on, to protect himself from this ninety-five-year-old biddie.

"Please, Mr. Ng, please give Mr. Koodles back. I love him," Mrs. De Mille begged in her gravelly chain-smoker's voice.

"No! His incessant meowing is killing me. I told you to have him de-meowed."

"The vet said he was too old for the operation. I tried."

"For God's sake," Michael said. "Mrs. De Mille, allow me."

Renata was excited to be in the midst of all this drama. She couldn't wait to write about it in her diary. Mr. Drummond was about to be a hero. She thought something like this happened on *Family Affair* once. But it was Buffy who was kidnapped and Mr. French who saved the day. Or, maybe it was her doll, Mrs. Beasley, who disappeared and Uncle Bill who came to the rescue. She couldn't remember for sure.

"Mr. Ng, please, open the door. You've already kidnapped the cat. You don't want to add murder to your crime."

"The cat's a nuisance. It deserves to die. I've called the pound. They're on their way."

"Nooooo," Mrs. De Mille gasped. She leaned against the wall like she was about to faint. Renata fanned her with a Chinese food menu she found on the floor.

"Mr. Ng, Mrs. De Mille is ninety-five. Look at her. How can you disrespect your elderly neighbor like this?"

"I don't care if she's a hundred. She deserves it for not shutting up the damn cat."

"Mr. Ng, take the chain off. At least let me come in and talk to you. Man-to-man. Come on."

Mr. Ng hesitated, then unlocked the door. Michael stepped inside while Renata stayed with Mrs. De Mille, fanning and comforting her. A few minutes later, Michael walked out holding a huge orange tabby cat out in front of him like it was a bomb about to explode.

Renata squealed and Mrs. De Mille let out a cry of relief. "Thank you, thank you. You saved my Mr. Koodles!" Michael hustled the two back to Mrs. De Mille's apartment.

Once inside, he asked, "Are you okay, Mrs. De Mille? Can I get you some water?"

"I'm fine. Thank you again," she said. "What did you say to him?"

"I promised we'd take the cat to our apartment so he wouldn't hear it meowing anymore."

"What! Never!" Mrs. De Mille said, holding Mr. Koodles tightly.

"Don't worry." Michael smiled. "I didn't mean it."

"You lied?" Renata said, her eyes wide. "On purpose?"

"I did, but I shouldn't have, Renata. It's not right to lie, but in this case, Mr. Ng was a thief, a kidnapper, and a possible cat murderer. I had to do something drastic."

"Don't worry, I won't start lying. Unless it's an emergency," Renata said solemnly.

"Mrs. De Mille, you better be careful. Mr. Ng is crazy."

"Don't worry about me. I've been a city girl my whole life. I know how to handle nut jobs like him." Mrs. De Mille hugged Mr. Koodles tightly.

"You're *my* hero," Renata whispered to Michael, batting her eyes.

"No big deal," he said, as they started back upstairs.

Mrs. De Mille cracked open the door again. "Mr. Drummond, would you consider buying my apartment and then leasing it back to me for life?"

"Well, I'll definitely give it some thought," Michael said in an interested voice. "But why would you want to do that? Do you need money to live on?"

"No, it's not that. Mr. Ng has been scheming to buy my apartment for years. I'll be Goddamned if I'll have my money-grubbing heirs selling my home to that fucking cat snatcher." She smiled at Renata. "Pardon my French, dear."

∽

DEAR DIARY,

   I 'LL NEVER FORGET LAST NIGHT AS LONG AS I LIVE. MICHAEL SAVED MR. KOODLES FROM CERTAIN DEATH AT THE HANDS OF AN EVIL MANIAC. IT WAS A HORROWING EXPERI-ENCE THAT BROUGHT ME AND MICHAEL TOGETHER AS FATHER AND DAUGHTER. NOTHING CAN TEAR US APART NOW.

      YOUR HOPEFUL FRIEND,
      R. E. RUIZ

Renata Spies While Christy Shops

DEAR DIARY,
   THIS MORNING I HID INSIDE THE PANTRY WHILE YOK WAH
MADE BREAKFAST. NOTHING OF INTEREST HAPPENED. BUT I
GOT IN AND OUT OF THE PANTRY WITHOUT HER SEEING ME.
IT WAS GOOD PRACTICE.
      LOVE,
      RENATA THE SPY

∞

Christy slipped on the red double-breasted jacket and admired herself in the mirror. "So, what do you think?"

"It's not quite right," Katherine mused. "You need something a little more feminine. Too bad Ophelia went out of business. Their jackets were so beautiful."

"What about something vintage?" Ava suggested. Ava was Christy's stylist, usually called in for big photo shoots for *Fortune*, *Wired*, the *Wall Street Journal*.

"No, not vintage. I want to go with a current designer. These are the Matrix Awards. I can't get too funky. I'll wear an antique brooch or something," Christy said.

"Then try the Dolce and Gabbana suit," Ava suggested.

"Now *this* I like," Christy said, unzipping the skirt, a fitted, retro-looking tweed with a row of leopard silk ruffles peeking out from the hem.

"I have the perfect brooch you can wear with that," Katherine said. "It's a Cartier piece from the fifties, a sculptured ivory rose with diamonds. My mother gave it to me before she died."

"You'd lend that to me?"

"Of course I would. You're my best friend. This is a *huge* occasion. I can't believe you're getting a Matrix."

"What exactly is a Matrix Award?" Ava asked. "I know they're prestigious. I just don't know why."

"They're for women who make outstanding achievements in communications," Christy said, examining the back of her suit in a three-way mirror. "We're getting one for sponsoring Columbia scholarships for girls going into sports journalism. It's the community service award," Christy said.

"Did you tell them we're both involved in that?" Katherine asked.

"Of course. But they could only take one person, so they went with the CEO. Sorry." She gave Katherine a sympathetic smile. She really did wish she could share this.

"That's okay. I'm happy for you. My day'll come. You're in good company this year. Did you see who else was getting an award? Diane Sawyer, Bernadette Peters, Galit Portal."

"I have to try to bond with Galit. Maybe she'll write more flattering articles about me if we're honorees together. What do you think?" Christy asked, modeling her suit. "Very hip, right?"

"It looks sexy but serious at the same time. I love it. Let's get a man's opinion," Katherine said, dragging Christy out of the dressing room to find Skip Heller. He had followed them into the dressing room, but Christy shooed him away. Maybe it was that he wore Nikes, maybe it was that he was pushy, maybe it was that he was a reporter, but something about him made Christy very uncomfortable. She was elated that this was his last week. Skip Heller was living up to his name—he was like the houseguest from hell.

Much Ado About Nuts

S o you see, gentlemen, even though the industry is in an overall downturn, eighteen- to twenty-five-year-old women are buying six percent *more* this year than last. Our market is eighty-three-percent women, and of that, more than half are in the eighteen- to twenty-five segment. It's our biggest audience. That's why *our* profits are going up while most retailers are losing ground," Christy explained.

Christy was having lunch at the Four Seasons with Jeremy Moran, Dan Patterson, and Calvin Wolff, three of Wall Street's most influential retail analysts. Of course, Skip "Pretend I'm Not Here" Heller was there as well, the fly on the wall.

"What can I bring you?" the waiter asked.

"We've been so busy talking, we haven't looked at our menus," Christy said. "You'll have to give us a few minutes."

"No rush."

"Could you bring me a glass of red wine? Whatever's your best wine by the glass," Skip whispered to the waiter.

"Certainly, sir."

"Why do you think you're so attractive to that segment?" Jeremy asked. He was with Goldman Sachs and hadn't been high on Christy's stock since they went public. She intended to turn him around today.

"With a lot of foresight and lucky breaks, we've managed to keep the buzz going for the brand. It started with Sasha, you know, when she first got so big. She was always being photographed wearing our street-inspired sneakers. After she died, they took on a kind of mystical significance. Since then, we've had excellent results placing our clothes on some of the most admired women in movies and on TV, and of course, athletes. The brand is considered hip, which is tough to achieve in athletic wear. Excuse me." Christy's cell phone was vibrating. In the past she would have turned it off for a business lunch, but now that she had Renata, she had to be reachable. Colby demanded it.

Damn, she thought when the school's number popped up. "Hello," she stage-whispered.

"Mrs. Drummond, this is Mrs. Smart, Renata's teacher." Christy thought it was weird that Renata's teacher had that name. She wondered if the woman had changed it when she went into the profession or if she went into the profession because she had the perfect name.

"Yes."

"This morning you sent a peanut butter sandwich for Renata?"

"Did we? Is there a problem?"

"Mrs. Drummond, Colby is a nut-free school. Do you realize how deadly it would be if Renata touched an allergic girl after eating the sandwich? Or worse, what if she'd traded lunches with an allergic child?"

Christy needed to find a private place. She looked at her lunch guests and mouthed "just a minute." Slipping out to the restroom, she sat on the closed toilet in one of the well-appointed stalls.

"I'm sorry, Mrs. Smart. Is someone allergic in the class?"

"No."

"Is someone allergic in the school?"

"Not this year."

"So why is this a problem?"

"I told you: *we're a nut-free school*. It's our policy *never* to take chances. Have you ever seen an allergic child go into anaphylactic shock after ingesting even a crumb of a nut?"

"No, I haven't."

"Their throat swells up until they can't breathe, their skin turns blue. It's a horrific way to die. You don't want to be responsible for that, do you?"

"No, of course not. What can I do?"

"Can you bring a replacement lunch?"

"I can't right this second—"

"Shall I call Mr. Drummond?"

"*NO*. I'll send our *nanny* immediately," she whispered, as if she was doing something she'd rather not publicize, like trying to score drugs or Wayne Newton tickets.

"Mrs. Drummond, do you think it's *appropriate* to send a nanny instead of a parent? I realize you're new to motherhood . . ."

"Okay, fine. I'll figure something else out," Christy said, ending the call.

On her way back to the table, she talked to Eric, the maître d'. He understood. Quickly, the kitchen prepared a bagged lunch of chicken salad and a fresh piece of strawberry shortcake, all for a mere $36. It was whisked out to Steven with coded instructions he would understand. After all, he wasn't a nanny. Problem solved.

"Guys, I'm sorry. Emergency, you understand," she said,

hoping they would assume it was work-related. Then she realized an emergency would send the wrong signal about the business. "Personal. Personal emergency."

The guys all nodded like they understood, but Christy knew they didn't. They had buffers between them and personal crises during working hours. She picked up where they had left off. "We save money on marketing since almost all of our promotion is done by billboards or celebrities wearing our products. Both cost less than TV."

She could do this.

Déjà Vu on Fifth Avenue

S o, Steven walked into the class with the chicken salad and strawberry shortcake, and do you know what Mrs. Smart said to him?"

"I have no idea," Michael said.

"She said, 'Sir, Colby is a strawberry-free school. Do you know how *deadly* a strawberry could be to a child who's allergic?' Can you believe it?"

"I can't. Hon, would you pass me some of that fish?"

"Sure." Christy passed the trout almondine. "Potatoes?"

"No, thanks, but I *will* have some wine."

Christy poured him another glass. "So, anyway, guess what he did?"

"What?"

"He went to the Food Emporium and bought Renata a plain piece of vanilla cake *without* nuts or strawberries from their bakery."

"Fascinating," Michael said, suppressing a yawn over a conversation that was feeling oddly familiar.

"Am I boring you?" Christy asked.

"No, not at all. I'm a little tired. Tell me, what kind of frosting was on the cake from Food Emporium?"

"Just the regular vanilla kind they make with powdered

sugar and shortening. Steven said it looked like something a kid would like."

"Uh-huh," Michael said, half listening.

"And Mrs. Smart went ballistic over the fact that a driver was sent instead of a parent."

"Why would she even care who delivered the food?"

"I think she's made it her personal mission to teach me how to be a good mother. But I wasn't going to blow my chance to get our stock price up. Anyway, she bawled Steven out right in the classroom. He said all the kids were cracking up. Don't teachers understand that mothers have more important things to do than to bring replacement lunches to school?" Christy said.

"Beegee, I think at *that* school, the mothers *don't* have more important things to do," Michael said, appearing surprised by his wife's naïveté. "Anything for dessert?" he asked, changing the subject.

"I have a wonderful piece of strawberry shortcake from the Four Seasons. You're not allergic, are you?"

Michael wheezed, grabbed his throat, and pretended he couldn't breathe. "No, not strawberries, but were those nuts on the trout? I'm allergic to nuts." He fell to the floor, took a few last breaths, and then pretended to die with his tongue hanging out.

"Cut it out. You're making fun of me now. You're gonna regret it." She jumped on his chest and tickled him until he yelled "*UNCLE!*"

Christy rang the bell, signaling to Yok Wah that she should clear the table. This was a tradition the cook insisted on even though Christy and Michael found it pretentious. Once Christy had tried to carry a few dishes into the kitchen herself, but Yok Wah practically tackled her with her whole four-foot-ten-inch, eighty-three-pound bulk, swearing in Chinese. After that, they both learned their place.

"So, tell me, what else is going on with the rest of your life? There still is a rest of your life, isn't there?"

"Well, I'm gonna meet with Brownie on Thursday so she can brief me on the graduation."

"Did you hear that Hicham El-Guerrouj won the fifteen hundred *and* the five thousand meters at the New Balance meet this weekend?" Michael's voice sounded almost angry.

Christy looked at him, wondering where this was coming from.

Renatus Interruptus

ook, Chapman, it's bad enough that you didn't un-
cover the loans they failed to book, *but to pay them
off by borrowing against mortgaged assets,* that's so
fucked up . . ." Michael said, his face red, his hair a mess.

"Mr. Drummond, Mr. Drummond, I need you," a little
voice said.

Michael put Andy on hold and turned to Renata, who
was, once again, jumping up and down in the library doorway trying to get his attention. "Renata, you're *really* not supposed to be in this part of the house, remember? We *talked*
about this."

"I know, but I need your help," she said.

"I'm on a very important call. I can't help you right now.
Find Nectar." He went back to the phone.

Renata stood firm in the doorway, boring her eyes into
Michael's face like a laser beam, willing him to look at her.
The child was furious, but trying not to show it. Hadn't she
and Michael formed an unbreakable bond when he saved
Mr. Koodles? He was acting like that night never happened.

"Thanks to *your* sloppy due diligence, we completely over-
paid. And repaying their debt by pledging assets we don't
own, what the hell were you thinking? I gotta tell you,

Andy . . ." Michael cupped his hand over the receiver. "Renata, can't you see I'm on a call?"

"Yes, but Christy and Nectar are out and I need to get on AOL for my science report on weather patterns, but I don't have an AOL account and if I don't turn this in tomorrow . . ."

Michael gestured to the computer that was set up on the library table. "Just use my account. It's Michaeldrummond@aol.com. The password's 'Christy.'" Michael went back to his call, looking irritated by the interruption.

Renata, who was proficient on the computer, got right on AOL and began looking up current and upcoming weather in cities across the country. As she worked, she'd steal glances at Michael, who was so absorbed in his conversation that she may as well have been invisible. Renata wondered if Michael would ever like her. She wasn't so bad. Grandma used to say she was "trrrrific." Why couldn't Michael see her "trrrific-ness?" Why? Because he wasn't looking, that's why. Renata frowned. Then she coughed. Then she knocked a stapler onto the floor. "Sorry," she said to Michael, who was oblivious to the noise. Finally, Renata completed her assignment and left the room. Michael didn't look up.

A Confederacy of Caregivers

On the morning Christy was to receive her Matrix Award, she held a seven A.M. breakfast for Renata's team of caregivers in the library. It was important to stay current on the child's progress. The following individuals were present: Nectar Freedom, nanny; Dr. Ruth Perlmutter, psychiatrist; Eve Hamilton, assistant; Junior Fritz, Renata's new driver; Yok Wah Lim, family cook; Cynthia Rodriguez, maid; Leo Morgenstern, tutor. Renata Ruiz lay silently in the closet with her ear pressed against a glass pressed against the bottom of the door. Eve led the meeting, since she was responsible for overseeing the girl's care. She stood up to make an announcement. "Would anyone like some more coffee before we start?"

Dr. Perlmutter scribbled something in her diary. Putting her pen down, she said, "I'd like a cup. But I can get it myself."

"Oh, would you pour me one?" Cynthia asked.

"My pleasure."

Eve called the meeting to order. "Let's go around the table. Each of you can give an update on how you think Renata is doing vis-à-vis your area of responsibility. Leo, how's the tutoring?"

"Well, as you know, we're trying to catch her up academically with her new classmates, and I'm happy to say that she's made great progress. We're working mostly on math because that's where she's behind. Right now, we're reviewing long division."

"Eve, what did her teacher say at the parent conference?" Christy asked.

"She's doing well, considering she's only had a public-school education. I've written a full report on the meeting. It's on your desk. There *was* one problem, though."

"What?"

"Next time, either you or Michael *must* attend. Mrs. Smart said she wouldn't do any more parent-teacher conferences without a parent present."

"Even though I sent written permission?"

"Doesn't matter. They're adamant about having an actual parent there."

"Hmmm. I guess I can understand that," Christy mused. She had hoped to spend all her Renata-designated time doing things with the child herself. But she could see that more would be required. That's okay, she thought. I'll just sleep less.

"Cynthia, do you have an update?" Eve asked.

"I've been cleaning her room and bathroom. At first, she left everything perfect, the way Maria taught her. I told her if she kept that up, I'd be out of a job. Now, I'm making her bed and picking up her clothes. She's leaving the sink dirty for me, too."

"That's wonderful," Eve said.

"*Wait*," Christy said, "shouldn't we expect her to clean up after herself? She doesn't have to iron her uniforms or vacuum, but making her bed and picking up clothes—she should do that herself."

"If you insist," Cynthia said, stiffening. "But most girls who live in this neighborhood have help for that sort of thing."

"That may be true, but I'm not comfortable with it, and I know Maria wouldn't be. Eve, would you let Renata know that we expect her to take on those chores?"

"Of course. It's perfectly ridiculous for children not to help around the house," Eve snipped. "Dr. Perlmutter? Your update?"

"Well, as you know, anything Renata tells me is confidential. I just want to say that, in general, she's adjusting to the many changes in her life as one would expect. She's grieving the loss of her grandmother, of course. I think it would be therapeutic to let her visit the cemetery. She hasn't been there since the funeral."

"Good idea," Christy said. "Junior, would you drive her there after school today?" Sorry, Maria, she thought. I'll make sure she visits you regularly.

"My pleasure, Mrs. Drummond," Junior said.

"Also, she seems to have forged a relationship with Mrs. De Mille, the ninety-five-year-old woman who lives below you. My sense is that she sees her as some kind of replacement grandmother figure."

"Transference," Junior observed. "It's to be expected."

"Yes, well . . . it's a bit more complicated than a layman can understand," Dr. Perlmutter said.

"Excuse me. Mr. Fritz studied psychology at the Learning Annex," Eve said, in defense of Junior.

Dr. Perlmutter continued as if Eve hadn't spoken. "I'm not sure it's healthy for Renata to pursue a relationship with such an old woman. I think we may want to limit her time with Mrs. De Mille and increase her sessions with me so we can explore the transference more fully. Did I mention that my fees are going up?"

"What are they going up to?" Eve asked.

"We can discuss the specifics privately," the doctor said.

"Give me a ballpark," Eve pressed. "While Christy's here."

"Three-fifty an hour."

"Three-fifty, from two-forty? That's steep," Eve said.

"Well, I haven't raised my rates in years," Dr. Perlmutter said. "You've been paying artificially low prices."

"Low? I don't know, Doctor—at those prices, maybe we should work with someone else," Christy said. She wanted to do right by Renata, but she hated being taken advantage of.

"I'll give her therapy for two-forty an hour. Heck, I'll do it for one-forty," Junior said.

"No, no, no. Switching doctors would devastate Renata. She might never recover," Dr. Perlmutter explained.

"I think we'll pass on increasing the sessions, Doc. Three times a week will have to suffice. Maybe we should invite Mrs. De Mille to our next update and get *her* thoughts; what do you think, Eve?" Christy said.

"Good idea. Let's do it," Eve said.

Michael poked his head in to say good-bye to Christy. "Don't stop," she told everyone as she slipped out to give her husband a kiss.

"What's going on in there?" he asked.

"It's a meeting of Renata's caregivers. I'm holding a quarterly review of her progress."

Michael gave his wife a strange look.

"What?"

"You don't think that's a little weird?" he asked.

"No. These are the people I've entrusted with her care. They have to be managed."

"Okay, fine, whatever," he said.

"You don't think I'm doing a good job?" Christy snapped.

"I didn't say that. I just think it's an unusual way to raise a child, that's all."

"Well, since you don't want to be involved, this is how it has to be. Unless you've changed your mind."

"No, no I haven't. She's your responsibility. Listen, Beeg, I'm not going to be able to make the ceremony today. I have to go to L.A. We're having problems with the Anipix acquisition. I'm really sorry."

Christy noticed that Michael looked worried. He was usually pretty undaunted by work stuff. "I'll miss you. I promise to thank you in my speech."

"Would you?"

"Of course."

"Do me a favor," Michael said. "Call me on your cell phone right before you speak. Then leave it on so I can hear what you say."

"Of course I will." Christy kissed Michael good-bye and rejoined her meeting.

"We're just getting to Nectar, Christy," Eve reported. "Nectar? Nectar, are you asleep?"

Nectar awoke with a start. "Sorry, I was just checking for holes in my eyelids. As you know, I'm with Renata most of the time. I take her near about everywhere she needs to go. Bad as I hate to say this, the child is hurtin'. It's like she fell outta the lonely tree and hit every branch on the way down. She needs a mama."

Christy was transfixed by Nectar. She was the least-educated person in the room, but Christy felt she was, in many ways, the smartest. They were lucky to have her on the team.

"Isn't it *your* job to nurture her, Nectar?" Eve asked, her eyebrows raised.

"Yes, but I'm not her mama. The child needs someone

who's not *paid* to be her parent. " 'Tis such fools as you that makes the world full of ill-favored children.' "

"Let me guess," Eve said, "Shakespeare."

"I have to agree with Shakespeare . . . I mean Nectar," Dr. Perlmutter added.

"Me, too," Junior added.

"Me, too," said Yok Wah.

"Point taken," Eve said officiously. "Christy, why don't we meet after everyone leaves? We'll juggle things around, schedule more bonding time."

"Right," Christy said, feeling a sense of emptiness without knowing why. "Block out two hours for me to take her to the cemetery today." Is Michael right? she wondered. Maybe this *is* no way to raise a child. But what can I do? There isn't enough time in the day. Maria, what were you *thinking*? I don't want to let you down. And I *really* don't want to let Renata down. Could I be missing the basic mommy gene?

Halibut, Honor, and Humiliation

The theme of the Matrix Awards this year was "Fearless Women." The luncheon was as glitzy as ever, with awards presented by media luminaries even more impressive than the winners. Goldie Hawn was giving Christy her award. She was inhibited to be in the presence of such a celebrity, but she tried to act like this was an everyday thing. Still, she knew that no matter how hard she tried, she would never be as fabulous as Goldie. Christy wondered if there would ever be a day when she wouldn't feel inadequate. Where was that unbridled confidence that was supposed to go along with being a CEO?

At the last minute, Katherine couldn't make the ceremony. Some sort of problem with Alex at school. Katherine had her assistant let Christy's assistant know. Christy understood these kinds of emergencies now. But she was disappointed.

When no one was looking, Christy rearranged the place cards to seat herself next to Galit at the luncheon. She would crack that reporter if it killed her. Galit was one tough lady. Although, Christy supposed, you had to be tough to serve in the Israeli elite forces. She could just imagine Galit in a camouflage miniskirt brandishing an Uzi and wiping out a band of angry insurgents.

When they first sat down, Galit didn't remember who Christy was. This was doubly maddening because Christy was wearing a name tag. Once she was reminded, Galit asked how things were at the company.

"Great, things are just great. Sales are up. Profits are up."

"Mmm-mmm," Galit mumbled.

Mmm-mmm? What does that mean? Christy wondered. "How are things at the *Journal*?" she asked.

"Busy as always. Companies are coming out with earnings statements. It's our version of Christmas season."

"Yes, I guess it is," Christy said, willing herself to be interested in this creature whose job it was to make CEOs' lives a living hell. "I'm surprised at how bland the food is, aren't you? I'd expect more from the Waldorf." Jeez, did I really say that? Christy was unable to muster her legendary charisma in the face of this cold fish.

"These lunches are all the same. Poached salmon. Roasted potatoes, steamed carrots, coffee, and a fruit tart. I always eat before coming," Galit said, in the tone of a woman who would never leave any detail of her life to fate.

"That's smart. I should do that." Christy wasn't giving up, no matter how unlikable Galit was. Charming her would do more for her business than a string of perfect quarters. "Tell me, are you working on a book these days? I enjoyed your Ian Malik bio."

"Thanks," Galit said coolly. "I haven't settled on a subject yet. I like covering business leaders who aren't overly publicized."

"Malik's had his share of media attention," Christy said.

"Yes, but he rarely gave interviews. Malik 'the man' was still a mystery to most people."

"You should consider doing my husband, Michael Drummond," Christy said, trying to melt the icicle sitting next to her. "He's a complicated guy, very interesting, always follows his own path."

"Michael's the ultimate outsider, that's for sure," Galit said. "He keeps a low profile."

"He's been burned by the press, so he's cautious about being too public. Anyway, he doesn't need the exposure. He owns the majority shares of his company, and his products speak for themselves."

Galit's demeanor changed. "Do you think he'd be interested in cooperating on a biography?" she asked, leaning in, giving Christy's arm a meaningful touch.

"I could ask. Or, better yet, here's his private number," Christy said, reaching into her purse for a card. "Give him a call and tell him I suggested it. I'll mention you might call. But don't try till next week. He's in California for the next few days." Christy knew she was being worked, but somehow Galit's attention was like a potent drug, even on her. And she needed this woman.

"Listen, Christy, I want to give you a heads-up. The *Journal*'s going to press with a pretty damaging article about you. It's scheduled to run tomorrow."

"About *me*? What are you talking about?" Christy asked.

"I'm talking about your sex life," Galit explained.

"*Sex life?* The *Financial Journal*? Why on earth would a business paper run an article about my sex life? Did *you* write it?" Christy asked.

"No, it's not me. No one called you for a quote?"

"I've been out all day, but the office has my cell number."

"They probably left a message. The reporter is Alan Hooper. I'll write down his number for you." Galit took a pen out of her purse and jotted the information on her card.

"Do you guys have something against me? Why all the negative press?"

"When we get a newsworthy tip, we investigate. That's our job. Give Alan a call. Maybe you can offer some balancing information." Galit looked at her with such empathy that Christy knew she was in deep shit.

"Thanks, I'll do it." *Damn*, Christy thought. This was supposed to be my day. A day of kudos, glory, and recognition. Instead, I have to go out and defend myself against some nasty reporter with nothing better to do than tell lies about my sex life. What could this possibly be about? Sometimes I hate playing in the big leagues.

Twenty minutes later, with Michael listening in on his cell phone, Christy got up and gave her acceptance speech. Somehow, she pulled herself together and managed to sound completely unshaken. Even she was impressed.

৶৹

Christy left the Matrix Awards with Skip Heller by her side. The time had come to say good-bye to the pesky weasel. It was a good thing. Christy was getting annoyed by Skip's constant presence, and further pissed off by his Nikes. "So, I guess this is it," she said. "Do you have much more to do on my story?"

"No, not really. I just have to interview your friends and enemies."

"I don't *have* enemies," Christy said, fervently hoping that was true.

"Every CEO does," Skip said.

"Skip, please be gentle," she said, hating the power that people like him had over her.

"Of *course* I will."

Christy was relieved not to have him looking over her shoulder while she dealt with this latest press attack. She called Randi, her office assistant, to see if the *Financial Journal* had called. Sure enough, Alan Hooper had phoned hours ago. He said he was on deadline.

"So, did you put him through to Rick Slotnik?" Christy asked.

"He was out today."

"What about Katherine?"

"She was out, too."

"Why didn't you call me here?"

"I didn't want to bother you while you were getting an award."

"Randi, why do you think I carry my cell phone with me? It's so you can reach me in emergencies."

"Was it important?"

"YES! Alan Hooper's a reporter at the *Financial Journal*. Apparently he's filing some kind of negative story. Give me all the numbers he left. I'll try to catch him."

Christy dialed Alan's office and cell numbers. Both calls went to voice mail. Damn, why do we bother carrying these phones if they don't do us any good when we need them?

That evening, after dinner, Hooper called her at home. He said he'd tried to reach someone in a position of authority at the company, but couldn't. The article was running in tomorrow's edition.

"What's the gist of it?" Christy asked.

"You're part of a broader story we're breaking about female CEOs who traded sexual favors for initial capitalization."

"*What?* You *can't* be serious." Christy was incredulous. If they were accusing Katherine, yes, she could understand, but *her?* This was nuts.

"Of course we're serious. We're the *Financial Journal*. We have witnesses who claim you provided sex to influence their investment in your company's privately held stock."

Christy was furious. "Witnesses? To what? First of all, Mr. Hooper, this *never* happened. Second of all, no banker would decide to fund a company in exchange for a fuck."

"Can I quote you on that?"

Christy took a deep breath. "Mr. Hooper, this is a serious accusation you're making. I suggest you not run the article or you'll be facing a libel suit."

"We're extremely comfortable with our source, Ms. Hayes. Tell me, do the names Ty Jennings and Robert Peale ring a bell? *Hmmmm?* Why don't you give me a call tomorrow. Maybe we can do a follow-up and keep the dialogue going."

Oh, yeah, Christy thought, great idea. Let's string this story out for days in the press. "I'll get back to you," she said, slamming the phone down.

Oh, man, she thought miserably. Now I know what those movie stars are always complaining about. Lies in the tabloid press. But the *Journal*'s no tabloid. Why would they believe this trash? The world's gonna think I'm a whore. Then she remembered her husband, who was still in Los Angeles. Forget what the world thinks. She reached for the phone. I'd better clear this up with Michael.

Mean Girls

DEAR DIARY,

NOW I GO TO THE COLBY SCHOOL. THESE ARE THE GIRLS IN MY CLASS:

1. LANGLEY STOKES-SHE HAS THE SMELLIEST FEET EVER. I SWEAR SHE WASHES THEM IN VOMIT. NEVER TRUST A GIRL WITH STINKY FEET.
2. JADA SHIFF-HER PEN EXPLODED IN HER MOUTH AND MRS. SMART WOULDN'T LET HER WASH OFF THE INK SO SHE'D LEARN A VALUABLE LESSON. BUT JADA LOOKS AWESOME IN BLUE LIPS SO HA! ON MRS. SMART.
3. PIPPA TILBERRY-SHE FEELS SORRY FOR ME BECAUSE I'M MEXICAN. I FEEL SORRY FOR HER BECAUSE SHE'S STUPID.
4. MICA MORGAN-SHE BRAGS ABOUT HER DOG WHO IS GAY. HOW DOES SHE KNOW?
5. BUNNY PRATT-HAS A MOLE ON HER FACE WITH HAIR GROWING OUT OF IT. PEOPLE LIKE THAT ALWAYS THINK THEY'RE BETTER THAN EVERYONE ELSE.
6. STEPHANIE RICH-TRIES TO BE TEACHER'S PET. I DON'T JUDGE HER FOR THIS.
7. MUFFIN WOJTKIEWICZ-HER ARMPITS ARE SO DEEP, IT'S HAIRY (GET IT DIARY? HAIRY INSTEAD OF SCARY!!!).

8. YANNA SEVIGNY-ALWAYS WHINING. BUT EVERYONE LIKES HER BECAUSE HER DAD'S A MOVIE STAR. BIG DEAL.

9. SOMERS BURDEN-SHE CAN WIGGLE HER DOUBLE CHIN LIKE JELL-O. WHAT A SHOW OFF.

10. TARA MCBEE-SHE CUT A HOLE IN MY UNIFORM JUST TO BE MEAN. I HATE HER. HER MOM HATES HER TOO. I KNOW THIS FOR A FACT.

11. DESIREE DEEDER-HAS A REALLY LONG TOUNGE THAT WILL PROBABLY HAVE TO BE SHORTENED SOMEDAY.

12. ARIEL SANDBERG-SHE KEEPS ACCUSING ME OF LIKING BOYS WHICH IS NOT, I REPEAT, NOT (!!!!!!!!!!) TRUE.

13. ME-SMART, CUTE, ZANY, NORMAL.

༖

The car was stuck behind a moving van on East Seventy-sixth Street. People were honking. Tempers were exploding. Christy was oblivious. She had her PR guy on the line. "Rick, where *were* you yesterday? Why weren't you reachable?" Christy demanded.

"I was at a funeral, I—"

"Did you see the story this morning? Do you *know* how much damage it'll do? From now on, someone from your department *has* to be on call to back you up. I can't believe I have to tell you this."

"I'm sorry, Christy."

"Where's Katherine?"

"She's in her office."

"Well, transfer me."

The phone rang, and Katherine picked up. Christy launched into her. "Katherine, did you read the article? What do you propose we do about it?"

"Deny, deny, deny. It's your word against theirs."

"But did you *see* who they named? Ty Jennings, Robert Peale? Aren't those guys *you* slept with?"

"Yes, but *you know* I didn't do it to get funding. I just did it because . . . because they were cute. I was young. I was single. What do you expect?"

"You were married."

"Whatever. I must have been having marital problems."

"Aaargh. Katherine, how do you think the *Financial Journal* got the names of two men you slept with? Don't you find that odd?"

"Yes, I think it's odd. And I have calls in to both men trying to get an explanation."

"Could Malcolm be behind this? Is this somehow related to your divorce? Because if it is—"

"No, he wouldn't do this. Stop acting like it's my fault."

Christy took a deep breath and composed herself. "Katherine, it's *not* your fault. I'm just trying to understand *how* the *Journal* got the information so we can deal with it."

"Well, obviously they contacted the banks we approached for our first round of financing. Someone there must have something against *you*."

"But *who*? *Why*? I don't get it. And what am I supposed to do? Deny that I slept with them and explain that it was *you*?"

"No, of course not. That's just as bad."

"Then *what*?"

"When'll you be in? Why don't we powwow with Rick? We have to prepare for the board anyway."

"The board?"

"They called an emergency meeting for four o'clock. Where *are* you?"

"I'm in the car on my way to Colby. I have an appointment with Brownie. Look, get things started with Rick and

I'll be there as soon as I can." Christy clicked off her phone. Her head was pounding. She wanted to scream. *What* was Rick's problem? Lately, he's been asleep at the switch. Maybe she should fire him. Of all days to have these school meetings. She realized she could have run to Colby in about ten minutes, and it was taking her half an hour by chauffeur. Oh, the perks of the rich.

This morning, Christy was getting her fifth-grade graduation marching orders from Brownie. Then, after school, there was the formal kickoff with all the volunteers. Steven pulled up to the entrance, and she got out. "This should take about an hour, no more. I'll call you when I'm finished."

Christy walked purposefully through the flock of stay-at-home moms who congregated in the entry hall of the school, chatting away with nary a care in the world. In her black take-no-prisoners suit and stiletto heels, Christy may as well have been wearing a sign that read LIVE SMALLPOX VIRUS — STAY BACK. The Mommies wore neutral-colored designer slacks, Prada sports shoes, cashmere tops, Hermes scarves, full makeup, and model-straight hair. The required look was one of accidental chic, a presentation that whispers, "for a girl who didn't even try, don't I look rich and perfect?" And they accomplished this expensive, time-consuming nonchalance before eight in the morning.

How do they do it? Why do they do it? And don't they have anything better to do? Christy wondered, wearing a brave half smile. She nodded at the Mommies, a few of whom were actually leering at her. The least they could do is hide their contempt, Christy thought. That's only polite. She wondered, do they hate me because of the *Financial Journal* article or because I'm a working mom? Then she decided it had to be the latter, because no woman could read the paper *and* make herself look like that before breakfast. It wasn't physically possible.

Christy looked around the foyer, marveling at the beauty of the interior. The floors and walls were marble. An enormous crystal chandelier hung in the center of the entryway. The grand staircase was lined with important oil paintings of dead Colby headmistresses and trustees. What I would have given to come to a place like this for school every day, Christy thought. She wondered if the girls knew how lucky they were.

"Oh, my goodness gracious," the woman behind the antique Louis XV desk proclaimed. "*You're* the mother who sent her daughter lunch from the Four Seasons, aren't you?" The marble in the room served as a natural microphone.

Christy felt the other mothers' eyes boring into her back. She was ashamed, as if sending a child lunch from a five-star restaurant was something a good mother would never do. "Yes, that would be me. I'm here to see Brownie Rich."

"Oh, she's expecting you. Her office is at the top of stairs to the right."

"She has her own office?"

"Yes, well, Brownie's the only mother who does. She's so involved with the PTA and, of course, the board. She has one of the best views. You'll see."

Christy walked up the stairs, past a Pilates studio where trainers were working with girls on the equipment. She found Brownie's brass nameplate and knocked on the door.

Brownie's parent-volunteer secretary stuck her head out. "Can you take a seat? She'll be with you in a few minutes." She pointed to the three wooden desk chairs across from the office.

"Sure," Christy said. She sat down and decided to make use of the time. Dialing Katherine, she was relieved to catch her in person. "Kath, are you with Rick?"

"Yes."

"Why don't you put me on speaker so I can be part of the conversation."

"Oh, sure. But I have some bad news. The wires picked up the story. By tomorrow, it'll be in every paper in the country."

"*Every paper?* Oh shit, don't tell me," Christy cried.

"*Excuse me.*" A primly dressed woman tapped Christy on the shoulder.

"Just a sec, Katherine. Yes?"

"You'll have to turn that off and watch your language. We're a curse-free *and* a cell-phone-free school," the woman said.

"I'm sorry," Christy said. "Can I just have a minute? It's urgent."

"If we made an exception for you, we'd have to make it for everyone. Our policy is zero tolerance. Do you know what the effects of hearing curse words are on young, impressionable girls?"

"Oh, no, I don't want to curse. I just want to finish my call."

"Ze-ro tol-er-ance," the woman said, pronouncing every syllable so there could be no misunderstanding. "No exceptions. Turn it off, or I'll have to summon the headmistress."

"Katherine, I'll get back to you," she said, snapping the phone shut. "See, phone's off. Sorry. Won't happen again." Christy smiled at her.

"Hrmmmph," the woman snorted as she disappeared down the hall.

Christy waited a few more minutes and checked her watch. Why hadn't she brought work with her? Surely, *that* wouldn't be against the rules. Watching the girls walk by as they changed classes, Christy noticed that there wasn't an extra pound or pimple in the bunch. Whatever happened to knobby knees, headgears, braces, and geeky glasses? she wondered. Every one of these girls looked like she could star in her own show on the Disney Channel. Christy wondered why that was. Was it the result of some manner of upper-class natural selection? Rich men mating with beautiful women who bear them equally gorgeous children? Maybe this isn't such a good place for Renata, she thought. She checked her watch. Twenty minutes had passed, so she knocked on Brownie's door once more.

Parent-volunteer secretary stuck her head out again. "Yes?"

"Do you know how much longer this'll be?" Christy asked. "I need to get to work."

"It could be a while," she said. "We're having a minor crisis." She lowered her voice. "A hundred and forty-eighty dollars is missing from the PTA treasury."

"Gosh, that's bad," Christy said.

"Tell me about it."

"Maybe I should reschedule," Christy suggested.

"That depends. What's more important to you, your daughter or your job?"

"Obviously, my child," Christy said, even though that wasn't technically true at the moment. "It's just that I'm in the middle of a crisis today."

The woman sighed. "Let me get Brownie's calendar." She closed the door, then returned a few minutes later with a black Day-Timer. "I can give you something four weeks from tomorrow, same time."

"But I'm meeting all the volunteers today. I have to see her first."

"Brownie's a busy woman."

Christy thought for a moment. She reached into her purse and counted out four fifty-dollar bills. "Here. Here's two hundred dollars for the treasury. Problem solved. Now can I meet with Brownie?"

"Mrs. Drummond, it's not the money. Any one of us could replace *that*. It's the fact that it's missing. We need to know what happened. Was it stolen? Was it never paid? Was it accounted for incorrectly? Was it lost? *That's* what we need to get to the bottom of."

"And the world can't go on until this is handled?" Christy asked, amused in spite of the fact that her own world was crashing down.

"I'm afraid it can't. You just be patient and we'll get to you as soon as we can. I'll tell Brownie you're in a hurry." She shut the door.

Christy went back to the chair and checked her messages, using her bag to cover her cell phone. Rick Slotnik had called. Alan Hooper from the *Financial Journal*. Bill Ritter, the business reporter from the *New York Times*. Michael had called. "Fuuuuck," Christy moaned.

"Excuse me!"

Christy looked up. Busted again. "Sorry," she mumbled.

After half an hour, parent-volunteer secretary opened the door and invited Christy to enter Brownie's magnificent digs. With million-dollar views of Park Avenue, the room was filled with antiques, Oriental rugs, and more oil paintings of important nineteenth-century dead people. Christy could see that the office was a beehive of activity. But as soon as she walked in, Brownie dismissed the other volunteer-workers. They obeyed as though Brownie was the queen.

"Christy, how *good* to see you." Even though her suit was yellow, Brownie still gave the impression of being a formidable woman. Surprisingly, her lumpish body and un-made-up face added to her majestic vibe rather than diminished it. You just knew that if you crossed her, she'd come at you with that stinger she kept tucked in her Playtex girdle.

Christy reached out to shake her hand, but Brownie didn't return the gesture. "May I sit?" she asked, figuring this was appropriate etiquette for meeting the queen.

"Be my guest."

Christy sat on the needlepoint cushion on the French provincial chair across from Brownie. She pulled a notebook and pen from her bag. "So, we're here to talk about graduation."

"Yes," Brownie said, putting on a pair of power reading glasses. "But before we get into that, there are a few ground rules you need to know about working with the Colby PTA."

"Of course."

"As you know, I'm the president. That means I call the shots. Here's a directory of the PTA representatives and their numbers. That's where we recruit our army of volunteers." Brownie handed Christy a thick notebook. "In the back, there's a highly confidential list of all the Colby families, their ENW, the father's occupation, the amount they've contributed to the school each year, and any major celebrity or professional sports connections we know they have. That should help you with commencement speakers."

"Why don't we list the mother's occupation?" Christy asked.

Brownie scoffed. "In the families that matter, the mother doesn't work, trust me."

"Right," Christy said, her face burning. "And what's the ENW?"

"Their estimated net worth."

"We *know* that?" Christy opened the book to the page listing her and Michael. It was as though the PTA had seen their tax returns.

"The development office makes it a point to find out what families are worth."

"Why would a family's net worth matter? I'm in charge of graduation."

Brownie gave Christy that *what Greyhound bus did you just ride in on* look. "*Everything* we do at Colby is a fund-raiser. You'll solicit donations in honor of each of the twenty-four graduates."

"Oh, I see," Christy said.

"Last year's class raised one hundred and eight thousand dollars for the fifth grade gift. Your goal is to raise one-fifty. Questions?"

"With twenty-four girls in the grade, that's over six thousand dollars a family. Is that realistic?"

"Of course. The girls are listed in the program from highest donation to lowest, with the amount given in their honor next to their name. Everyone wants her daughter to be at the top of the giving tree."

"What about the girls on scholarship?"

"They'll be at the bottom, of course."

"Naturally," Christy said. She silently vowed to make anonymous donations in the name of each girl receiving aid.

"In fact," Brownie said, "you can put me down for twenty thousand dollars. If anyone gives a bigger pledge, let me know immediately and I'll better it. We really can't do enough for our daughters' school." Of course you can't, Christy thought, as she got her first real taste of competitive mothering.

"If you'll turn to page eight, there's a listing of the fifth-grade-graduation committee members. You'll be seeing them today. If you schedule a meeting, I need to be included. Should you arrange a conference call, make sure it's on my calendar. If you want to send a note or e-mail, clear it through me first. I need three days' notice."

"I can't send e-mails on my own?" Christy wondered if this woman was for real.

"Not without my approval." She handed Christy a thick accordion file. "Here's the documentation from the last graduation. All the communications are filed in date order, including the e-mails the last committee chairwoman sent. They were approved by me, so I suggest you use them as models."

"If I send e-mails you've already approved from this file, do I need to get your approval again?"

"Of course. When you make the changes I suggest, send me the revised communication and I'll approve it within two days."

She has got to be kidding. "That seems so inefficient. Can I suggest another approach?"

"No, this is how we do things at Colby."

"Can I at least call members of the committee without first getting your approval of what I plan to say?"

"That's a great idea. The more you include me, the better."

Damn, why did I ask that? Christy thought.

"I suggest you read the file before your meeting this afternoon. You'll need to be prepared if you want to win the respect of the committee. They're going to be skeptical of you. You know, working mom, face on billboards, the way you look. That's three strikes."

Christy wondered what was the matter with the way she looked. "Uh, sure, I'll keep that in mind."

"And Christy, one more thing," she said.

"What?"

"*Don't* make a mistake. The parents at Colby have long memories."

Boardroom Brouhaha

On the way to the office, Steven and Christy swung by the apartment to pick up Eve for her afternoon briefing. Christy wondered if this day could get any worse. But she relaxed when she saw Eve. The cavalry had arrived.

"I brought you some food," Eve said, handing her a box lunch from Yok Wah. "Soba noodles, miso soup, hijiki. Yok Wah says you have to eat it all." Christy had the feeling the staff had held their own powwow about her crisis and were now executing an action plan.

"That was sweet of her, but I don't feel hungry." She knew she would have to pour it all out and return the bowls empty or she would get one of Yok Wah's Confucian lectures.

"Eve's right," Steven shouted from the front seat. "How do you expect to perform on an empty stomach?"

Christy's cell phone rang. It was Michael, wanting to know how she was holding up. He told her to hang in there and that he loved her. There was a lump in her throat when they hung up. She was so lucky to have him. Most husbands would come unhinged after seeing the sordid accusations the *Financial Journal* had leveled at Christy. Not Michael. He'd read enough half truths about himself through the years to mistrust the press implicitly.

Christy took a few bites of her noodles, and then stuffed the leftovers back in the box. They turned onto Thirty-seventh, where Baby G had its offices. Eve was taking down Christy's to-do list. "Can you pick up a gift for the Godfreys? We're having dinner with them on Friday. Michael has an important deal heating up with Samuel, so pick something really nice. Also, I left some questions from the adoption lawyer on the kitchen table. They want proof that we exhausted every avenue for finding Renata's next of kin. And the number for the terrace landscaper is on the fridge. You just need to set up time for us to meet. Oh my God, I just realized—Eve, you have to do me a huge favor while I'm in with the board."

"Name it."

"I'm supposed to meet with the graduation committee at four. I can't be in both places. Here's the file. Will you read through it and handle Colby for me?"

"Is that okay?"

"Not really, but we don't have a choice. I'll need you to assist me with the project anyway, so this'll give you a chance to meet everyone who'll be working with us. It should be fun. Steven'll drive you there."

"I can hardly wait," Eve said. "I think I'd rather face your board."

Oddly enough, Christy agreed.

Steven chuckled from the front seat. He pulled the car in front of the office building and opened the door.

"Wish me luck with the board."

"Luck," Steven and Eve yelled in unison.

⚭

"The two other CEOs who were accused of offering sexual favors for investments have already issued denials," Christy explained to the board. "The men mentioned in association with me called the accusations 'ridiculous.' We're about to do the same."

"There's no truth to this, is there?" Karl Lehmann asked. "If we deny it and they come back with proof, you know, like one of those Paris Hilton videos or something, we'll look like idiots." Karl had been one of Baby G's first directors. Usually, he was easygoing and supportive. Today, he was a pain in the ass. Obviously, he was stressed out by this. He had stuck his neck out on their investment in the company, and with the stock down, Christy knew he was getting a lot of heat from his fellow sheep.

"No," Christy said. "I never slept with anyone we were pitching." *Of course, our COO did, but that's not what we were accused of*, she thought. She was hoping that Katherine would do the right thing and come clean on her own with the board. But her longtime partner was just giving her a concerned and supportive look.

"I'd like to say that Christy was entirely professional during all our dealings with her. And, at the time, she was desperate for our infusion of funds. There was *never* a hint of impropriety," Niles Raines said.

"We have similar statements from other first-round investors who don't have seats on the board," Rick Slotnik said. "They're entirely objective and completely outraged by the accusations."

"I find the whole thing disgusting," Katherine added. "Even if the story *were* true, which it isn't, *so what*? It hasn't affected Christy's ability to lead the company."

"Yes, but it says something really bad about my character, so we have to deny it," Christy said, wishing Katherine had a clue that there was a connection between sexual forays and character.

"The stock dropped two points when the story broke. It'll

probably drop some more on news of your denial," Richard Bender said. Richard was their most pessimistic director.

"I'm not so sure," Niles said. "The market may have already reacted as much as it's going to."

"It was just reported on the wire that the chairman of UVA and his entire management team were killed today when their plane crashed near Jackson Hole. That'll pull attention away from this story," Rick said.

"*That* was a lucky break," Karl said, cheered by the news.

"I've always said you and I shouldn't travel together," Katherine said to Christy. "Now do you see why?"

A temp who was covering for Randi interrupted. "Excuse me, Christy, there's an urgent phone call on line two."

"Ah, must be Joe Navarrato," Christy said. He's giving the *Journal* our statement. I'll put him on speaker." Christy pressed line two.

But it was Brownie Rich. "Christy Hayes, in all the years I've worked on the PTA, and I've worked on the PTA for many years, I have never seen *anything* this disrespectful. Every single graduation committee member took the time to come to our meeting today. And are we women with time to spare? NO. We're active, busy wives, mothers, and volunteers. Here we sit in the Gloria Vanderbilt PTA Conference Room waiting for our committee chairperson to kick off our fifth-grade-graduation extravaganza and who walks in? *Our committee chairperson's assistant.* Are you unable to lead this committee, Christy Hayes, because if you can't do it, say so now."

Christy lunged for the phone to take the call privately. There was no headset. The phone worked only on speaker.

"Brownie, can I call you back in a few minutes? I'm in the middle of something right now."

"*NO YOU CAN'T CALL ME BACK.* I'm here with a room

full of dedicated volunteers who have no leader. Your daughter's admission to Colby was predicated on your overseeing a major committee. If you can't fulfill *your* part of the bargain, I'm sure you'll understand that Colby will need to revisit whether or not your family belongs here. You have twenty minutes to get to this meeting." Brownie slammed down her end of the phone. At least that's what it sounded like on speaker.

"I'm sorry," Christy said to the board, her face burning. They were staring at her in stony silence. "You didn't need to hear that."

"Let's take a five-minute break," Katherine suggested. Everyone nodded in agreement. There was an embarrassed scramble to the coffeepot.

As the room broke up, Katherine approached Christy. "Maybe you'd better go to Colby. You don't want to screw around with Brownie Rich."

"I can't leave. This is *way* too important."

"Christy, let me take it from here. I have the same information as you. I know what decisions need to be made. That's why you made me COO, so I could back you up in crucial matters."

"Are you sure?" Christy asked.

"I'm positive."

"Okay, but Katherine, would you *please* tell them where the accusations are coming from? At least let the board know that *you* had relations with those men."

"I will. I'm just trying to get up my nerve. Now go. I don't want to see Renata lose her place at Colby."

Christy made it all the way to the elevator before she realized what she was doing. Then she turned around and walked back into the meeting just as it was coming to order again. "Now, here's our plan . . ." Christy said, taking control. She couldn't believe she had almost walked out on her board in the middle of a crisis just to satisfy Brownie Rich.

∽

DEAR DIARY,

YESTERDAY I MADE A SPESHAL INVITATION FOR MICHAEL TO
COME TO DINNER WITH ME IN THE KITCHEN. YOK WAH PUT IT
ON HIS CHAIR AT BREAKFAST. MICHAEL ASKED IF HE COULD
BRING CHRISTY. I SAID YES OR HE'D THINK I DIDN'T LIKE HER
WHICH I DON'T. I MADE MY FAMOUS CHICKEN TACO CASSE-
ROLE THAT GRANDMA USED TO LOVE. NECTER NECTAR
HELPED ME SET THE TABLE WITH THE GOOD CHINA. DINNER
WAS READY AT 7. CHRISTY CAME ON TIME. MICHAEL WAS 20
MINUTES LATE DUE TO TRAFFIC. I WORE MY WILLY WONKA
OOMPA LOOMPA GOGGLES AT THE BEGINNING SO MICHAEL
WOULD THINK I WAS CUTE (WHICH HE DID). DINNER WAS
MOSTLY FUN. WE TALKED ABOUT WHAT I WAS STUDYING IN
SCHOOL (THE INDIANA CORNBELT), OUR FAVORITE SHOWS,
AND HEADLICE (WHICH MICHAEL HAD AS A KID-ME TOO!!!!!
WE'RE SO ALIKE!!). I'M HOPING THIS GIVES MICHAEL AND
CHRISTY THE IDEA TO INVITE ME TO DINNER WITH THEM WHICH
WOULD BE THE POLITE THING TO DO AT THIS JUNCTURE.

I'VE DECIDED TO CHANGE MY NAME TO STRINGBEAN.
THAT'S BECAUSE MICHAEL LOVES PEOPLE WITH NICKNAMES
(LIKE HOW HE LOVES CHRISTY WHO HE ALWAYS CALLS
BEEGEE). I DON'T KNOW WHY I DIDN'T THINK OF THIS BEFORE.

MRS. DE MILLE INVITED ME OVER FOR TEA AFTER SCHOOL
TOMORROW. THAT'S ONE OF MY FAVORITE THINGS TO DO
BECAUSE HER BUTLER SERVES MINI SANDWICHES AND STUFF
LIKE THAT ON BEAUTIFUL SILVER TRAYS THAT USED TO BE-
LONG TO THE RUSSIAN ROYAL FAMILY.

LOVE,
STRINGBEAN

Reunited and It Feels So Good

Christy stood outside the limousine on the tarmac at Teterboro waiting for Michael's jet to come to a stop. He had been in Geneva for three days, and she was determined to show him just how much she had missed him. Michael's driver stashed an ice bucket with a six-pack of Amstel in the backseat. Christy popped the top and poured a glass. She stood outside the car holding the beer, and wearing the black Russian sable coat Michael had bought her, with nothing underneath. Her plan was to flash Michael as he deplaned so he would know she meant business. I'll bet his ex-wife never did this, Christy thought.

Christy was doing her best to remain Michael's irresistible lover. But what she really wanted to do was hide under the covers and sleep for eighteen hours. The sex-for-capital scandal just wouldn't go away. The company's stock had dropped five points since the story hit the papers. Even though they'd denied everything, the *Journal* just ran an article where another of Katherine's ex-lovers claimed Christy had offered him sex if he'd invest in her company. A bad picture of Christy appeared on top of the story. Why does the paper print lies like that? And couldn't they have used a more flattering photo? she wondered. It was all so humiliating. A few board members expressed concern about Christy's ability to lead.

On top of that, Brownie was micromanaging her project. Christy told her that if she could build a three-hundred-million-dollar company, she could run a fifth-grade graduation. But Brownie was having none of it. Every comment she made seemed to imply that Christy wasn't cutting it as a Colby Mommy. And then there was Renata. Christy had managed to outsource most of her care. Eve was scheduling a few hours a week for the two of them, but it wasn't working. Renata just didn't want to be with Christy. They ate lunch together yesterday and barely spoke. Renata's class had a science fair on Monday to which all the parents were invited. Renata asked Nectar to come but didn't mention it to Eve, so she couldn't schedule it on Christy's calendar. Mrs. Smart called and chided Christy for not being there. Next week, Colby was having a special mother-daughter assembly. Christy would have to write a letter to Renata extolling their special bond. But there was no bond to extol yet. Christy was lost. Mrs. Smart had made a point of telling her *not* to send Nectar or Eve in her place.

Michael stepped out through the door of his plane, beaming at her before he realized she wasn't looking at him.

"Beegee, I can't believe you met me here," Michael said, breaking Christy's train of thought. "And you brought me an Amstel. I *love* you."

Dammit, she thought when she realized she had missed her chance to flash him. He took the glass from her hand, then kissed Christy with the passion he'd shown when they were first married. She returned the sentiment as enthusiastically as she could. Christy would have given anything to feel amorous at this moment. If only she weren't so tired. When

Michael finally let go, Christy stepped back and discreetly opened her coat, revealing his prize.

"You are *so* sexy," he said.

"Come in the car and let me show you just how sexy I can be," she whispered.

Anthony put Michael's bags in the trunk as the couple piled into the backseat. "I'll put up the partition," Michael said, pressing the button to raise the soundproof privacy window.

Michael downed his beer and opened his wife's coat, burying his head in her breasts. "God, how I've missed these." Christy closed her eyes and moaned as though she was turned on even though she was thinking about firing Rick Slotnik, who was doing a terrible job making the sex scandal disappear. Michael pulled Christy's coat off entirely and admired her body. "Mmmm, you're *so* hot." She moaned as he ripped off his clothes. In a frenzy, Michael kicked over the ice bucket. Christy made fake orgasm sounds, all the while wondering which of Katherine's ex-lovers would come out of the woodwork next and why they were claiming to have had sex with Christy. Was it possible that Katherine was behind this? She felt Michael's heart pounding as he lay next to her.

"You are a goddess, Christy," he said. "I thought I might be losing you. You just haven't seemed so glad to see me lately."

"Oh, honey, I'm sorry. I've been distracted. But that doesn't mean I haven't been lusting for you since you left," she replied, trying to sound all hot and steamy. She hated faking it with Michael, but the alternative was worse.

"I can't wait for next week," he added.

"What's next week?"

"You know, you and me, Chamonix. Climbing Mont Blanc."

Oh no, Christy thought. I totally forgot. "That's next week . . . ?"

"*Finally*, we'll be alone. No work, no responsibilities, no cell phones. It'll be fantastic."

"I can't go."

"What? Why not?" There was genuine disappointment in Michael's voice. He sat up and reached for his clothes. His hair was as scruffy as a pound puppy's. It was Christy's favorite look for him.

"Things are just too tenuous at work, babe. And I've got that mother-daughter assembly on Wednesday. Mrs. Smart said I *had* to be there," Christy said, putting on her coat.

"Oh, if Mrs. Smart said you had to be there, then I guess you do." She could see Michael going to a very dark place.

"Michael, please. I'm trying to do right by Renata. I'm trying to run my company. I'm trying to be a good wife to you. I'm doing the best I can."

"Beegee, you said things weren't going to change. Well, they've changed. We should think seriously about boarding schools. At least get Renata off your plate."

"I don't want to get her off my plate. I just want to figure out how to be her mom. I have no idea how to do it, and I can't make everything slow down. Give me time. I'm not used to all this juggling." It felt good to finally admit at least this much. "Oh, and Renata wants to be called 'Stringbean' from now on."

"Stringbean? Why?"

"I have no idea. Maybe she really likes vegetables."

"Stringbean, eh." Michael nodded and changed the subject. "Galit Portal called today. She wants to write that book about me."

"See, I told you she was gonna call. Did you say yes?"

"Not at first, and I said it was because of the way the *Journal*'s been treating *you*. But she assured me she'd be fair, even had Ian Malik call to tell me how pleased he was with *his* book. So I agreed. I figure if I build a good relationship with her, it could end up helping you. I hope I'm making the right decision."

"You are, I'm sure of it. A positive biography will be great for the company. And you know you've arrived when you become the subject of a Galit Portal book. Plus, it's nice of you even to think about saving me from those mean people at the *Journal*." Christy was proud of Michael. For a few moments, she felt like a newlywed again, nestled safely in her hero's arms.

Renata Uses Inappropriate Language

DEAR DIARY,

I AM SO GHETTO COMPARED TO EVERYONE ELSE AT MY SCHOOL. I WISH PEOPLE WOULD STOP TEASING ME ABOUT THAT. I WISH IT WAS A YEAR AGO. THEN GRANDMA WOULD BE ALIVE AND I'D BE GOING TO SCHOOL WITH KIDS WHO WERE JUST LIKE ME. EXCEPT FOR MAYBE THEY WOULDN'T BE AS NATURALLY TALENTED.

YOUR FRIEND,
STRINGBEAN

❧

The mothers and daughters assembled in Mrs. Smart's classroom. It was a good thing she'd come, Christy thought. If she'd missed the event, she would have been the only mom absent. Each girl stood before the group to read the tribute her mother wrote her. Then the mom reciprocated by sharing her child's letter of homage. It was as close to a lovefest as they ever throw on the Upper East Side. Christy couldn't help but notice how Brownie beamed when she read Stephanie's laudatory essay. She may be a bitch, Christy thought, but she's a bitch who has a better relationship with her daughter than I have with Renata. Of course, there had to be some exaggeration going on. Mothers and daughters don't get along this well. Do they? Christy wasn't sure. She could barely remember what it was like to have a mom.

When it was Renata's turn, she walked to the front of the room, opened Christy's letter, and spoke:

Dear Stringbean,

Unlike your friends and their parents, you and I are just beginning to form a relationship. It is my greatest wish that someday, you will come to think of me as your mother. While I would never expect to take the place of your cherished grandma, perhaps there is room in your heart to love me in a different but special way. As I once told you, when I was a child, my mother died. So I understand that you will always miss Maria. When your grandmother asked me with her last breath to raise you, it felt like God was offering me a chance to give something back for all the wonderful blessings that had been bestowed on me. I only hope I am worthy of standing in the place of the only mother you ever really knew, Maria Ruiz. Have I told you how extraordinary I think you are? I think you've a wonder. You are a well-mannered, smart, and loving girl. Maria did a beautiful job of raising you. I will do my best to continue to bring you up in the way Maria would have wanted. While I cannot give you back the woman you loved most in the world, I can give you the world. That's what I intend to do.

All my love,
Christy

The classroom erupted in applause when Renata finished reading. It wasn't that Christy's letter was so heartwarming; the class clapped after each person completed her recitation. Christy stood and walked to the front of the room as Renata took her seat. She opened the sealed envelope and pulled out her child's letter. She read what Renata wrote and then, slowly, folded the letter and put it back in the envelope.

"I'm sorry, but this letter is just a bit too personal for me to read out loud. You'll have to excuse me. I'm overwhelmed." Christy raced out of the classroom, intent on making it to the car before her emotions betrayed her. Steven held the door as Christy dove headfirst into the backseat. She opened the letter again just to make sure she'd read it right:

DEAR CHRISTY HAYES,
   YOU ARE A RUDE, MEAN, SELFISH BICH.
   I HATE YOU.
      LOVE,
      STRINGBEAN E. RUIZ

It's Always Something

"The descent from Refuge du Gouter was a nightmare," Michael said.

"How come?" Christy asked. She was in her bedroom, sitting at her desk, wishing Michael weren't so far away.

"There was serious rockfall. Big chunks were flying everywhere. They were sharp and coming down fast."

"Was anyone hurt?"

"A woman in the party below ours was cut pretty badly. It was a good thing Galit was there. She was trained as a medic in the Israeli army."

"How's it going with her?" Christy said.

"Pretty good. We've gotten most of the background interviews done. She seems like a good reporter, but I wouldn't want to be her boyfriend. What a ballbuster."

"You're not too tired for interviews after climbing?"

"We did most of it on the flight over. She's my Skip Heller, only I have to come up with more stories, enough to fill a whole book."

"I'm not worried. When have you ever been at a loss for words?"

"I miss you. You should have come."

"I know. I wish I had. Remember that mother-daughter assembly I told you about?"

"Yeah."

"Well, it was a disaster."

"Beegee, wait, hold on. Someone's knocking." Michael left the phone for a moment. "I'm back. Sorry. I'm with our Italian magazine partner. He's here. We're having dinner. What were you saying?"

Christy's call-waiting beeped in.

"Nothing. It's not important. Go enjoy your meal. I'll see you Friday."

The phone rang immediately. It was Lisa Drapkin, Katherine's secretary. When Christy started Baby G, Lisa worked for her. After Katherine was named COO, she needed someone with Lisa's experience, so Christy graciously gave her up and hired Randi.

"Hey, Lisa, what's up?" Christy said, trying to sound more upbeat than she felt.

"Christy, I'm concerned about something. It's confidential. It may be nothing, but I think you should know."

"What?"

"Everyone's talking. They think Katherine's having an affair with Rick Slotnik."

"Rick?"

"Yeah. He's always in her office. *Always*. They've been spotted getting out of the same cab in the morning. Mindy Swearingen saw them having dinner at Chanterelle and said they were sitting real close and being all touchy-feely."

"I can't believe it. She would have told me. She tells me everything."

"You'd think. But there's *something* going on. And people are pissed because he reports to her. Pat Hughes in accounting says that Rick makes more than anyone on Katherine's staff, including Fern and Stacy, and they're the general counsel and head of operations. Their jobs are way bigger. It doesn't make sense."

"Pat shouldn't be gossiping about Rick's salary."

"*Everyone's* gossiping about Katherine and Rick. I think you should talk to her. If there's something going on, you have to get involved. Fern and Stacy are really upset about how much he's making. The whole thing is sordid, and you're the only one who can help."

Christy sighed. "Well, *if* it's true, it can't continue. But I don't think it is. Katherine always tells me about the men in her life. I know all the skeletons in her closet."

"Christy, *hello!* She'd *never* tell you if she was sleeping with a direct report. You may be her friend, but you're also her boss. You gotta talk to her."

"Fine. I'll talk to her. But you'll see. There's a reasonable explanation. I'm sure of it."

Christy felt a terrible aching in her heart as she hung up. What was happening to her company? Bad press. False rumors. Falling stock prices. Bosses sleeping with employees. It was starting to feel like too much. There was a tentative knock at the door. Renata stuck her head in. "Can I come in?"

"What is it?"

The girl came over to the writing desk where Christy had been on the phone. "You have a nice bedroom. It's a pretty color." Since it was gray, Christy waited for what she really had to say. "Maybe I'll do my room this color when we redo it," she said, looking around.

"If you want." Christy rubbed her temples. "Renata, this is a bad time for me."

Renata looked at Christy with a pained expression. "I'm sorry I wrote that letter. It was mean of me," she blurted.

"Yes, it was."

"Your letter was real nice."

"Thanks."

"I didn't think you wanted me here," Renata said.

"Why would you think that?"

"I don't know. You don't spend time with me."

"I know. I wish I could be with you more. But I have my job and Michael. It's tough to give everyone I love enough time."

"Do you love me?"

"I'm starting to. Do you love me?"

"No, not yet." Renata hung her head.

Christy bit her lower lip. Then tears began to drip down her face. It wasn't because Renata didn't love her. It was everything.

Renata walked behind Christy and started to rub her neck the way she used to rub Grandma's. "There, there. It's okay. Everything'll be all right." That's what Grandma always said to Renata when she was upset.

Christy wiped her cheeks. "You're right. Things will work out." She couldn't believe that less than three months ago, her life had seemed perfect.

"Christy, don't take this the wrong way, but are you really crying, or are you faking? Are you just trying to make me feel sorry for you and love you?"

"What?" Christy said, baffled.

"You know, you're the president of a big company. People like you don't care if their family loves them or not. They only care about money and power. And they definitely don't cry."

Christy chuckled at the idea. "Renata, I mean Stringbean,

even though I'm a company president, I need my family's love more than anything. When I'm at work, I have to act strong and powerful because that's what everyone expects. But when I'm home, I can be myself. And right now, I feel sad. Sad enough to cry."

"Crying's not presidential," Renata said.

"I don't feel presidential tonight," Christy said. "I feel like a girl who just wants her mommy to make it all better. But I don't have a mommy."

"I know how you feel," Renata said. "Neither do I."

Christy took Renata's hand. "But you have me, String-bean. I'll always be in your corner. I promise."

"Christy, don't call me 'Stringbean' anymore."

"I thought that's what you wanted."

"I did, but when I hear you say it, it doesn't feel like you're talking to *me*. I need to think of a better name. Like maybe 'The Whoopster' or 'Li'l Ren.' "

"Why do you want a nickname, anyway?" Christy asked.

"Michael calls you Beegee, and he loves you. I think he'd love me if I had a nickname, too. Not that I care if he loves me or not."

Christy didn't know what to say. How could she tell Renata that it would take more than a nickname to get Michael to love her?

Christy closed her eyes and tried to relax as Renata rubbed her back. After a while, she told the child to go to sleep. She had promised to take her for a haircut first thing in the morning, since school was closed for yet another teacher-enrichment day. Eve had marked it on her schedule: 'Haircut—bond with Renata."

Renata left. Christy climbed into bed and tried to sleep. She didn't remember the last time she had felt this alone.

DEAR DIARY,

CHRISTY WAS REAL UPSET TONIGHT. SHE CRIED WHICH
SHOCKED ME BECAUSE UP UNTIL NOW I THOUGHT SHE HAD A
HEART OF BONE. BUT I DID SOMETHING MEAN TO HER AT
SCHOOL, SOMETHING I WILL REGRET TILL THE DAY I DIE. THAT'S
ALL I'M GOING TO SAY ABOUT IT. FROM THIS DAY FORWARD,
DEAR DIARY, I VOW TO BE NICER TO HER AND MAYBE EVEN TRY
TO LIKE HER. I HATED STEPHANIE RICH THE FIRST TIME I MET HER.
I THOUGHT SHE WAS A STUCK UP SNOT HEAD BUT NOW THAT
SHE'S NICE TO ME, I LOVE HER. NOT LIKE A LESBIAN BUT LIKE A
BEST FRIEND. IN CASE YOU'RE WONDERING HOW I KNOW ABOUT
LESBIANS ITS BECAUSE WE STUDIED THEM IN SCIENCE. SPEAKING
OF SCIENCE, I'M DOING GOOD IN ALL MY SUBJECTS EXCEPT P.E.
SO EVE GOT ME A TUTOR BECAUSE I HAVE TO DO GOOD ON THE
PRESIDENTIAL FITNESS TEST. JUST BECAUSE CHRISTY WAS IN
THE OLYMPICS, EVE SAYS I HAVE TO EXCEL IN P.E. JUST WHAT I
NEED. ANOTHER EMPLOYEE.

YOUR FRIEND,
RENATA (DON'T CALL ME STRINGBEAN ANYMORE)

Bergdorf Bonding

On the way to John Barrett's salon, Christy dialed the office. "Lisa, call me as soon as Katherine gets in. I want to talk to her." Lisa promised she would.

At Bergdorf's, she and Renata were whisked up in the stark white elevator filled with elegantly turned matrons from Connecticut, Japan, and the Middle East. Renata was not happy. Her grandmother took her to the corner barbershop instead of a fancy salon. But Christy persevered, sure she would warm up to the adventure sooner or later. Besides, Christy didn't know any barbers.

She had been coming here for years, ever since Katherine brought her up and personally turned her over to John Barrett, the owner and a hairdresser so famous that he was introduced to Princess Diana at the Metropolitan Museum Costume Ball as the hairdresser of American royalty. John and his staff had taught Christy a lot about being a New York woman; they were almost like her own private finishing school. Maybe they could help Renata fit in with those overgroomed Colby girls.

The elevator opened on the opposite side, which Renata got a great kick out of. They entered a world of sparse elegance, with lavender walls and minimalist furnishings. It was completely quiet; everyone was speaking in their best indoor voices. The entry foyer was a wide-open expanse of marble floor, with hairdressers and their attendants, mostly young, all skinny, clad in black and white, rushing quietly from one side of the salon to the other.

Michelle greeted Christy like a long-lost sister, then introduced herself to Renata. She took their order for drinks and no-calorie salads. The walls were lined with black-and-white photos from fashion shoots, featuring beautiful young girls in candid moments behind the scenes. Renata, who was tough to intimidate, seemed cowed and said nothing.

A few minutes later, Michelle led them back to Anna, the gorgeous bronze-skinned redhead who would be cutting Renata's hair. Christy knew it wouldn't do to ask for John in this situation, and she didn't think Renata needed a $400 haircut. She wasn't convinced that she herself needed them. Anna and Renata started bonding immediately, both Queens-born and bred. Anna trimmed away at lightning speed, revealing a refined and even more lovely Renata. Looking at her, Christy realized with some pride that none of Renata's classmates had her natural beauty.

As Anna was finishing, Gabrielle walked over. At five feet nine, with four-inch heels and spiky hair, she was an institution all her own, harder to get in to see than John himself. She liked Christy, but Christy was left to wonder if it was because she was such a nice person or because she was plastered on billboards all over the city. Of course, at this salon, she was a very minor celebrity. Christy was grateful that her marriage to Michael had ensured her place as John's client.

As Gabrielle began plucking Renata's eyebrows with her awful instruments of torture, the child let out a wail. All heads turned, the soft hum of name-dropping and confessing all to one's hairdresser halted. Christy stifled a giggle, remembering her own reaction the first time. But then Renata saw the results. She looked regal, like a real Mexican princess. Anna had managed to tame her hair without sacrificing the dramatic impact of those long black curls. And Renata liked it. She smiled at herself in the mirror. Christy felt she had finally done something right.

James Bonding

Steven, can you drop me at the office, then take Renata to Stephanie's house?" Christy asked when they hopped in the car.

"No problem," he said.

"That was kinda fun," Renata said. "I'm gonna get my hair cut at beauty shops from now on."

Christy fluffed her curls. "You liked that, huh?"

Renata nodded. Steven observed the girls in his rearview mirror and chuckled.

"That's a pretty necklace," Christy said, admiring the gold chain and heart that Renata was wearing. "Was it your grandma's?"

"No. Stephanie Rich gave it to me. It means we're best friends."

"Really?" Christy said as her cell phone rang. She glanced at the caller ID: It was Lisa. "So where's Katherine?" Christy asked.

"Sorry I took so long to get back to you, but she just called. Said she had to go to Connecticut for a family emergency."

Christy thought for a moment. "Lisa, do me a favor. Go to the Nextel site, the mobile locator page where you can track a phone. Do you know how to do that?"

"Oh, sure. I keep that page on my screen all day so Katherine can track Alex."

"Can you use it to find Katherine?" Christy asked.

"Just give me a second here. I have to input her number," Lisa said while typing. "Well, what do you know?" she exclaimed.

"What?"

"She's not in Connecticut. She's home. At least, her phone is."

"Thanks," Christy said. "Remind me to thank Katherine for telling me about the tracking feature. I'll stop at her house. But don't let her know." Christy snapped her cell shut. "Steven, on second thought, take me to Eighty-fourth and Madison."

"Why don't you want Katherine to know you're coming?" Renata asked.

"I'll tell you, but you have to *promise* not to tell anyone."

"I promise," Renata said. She loved secrets.

"Some people at the office think that Katherine may be having a relationship with a man who works for her. If she is, that's not allowed. I'm going to her house to find out if it's true. So when we get there, you have to wait outside. Okay? This won't take long."

"Oh, okay." Renata didn't see why that was such a big deal, but whatever.

Steven drove up Madison to Katherine's town house on East Eighty-fourth Street. Two years ago, she had purchased the run-down town house for a song. It had been subdivided into small rent-stabilized apartments inhabited by activist tenants with no intention of moving. After much legal maneuvering, she'd managed to get everyone evicted, even the eighty-seven-year-old woman who had called the place home for forty-two years. That made the newspaper. Katherine had bought her a one-bedroom in a high-rise that was better suited to an old arthritic lady with a son who worked at the *Post*. Then she engaged in a major renovation that turned the former eyesore into a showplace with a perfectly manicured backyard.

While Renata and Steven waited, Christy walked up the stoop and rang the doorbell. There was no answer. She rang again. Nothing. Frustrated, she came back to the car. "She's not home."

"Is there a backyard?" Renata asked. "Do you want me to check?"

Christy considered the offer. "No, I'll go." She walked around the corner and up the narrow alley. As she approached the garden, Christy was stopped by familiar voices. She crept silently toward the sound and then hid behind the trees in the back corner of the lot, listening.

". . . make a move soon, she'll drive the company into the ground. Everyone's options'll be worthless," Katherine said.

Christy felt herself go cold. Then she heard footsteps coming down the alley. Renata was doing her patented secret-agent tiptoe down the narrow path. Christy gave her a disapproving look. "I thought you might need me," the child whispered. Christy scowled, then turned her head so she could hear better.

". . . make it seem like a planned transition instead of a coup," a man was saying. It sounded like Karl Lehmann, one of their directors. "We can't let the stock drop further."

"We negotiate a deal where Christy's made chairman and *I'm* appointed CEO. Then, six months later, she goes quietly into the night," Katherine said.

Why that double-crossing, conniving, scheming bitch. I'm

gonna kill her, Christy thought. She started to move in, intent on confronting the conspirators. Renata grabbed her wrists, shook her head urgently, and put her finger to her lips. Christy stayed put.

"Will she go quietly?" someone asked. It sounded like Richard Bender. *Traitor,* Christy thought. After all she'd done to help his son get that track scholarship!

"If we pay her enough she will," Karl said.

"I don't think we have to," Katherine said. "*Wall Street Week*'s about to publish a *very* unflattering profile on her."

"How do you know?" Karl asked.

Rick Slotnik piped up. "I've been working with the reporter since the story was proposed. He's already warned me the piece won't be pretty."

"Can't you *do* something?" the director who sounded like Richard Bender asked. "A hatchet job on our CEO will hurt everyone."

Thank you, Dick Bender, if that's who you are, Christy thought. You have slightly redeemed yourself.

"Believe me, I'm doing my best," Rick said.

Well, your best isn't good enough, Christy wanted to scream. How many times do I have to tell you that?

"What about the advertising?" Karl asked. "Christy's in all our promotions."

"That's covered. We're launching a new campaign using current Olympic athletes," Rick said.

"It's about time," Katherine added. "These new female athletes we're using have magnificent bodies. Finally a spokesperson who isn't as flat as a boy."

What! Christy thought. That hurts. That really hurts. You have crossed the line, Katherine Garcia Winslow Witherspoon Kilborn. There's no turning back now.

"I think she looks pretty damn good," Dick Bender countered.

Thank you, Dick Bender. You have redeemed yourself even more. If you weren't about to stick a knife in my back, I might go so far as to forgive you.

Christy wasn't sure what to do. Should she storm in on the clandestine meeting and say exactly the right thing to put the conspirators in their place? But what was the right thing to say? Christy knew she couldn't afford to blow it. Renata gently took Christy's elbow and led her out of the alley. Barely making a sound, they got back in the car. Christy's eyes were wide open. Her heart was pounding. She was dumbstruck.

Gently, Renata patted Christy's hand. "I don't think you're flat as a boy."

Solid as a Rock

To: Michaeldrummond@aol.com
Fr: Galit@TFJ.com

Michael, La Dame Blanche was great. I have missed climbing the last few years, the buzz and the risk. And we got a lot of good material to get started with. I will need about 10 more days in total from you for the overall effort. It helps that you know your mind and say what you mean. I will call your assistant and arrange some times—I think chunks of a day or two work best. It can be over 2 to 4 months. Galit

To: Galit@TFJ.com
Fr: Michaeldrummond@aol.com

Galit, I'm not sure I like talking about myself so much to a stranger, but your questions were pretty fair. I guess that's how you suck them in. Part of that famous Galit charm. Let's hope I survive it. Michael

∾

Steven dropped Renata off at her play date with Stephanie Rich, then drove Christy to Michael's office. This was the first time since their wedding that Christy had surprised her husband at work. But Michael was delighted to see her. His assistant and secretaries were so solicitous it almost made her uncomfortable. I am the boss's wife, she thought. I guess this is how wives of CEOs are treated. Under the circumstances, it felt good.

Michael walked her into the dining area of his office where they could talk. He held Christy's hand as they spoke. It felt good to have him on her side. That was the only thing keeping her together.

"Beeg, call Niles Raines. He's always been your biggest supporter. All we know is that two directors are with Katherine. Where do the others stand? Niles'll find out."

"And what if *everyone's* gunning for my head? How do I fight back?"

"Either you or Niles will go see each board member, one at a time. They need to be reminded that *you* started the company. That you've never let them down. *Ever.* That even at a time when industry profits are falling, yours are holding steady. And while, yes, you've been plagued with bad press lately, you believe Katherine and Rick are behind it."

"You don't think that'll make me sound paranoid? I need proof. Can you ask Galit who fed her that first story?"

"I can ask, but I don't think she'll reveal a source. What about Lisa? Could she check Katherine's phone records and see if there are any calls to reporters?"

"That's a good idea. She'll do that for me—at least I think she will."

"Come here," Michael said.

Christy moved to Michael's lap. He held her tightly, gently rubbing her back. She could feel his heart beating against her chest. "I love you so much," Christy said. "What would I do without you?"

"Luckily, you'll never have to find out," he said, holding her. Christy wished he would never let her go.

Renata Gets Caught with Her Pants Down (Literally)

*S*teven drove Christy to Raines Partners' offices. Niles would see her immediately. Meanwhile, Lisa was going through Katherine's phone records to see if there were calls to reporters that preceded publication of the negative press.

Christy's cell phone rang.

"You need to get to my house to pick up your perverted daughter. And make it snappy. I caught her *naked* with my Stephanie doing . . . things."

"Brownie, calm down. What are you *talking* about?"

"I'm talking about *you*. You have no control over that child of yours. She was naked. *NAKED* with my daughter."

Christy wanted to hide. Could this day get any worse?

"Renata was naked with Stephanie?" Christy said, hoping Steven wasn't listening. "Well, was Stephanie naked, too?"

"They were *both* naked."

"So how do you know it wasn't Stephanie who influenced Renata?"

"What, are you nuts? Stephanie comes from a good family. A vigilant mother raised her. Obviously, that little tart of yours was allowed to run wild in the projects and now she's spreading her smutty ways to the nice girls at Colby. Well, it's not gonna happen. Not on my watch."

"Brownie, calm yourself. Renata's not a . . . a tart. How can you talk about a child that way? Kids their age are curious. Didn't you play doctor when you were little?"

"NO, I DID NOT. And there's *more*. Your little chippy stole a necklace from my jewelry box. That was all she was wearing when I caught her acting inappropriately with my Stephanie. God knows how many years of therapy it'll take my baby to get over this."

"Renata's not a thief. I'm sure there's an explanation. Listen, Brownie, I'm on my way to an important meeting. But Nectar'll be there in a few minutes."

"Isn't that *juuust* like you . . ."

"What's *that* supposed to mean?"

"Isn't it just like you to send an employee to do a mother's job! Do you *really* think that maid of yours is equipped to handle a delicate situation like this? *Everyone* at Colby says you're a bad mother, Christy, but I've been defending you. I will *not* defend you any longer."

Brownie slammed down the phone. She did that a lot.

Somebody to Lean On

Christy sent Nectar to pick up Renata. She knew that even if she collected the child herself, Brownie would tell everyone that Christy *wanted* to send the maid but had only come in person after Brownie shamed her into it. The other mothers would be scandalized. Since she was destined to suffer the consequences no matter what, she might as well commit the crime.

Are people *really* saying I'm a bad mother? Surely they have better things to do than gossip about me. Then again, maybe they don't. Am I a bad mother? Christy wondered. Renata goes to a wonderful school, eats well, dresses beautifully, takes piano and tennis lessons, studies with an excellent tutor, sees a top psychiatrist. Only a good mother would provide all that, right? Then again, maybe Brownie has a point. After all, *she's* always there for her kids. Vigilant. On top of their every move. I know what Renata's up to only if Eve schedules bonding time or if we run into each other in the evening. And that doesn't happen every day. Brownie's right, Christy thought. I'm a terrible mother. I've got to make this better. She called Eve and told her to assemble Renata's team later this afternoon. Why did this have to happen today of all days? Having Renata is such an inconvenience.

No, no, I take that back, she thought instantly. Does thinking that make me an even worse mother?

Steven pulled the car up to Niles Raines's building. "Stay parked in front. This won't take long," she told him.

Niles's assistant escorted Christy into his boardroom. He came through the back door and kissed her cheek before sitting in the chair next to her.

"Thanks for meeting on such short notice. What have you found out so far?" Christy asked.

"I spoke to Warren Heider and Rami Shah. Apparently, Katherine has been meeting with each director individually to make her case for ousting you."

"Did she contact you?"

"Not yet. She knows we're close, so I guess she's waiting until the others have turned before approaching me."

"What did Warren and Rami say?"

"That stock prices have been down for months and you haven't done anything to rectify it."

"But sales and profits are up . . ."

"Let me finish. She's arguing that you were the right person to create and build the company, but that now that we're public, we need a stronger CEO to take us into the future. Baby G has become too complex to be led by someone whose greatest achievement was athletic. Katherine's got the Harvard MBA, the history of having been here since the beginning, and a plan to grow the company threefold over the next five years."

"She's presenting a business plan?"

"According to Rami."

"The company commissioned Bain to work with us on that. *I* initiated the project. She's holding it out as *her* plan?"

"She admits Bain was involved in devising the strategy.

She claims it was Bain's recommendation that you become chairman and allow a different kind of leader to take over the day-to-day."

"Those traitors."

"I talked to Warren and Rami at length. Neither is convinced that it's time for you to go. I'm meeting with Peter Thomas and Judith Maslin later. Let me plant doubts in their minds. You need to call a board meeting for tomorrow afternoon. We can't let this drag on."

"I'll arrange it. And Niles, thank you for everything you're doing for me. I should have listened when you recommended against making Katherine COO. You were right."

"Unfortunately, Christy, most of the things one needs to know in business are learned after the fact, and at a big price."

Behind Co-op Doors

*R*enata's caregivers gathered in the library for an emergency session to discuss the incident at Stephanie Rich's house. The following individuals were present: Nectar Freedom, nanny; Dr. Ruth Perlmutter, psychiatrist; Eve Hamilton, family assistant; Junior Fritz, driver; Yok Wah Lim, cook; Cynthia Rodriguez, maid; Leo Morgenstern, academic tutor; Jake Cross, new PE tutor. Renata eavesdropped from the closet.

"Dr. Perlmutter, did you have a chance to talk to Renata?" Christy asked.

"Just for a minute. And as you know, everything Stringbean tells me is privileged."

"She doesn't want to be called Stringbean anymore," Christy said.

"Yes, I think she does," the doctor said.

"No, really, she doesn't. So please don't call her that."

"Fine. Everything *Re-na-ta* tells me is privileged. So I can only say that *if* she was engaged in the behavior of which she's accused, it would be perfectly normal for a child of her age—"

"Well, what she tells *me* isn't privileged," Nectar interrupted. "She told *me* that Stephanie has her strip naked every time she goes to that child's house. And she *also* told me that Stephanie *gave* her the heart necklace as a symbol of their friendship. Renata didn't steal nothing from nobody."

"When I drove her home from Stephanie's, she was inconsolable," Junior Fritz added. "We can expect her to regress after this."

"Excuse me, *I'm* the psychiatrist here," Dr. Perlmutter said.

"You don't need to be a shrink to know that being called a nympho by your best friend's mother will cause a trauma," Junior Fritz said.

Yes, he's right, especially now, when I'm so impressionable, Renata thought. What *is* a nympho exactly?

"I agree with Junior, Dr. Putter. In fact, I have Renata in the back right now vacuuming all the rugs in the house. Vacuuming is *excellent* therapy for her," Cynthia said.

"That's Perl-*mutter*," the doctor clarified. "And I don't think you're qualified to know what is and isn't good therapy for the child."

"What-*ev*-er," Cynthia said.

"May I interrupt?" Jake Cross said.

"Excuse me, but have we met?" Christy asked, appraising the stranger in gym shorts for the first time.

"Oh, he's Renata's tutor for the Presidential Fitness Test," Eve said.

"She has a *tutor* for the Presidential Fitness Test?" Christy said. "Don't you think *I* could have tutored . . . trained her for that?"

"Well, yes, if you had time," Eve said. "I just didn't think—"

"Excuse me," Jake said. "May I—"

"Not now," Christy said. "I want to get back on track here. Nectar, did Brownie call her a nympho to her face?"

"Not to her face. But as we was getting in the car, she told me never to bring my little nympho to her home again. Renata would've had to be deaf not to hear that."

"I heard it," Junior said. "And I *am* deaf in one ear. Too many Grateful Dead concerts," he explained.

"May *I* say something?" Dr. Perlmutter said.

"Of course," Christy replied.

"I recommend that you triple her therapy. If I don't see her every single day, I cannot take responsibility for the consequences."

That did it for Christy. "Dr. Perlmutter," she said, "you should be ashamed. Just leave us. You're fired."

Dr. Perlmutter gasped, then sputtered like a car that was about to break down.

From the closet, Renata could hear the door slam as the doctor exited in a huff. She jumped up and did her patented secret-agent dance, the one that only highly trained spies knew how to do because it required such talent. In her head, she sang, "Go Christy, go Christy, you're m' hero, go Christy."

". . . there's only one thing this child needs, and that's attention from her mother," Nectar was saying.

Renata stopped dancing. By "mother," does she mean *Christy*? she wondered.

Eve spoke up. "But Nectar, Christy and Renata bond *regularly*. I should know. I schedule those moments. And I'll bet you sometimes connect with Renata spontaneously, too, don't you, Christy?"

"Yes, well, sometimes." Christy nodded. "And I think I *could* find the time to train her—"

"Add that to the attention *you* and the committee provide, Eve interrupted. She was on a roll. "Renata gets as much love and devotion as any other privileged child, based on what I've seen from the kids in her class."

"*Mmm-mmm-mmm*. Eve, a child can't be raised by a committee. Don't matter how expert they are." Nectar grabbed a pen and a napkin. "Christy, here's my letter of resignation. I love that child too much to be part of this abomination." Then she stood up and walked to the door. " 'Good night. Good night! Parting is such sweet sorrow!' "

Stop her, Christy, stop her, Renata begged silently from the closet.

Christy ran after her. "Wait, Nectar, *please*. Don't abandon me now."

"I'm sorry, Christy, but I can't stay."

Christy asked Nectar to follow her into the bedroom.

Renata scooted to the other side of the closet so she could hear better.

". . . a little longer," Christy was saying. "Things are real hard for me at work right now. By next week, it should be straightened out. Then I'll make Renata my first priority."

"Don't you see, Christy? Next week it'll be another emergency at work. You need to commit to Renata all the way or let her go. You're not doin' her any favors."

"Someone said the moms at school think I'm a bad mother. Do you think that's true?"

"No," Nectar said.

"Really?" Christy asked, sounding surprised. "I'm okay?"

"I didn't say that. I don't think you're a good mother *or* a bad mother. You're not a mother at all."

Christy groaned sadly.

"Do you really think this is any way to raise a little girl?" Nectar asked gently.

"No, of course not. It isn't ideal. But I have so many responsibilities. I don't think I could do it without staff."

"Christy, lots of women work and have kids at the same time."

"Then why is this so hard for *me*?"

"Maybe those women have husbands who help more."

"Even single women work and raise kids."

"That they do," Nectar said. "But they aren't the big boss of the whole shebang. Didn't anybody ever teach you the rule of two?"

"Is that from Shakespeare?"

"It's from my old boss, Lillian Kornblee. Love, career, children, pick two."

"You think I need to choose?"

"Yes, I do."

"But Renata's not even my child. I started Baby G. It means *everything* to me. I fell in love with Michael. He's my other half."

"Then I guess we know what you'll be choosing," Nectar said.

Renata gasped in the closet, almost giving herself away. Her heart beat frantically. If Christy follows the rule of two and I come out number three, where will I go? What will I do? Who'll raise me? she wondered. Not good. Not good at all. What if they send me to foster care? Renata remembered that some of the kids at her old school had been with foster families, and it sounded like the worst fate possible. She knew for a fact that foster parents treated their kids like slaves and slapped them around for fun and held them prisoner in cellars filled with piles of old yellow newspapers. Renata's nightmare fantasy was interrupted when she heard Nectar say she was going to pack her things.

"*Wait,*" Christy said. "Please. Give me a week. *Please,* Nectar."

Nectar was silent for a moment. "You seem to want to do right by Renata. Okay," she said. "One week. After that, you're on your own."

☙

DEAR DIARY,

YESTERDAY STEPHANIE'S MOM CAUGHT US PLAYING DOC-
TOR. SHE WENT MENTAL AND SNAPPED. I CAN'T PLAY WITH
STEPHANIE ANYMORE. NOT THAT I CARE. I WAS JUST FAKING
BEING HER FRIEND ANYWAY. LATER, CHRISTY HELD A BIG MEET-
ING WHERE EVERYONE TALKED ABOUT ME. DR. PEARLMUDDER
WANTED TO SEE ME EVERY DAY TO GET OVER MY CRISIS.
NOTHING PERSONAL TO DR. PEARLMUDDER BUT I HATE HER. I
HAVE HATED HER EVER SINCE THAT FIRST VISIT WHEN SHE
SAID GRANDMA WAS REALLY SMART FOR A MAID. ANYWAY,
CHRISTY FIRED HER SO HA! ON DR. PEARLMUDDER.

THE WORST PART OF THE MEETING WAS WHEN NECTAR
QUIT. I KNOW I DON'T NEED HER, BUT I LIKE HER. I MAY HOLD
A CANDLELIGHT VIGIL TO GET HER TO STAY. PLUS, AND HERE
IS THE ABSOLUTE WORST PART OF ALL, THEY'RE PLANNING
TO SEND ME TO FOSTER CARE!!!! NO ONE HAS COME RIGHT
OUT AND SAID IT, BUT I CAN READ BETWEEN THE LINES.

TODAY AT SCHOOL, STEPHANIE TOLD THE GIRLS I WAS A
FREAK. NOBODY WILL TALK TO ME. PIPPA TILBERRY POURED
ELMER'S GLUE DOWN THE BACK OF MY BLOUSE. ALL IN ALL,
TODAY WILL GO DOWN IN THE ANUS OF HISTORY AS A COM-
PLETE DISASTER. AFTER SCHOOL, I WENT STRAIGHT TO MRS.
DE MILLE'S HOUSE. AS USUAL, SHE IS THE ONLY ONE WHO
CAN FEEL MY PAIN. WHEN SHE WAS LITTLE PEOPLE HATED HER
FAMILY SO MUCH THAT SOLDIERS ROUNDED THEM UP AND
KILLED THEM (EXCEPT FOR MRS. DE MILLE WHO MADE A DAR-
ING ESCAPE THAT SHE CAN'T TELL ME ABOUT BECAUSE IF SHE
DID I'D BE A WALKING TIME BOMB). THAT CHEERED ME UP. MY
PLITE IS NOTHING COMPARED TO HERS.

> YOUR UNWANTED FRIEND,
> RENATA

Media Massacre

*C*hristy allowed the hot water to beat against the back of her head. Then, she let the jet stream massage her neck. As she used to do before a big race, she visualized the next few hours. At noon, the board would hold an emergency session. After all these years, it came down to this. Christy versus Katherine.

In her mind, Christy saw herself speaking calmly but firmly to the board. They would listen, nod their heads. It would soon become clear to them that she was the one best qualified to lead Baby G. There would be a vote. Everyone would congratulate Christy on her victory. They would shake her hand and smile. Meanwhile, Katherine would sit silently staring straight ahead at the conference room table. The board would leave the room, suggesting that the two ex-friends take a moment. Christy would walk over to Katherine and offer her hand. Katherine would stand up to shake it but instead of an empty hand, she would be holding a small black revolver. Christy, who had always had excellent reflexes, would knock the gun to the floor . . .

A pounding at the bathroom door interrupted Christy's fantasy. She poked her head out of the shower stall.

"Beegee, hurry. Eve's waiting downstairs. Says you should come now," Michael called to her.

Christy dried off quickly, put on a robe, and tied her hair back in a ponytail. She rushed down to see what was so important.

Michael stood at the bottom of their stairs and handed her the new *Wall Street Week*. Christy's face graced the cover and she looked . . . confused. Couldn't they have chosen a more confident shot? The photographer must have taken two hundred pictures. The headline read CHRISTY HAYES—TIME TO LET GO? Michael walked with her to the living room, his arm around her shoulder. Christy felt nauseated. She sat on an ottoman and put her head between her knees.

Michael rubbed her shoulders. "Take some deep breaths. I'll bring you some water."

Christy sat up slowly. "No, I'm . . . I'm fine. It's just . . . *that headline*. Let me see the article." There were two stories. The first was a profile of Christy, beginning with her mother's death, then outlining the early struggles in school and later successes in track and field. The piece cited her lack of an MBA and chronicled her most notorious relationships, from the bankers mentioned in the *Journal* scandal to Cantor Farrar's Francis Rich.

"You didn't really sleep with Fran Rich?" Michael asked. "That's a lie, right?"

"Where does it say *that*?" she asked.

Michael pointed to the section.

"Katherine must have told the reporter. How *could* she?" Christy said.

"Is it true?"

Christy spoke softly. "Yes. It happened before I met you. The man is *such* a worm. He led me to believe he was separated from Brownie. I never would have slept with him otherwise."

Michael gave Christy a strange look.

"What?" she said.

"Nothing."

"Say it."

"I can't believe you'd have sex with that guy. He's a notorious skirt chaser."

"It was a long time ago. Before we knew each other. I thought he was separated from Brownie. I'm so sorry. I hope I haven't embarrassed you."

"I'm fine," he said, looking anything but. "It's you I feel sorry for. Fran Rich is *such* a loser."

"This is mortifying," Christy said. "I can count on one hand the number of relationships I had before we got married. And now, thanks to the *Journal* and *Wall Street Week*, my reputation is ruined. I worked so hard for everything I got, but the world's going to think I slept my way to the top. All the mothers at Colby will read this. Brownie will read it." Christy threw her hands up in the air. "How could Katherine do this to me?"

Michael went back to reading the article, then moaned. "Jesus, it says here that you're in the process of adopting a child who's having *emotional problems*. They're reporting she's in therapy."

"*What?* How dare they invade Renata's privacy? We told the reporter that was off the record."

"Honey, nothing is *ever* off the record."

"Yes, but this is about my kid," she said.

"Look at the next page," Eve said. "There's a whole piece about whether it's time for you to step down. Listen. It says 'sources close to the board are questioning if Christy's entrepreneurial style, so vital to the start-up of the company, will be enough to move Baby G to the next level of expansion.'

Then they quote Karl Lehmann: 'Christy's strength is in pitching investors, not in tending to the details required to run a complex public company.' Karl says it may be time for you to become vice chairman and appoint a new CEO so you can concentrate on visionary pursuits and special projects."

"*Special projects?* Everyone *knows* that's the corporate equivalent of a mercy fuck," Christy said.

"At least you're in good company," Michael said. "Look here. They're talking about CEOs like Steve Jobs and Bill Gates who resisted stepping down."

"Bill Gates says you know it's time to step down when you're no longer having fun," Eve added. "Are you having fun?"

"Oh yeah, I'm having a *blast*. Can't you tell?" She put her head in her hands. Christy *knew* this was her fault. She'd been so distracted at work. When she hadn't been paying attention, Katherine had made her move. She didn't know which was worse, the possibility of losing her company or discovering that her best friend was a double-crossing liar.

"So, what are you gonna do, Christy?" Michael asked.

Christy was silent for a few moments. "Remember when Fatuma Mongaala tripped me at the twenty-two-mile mark in Barcelona? What did I do? You were there."

"You got up, took her on, and then mopped the floor with her," Michael said.

Christy looked at Eve and Michael with determination. "And that's exactly what I'm going to do with Katherine."

Galit Weighs In

To: <u>Michaeldrummond@aol.com</u>
Fr: <u>Galit@TFJ.com</u>
Michael, I saw the article. Ouch. It's bad enough when the press goes after you, but to have to endure it from two fronts—your wife as well. You need to help her. She is drowning, and you don't want it to tarnish you. Your reputation is unblemished, and you must keep it that way. Galit

To: <u>Galit@TFJ.com</u>
Fr: <u>Michaeldrummond@aol.com</u>
Galit, I can't say there is no truth to what you are saying, but I love Christy and would endure far worse to be part of her life. As for drowning, Christy has a lot of grit under that beautiful exterior. You have a bit of that, too, don't you? Christy's toughness is just less visible. I would never bet against her. Michael

To: <u>Michaeldrummond@aol.com</u>
Fr: <u>Galit@TFJ.com</u>
I don't know if I was just insulted, but growing up with enemies who want to blow you away in real life tends to do that. I just hope you are able to see Christy objectively. Galit

To: Galit@TFJ.com
Fr: Michaeldrummond@aol.com
I hope I never do. That's not what soul mates are about. Maybe one day you'll be lucky enough to find someone who can pierce that fierce exterior of yours. Michael

To: Michaeldrummond@aol.com
Fr: Galit@TFJ.com
I don't know. There aren't many like you around. Meanwhile, my armor serves me well. Just don't let Christy bring you down. It has happened to other CEOs too enamored of their wives or lovers. Galit

And the Winner Is . . .

When Christy walked through the open office, it seemed that everyone was pretending to be busy. She held her head high, focusing on what she had to do. Christy was dressed to kill, in her black Chloé suit, cream silk blouse, double strand of South Sea pearls, and Prada boots. Katherine had taught her well. A quick glance told her that her former friend was wearing the identical outfit, except that *her* suit was from Steve Tyler. To the untrained eyes of the board, it would look like they'd dressed as twins for their big showdown. Christy didn't care. She planned to bait, trap, and exterminate Katherine, exposing her for the dirty sewer rat that she was.

"Hello, Christy," Katherine said sweetly across the table.

Does she know that I know she's a traitor? Christy wondered. Yes, she has to. Never underestimate a smiling cobra, she told herself.

"Did everyone see that we made the cover of this week's *Wall Street Week*?" Katherine asked the group, batting her eyes. She pulled a stack of magazines out of her bag and passed them around. The directors flipped through the articles as if they'd never read them, which of course they all had.

Niles Raines slipped in the door at the last minute, waving

away the magazine Katherine offered him. He whispered in Christy's ear, "Bender, Thomas, and Lehmann are with Katherine; Maslin, Heider, and Shah haven't decided, and I'm with you."

"Thanks, Niles," she whispered. Christy stood up and addressed the group. "Thank you all for coming on short notice. I felt it was critical that we meet and discuss some of the press that's come our way lately. I know you're all concerned, as am I, that investors are losing confidence. We can't let it continue. It's time to take action."

Warren Heider interrupted. "Who is responsible for PR?"

"That would be Rick Slotnik," Christy said.

"He's not doing his job," Warren said. "He needs to be replaced."

"I agree," Christy said. "In fact, he's being terminated as we speak."

"Ex-*cuse* me," Katherine said. "Rick reports to me. I should have been consulted, don't you think?"

"Normally, I'd say yes. However, it's also my recommendation that Katherine be relieved of her duties as COO."

"Why?" Katherine said.

Because you're a double-crossing, lying bitch who drove our stock price down by spreading vicious rumors . . . Christy cleared her throat. "It has come to my attention that Katherine and Rick have been planting negative stories about me in an effort to harm my image so she can steal my job. By undermining me, Katherine has damaged investor and analyst confidence, causing the stock to drop. As proof, I have in my hands telephone logs that show phone calls from Katherine and Rick's lines to each reporter who filed a damaging story beginning weeks before each article was published. I've spoken with the reporters in question. They revealed that Katherine and Rick were the sources of their stories and that they continued to provide damaging details throughout their investigations." The last part was a lie, but Christy was hoping to inspire a boardroom confession.

"None of that is true," Katherine said. "Rick and I have never done anything to hurt you or this company. These are paranoid accusations."

"*Really,*" Christy said, slapping a stack of telephone records in front of Katherine. "Then how do you explain *these?*"

"Excuse me, but last time I checked, this wasn't a court of law," Dick Bender said. "It seems to me that, whatever the source, our stock is down as a result of the negative press. The *Wall Street Week* article says that you don't have the education or experience to take us to the next level. Investors and analysts will be reading this. Many already have. The stock dropped a point and a half this morning."

"I have to agree," Karl Lehmann said. "If we want to turn the stock around, we have to show ourselves to be an assertive board. The market is sending a message that it lacks confidence in our leadership."

"Not necessarily," Niles said. "Prices are down across the board in this industry. So are profits. But Christy's managed to increase our sales by eight percent."

"*Exactly,*" Karl said. "Logically, we should see a bump because of that, but we aren't seeing it—because of negative perception about Christy."

"I think we all know the time has come for Christy to step aside," Rami Shah declared. "I'm sorry, Christy, but we need more professional management. You could remain chairman and handle our big-picture issues."

"And our special projects," Karl added enthusiastically.

"But is Kathy capable of handling the CEO job? Maybe

we should conduct an external search and make the transition over the next six months," Niles suggested.

"My name is *Katherine*, not Kathy," Katherine said.

Christy jumped in. "If you think it's time for me to give up the top job, I'll accept that. But for God's sake, don't give the position to Katherine. She's shown herself to be loyal to no one but herself. That's *not* who we want running the company."

"That's *not true*," Katherine said. "I stood behind you for twelve years while this business was built. If it wasn't for me, Baby G would be a two-bit company that manufactured running shoes. I'm the one who pushed us to expand our product lines. I'm the one who should lead us into the future."

"Katherine makes a point," Rami said. "I do seem to recall that she always reported to us on expansion plans."

"Yes, because *I* gave her that part of the presentation to do. That doesn't mean she was responsible for it," Christy said. "And there's one more thing I have to say, something that reflects badly on Katherine's character. The article in the *Financial Journal* that accused me of trading sex—"

"Enough," Karl Lehman said. "We're not here to sling mud at each other. I have a motion. I move that Christy Hayes be promoted to chairman taking responsibility for special projects and corporate vision while Katherine Kilborn be given the job of CEO responsible for all daily operations of Baby G."

Special projects? Corporate vision? Right. Just take me behind the building and shoot me, Christy thought. That would be more humane.

Someone seconded the motion, and there was discussion about whether or not Christy and Katherine should leave the room.

Christy tried to pay attention, but instead she thought of the night Renata massaged her back when she felt so blue. What was it the girl had said? *You're the president of a big company. People like you don't care if their family loves them. They only care about money and power.* Christy looked around the table. I'm fighting this battle *why*, she tried to remember. Then she drifted into a state of tranquillity the likes of which she had never experienced. Is this what it's like to be in a crashing plane? she wondered. You know you're going to die, and yet you feel total peace? That must be what I'm feeling. *Que será, será.* Surrender, Dorothy. Let go and let God. Whatever happens happens.

"*Christy?*" Niles said.

"What? Sorry."

"The board's voting. You and Katherine need to step out."

Christy walked into the anteroom and sat down across from Katherine, who put on lipstick.

Neither woman spoke for several minutes. "Nice outfit you're wearing," Katherine finally said.

Christy looked at Katherine. She should have wanted to rip her apart, limb by limb, then drag her lifeless body to the city dump and gnaw on her bones. But instead she felt nothing. Could this be shock? "You know, Katherine, if you wanted my job, why didn't you talk to *me* about it? Maybe we could have worked something out and stayed friends."

"It's not that I *want* your job. I'm just the obvious candidate. They're drafting me."

"Right."

"Really, I would be just as happy to stay COO."

"Of course you would," Christy said.

"Christy, I'm as tough as they come. The board understands that no matter what happens to Baby G, *I* can handle it. And if it's bad news, *I* can turn it around and come out smelling like a rose."

Dick Bender stuck his head in the doorway and asked the women to step back inside. As they walked into the board-room, Katherine turned to Christy and whispered, "Don't let the door hit you in the ass on your way out."

Christy carefully shut the door behind her, making sure it didn't hit her on the ass. She felt that would be a bad omen. As she took her seat, she noticed that no one looked her in the eye.

Karl Lehmann stood up and cleared his throat. "The votes are in and the resolution passes six to one. Katherine Kilborn is our new CEO. Christy Hayes has been promoted to chair-man. Congratulations to both of you."

"I don't know what to say," Katherine said, fanning herself, her eyes misting. "Thank you *all* for the vote of confidence."

Christy stood up and looked at everyone. "I appreciate your offer of a promotion. But we all know what this is and what it means. So I'll save you the trouble of easing me out in six months. As of today, I am resigning my position with Baby G. If you prefer a CEO who puts herself above the good of the company, that's your prerogative. But it's my pre-rogative not to continue to work with such a person. I wish you all the best."

Christy was about to walk out when Katherine spoke up. "Christy, you may want to rethink that. If you resign, your op-tions vest immediately. The exercise price is two points higher than today's stock price. You'll lose just about every-thing." Katherine was trying to keep a neutral expression on her face, but Christy could tell that she couldn't contain her glee.

Christy smiled and said the one thing that she knew would

eat at her ex-partner as nothing else would. "I know that, Katherine. But unlike *you*, I wasn't just dumped by my second husband. No, *I'm* happily married to my one and *only* husband who's worth hundreds of millions of dollars. And what's his . . . is mine."

Katherine flinched as though she had been slapped in the face.

Christy knew she should say something to the rest of the board, something that she had been stopped from saying before, something that would restore a tiny shred of her dignity. "Oh, and by the way, I think you should be aware," Christy added, "that those men the media reported *I* slept with to get investors? Those were men *Katherine* slept with. But I guess you know this already, because she promised me she'd come clean about her unprofessional behavior."

The board members looked at each other blankly.

Christy moved on. "It has been a privilege to work with each of you. You've been terrific advisers and boosters of the company, and I know you're doing what you believe is right." She looked around the room one last time, making eye contact with each director. Then she stood very tall, with more conviction than she felt, and walked out.

Closing the door quietly behind her, Christy paused to take a breath. She shook herself. What had just taken place? Why hadn't she looked into what would happen to her options if she resigned? She had simply assumed that she would win today's battle. It never occurred to her to plan for defeat. She'd committed one of the cardinal sins of business that was expressed in the childish aphorism: Never assume—it makes an "ass" out of "u" and "me." How many times had she irritated Katherine by chanting that line? Could she have been this careless? Had she made an unconscious choice?

No. Never. Ridiculous.

And yet, in moments, she had transformed herself from a wealthy, independent, and powerful woman into a dependent with no identity outside her own home. After all she'd been through to build the company, it was pathetic to have to rely on Michael's money when the time came to hit the road. Oh well, she told herself. It is what it is. There's no way I could have stayed with Katherine running the show. And anyway, maybe there are more important things in life than running a company. Love, career, children. Pick two.

After the Fat Lady Sings

Carrying herself with the dignity of Mary, Queen of Scots on the way to her beheading, Christy walked through the open offices of Baby G for the last time. Some people stared; others pretended to be hard at work at their computers. Her oldest employees looked at her with such grave concern that she thought a few of them might cry. I can't walk out without saying anything, she thought. At the front door, she turned and faced everyone.

Her voice shook as she spoke. "As of today, I'm leaving the company, but I . . . I know you'll all be fine. You are the most talented individuals. I have such faith in . . . in all of you," Christy stammered. Her mind went blank. She became silent and looked the crowd over, the people she had cared so much about that she would probably never see again. "It has been a privilege to be your president. I . . . I wish you all success." Blinking back tears, she turned and walked out the door.

Steven, who had been reading the *Wall Street Week* article in the front seat, was waiting in the car. With great relief, Christy stepped inside. It was one-thirty.

Niles Raines ran out of the building and rapped on Christy's window. Steven lowered it. "Christy, are you okay?" he asked.

"Of course, I'm fine," she said, sounding shaky at best.

"I just . . . I can't believe those idiots would pick Katherine over you. It makes no sense." Niles shook his head. "Really, what are you going to do?"

Christy smiled. "Don't worry about me, Niles. I'm going to leave all this behind and focus on being a great wife and mother."

Niles gave Christy a skeptical look, then kissed her and said to call him anytime. "When you're ready, let's talk about your next chapter."

Christy raised the window and sunk into the seat.

Steven turned around. "Is it true? Did Katherine beat you?"

Christy nodded her head weakly, ashamed. She wished Steven wasn't there to watch the aftermath of her crushing defeat.

"That *bitch*," he said.

"Steven, really, she's not that bad a person—"

"*What do you mean?* She stole the company right out from under you. I *never* trusted her." Steven pulled out into traffic and drove north, mumbling under his breath.

Steven's right, Christy thought. Katherine is a bitch. Why am I defending her? I'm definitely in shock.

"Listen, Christy, I've known you a long time. You're a survivor. You're going to be okay," Steven said kindly.

Christy didn't respond.

Steven kept driving. Finally, he asked, "Do you want me to take you to Michael's office?"

"No!" she said. "Not Michael's. Please just . . . just drive." Christy immediately regretted losing her temper. But she couldn't apologize. She couldn't talk to Steven. She couldn't talk to anyone.

"Where to?" Steven said.

"I don't know. Wherever."

Steven drove north until they reached 125th Street. Then he cut over to the FDR Drive and cruised all the way downtown, looping around the tip of Manhattan, then going north again on the West Side Highway. He checked the rearview mirror on and off, but Christy kept a stoic expression. She was silent. As they exited the highway at Twenty-third Street, Christy glanced toward the river and caught a picture of herself on one of the few billboards that hadn't yet been replaced with one of the new ads. There she was, the face of Baby G.

Christy let out a wail and dissolved into tears, weeping like a mother at the grave of her child. Steven pulled the car over and stopped. He stepped out to give her privacy as she gave in to the grief. She cried until there was nothing left.

Finally, Steven opened the door and offered Christy a bottle of water, a package of M&M's, and a decongestant he had just purchased at a nearby deli. She thanked him, then pulled a mirror out of her purse and started to repair the damage. Christy looked nothing like the dressed-to-kill corporate warrior who'd left the house that morning. She was red-nosed and disheveled, with black mascara circles under her eyes. Steven handed her the box of wet wipes that he kept in the glove compartment, and Christy took the makeup off her face. She chugged the bottle of Evian.

"Do you want me to take you home now?" Steven asked.

Christy shook her head. "I can't go home *now*. What time is it?"

Steven checked his watch. "Two forty-five."

Christy wasn't sure what to do. Where do people go in the middle of the afternoon when they don't have jobs? Shopping. Yes, that has to be it. Christy never had time to shop. "Take me to Prada," she declared. She saw Steven raise his eyebrows in the rearview mirror as they took off in that direction.

She stared out the window as the car headed back uptown. Soon, they were driving on Park Avenue in the seventies. Women were pushing babies in strollers. In very few cases did their ethnicity match. Stay-at-home nonmoms in running clothes were jogging over to Central Park. Nipped-and-tucked matrons were dressed in luncheon couture for their afternoon of shopping. Dog walkers pulled seven purebred dogs apiece—worth a small fortune. Outside each building, doormen stood guard over their domains, buttressed in their authority by official-looking uniforms, supervising the hip-hop ensemble of delivery boys who handed off food, prescriptions, bags of designer clothes, flowers, bundles of firewood, pets returning from their day spas.

On every corner, children in private-school uniforms were being chaperoned home. Little boys with khaki pants and navy blue blazers. Young girls with light-blue pleated skirts, starched white shirts, and navy sweaters. One girl was showing a drawing to her mother, who bent down with enthusiasm and interest. "On second thought, Steven, take me to Colby. I'll surprise Renata," she said.

Mommy Mogul

C hristy smiled for the first time that day. This was good. She had never once had the time to pick up her girl. Quickly, she dialed Nectar and told her not to come. *She* would be meeting Renata.

"Mmm-mmm-mmm, why, that's wonderful, Christy. I'm so proud of you. Now that's what I call 'good mothering.'" Christy collapsed back in the seat as Steven drove to school.

When the car stopped in front of the Colby School, Christy opened the door and stared at the scene before her. She wasn't sure what came after getting out of the car. Disoriented but trying not to show it, she assessed her surroundings.

It was three o'clock. A small group of brown-skinned nannies in white uniforms gathered to await their charges. The young French and Swedish au pairs, whose like journeyed to New York every year to improve their English and see the world, stood in another group awaiting the children in their care. By far the biggest crowd was the size-two stay-at-home Mommies (size zero if they were European), ready to greet their daughters as they emerged from the mansion they called school. The Mommies all wore different versions of the same outfit—expensive khaki pants, Chanel ballet slippers, French striped T-shirts, white cardigans, and modest pearls. Christy realized instantly that her outfit was outside the dress code.

The uniformed darlings flooded out the front door, anxious to get to their after-school ballet, tennis, piano, and horse-riding lessons. The Mommies hugged their daughters and asked about the day. Girls gave the Mommies handmade pictures or spelling tests marked "excellent." The Mommies told the girls how proud they were and turned toward home, where nannies waited behind co-op doors, ready to give their young charges a healthy snack before lessons.

Christy stood in the neutral zone equidistant between the Mommies and the nannies, waiting for Renata to emerge. Out of nowhere, an exquisite blonde wearing a tweed orange-and-cream-check Escada suit with periwinkle python-print boots came running up to Christy. She was as striking as a runway model. "Am I too late? Are they out?" She spoke with an English accent.

Christy smiled, delighted that someone was talking to her. "A few are. But my daughter hasn't . . . uhm."

"Whew. I thought I was late." She pointed to her jaw. "Root canal."

"Ouch," Christy said. "I'm Christy Hayes."

"Andrea Hyatt. Happy to meet you," she gushed. "You look terribly familiar to me. Do I know you? Are you one of my kind?"

Christy figured she had seen her picture on billboards, but she didn't want to talk about that. "Your kind? What do you mean?"

"A working girl," Andrea whispered.

Christy looked down at her power suit. "Yes, I do. I mean I was. No more. It's a long story. I guess you work, too."

"Used to until I married Heinz Wendt. Not anymore."

"The financier?"

"Yes. He insisted I quit. Wanted my full attention like a good trophy wife," she laughed. "But I'm a working girl at heart."

"So how come you don't dress like them?" Christy motioned with her head toward the Mommies.

"Normally I do. I have a special wardrobe just for pickup. But I had breakfast with old friends at J. P. Morgan before the dentist. You can't go to Wall Street wearing the Mummy outfit."

"I guess I'll have to buy some of those," Christy said.

"You *must*. Otherwise, people will talk. They'll say you look like a Dalton mum."

"And that's bad?" Christy asked.

"Not bad if your child goes to Dalton. But if you're a Colby mum, it's social suicide. Tell you what." Andrea dug around in her purse and pulled out a diamond-encrusted compact. She handed Christy an engraved personal card with her contact information. "Call me. I'll take you shopping for everything you'll need to fit in. We'll have fun."

"Thanks. I've had a terrible day. Your kindness means so—" Christy unexpectedly burst into tears.

Andrea put her arm around Christy and led her away from the crowd. "Whatever you do, love, don't ever let them see you cry. They'll start gossiping about what you're upset about and next thing you know, everyone'll be saying you're sleeping with another mum's husband."

Christy looked behind her and noticed Brownie standing across the courtyard with one of her girls. Remembering that *Wall Street Week* had today accused her of sleeping with Colby's number-one Mummy's husband, she pulled herself together. "You're right."

The front door opened and a river of identically navy-clad little girls spilled out, at least a hundred of them. They talked on cell phones, gossiped in tight cliques, and hit each other with their book bags. Christy scanned the sea of bobbing heads in search of the one that belonged to her.

"Christy Hayes. Do my eyes deceive me?" Renata cautiously approached. She looked stunned. "Did Nectar die?"

"No, of course not. I just wanted to pick you up."

"But *why*?"

"Do I need a reason to pick up my little girl?"

"No," Renata ventured. "Wait. Is that a trick question?"

"I see my daughter," Andrea said. She put her thumb to her ear and her pinkie to her lips and mouthed the words "call me" as she ran to catch her little girl, who was cartwheeling across the courtyard.

"So, how was school today?" Christy asked.

"Fine," Renata said.

"Just fine?"

"Yeah."

"Did you learn anything interesting?"

"No," Renata said as she climbed into the backseat. "Let me clue you in, Christy. Ask me something like 'what was the most unexpected thing you learned today' so I can't give you a yes or no answer. That's what the other mothers do."

"Ah, okay. What was the most unexpected thing you learned today?"

"Dunno," Renata said.

Christy couldn't help but laugh and was pretending to strangle the kid when Andrea ran up to the car and knocked on the window. "Christy, there's something you need to know."

"What?"

"If you're going to have your driver bring you to school, have him park around the corner. I don't care, but everyone else thinks it's gauche to have a chauffeur."

"You're kidding."

"No, no, really. Trust me. It's kind of a rule."

"Don't most of these families have drivers?"

"Of course. But they're discreet about it. When you go around the corner, you'll see all their limos and town cars lined up. But *never* in front. Never."

"Wow. Thanks for warning me. Can I ask why?"

"Haven't a clue," Andrea said. "It's one of the many mysteries of Colby. Ta-ta, darling."

ↄ♡

DEAR DIARY,

DON'T FAINT BUT CHRISTY STOPPED WORKING. SHE'S STAYING HOME TO BE MY MOTHER FULL TIME. SAY IT'S NOT SO!!! NOW SHE WALKS ME TO SCHOOL AND PICKS ME UP. SHE WEARS THAT SAME WEERD OUTFIT ALL THE OTHER MOMS WEAR. SHE SIGNED UP FOR A BUNCH OF CLASSES LIKE BODY SCULPTURE AND TANTRIC SEXTACY (DON'T EVEN ASK). SHE WANTS TO JOIN THE MOTHER-DAUGHTER BOOK CLUB AT COLBY. I DIDN'T HAVE THE HEART TO TELL HER THAT THE GIRLS WOULD NEVER WANT ME IN THEIR CLUB. NOT THAT I CARE ONE BIT. BUT BACK TO CHRISTY, SHE'S NUTS I TELL YOU. SHE FIRED JAKE AND STARTED TRAINING ME FOR THE PRESIDENTIAL FITNESS TEST. LIKE I NEED THAT KIND OF PRESSURE. I THINK SHE'S HAVING A MID-LIFE CRISIS. IT WAS BETTER WHEN SHE IGNORED ME AND I COULD HANG OUT WITH THE PEOPLE WHO WORK HERE INSTEAD OF THE FAMILY THAT LIVES HERE. NECTAR'S GOING TO STAY WITH ME WHEN CHRISTY AND MICHAEL GO TO PARIS THIS WEEKEND. FINALLY!!! A BREAK FROM THE MADNESS.

YOURS TRULY,
RENATA E. RUIZ

PART 2

Uptown Wife

We'll Always Have Paris

To: <u>Michaeldrummond@aol.com</u>
Fr: <u>Galit@TFJ.com</u>
Last week was a good session. I don't think I have ever interviewed someone who is so direct. It saves a lot of time. It was
nice skiing, too. I saw your Master of the Universe instincts let
loose on the double diamonds. Usually they lie under the cover
of your regular-guy thing, which is very disarming, by the way.
You will have to tell me more about how you got back on those
steep slopes after your accident. But maybe we should take a
break for a few weeks. I have enough material to work on. I can
see you have your hands full with Christy's situation. Michael, I
have an idea. Why not call Jerome Fudderman and ask him to
help? He has successfully repackaged a lot of powerful people
after they crashed and burned. Let's face it. At this point, her
status affects you. Galit

To: <u>Galit@TFJ.com</u>
Fr: <u>Michaeldrummond@aol.com</u>
Don't agree with your premise. But I do like your suggestion. The
skiing was great. I couldn't live without it, so I had to get my nerve
back. It was that simple. Michael

❦

Michael had arranged for a candlelit dinner to be served on the terrace of their suite overlooking the Tuileries at the Hôtel de Crillon. A violinist stood in the candlelight playing soft classical music.

"I love escargot," Christy said. "The first time I tried it was on a dare at an Olympic dinner. Here, taste," she said, stabbing a succulent morsel and feeding it to her husband.

"Mmm," he said, "chewy yet delicious. Just for that, I have a surprise for *you*."

"What?"

"Tomorrow morning, I'm taking you on an eight-hour shopping spree. You can buy anything you want, anything at all, for eight hours. We'll start at Avenue Montaigne and see where that leads us."

"Oooh, sounds fun. I need to get a simple Mikimoto pearl necklace to go with my new Colby Mommy wardrobe."

"Does it have to be Mikimoto?" Michael asked. "Who would even know?"

"Honey, nothing gets past the Mommy Mafia," Christy said.

"Sounds awful. Like a uniform," Michael said, indignant that he should be bankrolling her new neutered look. He had in mind spike-heeled boots, Versace dresses, sexy lingerie.

"It is, kind of. But I want to fit in, you know? I'm watching the Colby moms to learn the best practices for raising a daughter in Manhattan." Christy reached behind her chair for her jacket, then slipped it on. The night air had gotten chilly.

"Honey, I'm not sure best practices applies to raising kids," Michael said.

"*Au contraire, monsieur*. I've already learned a lot. Did you know that Colby moms give their nannies lists of permissible nonstructured outings they can take with their kids? You know, places like the Frick, the Metropolitan Museum, the Planetarium. I'm going to do that with Nectar."

"Sounds like a good way to bore the kid to death. And I thought Nectar was leaving."

"No, well, maybe. I'm hoping to convince her to stay."

"How are you doing that?"

"First, I'm trying to charm her. If that doesn't work, I'll beg. Money doesn't move her, but she cares about Renata. And she's worried about my mothering capabilities, although every day I learn more. For instance, Andrea told me that every Colby mom gets her portrait done in oil. And portraits of her kids, too. They all use the same artist. What do you think? Should I do it?"

"Sure, if you're naked," Michael said, smiling.

"*Michael*. You're such an animal. That reminds me, now that I'm not working, I'm gonna be your full-time sex slave."

"Did you learn that from the Colby moms?"

"Oh, God, no. Andrea thinks that only women who look like they never have sex—except for procreating, of course—can ever be fully accepted into the Colby power elite."

"Did you know that the only Barnes and Noble store where sex books don't sell is on the Upper East Side of Manhattan?" Michael said. "That's a fact."

"Really? Well, I'm a downtown girl at heart," Christy purred.

Michael came over and gave his wife a slow, sexy kiss.

"Delicious garlic," Christy said.

"You're not leaving that piece, are you?" Michael asked.

"Open wide," Christy said, and fed him the last snail.

Michael got serious. "Christy, I know how upset you are about losing the company. But selfishly, I'm happy to have you to myself for the first time."

"I know. It's just sad, that's all. I worked so hard to build that company, and to walk away with nothing . . ."

"Think of it *this* way. If you hadn't started Baby G, you wouldn't have been at Davos. If you hadn't been at Davos, we wouldn't have found each other. You didn't walk away empty-handed."

"That's true. I got first prize. It's just . . . I'm worried that you won't find me as interesting now that I'm not the big-time player I used to be."

"Beegee, you've done the warrior thing. You've made a name for yourself in athletics. You've kicked ass in the world of men. For the first time in your life, relax. Let *me* take care of you. We can travel, run, climb mountains, enjoy each other."

"You're right. It'll be great. You're sure you're not disappointed that I'm not the powerhouse you married? All that nasty press about my downfall doesn't embarrass you?"

"Look. Fireworks by the Eiffel Tower," Michael said. The couple stood up and walked to the balcony. Michael put his arm around Christy's shoulders.

"Beautiful," Christy said.

"Just like you. My beautiful wife who has *not* let me down or embarrassed me in any way. The truth is, I'm jumping for joy. I want to take care of you. I want you to lean on me. I adore you, *ma chérie.*"

"Me, too," Christy said, kissing Michael softly.

Michael looked up and spoke to the waiter who had arrived with the second course. "*Servez-nous, garçon, s'il vous plaît.*" They sat down again and the waiter refilled their wine-glasses.

"To our new life together," Michael toasted.

"To our new life." They clinked their glasses and took a sip.

"Oh, I forgot to tell you. You've got a meeting with Jerome Fudderman on Wednesday, *if* you want it," Michael said.

"No way! That's like having an appointment with the Wizard of Oz."

"Yup."

"He agreed to represent me?" Christy asked.

"Not yet. First, you have to convince him you're worth representing. But you can do it."

"Wow." Christy couldn't believe that she had an appointment with the spin doctor to the stars. "But if I'm going to stay home and be your sex slave, how would I use him?"

"Think of Jerome as a very special shrink who can guide you toward your next chapter," Michael said. "His specialty is helping public failures overcome their bad press and move forward with new lives. Isn't that what you need?"

"I guess," Christy said, trying to ignore the fact that her husband had called her a failure without even noticing it. "Have you spoken to anyone who's worked with him?"

"Only George Wells. He told me that if they give you a meeting with Fudderman himself, you're halfway there. He's going to ask you to tell him your life story. Don't hold back. He has to know everything. He'll decide if you're worth saving."

"Okay. I'm flattered that he'd agree to see me."

"You're as powerful as any of his other clients were before *they* self-destructed. I'm not surprised at all that he'd see you."

Christy flinched as he said "self-destructed." Somehow she had hoped that Michael hadn't seen it that way. At least he thought she was powerful.

"So you really think I can turn the damage around?"

"Of course you can," Michael said. "Everyone can. That's the beautiful thing about America."

"All right, I'm in. Now hurry up and finish your coq au vin. Let's take a walk along the Seine. I love this city."

Mr. Second Chance

*C*hristy sat in one of the giltwood armchairs across from Jerome Fudderman's ornate antique desk in his palatial Fifty-seventh Street office. Surrounded by his French chandeliers, nineteenth-century Russian carpets, and satin wall coverings, she felt like a lowly commoner awaiting an audience with her king. Most of the wall space was covered with elaborately framed oil paintings, each with its own light. Pictures of Jerome standing with his infamous clients covered the entire south wall. There he stood with some of the greatest public failures of all time—the wall of the fallen. Many had successfully rebranded themselves; others had not.

"Helloo, helloo, I'm Jerome Fudderman. You must be Christy Hayes." Jerome stormed into the room like a tornado, his note-taking assistant at his heels. A tall, bald, barrel-chested man with heavy jowls and pudgy hands, Jerome seemed like your average grandfather, only with a Savile Row suit and handmade tassel loafers.

Mr. Second Chance wasted no time. "So, Christy Hayes, the latest of the mighty to be chewed up and spit out. Tell Uncle Jerry everything. Why I should bother to save that lovely ass of yours."

Christy hesitated. She wasn't sure her ass *was* worth saving. She had no idea what she wanted. Hiding sounded good.

Jerome interrupted her thoughts. "Just start from the beginning. Tell me your story, dear."

Christy sat up straight. "Well, I became a runner when I was twelve."

"No, not *that* beginning. I have your history here. Tell me about the last year, year and a half. You've fallen hard, and I need to know what happened."

"Oh, sure. About a year and a half ago, I met the man of my dreams, Michael Drummond. You've probably heard of him."

"Everyone knows Michael Drummond, dear."

"Right. Well, we met, fell in love, and were married not long after. Our life was perfect. Perfect! I continued to run Baby G while he managed his companies. We were like two kids in a candy store, and the world was the candy store. We did whatever we wanted, with just one rule: we always did it together. It took us so long to find each other, we didn't want to be apart if we could help it."

"So, you ignored your company while you were busy playing nookie with your new husband, heh-heh-heh?" Jerome had one of those annoying perverted laughs.

"No. I was an excellent CEO. Very attentive. Our sales were up eight percent last year. Our stock was down, but that was because my partner, who wanted my job, was busy planting negative stories in the press about me. Anyway, several months ago, my housekeeper died. She was the grandmother of an eleven-year-old girl, who I, um, kind of inherited. I've filed for adoption. In six months, it'll be final, and Renata will be my daughter."

"So you ignored your business while you were busy playing mommy to your new little girl, heh-heh-heh?"

"You could say that, yes. While I was getting her settled, Katherine Kilborn, my COO, was secretly trying to steal my job. Ultimately, I lost the battle for CEO. They offered me the chairmanship, but I said no. I couldn't work with Katherine anymore."

"What reason did they give to the press as to why you left?"

"They said I wanted to spend more time with my family. But there was speculation that I didn't leave of my own accord. There were some mean-spirited stories."

"Yes, well, the media always has a collective orgasm when successful executives go down hard, especially women." Jerome stood up and walked over to his refrigerator. It was hidden inside a cabinet that blended perfectly with his bookcase. "Soda, dear?"

"Sure, anything." Christy wondered how she was doing. Jerome wasn't giving any hints as to whether he deemed her worthy of his services.

"I take it you walked away with a big cash settlement?"

"No, that's the terrible part. My options were underwater when I walked out. After working so hard for so long, I left empty-handed."

"Oh dear," Jerome said. "Humpty Dumpty had a great fall, didn't she?"

Christy sighed. "That's an understatement."

"So tell me, what needs to happen for your story to have a happy ending?" Jerome asked. His assistant handed her a glass of Pepsi.

Christy took a sip, stood, and walked to the window. An empty Food Emporium bag was dancing through the air as the wind blew it about sixty stories above the Manhattan sidewalks. That's exactly how I feel, Christy thought. "I don't have my footing anymore, Jerome. I just need a safe place to land, where I can create a new life that's worth living. But I'm not sure a spin doctor like you can help me do that. Nothing personal. I appreciate your seeing me."

"My dear," Jerome said, "don't you understand that for certain echelons in New York society, the unspun life isn't worth living?"

"You think that applies to me?" Christy asked, walking back to her chair.

"You *have* been in the public eye your whole adult life," Jerome said.

"I suppose I don't want to completely disappear," Christy said. "So how could you help me reinvent myself? I wouldn't know where to begin."

"Tell you what," Jerome said. "Take a few moments and study my before-and-after book. It shows what my clients were known for before their downfall, what blew up in their life, and how we reframed them."

Jerome handed Christy a thick leather binder. She placed it on her lap and began to peruse. Each page contained a photo of the client along with a brief sketch of their before and after personas.

Juliana Elena de Marichalar y de Borbón. Before: Thrice divorced, laughingstock heir to the Spanish Crown. After: writer, spokesperson for Chrysler, host of reality TV show.

Funkmaster Four-Four. Before: Rapper/Producer accused of masterminding the drive-by shooting of MC Two-Bit. After acquittal: Rapper/Producer, clothing designer.

Lizzie Kayan. Before: Publicly reviled mistress of the Speaker of the House. After: Handbag proprietor, memoirist.

Lolhanna Wentworth. Before: "It" girl, radical arsonist. After prison term: Author, socialite, motivational speaker.

Brooklyn Goldstein. Before: Rock star, heroin addict. After: Swimsuit designer, antidrug activist.

Alfred Silverglad. Before: Scion of Silverglad Enterprises, accused of rape. After acquittal: Congressional candidate. After election loss: Pundit on *Meet the Press*.

Baroness Claudia Von Frick. Before: Madam. After prison term: Author, manners and etiquette expert.

Christy looked up from the book. Jerome was talking on the phone to someone named Brittany. Or Britney? Could it *be*? She waited for him to end his call. "So this is supposed to give me ideas on how to reinvent myself."

"Exactly," Jerome said.

"I could design purses or swimwear, run for Congress, write a book, become a socialite, or host a reality TV show."

"The possibilities are endless."

"You know what I *really* want to do?" Christy said thoughtfully. "This may sound crazy, but I want to be as accomplished a wife and mother as I was an athlete."

"And you want to write a book about that? Appear on *Scottie Childs Live* and *Robert Beck* telling working women everywhere what it's like to go from being an important businesswoman to an anonymous wife and mother?"

"I do like the idea of being a voice for working women who choose to put family first. Although it wasn't really my choice," Christy said.

"Details, details. With my help, everyone will believe you left of your own accord. Yes, I like this. We'll start with a profile in the *Times*, maybe *Newsweek*. I'll get you a book deal. If things break as I plan, you can have your own reality show. Kind of like *The Simple Life*. Only *your* show will be about how a woman who has known only the world of business bumbles about as an inept wife and mother. We'll film you botching your family's Thanksgiving dinner, greeting your husband wearing Saran Wrap after he's had a hard day, putting your foot in your mouth when you volunteer at your kid's school. It'll be hil-*air*-ious, heh-heh-heh."

"I don't want a reality show, Jerome."

"Honey, everyone wants a reality show these days."

"I don't. Will you take me on anyway?" Christy asked.

"Yes, I believe I will, dear. My fee is fifteen thousand a month and I require a six-month retainer."

"Thanks. I really am grateful to be working with you." Christy felt a weight lift off her shoulders. With Jerome's help, she would turn this disaster around.

"By the way, now that you aren't employed, you need to be seen at the right places. I'm going to make sure you're put on the guest list for Mimi Kimble's power-girl salons."

"What are those?"

"She invites only the most fabulous women in the city to lunch at her house. Usually there's a speaker who talks about an important issue of the day. That's followed by meaningful conversation among the guests. It's like an old-fashioned salon. The most important women in media will be there. Get to know them. You'll need their support when we go public with the new you."

"Sounds exciting. Thanks." The idea of being included with such a respected group of women was enticing.

"One more thing. Can you put on about ten, fifteen pounds?"

"No way. Why would you ask me to do that?"

"The public is more sympathetic to plump girls. That's why it was easy to generate good feelings about Lizzie Kayan, but that goddamn bag of bones Claudia Von Frick was near impossible."

"I have no sympathy for Baronness Von Frick," Christy declared.

"See what I mean?" Jerome said, shaking his head sadly. "See what I mean?"

Begging Brownie's Pardon

Christy sat in the hard wooden chair outside Brownie's office at Colby. It had been forty minutes since the parent-volunteer secretary announced her. She wondered if she should knock again just to see how much longer it would be but decided against it. If Brownie knew she was in a hurry, she would keep her waiting longer.

It was Michael's idea that Christy make amends with Brownie. She still had to report to her for the fifth-grade-graduation extravaganza. Brownie was the Mother of All Mommies at Colby, and it behooved Christy to get along with her. After an hour, the parent-volunteer secretary summoned her inside.

Christy had met a lot of important people in her life. No one had ever kept her waiting this long. Following her second Olympic victory, she and the other medalists got to meet the president. Even *he* didn't keep them waiting. But she refused to let her frustration show. "Hello, Brownie," she said, extending her hand.

Brownie didn't take it. Instead she sat down and said, "So, tell me how I can help you."

Christy made herself at home in the visitor's chair. She cleared her throat. "Brownie, I came here today to make sure you and I are square. I know we've had a few rough patches, but our girls go to the same school, and our goals are the same for the PTA. Can we make peace?"

"That depends. Is that *Wall Street Week* article true? Did you sleep with my husband?"

Christy took a deep breath, not sure how to respond. "I thought you two had separated. I had relations with Fran . . . once. It was a terrible mistake. I'm sorry, Brownie."

"Hmmph," she snorted. "*He* said the article was a crock. Now I don't know whom to believe."

Dammit, Christy thought. *I should have known the bastard would lie.* "I pose no threat to you, Brownie. I'm happily married to Michael. And I wish you'd reconsider letting Renata play with Stephanie. She misses her so much."

"I will not have that strumpet in my home."

Strumpet? How dare you call my daughter a strumpet? Christy wanted to leap over the desk and choke the haughty cow until her turtlelike face turned blue and her bug eyes popped out of their sockets. But she sat on her hands and took deep, cleansing breaths instead. She thought of all the annoying people she had tolerated to build her business. She could do this. "We need to work together on the graduation," Christy said. "Can you at least agree to give me your support on that for the good of the school?"

"Yes, for the good of the school. But don't get any crazy ideas. You and I will *never* be friends."

Christy wanted to dance the hokey-pokey on that news flash. But she continued to sit on her hands and took more deep, cleansing breaths.

"Are you available two weeks from Wednesday?" Brownie asked, consulting her calendar.

"I could be."

"Fine. I'd like to hold a luncheon at my home in your honor since you're chairing the graduation. We'll invite the fifteen make-it-or-break-it fifth-grade Colby mothers. If you have *their* support, the event will be a success. Without it, you're doomed."

"Thank you. I don't know what to say." Christy was struggling hard to keep a straight face.

"Just show up and I'll take care of the rest. Oh, wait. There's one thing you could do."

"Anything."

"You can be responsible for the flowers. We'll have two large oval tables. The colors in the room are blue and yellow. I'd recommend blue hydrangeas mixed with white peonies, with a spray of yellow delphinium. Do you think you can you manage that?"

"Yes, Brownie, I *think* I can order a couple of flower arrangements." Give me a break, Christy thought. In all her years in business, she didn't think she had met anyone as annoying as this Duchess of Do-Goodism.

"Fine. But don't get any ideas about our becoming friends. It's *not* going to happen. I could probably get past your having carnal relations with my husband. But I'll never forgive you for getting it splashed in the press."

"Brownie, if I'd known Fran was still with you, I wouldn't have given him the time of day. I'd do anything if you'd forgive me."

Brownie was silent for a moment. Then, slowly, she turned her thin lips upward into a sort of snarl smile. "There *is* one thing."

"There is?"

"Your husband is big in the media world, right?"

"Yes."

"Does he know Scottie Childs?"

"I think so, why?"

"I want to be invited to dinner with Scottie. I want to meet her."

Christy just about lost her lunch. Scottie Childs was famous beyond fame, one of the richest women in the world, a daytime-TV idol and media mogul who had risen from poverty to the stratosphere of power and success. Dinner with Brownie? Sure. No problem. "Well, you know, she lives in L.A. It may be hard to get her to New York for a dinner."

"I know for a fact that Scottie has a standing monthly appointment to have her eyebrows groomed by Gabrielle at John Barrett's. You asked me what you could do to help me move past your quote-unquote mistake. I told you. That's it," Brownie said.

"Well, I'll ask Michael. Just out of curiosity, why do you want to meet her?"

"It's a charity thing. I'm chairwoman of an organization that provides psychological counseling for children with self-esteem issues."

Christy stood and curled her lips into a nervous smile. "Well, hmmm . . . I know Scottie cares about children. I'll see if Michael can arrange something."

◌

Michael laughed so hard at Brownie's request that Christy was worried he might not come through for her.

"Ha-ha, crazy, huh?" Christy laughed.

Michael started howling all over again. He was holding his stomach. Tears were streaming down his face.

"It's not *that* funny," Christy said.

That got Michael started again.

"She is too much, too much," he said, wiping his eyes.

"But you'll do it, right?"

"Beegee, if I make Scottie listen to a pitch from Brownie, I'll lose all credibility with her. Don't ask me to do that."

"Pleeeeeease. I'll beg if you want," she said seductively.

"Oh, God. I'll see what I can do, but *only* because I know it's important to you. Why, I'll never understand."

"You're such a good husband. Here, let me massage you," Christy said.

Michael lay back down on the bed and Christy started rubbing his feet. How she loved those feet.

"Mmm, don't stop," Michael said.

"Do you think I should take a sensual-massage class?" Christy said.

"I'd love it. Between that and your tantric sex lessons, I'll be one happy puppy." He grinned with satisfaction.

"Done. I'll look for a program tomorrow. Speaking of tomorrow, are you still going to L.A.?"

"Yeah. We're trying to interest Disney in a partnership with Anipix. They're no Pixar, but they're close. And some of their technology is superior."

"Ooh, does that mean I can get access to their equipment?"

"Whatever you want," he said, laughing.

"Maybe I can use it for the school," she added thoughtfully. "They're starting a film program."

"Ugh, stop. You are turning into such a Mommy."

"Oh God, you're right. Sorry. Here, kiss me, baby. I'll show you who's not a Mommy."

∽

DEAR DIARY,

MICHAEL'S IN L.A. SO CHRISTY WANTED TO TAKE ME TO SOME BORING MOTHER-DAUGHTER FASHION SHOW BUT I TALKED HER INTO STAYING HOME AND WATCHING TV. SHE SAID NO AT FIRST BECAUSE OF HOW MIND NUMMING TV IS, BUT THEN SHE AGREED TO TRY IT. NECTAR MADE US BISCUTS DRIPPING WITH SORGUM MOLASSES. HER MOM USED TO MAKE IT FOR HER AND HER SISTER (MAY SHE REST IN PEACE) AND WE ATE THE WHOLE PAN, PLUS WE EACH HAD A TUB OF BEN AND JERRY'S. I HAD CHERRY GARCIA AND CHRISTY HAD CHUBBY HUBBY. WE DECIDED TO WATCH TV AND PIG OUT EVERY NIGHT UNTIL MICHAEL COMES HOME. YAY! AN EXCELLENT PLAN! I FINALLY TOLD CHRISTY HOW THE GIRLS AT SCHOOL ARE SO MEAN TO ME. SHE SAID THE KIDS TORTURED HER WHEN SHE WAS MY AGE. WHAT SHE DOESN'T UNDERSTAND IS THAT PRIVATE SCHOOL GIRLS OF TODAY ARE CRUELER THAN OLDEN DAY KIDS OF YESTERYEAR. NECTAR TOOK ME TO GRANDMA'S GRAVE TODAY. IT MAKES ME CRY TO VISIT, BUT I WILL NEVER ABANDON GRANDMA. DID I MENTION THAT NECTAR'S ABAN-DONING ME AT THE END OF THE MONTH? FIRST GRANDMA, THEN NECTAR! WHY, NECTAR, WHY?

      LOVE,
      RENATA RUIZ HAYES

Mimi's Power-Girl Salon

Christy rang the doorbell of Mimi Kimble's limestone town house. While she waited, she noticed two secret-service agents trying to look inconspicuous even though their curly-wired earpieces and cheap suits were a dead giveaway. She wondered who at the salon needed secret-service protection.

A waiter answered the door, and Christy waited for her sable to be taken and hung on a coatrack stuffed with minks, beaver, fox, and other assorted animal skins. Only the woman standing ahead of Christy wore cloth. She turned. It was Hillary Clinton, which explained both the secret-service protection and the modest wrap. They smiled at each other.

"Hi, I'm Christy Hayes."

"Hillary Clinton."

"Of course I know who you are," Christy said, trying to keep the reverence out of her tone.

"And I know who *you* are," Hillary said.

Christy was stunned. Hillary Clinton knew who she was? This was exciting. She followed the senator upstairs to the parlor floor, where the women were feasting on a lunch of salad, filet mignon, and lobster tails—emphasis on the salad. Christy found her place card and grabbed a white wine.

The room was full of women she recognized. Just as Jerome promised, there was the holy trinity of newswomen—Katie Couric, Diane Sawyer, and Meredith Viera—and their patron saint, Barbara Walters. Peppered about the room were other professional luminaries whom Christy had heard of but never met. A gaggle of grasshopper-thin socialites were present—from Maude Astor to Denise Zwerble and everyone in between. Christy was amazed at how beautifully these women put themselves together. Even the plainest guest managed to look stunning. Their clothes and handbags were couture or vintage au courant, their hair and makeup society-page-ready. A photographer was snapping pictures of everyone. What am I doing here? Christy wondered. I could be one of them, a lady who lunches. Then she shivered. This looked harder than working, and, certainly, more pointless.

Christy's thoughts were interrupted by Mimi, a raven-haired wisp of a hostess, who was ringing a delicate silver bell. "Ladies, ladies, if I can have everyone's attention." She put her arm around a woman wearing a bright yellow-and-orange African *khanga*.

Mimi then spoke in an urgently dramatic voice, the same one she used for her show on cable TV. "Ladies, I'd like to introduce you to Ya'a Boushra, a young woman from Dodoma, Tanzania, who has come all the way to New York to talk to us about the barbaric practice of female circumcision in African countries. It is *so vital* that women around the world understand this travesty so we can use our power to unite and stop this brutality from continuing."

"Hear, hear!" a lady in Versace said. "Stop the violence." Other women nodded their heads and raised their crystal champagne flutes in solidarity.

Christy reached for a glass of Dom Pérignon, which a

waiter in black tails was offering. As she watched the women who were watching Ya'a with expectant faces, she wondered if a person could find happiness through physical perfection and social triumph.

"Thank you, ladies," Ya'a said. "Thank you, Mrs. Mimi, for bringing me to your great country so that I can share my story. As you may have heard, it is common in Africa to give girls as young as eight and as old as eighteen clitoridectomies. When I was twelve, four older women came to my home. They took me against my will into the desert, to a special tent, where I was stripped naked and tied up. With no anesthesia, the oldest of the women used a sharp knife and cut off my clitoris."

There was a collective gasp from the audience. No one could stomach the hand-decorated petit fours Mimi was serving for dessert.

Ya'a continued to tell her story. "I was given no pain medicine, nothing to stop infection. For four days, I was left in that tent. I tell my story today so that you, my American sisters, will be aware of the abuse we suffer in Africa. It is my greatest hope that you will tell the world of this injustice and help me make it right."

Mimi walked up to Ya'a and hugged her tightly, her eyes moist with emotion.

Livia Schorr waved her hand, which really wasn't necessary. It was hard to miss her in that chartreuse suit.

"Yes, Livia," Mimi said.

"This is *so* terrible. I applaud you for coming forward and sharing your pain. Tell me, *what* can we do to support your cause?"

"You can talk about the practice wherever you can. The more women who know about this, who protest this practice, the better chance we have of someday ending it," Ya'a said.

"Also, perhaps when Mrs. Senator Clinton becomes president, she will be able to mobilize a global campaign against such violence."

Hillary smiled modestly.

"Would you be interested in speaking at the Junior League tea next week? I could arrange it," Livia offered.

Seeing Livia step up so selflessly, Christy realized there was more to being a socialite than playing dress-up. These women spend thousands of hours on benefit committees planning events that raise millions for charity. The joy of giving back must be the ingredient that brings meaning to lives of these privileged women, she thought. Yes, that's it. The lure of this life must be the prospect of sisters working together toward common goals. I could get into that . . .

Mimi turned red and spoke up for Ya'a, who looked like she was about to agree to Livia's Junior League gig. "I'm sorry, but Ya'a's tied up next week. Maybe you can find your own East African speaker. Or look for someone from the Middle East. I've heard female circumcision is a problem there, too. Anyone else? No? Well, thank you, ladies. Let's have another round of applause for Ya'a Boushra, our brave victim," Mimi said.

Everyone applauded enthusiastically. Several women went over to Ya'a to talk with her personally. Eventually, people began milling about and forming little cliques. A petite redhead in pinstripes and pearls touched Christy's shoulder. "Don't you love these salons? It's such an honor to be able to help others in this way."

"Yes, it is, isn't it?" Christy said. She couldn't figure out how they were actually helping.

"You know, you look *so* familiar to me," the redhead said. "Do I know you? You're *somebody*, aren't you?"

I used to be, Christy thought. She smiled at the woman. "I

heard everyone had to be special to get invited to Mimi's salon. Now, if you'll excuse me." She walked toward the kitchen, intent to introduce herself to any one of the holy trinity of newswomen. Jerome had made her promise to do that. She headed for Diane Sawyer, then stopped short. Who's kidding whom? She was a fish out of bottled water here. Glancing at her watch, she realized she would have just enough time to pick up Renata. With that, she dashed down the stairs, relieved that no one had brought up her recent ordeal.

She stood in the coat line behind a blonde in her fifties. The woman turned around when she heard Christy's voice, looking a bit embarrassed. It was Anne Gregory, New York City's number-one civic volunteer.

Christy raised her chin and smiled.

"Why, Christy, how good it is to see you, dear. It's so smart and courageous of you to come out after all that nasty press."

"Well, it's just press, Anne." Christy hated that attention was being drawn to her humiliation. Anne didn't seem to mind.

"Well, dear, I'm afraid in this city it goes a bit deeper than that. I was going to call you this week. I'm sorry to say that the committee decided they couldn't have you as the honored speaker at the Up with Girls lunch next month. You know, the whole sex thing just doesn't send the right message to our young women." She waited expectantly for Christy to see the reasonableness of her position.

Christy felt as if she had been sucker punched. This chance to reach out to eight hundred teenagers from all over the country had been proof to her that she still mattered in this city, CEO or not. She wanted to shake this woman by the shoulders and ask her how it felt to be a heartless, social-climbing hypocrite. But she simply said, "No problem, Anne," and turned to leave, hungry for the sight of Renata's face.

Meet the Press

The house was immaculate. Yok Wah was gone after having prepared a meal of lemongrass soup, salad, and poached salmon that Christy would pretend to have made herself. Christy had told her to leave the tomatoes so she could slice them in front of the reporter. The sauce for the fish was made except for the olive oil, which Christy was planning to add when the reporter was watching. The rest of the staff had also departed. Renata was in her room, awaiting her cue. Michael would be home in an hour or so. All was ready for the arrival of Dina Gladwell, Lifestyle reporter for the *Times*. Jerome had worked his magic, and a five-column spread with color photos would appear on Sunday.

"This is *huge*," Jerome said. "I've earned my fee on this one."

"You are amazing, Jerome. Nobody but you could have made this happen for me," Christy said. She had already learned that it only took a few compliments thrown Jerome's way to warm his ego.

"Don't blow it," he said. "Keep your guard up at all times. Nothing gets by Dina. She was a front-page reporter until her second kid was born. Then she moved to Lifestyle."

"Don't worry. I can do this," Christy said.

"Just make her like you, that's half the battle," Jerome advised. "What are you wearing?"

"My brown Valentino pants with a Dior leopard-print chiffon shirt. Miu Miu moccasins."

"Put on heels—something sexy," he advised.

"Don't you think it would be more realistic if I looked comfy, like she just happened to catch me on a normal day?"

"This isn't about what's *real*, dear. It's about repackaging you from a tough corporate warrior to a glamorous housewife who finally got her priorities straight. The article will describe how you look and what you're wearing. Put on spiky shoes right now. That's an order."

As she waited for Dina, Christy wondered, *could* she do this? She knew how to handle a business interview, but this would be personal.

The doorbell rang. Christy ran to answer it. It was the first time she'd answered her own door in months. I should start doing more chores around the house, she thought. When did I turn into a person who needs ten people to help her put on her pants in the morning?

"Hello-ow!" Christy said, greeting her visitors. "So nice to finally meet you in person. I've been reading your byline for years. Let me take your coat." Christy tried to remember where the maid usually hung the coats. That's it, she vowed, I'm cutting my staff in half. She laid Dina's coat over a chair in the living room.

"You have a lovely home," Dina said graciously. She was trailed by a hunky photographer, who was introduced as Wolf. He was already shooting pictures of the place.

"Would you like the grand tour?" Christy asked. Of course she would. No one passes on a chance to see a semi-celebrity's Manhattan apartment. Christy explained that they were planning a complete renovation.

Dina made herself at home at their glass dining room table. Yok Wah had done a beautiful job with the place settings. After Christy brought the tray of soup, salad, and salmon to the table, she went back for the tomatoes and a cutting board. Then she carefully sliced them into wedges, mixing them into the already dressed salad.

"So," Dina said, "do you mind if we go ahead and start?"

"No, not at all. Fire away," Christy said, serving the greens and fish on two small plates, pouring sauce over the salmon.

Dina set a tape recorder on the table and hit the record button. "What made you decide to leave Baby G?"

"I'd been there for almost fifteen years. And to tell you the truth, I'd had my fill of all that responsibility. Then last year, I married Michael. A few months ago, we took in Renata after her grandmother died. I realized that I just couldn't do *everything* well. More than anything, I wanted to be a good wife to Michael and a mother to Renata. I came face-to-face with the rule of two and had to choose."

"The rule of two?"

"Yes. Love, career, children: pick two. A very smart person taught me that," Christy said.

"Ahh, how true that is," Dina said, nodding wisely. "After I had children, I kept working fourteen-hour days. That's when my marriage fell apart."

"I'm so sorry," Christy said sympathetically, pleased that she and Dina were starting to bond. Biting into the salmon, Christy's cheeks puckered. The sauce was sour. *Damn*, she thought, I forgot to add the oil.

Dina took a bite of her fish and chewed it slowly. Christy took another bite, smiled at her, and pretended it tasted just fine. Wolf took pictures of the two women as they chatted and chewed.

"But most women aren't lucky enough to make the choice you made," Dina said. "Let's face it. You lead a privileged life."

"I do now, Dina. But I didn't always. I grew up in a midwestern family, and my mom didn't work. My dad was a high school coach. We weren't rich. Our house was small, and we never took vacations. The whole family sacrificed so Mom could be home for me." Christy decided to skip the part about her mom dying when she was ten.

"Your salmon is delicious, by the way," Dina said. "Can I have the recipe? Maybe I could put it in the article."

Is she making fun of me? Christy wondered. "I wish I could share it, but it's from an old family recipe. Top secret, you understand," Christy said, since she had no idea how to make the sauce, and, even if she did, she wouldn't know whether to give the recipe with or without the oil. She immediately vowed to take a cooking class.

"Of course. Here's what I wonder, Christy. You used to be such an extraordinary person. Now you're an ordinary wife and mother. Don't you miss the limelight?"

How would I know? Christy thought. I left work a month ago and here I am doing an interview with the *Times*. "Oh God, no. I consciously chose this path. I'm putting the same energy into being Michael's wife and Renata's mother that I put into being an Olympic runner. We have a beautiful life together."

"So you advocate traditional roles for women?"

"I believe it's a choice as valid as working. At the end of the day, there's no right way to go," Christy said. "When I was an Olympian, high school athletes constantly told me how they wanted my life. They didn't see the hours of training behind the glory—how much I'd given up to be a champion. I ate, slept, and ran. That was it. Later, when I was a CEO, young women would come up to me and say they wanted to be me. Again, all they saw was the glamour. They didn't know that my whole life was about working. No relationships. No fun. Then I married Michael. Now powerful, independent women in their thirties and forties tell me they want to be me. Once again, they don't see the effort I put into keeping our marriage alive and exciting. But you know what? I've never been happier. When I was an Olympian or a businesswoman, I jetted around the world, had lunch with business leaders, and knew all the world's top athletes. I don't do that anymore. But I don't miss it. I've *had* that life. I get more pleasure out of washing my husband's dirty laundry than having lunch at the White House." Did I really say that? Christy thought.

"Lunch at the White House can be so stressful," Dina said.

"Don't I *know* it," Christy agreed. She was glad Dina didn't ask more about washing Michael's laundry, since she didn't even know how to use the fancy European washing machine they'd just bought. She decided then and there that she needed to learn.

"You know, the reason I couldn't give up my work was because I get such a charge out of touching millions of people. You were able to do that at Baby G. Is it enough for you to make a difference in the lives of only two people?" Dina asked.

This was the burning question that Christy had been asking herself. "Working as hard as a CEO has to work, I could never have sustained a warm and loving marriage. I couldn't have put my stamp on Renata as she grew up. Anyone can run a company. I'm the only one who could do those things."

"You make me want to quit my job and stay home," Dina said.

"Would you like to meet my daughter?" Christy asked.

"Absolutely!"

"I'll be right back." Christy walked down the hall to Renata's room and opened the door. The child stood in front of her vanity mirror making odd facial expressions. "What are you doing?" Christy asked.

"I'm practicing my bedroom face," she said. "Mrs. De Mille's been giving me lessons. Look at this." Renata lowered her eyelids and made her lips all pouty. She looked pretty darn sexy, and Christy realized that she would have her hands full in a few years.

She laughed because she didn't know how else to react. "Come on, gorgeous. I need you in the living room. The reporter's here. But don't mention your bedroom face."

"Remind me again why we have to pretend to be a normal family?" Renata asked.

Christy's face reddened. "C'mon Renata, work with me here."

Renata grabbed a math workbook and a Rubik's Cube and followed Christy out. As soon as they were in Dina's range, the child spoke. "Mommy, can you help me solve this Pubic Cube?"

Mommy! Renata had never called Christy "mommy" before. Did she mean it? Christy wondered. Dina met Renata. Michael strolled in at the right moment. He introduced himself to Dina and proceeded to charm her. Christy sat down with Renata and tried unsuccessfully to help her solve the cube. Wolf snapped pictures of the moment.

"Can we have some family shots?" Wolf asked.

"Oh, sure," Michael said.

Michael, Christy, and Renata posed in front of the fireplace like a Norman Rockwell family.

Soon, Dina and Wolf were saying good-bye. "Go easy on me," Christy shouted in jest (but not really) as they walked out.

The Best News Possible

DEAR DIARY,

I VISITED MRS. DE MILLE YESTERDAY. SHE'S BEEN SICK. ME AND MR. KOODLES SNUGGLED UP IN BED WITH HER. SHE TOLD ME THE STORY OF MRS. KOODLES (MR. KOODLES' WIFE CAT) WHO DIED A FEW YEARS AGO. SHE COULD TURN BACKWARD FLIPS LIKE A CIRCUS CAT. WHAT A FINE ANIMAL SHE MUST HAVE BEEN. MRS. DE MILLE ASKED ME IF I'D BE MR. KOODLES' GUARDIAN IF ANYTHING HAPPENED TO HER (LIKE IF SHE DIED). I TOLD HER IT WOULD BE MY HONOR.

BREAKING NEWS ON THE HOME FRONT! NECTAR DECIDED TO STAY! IT'S A MIRACLE. SHE SAYS CHRISTY'S NOT READY TO PRACTICE MOTHERHOOD WITHOUT SUPRAVISION. HELLO! THAT'S WHAT I'VE BEEN SAYING ALL ALONG. CHRISTY HAD A GOOD IDEA TO MAKE THE GIRLS AT SCHOOL BE NICER TO ME. FOR MY BIRTHDAY, WE'RE INVITING MY CLASS TO THE GWEN STEFANI CONCERT AT MADISON SQUARE GARDEN. I'M GOING TO SURPRISE EVERYONE WITH CUPCAKES AND STICK THE PARTY INVITATIONS ON TOP. IF THAT DOESN'T MAKE THEM LIKE ME, NOTHING WILL. YAY ME!!!

XXXOOO,
RENATA RUIZ HAYES

Cupcake Catastrophe

As Renata poured cake mix into the cupcake papers, Christy licked the beaters clean. No point letting all that mix go to waste.

"Aren't we supposed to use a special cupcake pan?" Renata asked.

"I don't think so," Christy said. "As long as you pour the batter in those paper things, it'll be fine."

"Grandma always used a muffin tin."

"Ah, well, to each her own. I prefer to set my cupcake papers on a flat cookie sheet."

Renata stuck the cupcakes in the oven while Christy put the ingredients together for vanilla frosting. Then she let Renata mix it all up.

"Stop for just a second," Christy said. She poured in a few drops of yellow and blue food coloring. Then Renata stirred until the colors blended. "The perfect shade of green for frosting."

Renata flipped the oven light on to check the cupcakes. "Oh no," she said. "Look."

Christy glanced in the oven and saw the cupcakes had flattened into pancakes. Just as Renata had feared, the papers weren't strong enough to maintain their proper shape without a muffin pan. Everything had run together to make one big cake with a lot of papers stuck underneath. Christy started to laugh. "Have you ever met a worse cook than me? Next time, remind me to listen to you."

The phone rang, and Christy picked up. It was Brownie calling about the seating chart for tomorrow's luncheon. "Well, there's a problem, Brownie. Your assistant told me that only half the women RSVP'd." Christy prayed they weren't boycotting her lunch for some unintentional social crime she had committed.

"And you didn't *think* to call the ones who didn't respond to see if they were coming?" Brownie said.

"Well, I called to ask you if I *could* call them, since I'm not allowed to contact people without your permission, and you didn't call me back."

"I *did* call you back. That incompetent maid of yours didn't give you the message."

"Right. Well, even if I knew who was coming, don't you think *you* should make the seating chart? I haven't met most of these women. I wouldn't know who to seat together and who to keep apart."

Brownie let out an exasperated sigh. "Fine. I'll do it myself." She slammed down the phone as usual.

Yay! I don't have to do it. I don't have to do it, Christy sang to herself. She made horns with one hand and a tail with the phone.

Renata cracked up. "Yeah, she's kind of a—"

"Renaaaata . . ." Christy stopped her from saying it, though she couldn't have agreed more.

As Renata took the cupcakes out of the oven, she announced, "Oh, I forgot to tell you. Mrs. Rich called this afternoon."

"Thanks for the message."

After the flattened cakes cooled, Christy and Renata cut them apart, peeled off the paper, and iced them anyway. "No sense letting these go to waste, don't you think? I mean, they're still cupcakes."

"And we need something to eat while we watch TV," Renata agreed.

"Don't worry. I'll have Yok Wah whip up a new batch tomorrow. You can decorate them yourself and take them to school with your invitations."

Renata smiled as they settled in to watch back-to-back episodes of *The Cosby Show*. By the time Rudy gave Cliff that "all's well that ends well" hug at the end of the second episode, the cupcakes were gone.

Where Have All the Flowers Gone?

There was a major snowstorm on the day of Christy's honorary luncheon. But Christy wasn't worried. All she had to do was get the flowers there. Brownie was in charge of the rest. Still, she felt more trepidation about this event than she used to feel about business meetings with real stakes.

"It's at Fifth Avenue between Seventy-eighth and Seventy-ninth, the limestone building with gargoyles in the front," Christy said. She was determined to do her part perfectly.

"We can find the building," the floral clerk said. "We just don't think we can get there in this weather. Our van just had a collision because the streets are so slick."

"But the flowers *have to be* delivered. If they aren't, I'll be ruined," Christy whined.

"No, our driver was fine. Thank you for caring," the clerk said.

"I'm really sorry," Christy said. "For reasons you'll never understand because I don't, these flowers have taken on a ridiculous level of importance."

Christy called five other florists in the city, ordering four arrangements of blue hydrangeas mixed with white peonies and a spray of yellow delphinium from each. No one would guarantee delivery. Conditions were so unsafe that the mayor had declared a state of emergency. Schools were closed. Businesses shut down. People were told to stay indoors unless it was a medical necessity. Brownie called her luncheon guests to say that *they* could ignore that directive. She said she had personally asked the mayor to make an exception for their lunch. What a show off, Christy thought.

The flowers arrived just as the guests did. The hydrangeas were pink instead of blue, but Christy was relieved. She tipped the driver handsomely for coming out in this weather, then quietly placed a centerpiece on each table, the dais, and the buffet line.

Christy sat at the head of the table with Brownie and her two minions. She didn't know their names, nor could she tell them apart. They were the efficient gatekeepers who kept Christy waiting outside Brownie's office for hours at a time. On other occasions, she had seen them walking two steps behind Brownie taking notes, carrying her stuff, or sucking up in assorted and pathetic ways. You can't tell where Brownie's butt ends and their noses begin, Christy thought, right before complimenting Brownie on her vintage Pucci dickie. "Someone's been shopping in Palm Bee-each," she said, giving her a playful finger wag. Ugh. Tell me I didn't just do that.

The other two tables were filled with fifth-grade moms, most of whom Christy had met at the assembly when the mothers and daughters read their tributes to each other. At least Andrea was there. Christy gave her a friendly wave. Andrea made the thumbs-up sign.

As lunch was being served, there was a knock at the door and a man entered with four vases brimming with yellow roses. Oh Lord, Christy thought. She quietly intercepted him and placed each arrangement on any flat surface she could find. "Thanks for making the delivery," she whispered, handing the guy twenty bucks.

Brownie stood to welcome everyone and introduce Christy. "Ladies, thank you all so much for coming today in such nasty weather. It is a tribute to all of you as mothers that you would risk life and limb to attend a school function supporting such an important cause, our fifth graders' graduation. And—"

A rapping sound interrupted Brownie's speech. The door to the room burst open and two flower-delivery men in Arctic parkas walked in, each carrying multiple centerpieces—pink and white chrysanthemums, purple irises, peach lilies. Everyone turned to see who it was. Christy discreetly directed each man to line the back wall with his flowers. She reached into her wallet for a tip, but was out of cash.

"I'm sorry," she whispered to the two men. "I don't have any money. If you'll write your names here, I'll mail you a tip." She offered up a paper napkin and a pen.

"I don't think so, lady. If I don't collect now, I don't collect," the first man said, a wee bit loudly.

"Is there a problem?" Brownie asked from the podium, her right eyelid twitching in burning rage.

Christy looked sheepishly toward the podium. Her burgeoning career as a Colby Mommy was disintegrating before her eyes.

"Um, we received some extra flowers, and I'm out of cash for tips. Can I borrow a couple of twenties from anyone?" Christy asked.

The ladies started digging in their purses. Three women got up and pressed twenties into Christy's hands. "Thank you," she mouthed.

Brownie was red-faced, but she went on with her speech.

"As you know, our fifth-grade graduation is a huge celebration for us all. The commencement exercises and address. The honorary donations. The graduation tea. This year, our goal is to raise one hundred fifty thousand dollars. Lucky for us, a brand-new Colby mother volunteered to oversee the festivities . . . a-choo . . . ah-CHOO. Fortunately, because of certain events that I'm sure you've all read about, she now has full time to devote to our cause." One of the minions appeared at Brownie's side with a handkerchief. "Thank you. Let us all welcome Christy Hayes Drummond, who will tell us what she has planned for the event." Brownie started clapping and others politely followed suit.

"Thank you all," Christy said. "I'm honored to be here. It was so generous of Brownie to offer her home for this event. And for her to convince the mayor to let us come out today. Well, that's power, let me tell you."

Brownie stuck her chest out and nodded her head a few times like Queen Elizabeth.

"Anyway, I want to thank you all for volunteering to help with the fifth-grade-graduation extravaganza. This year's event promises to be better than any ever given. Just yesterday, tennis-great LaShaun Mason agreed to speak at the commencement exercises. Ah . . . ahh . . . choo! Excuse me, but does anyone have any Benadryl or Claritin?"

"Oh, I do," Bunny Pratt's mother offered.

"Can I have one?" Jada Shiff's mom asked, walking over to her table.

"Me, too," said a woman wearing dark glasses and a chin girdle. Christy didn't know her name.

"I have nondrowsy Allegra if . . . ha-*choo* . . . anyone wants it," Andrea offered.

"I have some Flonase," one of the minions said. Brownie

gave her a searing stare. The luncheon was disintegrating into an antihistamine swap meet.

Yanna Sevigny's mother pulled out her asthma inhaler and pumped vigorously. Then she left the room with a friend helping her walk. Dear God, don't let me kill anyone, Christy thought.

"Ladies, ladies," Christy said, getting everyone's attention. "I'm so sorry about all these flowers. Ahh-CHOO! All the florists said they couldn't deliver because of the weather. So, I ordered extra arrangements thinking that maybe *one* of them would get through. And wouldn't you know it, they *all* showed up. Anyway, I promise, the fifth-grade graduation will be more organized than this. And I apologize to anyone who's having an allergy attack. The good news is, there is at least one bouquet for each of you to take home. Thank you."

Christy started back to the dais and then remembered one more thing. "Oh, for those of you who tipped deliverymen for me, I appreciate it. If you'll give me your name and address, I'll send you your money back along with Knicks tickets as a token of my thanks."

The mothers clapped enthusiastically. Every mom at the event took home a basket of flowers and gave Christy her engraved personal card for the return of her tip and the thank-you Knicks tickets. Christy knew that most of these ladies hadn't tipped anyone, but what the hell.

"You just *couldn't* get it right, could you?" Brownie said.

"Excuse me?"

"I gave you one simple job, and *you* with your big career and your Olympic gold medals—you couldn't even get the colors right. And your delphiniums, they weren't even fresh!" Brownie accused.

Christy stiffened. Well, maybe if you'd stick them up your

airtight butt, they would be. She didn't think she said that out loud. Christy was determined to find the reasonable person who had to be hiding somewhere beneath that unbearable exterior. "Wait a minute, Brownie," she said. "I'm sorry about the flowers. We'll probably laugh about it next year . . ."

Brownie appeared to have been struck dumb by the audacity of the remark. "Christy," she said evenly, "this is *no* laughing matter." Then she executed a perfect pivot and made her exit, minions in tow, leaving Christy to find her own way out.

◌

Christy immediately dictated her thank-you notes in the car on the way home. Leaving instructions for Eve to handwrite the notes and include a twenty-dollar bill plus four Knicks tickets with each letter, she tried to think of something personal and complimentary to say to each woman who had come. That seemed to be the protocol, based on the thank-you letters Christy herself had received. The problem was, she barely remembered anything other than Brownie's steely gaze.

Cupcake Catastrophe . . . (Continued)

After the bulletin-board meeting broke up, Andrea and Christy walked out together. "Can you *believe* that? Eight meetings for *one* bulletin board," Andrea said, rolling her eyes and laughing. "I'm sorry I got you into this. Say, why don't you come over for lunch?"

"Sure," Christy said. "I'm starved." As they walked toward the front door, Christy heard someone calling her name. It was Mrs. Smart, Renata's teacher. She ran after the two mothers.

"Mrs. Drummond, I'm so glad I caught you. We need to speak about the cupcakes Renata brought in today." Mrs. Smart was winded from running in her half-inch heels.

"There weren't any nuts in them," Christy said.

"No, nuts weren't the problem," she said. "The thing is, the cupcakes were entirely too much. First, chocolate cake. Then green icing, at least twice as much as was necessary. Topped with all those M&M's, plus that envelope stuck in the center. You went way too far, Mrs. Drummond," Mrs. Smart said in a grave tone.

"You mean, they were gaudy or there was too much sugar?" Christy asked.

"Both. You have to understand, Mrs. Drummond. This is Colby. We're all about understatement."

"I see. But Renata decorated them herself. If they were overdone, it was out of a little girl's enthusiasm. She wanted to surprise everyone."

"That's another thing: Cupcakes should *never* be a surprise. We must *plaaaaaan* for them. I talked to Renata about it this morning. She'll be taking them home."

"You didn't let her serve them?" Christy asked, her heart aching for the little girl who just wanted her classmates to give her a second chance.

"How could I?" Mrs. Smart said.

"Right, how could you?" Christy said, her annoyance breaking through, as Andrea signaled "cut" behind Mrs. Smart's back.

"She obviously couldn't," Andrea piped in, to give Christy time to calm down.

"Did Renata hand out the party invitations, at least?" Christy asked.

"No," Mrs. Smart said. "They were part of the overall cupcake problem."

"Right, overstated." Christy said.

"*Ex-aaaaaactly.*"

"Well, thanks for letting us know. Christy'll be more careful in the future," Andrea said.

"Soul murderer," Christy mumbled, as Mrs. Smart walked away.

Andrea shook her head. "Colby is one hard place to understand, but don't worry. We'll crack this nut."

"No, we won't," Christy said. "Didn't you know? Colby is a nut-free school."

Tawdry Tales

T he phone rang while Christy was waiting for Renata to come home. It was Brownie.

"Christy," she said, "Your thank-you note arrived today."

"Oh, I'm glad you got it," Christy said. Finally, she thought, I did something right. Lovely thank-you notes, personal messages, mailed immediately, on perfect stationery, containing much-appreciated Knicks tickets.

"The other ladies also got notes. Why weren't they sent to me for vetting?"

Christy started to laugh and then covered it up with a cough. "You need to approve my thank-you notes?"

"They were written to the graduation committee, were they not?"

"Well, yes," Christy said.

"Have you forgotten our conversation? I told you I had to see and approve all communications to the committee, that I needed three days' notice. Is this *not* a communication?"

"It's a thank-you note."

"A thank-you note *is* a communication. If you *ever* pull a stunt like that again, you'll be fired," Brownie said.

Christy didn't understand how she could be fired from a

nonpaying job, but she kept her mouth shut. She now considered it a personal challenge to keep her cool with this woman.

"Have you made progress on my dinner with Scottie?" Brownie asked.

It amazed Christy that Brownie could bawl her out in one breath, then ask for a favor in another. "Michael's working on it," she said noncommitally.

The front door opened. Renata and Nectar came in. Nectar was holding the Tupperware box of cupcakes. The invitations had been removed and stuffed inside the container.

"Gotta run, Brownie," she said, happy for an excuse to hang up.

"Can you believe Renata's teacher wouldn't serve these beautiful cupcakes?" Nectar said. "Now what kind of teacher would tell a child that her cupcakes were overdone?" She tilted her chin up to snob level and stuck out her bottom jaw. " 'We're all about understatement here at Colby,' " Nectar said, capturing Mrs. Smart's upper-crust tone perfectly. Christy cracked up.

Renata walked over to the couch and sat down. She looked at Christy glumly. Her chin started to quiver.

"Well, I for one am *glad* Mrs. Smart wouldn't serve your cupcakes. You know why?" Christy said.

Renata shook her head silently.

"Because there's more for us! C'mon, girls, let's have a cupcake party."

Renata made half a smile. "Can we invite Mrs. De Mille?"

"That's a great idea. Shall I call her?" Christy offered.

"No, we have to go to her house. She can't get out of bed," Renata said.

"I'll get the milk and meet you downstairs," Nectar offered.

That afternoon, Renata, Christy, Nectar, Mrs. De Mille, and Mr. Koodles had a party on Mrs. De Mille's soft and cozy queen-size bed.

"What a beautiful boudoir jacket, Mrs. De Mille," Christy said, complimenting her baby-blue satin-and-lace cover-up. She was impressed that, as sick as the old lady was, her long salmon-colored hair was brushed and shiny, framing her made-up face. Close up, the white powder and eye makeup were slightly alarming, but the old girl was still in the game.

"Thank you," she said primly. "It was given to me by one of my favorite lovers, Captain Louis Francisco Grant of the Canadian Mounties. He bought it for me at Lord and Taylor in 1955."

"Is he still one of your boyfriends?" Renata asked.

"Oh no, child. He died in the eighties. I do miss the bastard," she said with regret. "I may be a wrinkly old dinosaur, but I'm still horny as hell."

Christy blew a mouthful of cupcake across the bed when she heard that. Luckily, it hit the wall behind Mrs. De Mille and stuck. Christy ran to the dresser to grab a Kleenex and wipe it off.

"What does 'horny' mean?" Renata asked.

"Never you mind, child," the old lady snorted. "You're too young to know about these things."

"Mrs. De Mille, you should *not* be eating in bed," her nurse interrupted. "It's unsanitary."

"You think I give a pygmy's ass? Pardon my French, dear," she said to Renata, patting her hand gently. "We're having fun. Go away, you party pooper."

"This is *too* much excitement for you," the nurse said. "I'm calling your son."

"He won't care. The greedy bastard can't wait till I'm dead. Just wants to get his goddamn bony hands on my money."

"Another cupcake?" Christy interrupted.

"No thank you, dear," she said primly.

Nectar ate two cupcakes. Renata ate two. Mrs. De Mille ate a half. Mr. Koodles ate the other half. The nurse ate one. Christy ate the rest. She didn't want any of Renata's cupcakes to go unclaimed, lest the girl's feelings be hurt even more.

"You do have an appetite," Mrs. De Mille said to Christy.

"Yes, well, I used to be a runner. I had to eat four thousand calories a day just to maintain my weight."

"Do you still run?" Mrs. De Mille asked.

"No, not lately," Christy said.

"That's why she's looking so plump," Nectar explained.

"I don't look plump," Christy said.

"Oh, yes, you do, child. But it suits you. Mrs. De Mille, when I first met Christy, there weren't an ounce of meat on those bones of hers. But now, 'Sweep on, you fat and greasy citizens.' That's a direct quote from *As You Like It*."

"Was that really necessary, Nectar?" Christy said, running into Mrs. De Mille's bathroom to see if she *was* looking plump. She stepped on the scale that sat in the corner. Aaahhh! Christy ran back in the bedroom. "I've gained *twelve pounds*." She immediately resolved to diet and start running again.

Mrs. De Mille weighed in. "Did I ever tell you about my first husband, Mr. Henry De Mille? Henny. I called him 'Henny.' He was handsome and charming, other than his hairy fingers, which were disgusting. But in those days, what could you do? He refused to shave them, which I never understood. Now why was I telling you about Mr. De Mille?"

"Did it have something to do with my gaining weight?" Christy asked, feeling disgusted by her lack of discipline.

"Right. Yes, of course. That's it. Henny left me for a skinnier girl in 1952. But God punished the son of a bitch. He collapsed on top of her after a night of mattress mambo, if you know what I mean. Suffocated the whore. She was too damn weak to push him off. He did five years in Sing Sing for involuntary manslaughter. That rat bastard adulterer," Mrs. De Mille said, shaking her head in disgust. "Pardon my French, sweetheart," she added to Renata.

Christy smiled. "Mrs. De Mille, is that a *joke*?"

"No, it's the God's honest truth. *Nurse Ratched*," she shouted. "*I need you*."

The nurse stuck her head in. "My name is *Hatcher*, not *Ratched*," she said.

"Hatched, Ratched, Bastard, whatever. Bring me my orange photo album," Mrs. De Mille said.

"*I can't find it*," the nurse screamed after less than a minute of looking.

"*It's in the freezer*," Mrs. De Mille yelled back.

The nurse brought the ice-cold album along with a Dixie cup full of colorful pills. Mrs. De Mille shooed her away when she tried to get her to take them. She began turning the book's pages. It was filled with yellowed newspaper clippings. "See, see," she said, pointing to an article that looked like it had come from the *Times*. The headline read, LOVE TRYST TURNS DEADLY."

"Well, I'll be," Christy said.

"It *is* rather funny. *Now*. It wasn't then. Anyway, the point is, watch yourself, girlie. You don't want that husband of yours trading you in for a skinnier dame."

"You are *so* wise, Mrs. De Mille," Renata said reverently.

"I'm not just another pair of perfect cheekbones, Dolly," the old lady said.

Christy knew what was coming next.

" 'Compare her face with some that I shall show, and I will make thee think thy swan a crow,' " Nectar recited with fervor. "That's from *Romeo and Juli-ett*."

Christy just stared at the three of them and tried to reconstruct exactly how many cupcakes she had consumed.

Things Are Looking Down

DEAR DIARY,
MICHAEL TRAVELS ALL THE TIME. SOMETIMES CHRISTY
GOES WITH HIM. SOMETIMES THIS REPORTER NAMED GALEET
GOES. SHE'S WRITING A BOOK ABOUT MICHAEL. SHE INTER-
VIEWED ME ABOUT HIM. I TOLD HER WE EAT DINNER TO-
GETHER EVERY NIGHT AND PLAY BASEBALL ON SATURDAYS.
IT'S A LIE BUT I WANTED MICHAEL TO LOOK GOOD. WE ARE
GOING ICE SKATING ON FRIDAY NIGHT SO THEY CAN TAKE
PICTURES OF ME AND MICHAEL HAVING FUN TOGETHER FOR
THE BOOK. ONCE AGAIN, WE ARE PRETENDING TO BE A NOR-
MAL FAMILY FOR THE PRESS. I PRAY FOR THE DAY WE CAN
STOP LIVING A LIE SO THIS HOUSE OF CARDS KNOWN AS
OUR FAMILY DOESN'T COLLAPSE IN MORTAL DECAY.
UNTIL TOMORROW,
RENATA

"So, Brownie tells me that I have to clear my thank-you notes
with her before I can send them out. Can you believe that?"
Christy said.

"Unbelievable," Michael agreed, breathing hard. Christy
was sitting next to him as he worked out on the elliptical
trainer.

"I can't stand her. I'm thinking of quitting the graduation committee. Do you think I should?"

"Maybe you should," he said.

"No, I can't. Heading the committee was the quid pro quo for getting Renata admitted. I made a commitment."

"Then you shouldn't," he agreed, flicking sweat off his face with his hand.

"And what's your take on the cupcake incident?" Christy asked. She had sent him a BlackBerry message about it when he was coming home from the airport.

"Shocking," Michael said. "Maybe we should put Renata in public school."

"*Michael!* We can't disrupt her life again. Besides, she's getting a wonderful education at Colby, no matter how crazy the place is for grown-ups. Here, use this towel."

"Thanks. She may be getting a good education, but what kind of values will she learn at a place that doesn't approve of children making their own cupcakes?" he asked.

"Oh, that reminds me. I didn't even tell you about the bulletin-board committee. Wait'll you hear *this*." Christy went on to tell him how the committee was meeting eight times to make the board even though they were having it professionally designed and constructed by an advertising agency.

Michael shook his head in wonder. "Hon, why don't you work out with me anymore?" he asked.

"Oh, didn't I tell you? I'm gonna start running again. First thing tomorrow morning. Why do you ask?"

"No reason."

"You think I'm looking fat, don't you?"

"No, I like a woman with a little extra meat on her bones."

Since when, Christy thought in a panic. "Honey, I know

I've put on a few pounds. It's the stress associated with all this school business. But I'll take it off, don't worry."

"Speaking of school business, did you hear from Eve?"

"No, not yet. You?" Christy asked.

"Yeah. Three times today. There were a bunch of sticking points she needed my advice about. But they seemed to be close." Michael had sent Eve to L.A. to negotiate with Scottie's people over the terms of the dinner invitation he had extended.

"If she makes it happen, you should do something really special for her as a thank-you," Christy said.

"I will," he said. "And you should do something really special for me," Michael added.

"Oh, don't worry, I will, you sexy thing," she said making the bedroom face Renata had taught her.

Michael got off the machine, dripping with sweat. "Come here, you," he said. "Kiss me."

Christy screamed and ran out of the room with Michael on her tail.

Christy Hayes—New and Improved

*E*arly Sunday morning, Eve knocked on Michael and Christy's door. The *Times* had arrived, and in it, Dina's story. Christy brought it into bed where she and Michael snuggled together to read:

WHERE IS SHE NOW? CHRISTY HAYES

by Dina Gladwell

Olympian tycoon trades glamour for family life

A year ago, the last place you'd expect to see Christy Hayes was preparing poached salmon and Asian salad for guests in the middle of the day. But that's where we found her one recent rainy Tuesday afternoon.

Last year, Christy Drummond (yes, she took her husband's name), the two-time Olympic marathon champion and the founder, CEO and spokesperson for Baby G Sports, met and married wealthy entrepreneur (and one of *People* magazine's ten most eligible bachelors) Michael Drummond. Tall and lithe, and living in a magnificent Fifth Avenue penthouse with views to die for, Christy would be easy to hate if she wasn't so nice.

Wearing brown Valentino pants, a Dior chiffon blouse, and spiky Jimmy Choos, she spoke as she expertly sliced tomatoes to top the salad. "After I met Michael, my housekeeper, Maria Ruiz, passed away, and I was left responsible for her granddaughter, Renata. All of a sudden, I was faced with trying to be a good wife, mother, and CEO. That's when it hit me. I'd had my fill of the jet-set life. What I wanted to do more than anything was to take care of my husband and child. I vowed to be as good a wife and mother as I had been an Olympic athlete."

With that realization, Christy said good-bye to Baby G and never looked back. Overachiever that she is, however, Christy isn't stepping quietly into the role of wife and mother. No, she has taken it upon herself to become a spokesperson for women everywhere who choose old-fashioned domesticity over making it in the traditional world of men.

Mrs. Drummond served poached salmon with a tangy orange vinaigrette, presenting this reporter with a lunch that would delight the most discerning critic. "I think the hardest part of being a housewife and mother in our culture is that there are so few accolades for a job well done. In business, you get a bonus or an award when you do something noteworthy. With family, maybe your husband or child thanks you for making a tasty meal or running an errand, but that was the job you signed up for. It's what they expect. In my new universe, there is no Best Supporting Wife trophy, no profile in *People* magazine. As someone who spent her whole life working for recognition, always being singled out as someone special, that's been an adjustment for me."

Christy was thoughtful when asked what she would tell her own daughter about career versus family priorities. "Of course I'll make sure she gets the education and training she needs to take care of herself financially. But if she works for a while and then wants to take time off to raise a family, I'll encourage her. If you love being with your children, it's not a sacrifice. You can always go back to work later."

So does Christy believe this is the beginning of a trend—women choosing old-fashioned wifehood over independence? "I'm not the only high-achieving woman who feels this way. I can't tell you how many famous, powerful women come up to me to say they want my new life."

What's not to want? Who among us wouldn't take the life of a Fifth Avenue princess caring for one of the country's richest, most powerful men?

Does Christy have any regrets? "Not a one. I could never have kept my old job and sustained a warm and loving marriage. I couldn't have been there for Renata as she grew up. I couldn't have devoted myself to Michael's happiness. A hundred interchangeable people could run Baby G. I'm the only one who could do these things."

Michael put the paper down. "Wow. That's a great article. I'm so *proud* of you."

Christy smiled. "Thanks. It's the new reinvented me. What do think of that family picture of us?"

"Nice," Michael said.

"Do I look chubby to you?"

"Well you know, the camera puts ten extra pounds on anyone," Michael said.

"Michael! You're supposed to say I look beautiful."

"That goes without saying."

The telephone rang. Christy grabbed it. She never made Michael do anything resembling work when he was home. It was Jerome Fudderman. He was beyond thrilled.

"You done it, Christy," he said. "You done it!"

"No, *you* done it, Jerome. *You're* the genius."

"Yes, well, I am, aren't I, heh-heh-heh?"

"Absolutely."

"Guess what? Robert Beck wants you Wednesday night," he said.

"Robert Beck wants me on his show Wednesday," Christy whispered to Michael. "That's great, Jerome. The *Times* and Robert Beck in the same week. You're amazing. *Amazing!*"

"That's just the beginning, kid. *People's* covering you in this week's issue. With my help, we'll make you the most revered domestic diva on the planet."

"Thanks, Jerome. Love ya."

"Love ya, too, kid."

Once Again, Galit Weighs In

To: <u>Michaeldrummond@aol.com</u>
Fr: <u>Galit@TFJ.com</u>
I just spoke to Jerome. He seems pleased. She comes off as the classiest housewife on earth. I bet other guys are eating their hearts out right now. You have a sexy CEO wife who gave it all up to wait on you hand and foot. Galit

To: <u>Galit@TFJ.com</u>
Fr: <u>Michaeldrummond@aol.com</u>
Galit, I know this is good for Christy, but I assure you, the last thing I want is a classy housewife. I married Christy for her brains, her guts, and her awesome accomplishments. And those stand, no matter what she does or doesn't do for a living.
Michael

To: <u>Michaeldrummond@aol.com</u>
Fr: <u>Galit@TFJ.com</u>
I just hope you won't find yourself missing the Christy you married. By the way, I will be asking for a review of your company's financials as background for the book. Can I meet with your CFO? Do you want to be there? Galit

To: <u>Galit@TFJ.com</u>

Fr <u>Michaeldrummond@aol.com</u>

Sure, I will get back to you on how we'll handle the meeting. Give me a list of the kind of questions you will want to ask so we can put the right reports together. Michael

Christy Live and in Person

"Tonight. Exclusive! Christy Hayes Drummond. From Olympic star to high-flying CEO to traditional wife and mother. She'll open up about it all, take your calls, too. Christy Hayes Drummond, next on *Robert Beck Live*."

As Robert went to commercial, two people came on set, one to comb Robert's thick silver hair, the other to powder his face. Christy smiled uncomfortably. She tried to appear calm even though her nerves were frayed and her heart was racing.

The red taping light went on. "She's been a role model to girls everywhere for the last twenty years. First, she won two Olympic gold medals. Then she parlayed her endorsement fees into a small running-shoe company that grew into a multimillion-dollar operation. Last year, Christy Hayes married media mogul Michael Drummond and inherited a daughter when her beloved housekeeper died, naming Christy as her granddaughter's guardian. Christy then shocked the world by chucking her career and announcing that she was devoting her life to being a traditional wife and mother. Christy, do you realize that you've set the women's movement back thirty years?"

"Well, I hope that's not the case. It was the women's movement that gave me the ability to choose between being a corporate warrior and a traditional wife."

"So what was the impetus for this decision?"

When Michael and I were first married, there was plenty of time for me to be a world-class CEO and wife. But when a child was added to the equation, I knew I couldn't shine in all three events—work, wife, mother. Something had to give."

"And that was work?"

"Well, Michael's the love of my life, and I couldn't give him up. When Renata showed up, I knew I couldn't run the company and still pick her up at three o'clock every day."

"Let's be honest, isn't it more stimulating to lead a company than to wash your husband's dirty underwear?"

"Let me answer you this way. I'm trying to be as good a wife and mother as I was an Olympic athlete. I'm always trying to think of creative ways to please my husband. Here's an example. Not too long ago, I met his plane after he'd been on a long business trip. I was wearing a fur coat with nothing underneath. We couldn't get in our limo fast enough. That was one very sexy ride home, let me tell you. When you put *that* kind of energy into every domestic activity you do, life is anything but boring." Oh my God, did I just tell that story? Christy thought.

"I hope my wife is listening," Robert said. "San Antonio, Texas, hello!"

"Hi, there. Love your show, Robert. Christy, I was wondering what kind of staff you have now that you're a stay-at-home mom."

"Well, we have a housekeeper, a driver, a cook, a nanny, an assistant, that sort of thing."

"So if you have staff to wash your family's clothes, clean the house, cook, and drive your child to school and lessons, then what do *you* do?"

"A lot. I make cupcakes with my daughter. I volunteer at her school. I pick her up."

"Sorry, hon—that doesn't cut it. You're *nothing* like the rest of us. I'm sure it's really grueling having to juggle your stylist, your interviews, and your daughter's nanny all at the same time. Why don't you tell the rest of us, how *do* you *do* it?"

"Well, I never said I had a stylist—"

"New York City for Christy Hayes Drummond, hello."

"Hi, Robert. Christy, I read that article in the *Times* about you on Sunday. And nothing personal, but I think you're full of bull ca-ca. Can I say that on the air? You've been a mother for what, five minutes? I'll bet you've never washed your husband's laundry. In fact, I'll bet you don't know how to use a washing machine."

Christy took a deep breath. Busted. "I'll grant you that I'm not your typical wife and mother. But having worked *and* stayed at home, I can say with authority that the stay-at-home life is the harder choice." Okay, Christy thought. Good answer.

"Christy, you're not telling us anything we don't already know. You act like you discovered motherhood. I hate to break it to you, girlfriend, but a lot of us have been doing it for years, and without help, I might add."

"Sacramento, California, hello."

"Hi, Robert. I loved your show with Suzanne Somers yesterday."

"Thanks, what's your question?"

"Yes. Christy, I'm wondering if the fur you were wearing

when you met your husband's plane was real? And if it was, do you know how inhumanely animals that are bred for their hides are treated?"

"My fur was fake," she lied. Uh-oh, bad turn. Christy wondered if anyone would notice if she exited stage right. How many more minutes were left? Thirty. Ooooooh.

"Bridgehampton, New York, hello. Bridgehampton, are you there?"

"I'm here, Robert. Hello, Christy. You know, I read the article in the *Times* on Sunday and I found it so ironic that while you complained that there's no recognition for women who stay home, no awards, no profile in *People* magazine, *you're* all over the newspapers and TV. And imagine my surprise when I saw a profile of you in this week's *People*. I can't tell if you really want this domestic life or if it's just a publicity stunt to keep you in the news."

"You're awfully cynical," Christy said. If she could have made herself melt like the Wicked Witch of the West at that moment, she would have.

"New York, New York, you're on with Christy Hayes," Robert said.

"Christy Hayes, don't you think it's time to come clean with Robert's audience?"

Christy froze. That was Katherine's voice. Her heart pounded so hard, she felt certain her mike was picking up the beat. Don't puke, don't puke, don't puke, she silently chanted. This can't be happening. Why would Katherine call? Hasn't she hurt me enough? I can't think. Air. I need air.

"What do you mean by 'come clean,' Caller?" Robert asked.

"Christy didn't *choose* to become a reborn domestic goddess. She was *forced* out of her company because she wasn't up to the job," Katherine said. "Tell them, Christy."

"Those are some pretty serious charges, Caller. Do you want to answer the accusation, Christy?"

"Yes, yes I do, Robert. But first, let's go to commercial because *I'm going to throw up.*" Christy urgently whispered those last few words.

"I'm sorry," Robert said. "What did you say?"

"I think I'm going to puke," Christy wrote on a piece of paper.

"Aaaaaand cut," the director yelled.

Another Day, Another Daughter

ichael was in L.A. again. An FCC investigation of his West Coast radio stations required his presence, followed by more meetings with his animation company. He's so stressed out, Christy thought. I'm glad it's him dealing with business problems and not me. Renata was at school. Christy was in the library sorting bills for the accountant, a job that she had taken over after leaving Baby G. She found it amusing to see a bill for $54.95 instead of something like $5,495,000, which she was used to seeing at Baby G. Secretly, she loved this low-level finance. There was a tentative knock at the door. "Christy, I think you'd better come to the foyer," Cynthia said.

"Who's there?" she asked.

"I don't know, but you better come."

Christy walked to the front door, which was wide open, and saw a teenage girl lying in the hallway. Her blond hair was as limp and lifeless as her whisper of a body. She wore a blood-stained Juicy sweat suit. She had two black eyes, and her lips were swollen. Bandages were peeking out from under her top. The girl half opened her eyes and then shut them.

"Are you okay?" Christy asked. "Who *did* this to you? Should I call nine-one-one? Who *are* you?"

"Ali Drummond. Where's my dad?"

Christy was taken aback. She had seen pictures of the girl, but the photos looked nothing like this beaten-up child in front of her. Who had attacked her?

"Ali, your dad's not here right now. I'm calling emergency. You need a doctor. What happened to you?"

"Nothing. I had surgery. My nose got fixed and they added cheekbones and made my jaw stronger. I got my boobs done, too. And collagen in my lips."

"*What?* How old are you?"

"Sixteen."

"Sixteen? Does your *mother* know about this?"

"She arranged it."

"My God," Christy said. "You're too young for that."

"No, I'm not," Ali mumbled. "All the girls are doing it. Can I have a glass of water?"

"Yes. Sure." Christy helped the girl stand up and walked her into the apartment. Cynthia brought her Prada backpack inside. After making Ali comfortable on the couch and giving her a glass of water, Christy asked why she had come.

"It's that awful guy my mom married," she said. Then she began to weep. Christy sat next to her and held her hand until her tears slowed down. "I can't stand him. He just wants her money. It's *so* obvious. Plus he *hates* me. He never even talks to me."

"I'm sure he doesn't hate you."

"Yes, he does. He and my mom are always going away without me. They say it's because I have to go to school, but I know it's because *he* doesn't want me. Mom says I have to be more understanding. Enrique's her *future*. I'm gonna grow up and move away." The girl started crying again, and Christy hugged her, rubbing her back.

When Ali's staccato breaths finally slowed, Christy gently wiped the girl's runny nose with a Kleenex. It had to be sore.

"It's my sixteenth birthday today. I asked my mom to stay with me as a special treat. But she wanted to go upstate to look at some *racehorse* with *Enrique*. She says I'm selfish. That I don't appreciate that she got me all this plastic surgery. I hate them both. I want to live with my dad. He wants me, doesn't he?"

"Of course he does. He talks about you all the time," Christy said. "Your mom left town when you were in this condition?"

"I have a private nurse. Do you have any codeine?"

"Sorry, we don't keep drugs like that in the house."

Ali's eyes widened. "No pain meds in the house? That frightens me," she said.

"I have Advil. You want that?"

"If that's all you have," the girl said.

"Tell you what, why don't you go lie down for a while? Cynthia'll make you comfortable in the extra bedroom we have by the kitchen."

"Are you Christy?" she asked.

"Oh, sorry, we haven't been formally introduced, have we? Yes, I'm Christy."

"Funny, you don't seem like a bitch," Ali said.

Christy just smiled. Suzanna must be a real charmer, she thought.

෴

Christy checked her watch. It had been almost two hours. This was as nerve-racking as waiting outside Brownie's office.

"Oh, there she is," the doorman said, pointing to the middle-aged Barbie type who was emerging from the backseat of a black sedan. She was carrying large shopping bags from Bergdorf's, Bottega Veneta, and Versace. Call me a cynic, Christy thought, but last time I looked, they weren't selling racehorses at Bergdorf's. Christy stood between the front door and the elevator, intent on intercepting Michael's ex before she got upstairs. "Excuse me. Suzanna?"

Suzanna looked askance at Christy. "And you are . . ."

"I'm Christy, Michael's wife."

"I'm sorry, I have *nothing* to say to you," Suzanna said, trying to walk past her.

"Oh, but I have something to say to you. Ali showed up at our doorstep today," Christy explained. "I wanted you to know that she was safe, so you wouldn't worry."

"Thank you, God!" Suzanna said, waving her arms and packages. "Don't you worry about me. I won't worry about Ali. I'm sure you'll take good care of her." Suzanna pressed the elevator button.

"Suzanna, she says she wants to live with Michael. Don't you want to talk to her?"

"That's okay. Write to me when she graduates from college, or, better yet, when she marries her first husband." The elevator door opened, and Suzanna stepped inside.

Christy snatched the shopping bags out of Suzanna's hands. "Don't walk away from me," she said sharply. "We're talking about *your child*."

Suzanna stepped out of the elevator. "She's Michael's child, too. I've taken care of her for sixteen years. She's more than I can handle right now. Let Michael do it for a change."

"How can you turn your back on your own daughter?" Christy asked, aghast.

"You've obviously never raised a teenage girl or you'd understand," she said.

"No, I'll never understand abandoning your own child."

"Look, Christy, I'm a newlywed, okay? My husband has no interest in being Ali's stepfather. I'm not going to risk my new marriage over a daughter who doesn't appreciate anything I do for her."

Suzanna turned and stepped into the elevator. Christy started to follow. "Don't!" Suzanna commanded. "I'll send her things tomorrow." The door shut in Christy's face.

Christy stood in front of the elevator, in shock that a mother could so cavalierly dispose of her child. She had to admit that there had been a few dark days when she secretly wished Renata had never come into her life. That she and Michael could have their old carefree lives back. But she'd never abandon Renata. *Never.*

Christy left Suzanna's building and started to run across Central Park. "Shit," she said, stopping short when she realized she was still carrying Suzanna's shopping bags. She walked over to a bench and set them down. What *is* all this, she wondered, digging through the tissue paper. A cashmere sweater. Luscious Tasmanian woolen pants. A black fur jacket. She'd spent a fortune on herself, and on Ali's birthday no less. Christy shook her head.

A thin homeless woman approached her. "Excuse me, ma'am, spare some change? A quarter, a nickel, even a penny?"

Christy looked at the small weather-beaten woman. Her hard life had given her naturally what Suzanna probably paid trainers and surgeons thousands of dollars a year to achieve — a slender body and strong muscles. How ironic, Christy thought. "Here," she said, handing her the bags. "Wear it in good health."

∞

DEAR DIARY,

LOTS OF NEWS!!! MICHAEL'S DAUGHTER ALI IS LIVING WITH US NOW. HER STEPFATHER DOESN'T LOVE HER SO SHE MOVED IN WITH US. THAT IS SO SAD. MICHAEL HAS BEEN DOING LOTS OF STUFF WITH HER SINCE SHE CAME. I'M THINK-ING MAYBE HE'LL START SPENDING TIME WITH ME TOO. ALI IS RECOVERING FROM PLASTIC SURGERY AND SAYS SHES GOING TO LOOK JUST LIKE CHRISTINA AGULARI WHEN THEY TAKE HER BANDAGES OFF. THAT IS SO COOL. I'M GETTING PLASTIC SURGERY WHEN I'M 16 TOO.

CHRISTY WAS ON THE ROBERT BECK SHOW THE OTHER NIGHT. WHEN I TOLD HER HOW GOOD SHE DID, SHE CRIED. SHE'S BEEN REAL UPSET SINCE SHE DID THAT SHOW. I'M NOT SURE IF ITS BECAUSE ALI SHOWED UP OR BECAUSE OF THAT STUPID TALK SHOW. THE TRUTH IS, THE TV CALLERS WERE MEAN TO HER. NECTAR SAYS IF YOU CAN'T SAY ANYTHING NICE YOU SHOULD KEEP YOUR MOUTH SHUT AND I AGREE.

AND THERE'S MORE!!! SCOTTIE CHILDS AND HER HUSBAND ARE COMING TO DINNER TOMMORROW. STEPHANIE'S PAR-ENTS ARE COMING TOO. HER MOTHER IS SUCH A BICH (PAR-DON MY FRENCH).

SINCERELY,
RENATA

Ouch, She Did It Again

T here was a sharp knock on the bedroom door Friday morning. Christy dragged herself out of bed to open it. Eve stood outside, looking nervous.

"What is it?" Christy asked.

"Here," she said, shoving the *Financial Journal* into her hand. "There's an article about Katherine and Baby G that you might want to see."

"Thanks." Christy walked over to her stuffed chair and sat down to read.

BABY G SOARS UNDER NEW LEADERSHIP

by Dan Edwards

Christy Hayes may have founded Baby G, but the company is doing very well without her, thank you very much. In the short time since she left, the stock price is up 25 percent.

Since the day she took over, Katherine Kilborn, the new CEO, has shaken things up. The company has moved all its manufacturing to India. In announcing the relocation, Ms. Kilborn said that the move will allow the company to lower their cost for goods by 15 percent. "It should have happened years ago," says Jeremy Moran, a Goldman Sachs retail analyst. A smashing new advertising campaign was initiated, using fresh Olympic hopefuls instead of their former in-house Olympian, Hayes. Yesterday, the company announced that it was purchasing Rocky Mountain Wellness, a $60 million chain of health clubs located throughout the western United States.

Rumors abound that Baby G is ripe for a takeover. Should that happen, Ms. Kilborn stands to make a fortune given the options she has accumulated since the company went public and the large stock position she has taken in the weeks since she was named CEO. While Christy Hayes Drummond can be seen on every talk show evangelizing about her resurrection as a born-again housewife, Katherine Kilborn has focused her Harvard-trained, razor-sharp mind on turning around the company that some doubt her predecessor was ever qualified to lead. Katherine Kilborn is one CEO who is going places.

Christy threw the newspaper across the room. She looked at her husband, who was still asleep. "Damn," she said, pounding the arm of the chair over and over. "*Damn, damn, damn.*" Instantly, Michael was up and by her side.

"What's wrong?" he asked.

Christy looked at him and started to speak, but words wouldn't come. She wanted to trash her bedroom like an out-of-control rock star. To break the Tiffany lamps, smash the Venetian mirrors, throw the vase of roses against the wall.

"Did someone die?" he asked.

Christy shook her head. "No, no!" She retrieved the newspaper that she'd just thrown on the floor and brought it to Michael, poking angrily at the offensive story. He read the piece.

Closing the paper, he reached for his wife and held her. "I'm sorry," he said. "You know Katherine is behind this."

Christy nodded but did not speak. She was so furious, she couldn't.

"Should I have her killed for you?" Michael said.

Christy nodded. Michael continued to hold her, comforting his wife as if she were a child. "Come on now," he said. "Cheer up. Scottie's coming for dinner tonight, remember?"

This got Christy's attention. She pulled away from Michael. "*Nooooo!* I *can't* face Scottie after this."

"Of course you can," he said. "Scottie knows what it's like to be criticized by the press. She won't judge you."

"Brownie will."

"Who gives a shit what Brownie thinks?"

"I do," Christy said.

"Well, you shouldn't."

Christy crumpled up the paper and stuffed it into the trash. "Oh, Michael, what am I going to do now? My turnaround has been a disaster. I don't know which was worse, losing my company or losing my dignity trying to be the Fifth Avenue housewife spokeswoman for the masses. It's an oxymoron. What was I thinking?"

"Why don't you just be yourself for a while? Be Christy Hayes without all the bells and whistles. What do you need with all that publicity? Be my wife. Take care of Renata. Ali needs you, too. Relax and enjoy yourself for a change."

"I don't know *how* to be myself. I only know how to be special."

Michael laughed. "Well, I think it's time you learn."

The Joy of Stepmotherhood

o, absolutely *not*. That's ridiculous," Christy said to Ali later that morning. Both girls were home on spring break.

"It is not. Everyone at my school has hair extensions. And anyway, you're supposed to change your hair after cosmetic surgery. Then no one notices you had work done. That's, like, a total plastic surgery rule."

"Ali, hair extensions won't hide what you did," Christy said. "Your nose is different. Your boobs are bigger. You have cheekbones, a longer chin, luscious lips. Trust me, people will notice."

"Do you really think my lips look luscious?"

"Totally."

"But Tara Rubin's mom let *her* get hair extensions after *she* got her implants."

"I don't care if Honk the Wondergoose got hair extensions, *you* aren't getting any," Christy said firmly.

"But whyyy-yyy-yyy," Ali said. She had perfected the ability to turn any one-syllable word into a three-syllable whine. It was a gift.

"Ali, hair extensions cost over thirty-five hundred dollars. That's too much money to spend on a teenager's hair."

"It's not *your* money. It's my dad's! And he can afford it. I'm calling *him*."

"You do that," Christy said, confident her husband would back her up. Of course, she was happy for Michael that he'd gotten his daughter back, but Christy had never met such a brat in all her life. The kid spent money like it was tap water. She slammed doors and screamed like a two-year-old when she didn't get her way. She seemed to have never heard of the words "please" and "thank you." Making her bed was a foreign concept. A trail of towels followed her wherever she went. She preferred the floor to the trash can. And there was a permanent appendage on the side of her head that looked suspiciously like a cell phone. Worst of all, she was influencing Renata, who had begun to stuff her training bra and was agitating to buy a Prada book bag like Ali's. Michael felt guilty that he and Ali had been separated for so long. So he kept giving in to her ridiculous fits. Christy tried not to interfere. Ali was *his* daughter, after all. She stood in the doorway to the library, where the child was deeply engrossed in a telephone conversation with her father.

"And Daddy, when are you gonna talk to her about giving *me* Renata's room? If Mom knew I was staying in the servant's quarters, she'd go ballistic. Mmm-hmm. Yes, well, I *am* the real daughter in this family. Okay. Yeah, see you tonight."

Ali hung up the phone and looked at Christy with a smug expression. "Daddy said I *could* have the hair extensions, so give me the money and tell Steven to drive me."

"Didn't anyone ever teach you the magic word?" Christy asked.

"You mean 'black card'?" she said.

"No, I mean 'please.' "

"Oh, will you *please* give me Daddy's black card? Paul

Labrecque doesn't like it when you're late for your appointment," she said, rolling her eyes. "And while I'm gone, have Nectar move my things into Renata's room and give Renata the maid's quarters. Daddy said you *had* to do that."

"Did he now. Well guess what? Renata was here first, and I'm not moving her. So if you don't like it, I suggest you move back with your mother where you can have a dandy room." Christy stormed out of the library. "Goddamned brat," she mumbled.

"I heard that," Ali screamed. "I'm telling Daddy what you said."

"You do that," Christy shouted, frustrated with herself. She *was* the grown-up, after all.

ᦞ

When Ali returned from Paul Labrecque, she had Renata in tow. As if by magic, Ali's chin-length hair now reached the middle of her back. And Renata's beautiful curly black hair was now straight as an ironing board. The child could hardly contain her glee.

"Renata, *what* did you do?" Christy asked.

"Ali took me to get my hair Japanese-straightened. Do you like it?"

She *hated* it. *Hated it*. Renata's lovely billowing tresses were no more. The delicate corkscrew tendrils that framed that exquisite Spanish face were gone. She no longer looked like a beautiful woman-child from a Raphael painting. She looked like a Mexican Hilary Duff. "Do *you* like it?" Christy asked. "That's what matters."

"*I love it!*" she gushed. "Can I go show Mrs. De Mille?"

"Sure, go ahead."

As Renata skipped out the front door, Michael's demon-child made a beeline for her room. "Just one minute, young lady. *Not* so fast."

"What did *I* do?" she asked.

"How could you *do* that to her without checking with me first? You had no right."

"I knew you would say no."

"You should have given me a chance. You should have asked."

"Would you have said no?"

"You're frickin' right I would have said no. Just how much did you spend on Renata's hair?"

"Seven hundred and fifty dollars, but it'll last a long time."

Christy took a deep breath. "Ali, give me your father's black card."

She dug through her purse and handed it to Christy. "Sor-reee-eee," she said, in the universal teenage fake-apology tone.

Christy took the card, opened the credenza drawer, pulled out a pair of scissors, and cut the offensive plastic in half.

"How *could* you?" Ali said. "That's . . . that's like . . . that's like burning the American flag."

Christy heard the key turning in the lock, signaling that Michael was home. "Fine," she said to Ali, "we'll have this out right here and now."

Guess Who's Coming to Dinner

Michael walked in, followed by Brownie and Fran. "Look who I found in the lobby," he said.

Shit. Was it that time already? Christy hadn't even put her jewelry on. The discussion with Ali would have to wait. The child slunk off to her room, relieved to be off the hook.

Fran took Christy's hand in his. He looked her straight in the breasts and told her how good it was to see her again. Christy caught Michael glaring at him as if he wanted to pummel the man. Brownie, on the other hand, didn't find the situation the least bit awkward. She was the sort of wife who moved into her own bedroom as soon as her last child was born. Sex wouldn't even be on her radar screen were it not for all those tabloid reports of her husband screwing this one or that one. As she said to Christy, the fact that Fran cheated didn't bother her. The fact that his indiscretions hit the papers did.

"Brownie, you look very pretty tonight," Christy said, breaking the awkward silence. Brownie was wearing a pale green suit and a matching silk blouse, with wide-heeled khaki pumps. Brownie never felt dressed unless she was wearing some khaki.

"Thanks," Brownie said, inspecting Christy as if she were a bitch in the Westminster Dog Show.

"Would you like a tour of the house?" Christy asked, wondering if she had gotten too fat to wear her Helmut Lang stretch dress.

"Oh, no thanks," Brownie said. "We lived in this building when we were just starting out."

"Right," Christy said.

"Did you know there was an article about you in the *Journal* today?" Brownie asked.

"How about some drinks?" Michael offered, changing the subject. The group retired to the living room, where a bartender made cocktails to order. Christy had a double martini. Michael told her to slow down.

The doorbell rang and Michael answered it, greeting Scottie and her husband, Johnny. Christy walked up behind Michael and introduced herself. She had seen Scottie on television, she had watched her from afar in Davos, but she wasn't prepared for the three-dimensional manifestation of this living legend standing in her entryway. Scottie was smaller than Christy had imagined. Her smile was warm and radiant, surrounding her like a bright aura. At the same time, Christy sensed what a tough and determined woman she was. She had to be, to get where she was in life. Just being in her presence made Christy feel like a quitter. One hard knock and she'd gotten out of the game.

Johnny, an athetic-looking six-foot-six skyscraper of a man, introduced himself to Christy. He said he was looking forward to talking with Fran Rich, whom he'd never had the pleasure of meeting. Christy almost told him not to get his hopes up. It occurred to her that she and Johnny had a lot in common. He was with one of the most accomplished partners on the planet, as was Christy. But Johnny had found his niche in life as a hedge-fund manager. She decided to sit next to him at dinner and get pointers on how to find happiness as a high-class appendage. She wondered if it would be rude to ask.

Brownie and Fran stood side by side as Michael introduced them. Brownie actually curtsied when she met Scottie, which surprised Christy, knowing what a stickler she was for proper etiquette. Hello-ow, she's the queen of daytime TV, not of England.

Yok Wah announced that dinner was served and that everyone should move to the dining room. Christy grabbed another drink on the way in.

Michael proposed a toast to their famous dinner guests and thanked them for coming. As Italian salad was placed at each person's place, Brownie turned to Scottie. "So, did Michael tell you what was behind this dinner invitation?" Brownie didn't believe in waiting for just the right moment.

"Why no, he didn't." Scottie glanced at Michael, who smiled his guilty smile. Christy knew it well.

"I'd like to tell you about a *wonderful* opportunity to become the spokesperson for one of the world's most important children's charities," Brownie said.

"I'm all ears," Scottie said politely.

"Are you aware of how many New York City children of means come home to an empty apartment every day?" Brownie asked.

"No, I'm not," Scottie said.

"Thousands. Unlike my children, whose mother is entirely devoted to their welfare, many wealthy parents are so busy jet-setting around the world, they *ignore* their offspring."

"No," Scottie said.

"*Yes,*" Brownie said. "Even the most exquisitely decorated penthouse can be lonely for a child who has only her nanny to keep her company. These kids develop profound psychological problems. Some of them lie. Others steal. Many turn to drugs. The girls develop eating disorders. Most people think that being a child of wealth and privilege is one big party. They never see the dark side."

"That is *so* tragic," Christy said.

"Yes, it is. In order to save these children, we've started the Golden Latchkey Foundation. I'm the president," Brownie said.

"Of course you are," Christy added. Spare me.

"As president, I'd like to ask you to serve as our spokesperson," Brownie said to Scottie.

"I'm honored," Scottie said, looking pointedly at Michael.

"Yes, the board originally asked *me* to be the face of the charity, but I'm willing to step aside to let you have that honor," said Brownie nobly.

"Uhm, I'm just wondering," Scottie asked, "if these children have such wealthy parents, can't they afford their own psychological counseling?"

"They could if their parents were paying attention to their children long enough to notice the problem."

"I have an idea," Christy said. "Why don't you start an exchange program between the Latchkey kids and the hungry children of the third-world countries who truly *deserve* Scottie's help? I'll bet one week living in Africa or El Salvador would cure those ungrateful brats—"

Michael interrupted. "What Christy means to say is . . ."

Christy realized that she was a little tipsy.

Scottie couldn't contain herself any longer. She burst into laughter, sucking a large piece of salad up her windpipe. Her eyes widened, and she grabbed her throat. Her face took on a dangerous hue. Everyone at the table had a vague idea about how to do the Heimlich maneuver, but no one had actually done it before. They all sat there waiting for someone else to jump in to save Scottie.

Michael, his face ashen, finally took control. He helped Scottie to her feet and gave his best imitation of the Heimlich maneuver, which, to his surprise and relief, was close enough. Half a tomato wedge came flying out of her mouth, landing smack in the middle of Brownie's hairdo.

"Oh my God, are you okay?" Christy asked. It would be tragic to lose a national treasure over Brownie's silly charity.

Scottie nodded. "Let me just use the restroom," she croaked, as she left the dining room, coughing.

"Don't worry, I'm okay, too," Brownie said, fishing the tomato out of her hair.

When Scottie came back to the table, she told Brownie that she'd think about it. But Christy knew that the first thing she'd do when she got back to L.A. would be to send Brownie her deep regrets at not having the time to give to this very worthwhile cause. Christy was mortified. Scottie must think I'm the world's biggest nimrod to have introduced her to Brownie, she thought.

Scottie turned to Michael and mouthed, "You owe me."

He nodded. His color returned to normal, and the two of them carried on a lively conversation for the rest of dinner. Christy noticed sadly that Michael was as animated while talking with Scottie as he used to be with her. She wondered if he missed being married to Christy, the dynamo.

"Can I ask you something?" Christy turned to Johnny.

"Sure," he said.

She wasn't sure how to say this delicately. She had to be

tactful. Approach this with compassion, Christy thought. "Johnny, what's it like to live in the shadow of one the most celebrated women on earth? Do you feel like . . . like . . . kind of a loser?"

"Of course not," he laughed. "Do you?"

"Yes, I do," Christy said. "I *absolutely* do."

Johnny reached over and patted her hand. What a nice man he is, Christy thought. No wonder Scottie keeps him around.

"Christy, why in the world would you feel like a loser?" The server discreetly took away his salad plate and replaced it with seared tuna.

"Well," she whispered, "my best friend betrayed me and stole my company. I tried to reinvent myself and failed miserably and publicly. And did you see that awful article about me in the *Journal* today? I'm a laughingstock. I'm gaining weight. Meanwhile, I'm married to one of the world's most successful men. I don't know why he stays with me."

"Is that all?" Johnny asked, smiling.

"You want more?" Christy said.

"You know, Christy, believe it or not, I understand your feelings. Most people think being the partner of a celebrity is one big laugh riot. But you and I both know there's a dark side."

"Just like those Golden Latchkey kids," Christy said ominously.

"Exactly. All I can tell you is what I figured out after fourteen years of being married to Scottie. And that is, when you're completely at home in your own skin, Michael's success will be a nonissue. Trust me on this."

"Thanks. That makes sense," she said, grateful for the advice. "I guess I'm not comfortable with who I am right now. I'm still not sure where I'll land."

"Give it time," Johnny said. "You'll figure it out."

Christy glanced at Michael and Scottie, who were laughing about something. Those two were certainly acting chummy. Brownie and Fran were eating silently. Christy gave Johnny the eye signal to engage Brownie, which he did. Then she turned to Fran. "So Fran, you going to Davos this year?"

Let's Disagree to Agree

Brownie and Fran took off the minute Scottie and Johnny left. Brownie wasn't interested in spending any more time with Michael and Christy than she absolutely had to.

"So, did you accomplish your objective tonight?" Michael asked, pouring Christy a glass of wine. They sat at the kitchen counter.

"I don't know. When Scottie says no to her charity, which of course she will, and she should, Brownie'll take it out on me."

"No good deed goes unpunished. I've always found that to be true," Michael said, popping open a beer.

"Me, too. But don't think *I* don't appreciate what you did," Christy said, flashing a half-drunk, sexy smile. "I've had a little too much wine," she added.

"Why do you say that?"

"The room's spinning."

"Good sign. Here, give me your glass."

Christy handed it to Michael. He spilled what was left into the sink and offered her a box of mint Girl Scout cookies.

"Thanks," she said, taking five. "You and Scottie sure seemed to get along."

"We do. She's an amazing lady. Very attractive. So accomplished. Respected by everyone. A hoot to talk to. I'm glad they came."

Christy bit her lip, which had started to tremble.

"What?"

"I used to be *all* those things." Christy took his hand. "Are you sorry you married me?"

"No, I *love* you. You're perfect. I could never be married to someone like Scottie."

"Why not?"

"She's too successful. I'd feel like a glorified hood ornament around her."

"That's how *I* feel around *you*." Christy took three more cookies.

"*What!* How can you say that? You're everything I've ever wanted."

"Yes, but I used to be *special*. Now I'm nobody."

"Beegee, if I'd wanted a trophy wife, I would have married one."

"That's the thing. You *did* marry one. And *you* stayed a trophy, but *I* didn't."

Michael pulled his hand away from hers. "Christy, for God's sake, get a grip. I married you because I love *you*. And I love you with or without the company, with or without the money, with or without a few extra pounds, with or without the kid. I will *always* love you. Get that through your thick head. Now let's just go to bed."

"Okay," Christy said, sounding only slightly less needy than she felt. "Would you want to go to bed with Scottie?"

"Christy! *Enough.* Jeez, what has happened to you? You used to be so beautiful and confident. Where's the girl I married?"

Christy swallowed hard. "Michael," she said, barely breaking a whisper. "I'm confused. First you say you still love me with a few extra pounds. Then you say I'm not beautiful anymore. Which is it?"

Michael threw his hands into the air in frustration. "You know, Christy, when you *think* you're a loser, people around you pick up on that vibe. Don't think I haven't. I've been *really* patient with you until now. Did I stand behind you when the *Journal* made those sexual accusations? Yes. Was it hard for me to do that? You bet your sweet ass it was. You wanted the kid. You got the kid. You said that wouldn't change anything, but it did. You stopped exercising. You started eating too much. You don't travel with me anymore. You can't have a lucid conversation about anything but Renata and her goddamn school. You're turning into my ex-wife, and I gotta tell you, hon, that's not attractive."

Christy stared at him with her mouth open. She threw her remaining cookies into the sink in anger.

Michael started toward the kitchen door, then turned back and faced his wife. "You keep telling the press that you want to win a gold medal as wife and mother. Well, now you've got *two* kids to take care of. So why don't you just *be* what you told the world you wanted to be, and let's get on with our lives?"

"Michael, how can you expect me to be a mother to Ali when you won't be a father to Renata?" Christy was raising her voice, but she couldn't help it. She was sick of pretending that she was okay with the way he treated Renata.

"That's different. Ali's my *real* child. As long as you're not working, I'm asking you to pay attention to her while I'm not around."

Christy shook her head. "Your kid's impossible. The few

times I've tried to mother her by setting limits, which she desperately needs, by the way, you just give in to her."

"Well, I think you've made some wrong decisions. Like today. Ali wanted hair extensions. Why not let her have them? She needs to know that I'm in her corner right now, that I'll support her. She's just come from a home where her stepfather wanted nothing to do with her. Can you *imagine* how that made her feel?"

Christy stared at Michael in disbelief. "No, I can't imagine how that must have made her feel, but I'll bet Renata can. Why don't we ask her?"

"And that's another thing," he said, ignoring Christy's valid point. "I *don't* think Ali should be sleeping in the maid's room. She shouldn't feel like a second-class citizen in her own house. She is my *real* daughter."

"And Renata's not *my* real daughter?"

"No. You *know* she isn't."

Christy looked at Michael, who had turned into a ragged mess between the time Scottie left and now. For the first time, his scruffiness wasn't endearing to her. "Funny, I don't know that at all."

Michael, for his part, slammed his fist into the wall and walked out. That night, he slept in the library.

∽

MY DEAREST DIARY,

MICHAEL BLEW A CASKET AT CHRISTY TONIGHT. DON'T QUOTE ME, DIARY, BUT I FEAR THEY WILL GET DIVORCED. WHO WOULD TAKE ME IF THEY BREAK UP? WHERE WOULD I LIVE? AND WHAT ABOUT SCHOOL? HERE'S WHAT HAPPENED. ALI WAS IN HER ROOM LISTENING TO HER IPOD AS USUAL. ME AND CHRISTY WERE JUST SITTING AROUND WATCHING THE SIMP-

SONS. THEN MICHAEL CAME HOME FROM WORK AND ASKED
WHERE DINNER WAS. CHRISTY TOLD HIM SHE FIRED YOK WAH
AND WANTS US TO EAT TOGETHER AS A FAMILY EVERY NIGHT
(YAY I THOUGHT!!!). SHE WOULD COOK FROM NOW ON. NEC-
TAR SPENT ALL AFTERNOON TEACHING CHRISTY HOW TO
MAKE THIS SOUTHERN DISH SHE GREW UP ON-SHRIMP AND
LOBSTER GUMBO. SO WE SAT DOWN TO EAT AND MICHAEL
SAID, YOU <u>KNOW</u> I HATE SHELLFISH. SHE SAID NO, THAT HE
ATE IT ALL THE TIME. HE SAID SHE WAS WRONG AND HE
DIDN'T AND WOULD SHE PLEASE MAKE HIM A STEAK. THEN
SHE DUMPED THE WHOLE BOWL OF GUMBO IN HIS LAP. SHE'S
GONE MENTAL AND THAT'S A PROBLEM. I'VE NEVER SEEN
MICHAEL THIS ANGRY. HE PACKED HIS SUITCASE FOR ASPEN TO
WORK ON HIS BOOK WITH GALEET. CHRISTY SAID FINE! GO
TO YOUR GIRLFRIEND! MICHAEL SAID MY GIRLFRIEND!!!! YOU'RE
DREAMING, CHRISTY! THEN HE RAN OUT AND SLAMMED THE
DOOR. ALI LAUGHED WHEN HE LEFT BUT IT WASN'T FUNNY.
I'M WORRIED SICK ABOUT THOSE TWO. I WAS PLANNING TO
ANNOUNCE MY NEW NICKNAME TONIGHT (FRECKLES) BUT I'M
PUTTING THAT OFF UNTIL FURTHER NOTICE.

    YOURS,
    RENATA RUIZ HAYES

Thanks for the Memories

The next morning, as was the custom in New York, two thank-you notes with gifts were waiting for Christy with the building's doorman. First there was the obligatory flower arrangement sent by Brownie Rich. It came from Petals, the florist of choice for ladies of the 10028 zip code. The second, an antique silver compact, was sent by Scottie and Johnny, who did not feel compelled to follow the gift-code conventions of well-heeled New Yorkers.

Dear Christy,

Thank you for last night. As instrumental as I have been in helping you find acceptance in the Colby community, I was still moved that you would host a dinner in my honor. And how very clever of you to think of inviting Scottie and Johnny Childs. I'm so looking forward to Scottie's involvement in the Golden Latchkey Foundation. Wouldn't it be excellent if Scottie would devote a whole show to the unique problems faced by these children who are so rich and yet so poor? At your convenience, please call me with her personal telephone number so that I can propose that idea.

   Sincerely,
   Brownie Rich

Dear Christy,

   Many thanks for the lovely dinner you hosted. Johnny and I enjoyed getting to know you and Michael better. Don't worry, I will not hold that beastly Mrs. Golden Latchkey against you. Michael told me how much torture she has inflicted on you as you've tried to do the right thing by your daughter's school. Just don't ever send her my way again, or I will have to choke you with a tomato wedge (only kidding, NOT).

   It was terrific talking to Michael. You are a lucky woman to have a husband who loves you so much. No matter what subject we talked about, the conversation always came back to you. Johnny mentioned that you feel you're living in the shadow of Michael, who is so very accomplished. But from what I observed, you are the light of his life. How fortunate you are to have had it all in athletics, business, and love. Not many of us can make that claim.

   With appreciation,
   Scottie Childs

The New Trophy Wife

On Thursday, Christy pulled herself together to go with Andrea to hear Dr. Mindy Harris speak about the "New Trophy Wife" at the Yale Club for a Mount Sinai Medical Center benefit. At the last minute, Andrea canceled because Heinz's enlarged prostate had gotten even larger. Christy wore Gucci, Pucci, and Prada in order to blend in with the crowd. And blend in she did. The room was filled with designer-clad trophy wives.

Christy sat at a table of women who seemed to know one another. An elegant brunette suggested that everyone introduce herself. They went around the table. "Hi, I'm Chappy Reeves. I'm married to Henry Reeves."

"I'm Christy Hayes, married to Michael Drummond."

"Hi there. I'm Susan Gilbert, married to Jack Gilbert."

"Hi, Tiffany Underberg, married to Saul Underberg."

"Carter Jaeger, Jack Jaeger's second wife, although I really don't consider myself a trophy."

"Kathleen Stowers. I'm not a trophy wife yet, but I'd very much like to become one."

"Lilian Underberg. I'm an ex–trophy wife. I used to be married to Saul Underberg." She and Tiffany gave each other polite head nods.

A waiter came by with salads. Everyone took one, with dressing on the side. Nobody but Christy wanted the mimosas they were offering. The ladies chatted as they nibbled.

As Christy drenched her arugula-and-endive salad with dressing, she noticed that Lilian was pushing her greens around on the plate like a waifish model. "Not hungry?" she asked her.

"Nothing tastes as good as thin feels. That's my motto," Lilian said.

Christy put her fork down.

The waiters came by and replaced everyone's salads with white poached fish and steamed veggies.

The conversation turned to which charity committees everyone was on. Christy wasn't sure what to say when it was her turn to speak. Luckily, she wasn't the only one not involved in that endeavor.

"You know," Tiffany Underberg said, "I've been looking for a pet cause. Maybe you all can help me find a good one."

"There are so many wonderful organizations to support, dear," Susan Gilbert said. "Would you like me to take you under my wing, maybe mentor you through the charity circuit?"

"Would you?" Tiffany asked.

Lilian looked at Christy and rolled her eyes. "She's the same age as Saul's granddaughter."

"It must be hard," Christy said sympathetically. Okay, this is one weird scene.

"You don't know the half of it. The day I turned forty, Saul dumped me. Then he stopped financing my makeup line. That was the end of my career. These people"—she pointed to the women in the room—"used to be my friends. Now they avoid me. They all went to Saul's wedding. I hate them."

"I can see that you're bitter," Christy said.

"I'll be back. Don't you worry," Lilian said, fire in her eyes.

"No doubt," Christy agreed.

Before the charity conversation got around to Christy, the waiters picked up everyone's plates and offered coffee and chocolate cake. Most everyone said yes to coffee (with skim milk) and no to cake. Knowing this crowd, Christy wondered if the Yale Club had even bothered to bake the cake.

". . . and here she is, Dr. Mindy Harris," a beautifully dressed woman was saying. Everyone applauded. Christy turned her attention to the podium.

"Do you think she's had work done?" Lilian whispered. Christy just shrugged.

"When Kitty asked me to come speak about the 'New Trophy Wife,' I was happy to do it, because it's time to put that image to rest. You know the image about which I speak—the grotesque frog of a CEO married to the ravishing young bubblehead as a testament to his manliness. Well, let me be the first to tell you that the old-school trophy wife has been traded in for a newer model, no pun intended."

The trophy wives applauded nervously at the news. Most of them hailed from the old school.

"Yes, brain candy has replaced arm candy," Dr. Harris said. "Not that today's trophy wife isn't gorgeous—she is. But she is also accomplished, intelligent, well bred, and busy pursuing her own work. As I look around this room, I see women who personify exactly what I'm talking about. There's Chappy Reeves, Henry's wife. Chappy has a master's degree in political science, she's a writer, a senior fellow at Columbia, she serves on a variety of boards. At the same time, she is beautiful, entertains lavishly, loves her jewelry, has an extensive Impressionist art collection, never misses the opera. Who did you say you were married to, Chappy?"

Everyone laughed, including Chappy.

"And over there, I see Christy Hayes Drummond," Dr. Harris said.

Oh my God, she's talking about me, Christy thought. Please don't do that.

"Christy is an Olympic champion, an entrepreneur, a face we have seen on billboards across the country, a champion for women who choose family over work. She's also a mother. Christy Hayes Drummond is a wonderful example of the new trophy wife—a beautiful woman who has the perfect combination of brains, glamour, confidence, and achievements. She epitomizes what the powerful man of today wants, and it is *not* arm candy."

Christy smiled shyly. She didn't feel like the person Dr. Harris was describing. But maybe the doctor was right when she singled her out of the luncheon crowd. Maybe Michael *did* want her by his side for her intellect and accomplishments. Of course, it was kind of hard to hear that she didn't qualify as arm candy.

Dial "S" for Snoop

enata waited until Christy was gone before sneaking
into the library. First, Christy was going to some
luncheon. Then she was meeting with Mrs. Smart for
Renata's parent-teacher conference. She would be safe for at
least a few hours. To her surprise, Ali was curled up on the
couch reading *Cosmo* — not *Teen Cosmo*, normal *Cosmo*. She
didn't acknowledge Renata's presence.

Fine, Renata thought. Ignore me as usual. She turned on
the computer and went right to AOL. Michael's e-mail address came up, but the password space was blank. C-H-R-I-S-
T-Y, she typed in. Ta-da! She opened Michael's mailbox to
see what she could learn. He'd been gone for days, and
Christy refused to talk about it. Renata knew she could be arrested for this, but she just had to find out what was going on.

Most of the communications were from either Christy or
Galit. Skipping over the mail about Viagra, debt consolida-
tion, and adult XXX specials, she began opening the messages between Michael and Christy. Until the day he left,
they were all friendly. The older ones were just plain mushy
and gross. Christy had sent Michael a few notes about Renata. He always said the same thing: it's your choice. Whatever you decide is okay with me. This confirmed what

Renata suspected. Michael didn't care about her. She bit her lip and tried not to think about it.

"What are you up to in there, child?" Nectar was standing in the doorway.

"Nothing. Homework."

Nectar walked in and looked over her shoulder. What she saw didn't register. Renata was grateful that her nanny didn't know anything about computers. "Mmm-mmm-mmm, we didn't have those when I was a child," she said, clucking her tongue. "What do you want for dinner tonight?" Nectar asked. Christy hadn't cooked one thing since the shrimp-and-lobster-gumbo debacle.

"How about Shake 'n Bake?"

"Shake 'n Bake? I'll pick some up at the store." Now that Yok Wah was gone, so were the fresh, healthy meals.

Ali looked up from her magazine. "Shake 'n Bake? What are you? Trailer trash?"

Renata started to respond, but Nectar beat her to it. Snatching the magazine out of Ali's hands, she lit into the girl. "I'll have you know, child, some of the finest people I ever met grew up in trailers 'cause that's all their families could afford. Trash isn't where you come from; it's how you behave."

"Then I guess we know who's trash in this room," Renata said, happy that someone finally stood up to Ali.

"Shut up, Snot Breath," Ali said.

"I know you are, but what am I?" Renata said.

Ali rolled her eyes. "I want my *Cosmo*, Nectar," she declared.

"Sorry, you can't have it," she said. "Child, you have no business reading this magazine. What do you need to know about 'his secret sex zones'? You're too young."

"Hello-oh! I'm sixteen," Ali said.

"Sixteen! 'It is common for the younger sort to lack discretion,' " Nectar said. "That's from *Hamlet*."

Ali got up and stormed out of the room. "Hamlet," she shouted behind her, "Who's he? Some trailer-trash friend of yours?"

"Ali, Ali, Ali," Nectar said, shaking her head as she walked away.

Renata turned to the screen. Professional that she was, she refused to let the fight between Ali and Nectar distract her from her mission. Checking out the e-mails between Galit and Michael, she saw they were mostly about the book. Galit would ask him a question and he'd answer it, like an interview. There were a few notes that Michael wrote to Galit about Christy. Hmmph, she thought, Michael shouldn't be talking to Galit about Christy. It isn't right. *Whoa!* The newer mail was juicier. Galit was flirting with Michael. Then Renata found the smoking gun:

To: Galit@TFJ.com
Fr: Michaeldrummond@aol.com
Galit, could you call me? I'm thinking about a new
strategy for the TV side of my business, and I'd like your advice. I need a sounding board on some issues. Would you
mind? My beautiful wife is momentarily distracted by cupcakes. I'm assuming she will come to her senses soon. MD

To: Galit@TFJ.com
Fr: Michaeldrummond@aol.com
OK, I will call in a couple of hours. I am really looking forward to
Aspen, a chance to spend a little more time together. You know,
Michael, working on this book with you has meant a lot to me.
You aren't the average run-of-the-mill alpha male. Galit

To: Galit@TFJ.com
Fr: Michaeldrummond@aol.com
Galit, I appreciate everything you've done for me with the book.
But our Aspen meeting will be strictly business. As I've told you
before, Christy is the love of my life. Let's leave it at that.
Michael

Renata spun in circles on the ergonomic swivel chair as
she printed the telltale e-mails. My work here is done, she
thought proudly. Now it's all up to Christy.

Boulevard of Broken Dreams

Renata sat on the edge of the bed watching Christy pack. Ali sat across from her, in the easy chair, flipping through *Glamour*.

"How long will you be in Aspen?" Renata asked.

"A few days, maybe a week," Christy said. "Nectar will watch you both."

"I don't need to be watched. I'm sixteen," Ali said.

"All the more reason for Nectar to watch you," Christy said.

Ali rolled her eyes without taking her face out of the magazine.

"You'll miss my chorus recital," Renata said.

"Damn," Christy said slapping her forehead. "Pardon my French. Mrs. Smart'll kill me, won't she?"

"I'll make up an excuse, don't worry. You *have* to go see Michael." Renata had given the revealing e-mail to Christy. She felt she had no choice. Christy was about to blow her marriage. And while Renata wasn't too keen on Michael right now, Christy was a different story. When Christy asked how she'd gotten the e-mails, Renata said that she'd found them by the computer when she went to do her homework.

"*Oh, man, what have I done?*" Christy lamented. "I've

been so busy obsessing about not being important to the world that I forgot how important Michael and I are to each other. I'm such an idiot."

"You said it; I didn't," Ali offered, glancing up to catch Christy's reaction.

It was Renata's turn to roll her eyes. "Ali, didn't your mother teach you that if you can't say anything nice, don't say anything at all?"

"No," Ali said. "My mom *always* says mean things about people. Now shut up or you'll regret it, loser."

"Ali, don't tell Renata to shut up, and don't call her a loser," Christy said.

Ali stood up and yelled at Christy. "You're not the boss of me. I can say whatever I want."

"No, you can't," Christy said in a calm tone. "If you want to stay in *my* house, you have to be civil."

"This isn't *your* house. It's my dad's. And when *he* gets back, he's gonna leave you like he left my mom. You'll see. You're not good enough for him. Knowing Dad, he's got a new girlfriend already."

Christy took a deep breath. She got right in Ali's face. "Listen," she said evenly. "I'm here. And I'm here as long as I choose to be. So get used to it. If you get in the way, you'll be hurting yourself, not me."

"How dare you . . . you gold-digging wack job! That was verbal abuse." She turned to Renata. "Did you see what she did? She threatened me. You're a witness. I'm calling my mother." Ali ran out of the room.

"Here, use my cell phone," Christy said, tossing it after her. She shook her head and resumed packing.

Renata looked at Christy sympathetically. "Don't worry. You can get Michael back. He still loves you. Just wear something all see-through and fluffy to bed. The same thing happened on *The Cosby Show* once, and Cliff took Claire back." Or maybe it was Mr. French who took Mrs. Beasely back, she thought.

Christy looked up and smiled at her new love adviser. "Well, that's good to know. If Claire can do it, so can I."

Renata reached into Christy's suitcase and pulled out the overwashed New Balance T-shirt she had been wearing to bed recently. "This is *not* what I'm talking about."

"Oh dear, you're right. I won't need *that*."

౬౧

Christy spent the four-hour journey to Aspen obsessing about her life and her marriage to Michael. What happened to her vow to put all her energy into becoming a world-class wife and mother? Was she even capable of that? When did she stop putting Michael first? Why did she think she needed to reinvent herself? How could she have let herself get out of shape? Did she look as fat as she felt? Or did she look average? Was it so bad to be average? If she got back into shape, could she become eye candy again? Was it shallow to care about her looks when her life was falling apart? Had that doctor who spoke at the New Trophy Wife lunch had work done? Should *she* get work done? If so, what? And so it went, all the way to Aspen.

Christy asked the taxi driver to drop her off in town. She wanted to find that luscious lingerie store she had walked past last time she and Michael were here. Let's see, which way were we walking, she thought. West, toward the mountains. Yes, there it was: Anabella's. Christy stopped to admire the lace-and-silk teddies in the window. The store had the loveliest lingerie she'd ever seen, except for Paris of course.

She remembered the day she and Michael had gone shopping at Alice Cadolle on rue Saint-Honoré, the most amazing couture lingerie store in the world. Michael couldn't believe anyone would pay $700 for a bra, until he saw Christy's breasts showcased in such a magical undergarment. He insisted she take four. Then he bought her a beautiful black see-through teddy and a lace-and-pearl thong. They'd gone right back to the hotel to put it to good use.

Christy walked inside and set her suitcase in the corner. A mother and daughter were examining push-up bras. Looking around, Christy vowed to wear sexy clothes to bed every night. When did I start wearing T-shirts? She tried to remember. She picked out a few French lace chemises to try, a garter belt, some stockings, and a couple of camisoles. The saleswoman showed her to a dressing room.

Whoa! This was some kind of fitting room. The only lighting came from candles. The walls were red, and an elegant Persian carpet covered the floor. There was a daybed that looked like it belonged in a high-priced bordello.

Let's see, what shall I try first? She went for the transparent lace nightie. After taking everything off, she slipped it over her head. The neckline plunged in a deep V and the fabric left nothing to the imagination. She gave herself a thorough appraisal. This isn't so bad. I can't be more than a size eight, maybe ten.

She heard a muffled voice in the next dressing room, and a man responded, followed by bedroom laughter. Wow, they let couples in here? I'll bring Michael. He would love this. Wait. She *knew* that laugh. Without so much as a thought, Christy bolted out, walked next door, and barged inside. There was Galit, all six feet of her, facing the full-length mirror in a black G-string and sheer teddy, her sinewy ass inches from where Michael was sitting. He was still dressed, but obviously aroused. His pants spoke for themselves.

Michael sensed Christy before he saw her. He turned around. His mouth opened. His eyes widened. His penis deflated.

"She *is* your girlfriend," Christy said. "I was *right*."

"No, no, no, she isn't," Michael said. "We were shopping for lingerie *for you*. I swear it."

"Right, I'm sure you were."

As Michael and Christy argued, Galit reached into her purse, pulled out a cigarette, and lit up a smoke, acting annoyed by the interruption. Christy looked at her rival's perfect body, and then glimpsed her newly expanded self in the mirror. That made the situation all the more tragic. Galit sucked on her cigarette, looked up at the ceiling, half closed her eyes, and blew smoke out her nostrils like the evil fire-breathing dragon that she was.

"YOU *bitch!*" Christy screamed, lunging at her.

Big mistake. Acting by reflex, Galit performed some manner of Bruce Lee–James Bond karate chop on Christy, sending her flying out the door. She had forgotten about Galit's stint in the Israeli elite commando forces. Her body hit the wall across from the dressing room. Then Galit jumped her, pinning her to the carpet like an Olympic wrestler.

A few shoppers, already pressed together in the tiny shop, heard the commotion and sidled over.

"*Michael, get her off of me,*" Christy pleaded.

Michael grabbed Galit, who had Christy in some manner of Israeli Ramboesque stranglehold. Somehow, he separated the women.

"I'm calling the police," the saleslady announced.

"*No, don't,*" all three of them yelled. On that they agreed.

In pain, Christy picked herself up and staggered back into her dressing room.

Michael followed. "Christy, let me explain."

She turned around, gesturing to her sexy ensemble, which was now ripped. "This was for *you*, Michael. *For you!*"

"Please, hear me out," he said.

"There's nothing to say. I heard everything," she snapped.

"Galit has come on to me a few times, that's true. But we came to Aspen *to work*. I told her I wanted to buy you something after we had that terrible fight. She offered to help me. We ended up here. While I shopped for you, she went in the back to try something on. She called me to take a look. And then she tried to seduce me, but nothing happened . . ." he trailed off, aware of just how lame he sounded.

"So, it's all her fault, is it?" Christy said, buttoning her shirt. "And anyway, even if nothing happened, you *wanted* something to happen, didn't you?"

"No, of course not," Michael said sheepishly.

"Don't deny it, Michael. If I hadn't walked in, you'd be screwing her right now," Christy hissed as she zipped her jeans.

"Well, I—"

"I would *never* have pegged you for a cheater, Michael. *Never.*"

Christy craved air. Michael followed her through the store.

The bell rang as she opened the door. "*Wait!* Who's going to pay for the merchandise you ruined?" the saleslady demanded.

"He'll pay," Christy shouted, then slammed the door behind her.

You Can Run but You Can't Hide

As Andrea spoke, her *New York Post* was open to Page Six, where a picture of Michael and Galit looking all chummy on the slopes was front and center. "Christy," she said, "you can't come home. Not yet." Andrea didn't think Christy could handle the press that was exploding in New York.

Christy was at the Aspen airport, about to board Michael's jet back to New York. She'd called her friend for moral support. "What should I do, Andrea? I can't very well stay here."

"You must go somewhere to *heal*," she suggested.

"You mean like a spa? Will you meet me? God, I could so use a friend right now."

"I'm not thinking of a regular spa, Christy. There's a place, a sanctuary, for high-profile people like you who are in emotional pain. It's called Moonview. Heinz belongs. He was so burned out last year. The program was a lifesaver for him. You must go to Santa Monica immediately and check yourself in."

"What, is this like Betty Ford or something?"

"No. It's a mental-health clinic for executives and movie

stars. Moonview understands the special issues faced by people in the public eye. They'll take care of you, mend your soul, and other than their staff, you won't see another person while you're there. It's *completely* private. Jerry Levin started it, you know, the guy from AOL/Time Warner. Trust me on this. Go. Heal."

ര◌

Christy pulled away from Moonview's gate into the perfect luminous asphalt of the highway and took in the backdrop of black clouds. Rain and thunder hung in the air. The sky was as dark and gloomy as she felt.

Moonview was a bust. She should have asked Andrea a few more questions before flying all the way to California. The facility was beautiful. The atmosphere was peaceful and supportive, just like Andrea had said. The combination of Eastern and Western healing practices to promote harmony of mind, body, and spirit was made to order for a heartbroken wife who'd caught her famous husband cheating. But there was the small matter of the $175,000 fee (*not* including food and hotel). Christy couldn't bring herself to spend such an enormous sum on her self-esteem. To her, this fell into the same category as spending $3,500 on hair extensions for Ali's self-esteem. "But we have *equine* therapy," the counselor had said, as though that explained everything. "Do I get to keep the horse?" Christy had asked. No, Christy's midwestern values precluded her from dropping the cost of a small house in Glenbrook, Illinios, for a two-week psyche cleansing. It didn't matter that Michael could afford it.

Luckily, the concierge at her hotel recommended an ashram down the road for a little silent meditation therapy. At $500 for the weekend, it sounded like a bargain.

Christy turned onto a windy road and followed the sign to Dharmadhan Wilderness Center. After pulling up to the lodge and registering, she was directed to her monastic suite, which was more like a cell with its own tiny bath. A green cotton meditation outfit was laid out for her on the bed. No, *outfit* was too kind a word. It was more like a doctor's scrubs or a prison uniform. Think positively, Christy admonished herself. This is just like being issued a bathrobe at Canyon Ranch, she thought, hoping that the food here was just as good.

After dressing, Christy wandered over to the gift shop. There was a world-class candy-bar selection right next to the devotional objects and meditation cushions. She loaded up on junk food, a Dharmadhan Center sweatshirt, and a sexy T-shirt with a green goddess on the front. Realizing that she couldn't buy another thing without drawing attention to her desire to shop her way out of anxiety, she carried the loot back to her suite/cell.

Later, Christy wandered into the shrine tent, which reminded her of the one she and Michael had been married in. It was filled with people sitting on a sea of navy-blue cushions on the floor in front of an exotic-looking altar affair dominated by a large ancient Buddha. There were wildflowers in one chalice and cooked rice in another. The warming scent of incense floated over the whole space.

Christy selected a cushion in the back row and waited for the spiritual part to begin. From what she understood, most of these people had been sitting here silently meditating ten hours a day for two weeks. This being her first visit to an ashram, she awkwardly mimicked the little bows she saw going on, then sat down and watched everyone pile in. Wow, that guy is cute, she thought. Hmm, there are at least twice as many women here as men, maybe three times. You're once, twice, three times a lady, she sang in her head. And I lo-o-ove you-ou-ou. I don't care what anyone says, Lionel Richie's a genius. This deep reflection was cut short when the teacher began to speak. He sounded refreshingly normal, and Christy began to think that this might not be so bad.

The teacher, who was Christy's age, sat in a chair by the altar. He looked like he might have come straight from Park Avenue, and it turned out he had, several decades ago, from a New York family of distinguished lineage. He told the group that he recently overheard his father telling a friend, "Yes, Bill is still at that place in California. I wish he would come home and practice law, but he does seem less pissed off." Well, Christy thought, I would like to be a little less pissed off myself right now, so maybe *I'm* in the right place, too.

After Bill (which seemed to be his name despite an array of unpronounceable titles used to refer to him) welcomed everyone, he assumed the half-lotus position, and everyone followed suit. He demonstrated proper meditation technique, which boiled down to follow your breath, in, out, in, out, gaze three feet in front of you. Christy would do okay for three or four breaths. Then she would come to, having no idea how much later, midfantasy, where she would be chopping Galit's perfect body into tiny little pieces. Or dabbing acid on Michael's private parts while he slept. The more Christy tried to clear her mind the way Bill explained, the clearer the images of her SOB husband and his skanky slut. She finally forced herself to picture Renata, and that brought her into a more tranquil state. In, out, Renata, in, out, Renata, in, out, Renata—this went on for three hours. Including Renata in her meditation practice was cheating, but it calmed Christy and filled her with a sense of well-being.

After three hours a gong rang, signaling that it was time for dinner. Everyone stood up and walked in a stately way (the only way people walked there) to get their *oryoki* sets, little bundles of blue linen tied around chopsticks and a set of bowls. Christy got hers and sat back down, watching the person beside her for clues as to the next move. Suddenly they were bowing to each other, and the bundle went in front of them. Then they were untying the knot, laying out the bowls and chopsticks and the little spatula thing with white cloth tied around it. The person across the aisle looked hard at Christy, a meaningful insistent look. After staring stupidly back at him and intensely studying his arrangement, she realized what the problem was. Her spatula was turned the wrong way.

By the time Christy fixed her spatula, the chanting had started, and she quickly consulted the little card that came with the bowls, only to find that it was all in Tibetan. Okay, she moved her lips and fake chanted. As she did, a server was bowing to her and she handed over her bowl as she had seen the rest of the row do. They all seemed to be making little tripods out of their fingers as they held out their dishes, and using the spatula thing to indicate when they had had enough. By the time Christy got the spatula up and running, her rice was overflowing. As Christy tried to chase down the rice that had fallen into her lap, a bowl of condiments was offered to her along with a bow from the left. With one hand on her rice bowl, the other on her chopsticks, Christy was at a loss as to how to proceed. She was receiving lots of looks—helpful, disdainful, urgent—eyes that were trying to send a message in plain but unfortunately unspoken English. Finally, the tension ended when Christy's rice bowl flew out of her hands as she simultaneously bowed and reached for the condiments. The whole row cracked up, except for one man who glared at Christy, which, in her fragile state, unnerved her even more.

Now Christy understood the candy bars in the gift shop. They ate *oryoki* three times a day, and each time she took less food in order to avoid a mishap. After lunch the next day, she made a dash to her room and scarfed down all the junk food she had bought.

Following the break, Bill returned to the altar and assumed his half-lotus position, then invited those who had joined the ashram in the last day or two to raise their hands, come up to the mike, and say a few words about why they were there. Christy panicked and sunk into her cushion. She imagined herself speaking: "Hi, I'm Christy. I'm here because I caught my dirty rotten husband screwing his biographer. Okay, I caught him prescrew, but still." No, that won't do at all, she thought. Buddhism is about nonattachment. Say something more Buddhistically correct. Ah, I know, she thought, "I'm here because Moonview was too expensive." No, that makes me seem too attached to money. It hit Christy then that she had no idea why she was there.

Finally, it was her turn to take the mike. She looked out over the motley but surprisingly kindly sea of people, opened her mouth, and then closed it. C'mon, Buddha, she thought, help me. I'm dyin' up here. Christy took a deep breath and then spoke. "I came to the ashram," she started, "I came because, I came because I thought, I thought I could somehow mend my heart here. But I realize as I stand before you that I came to the wrong place. Over the last day and a half as I've meditated, one vision keeps recurring in my mind. And when I see it, I'm at peace. It's my daughter, Renata." As

Christy spoke, everything became clear. It was as though Buddha had given her a pair of magic spectacles and now she could see what had been a blur before. "I think I'm going back to New York now, to Renata. But you know, I believe I needed to come here, to this ashram, to open my eyes to how much my little girl means to me, so thank you for that." Christy smiled, waved, and ran out the door. If she hurried, she could catch the last flight home.

Reality Bites

Christy's plane arrived at La Guardia at five A.M. Rather than wake Steven, she grabbed a taxi. As the car sped down the Long Island Expressway, she made a mental list of ways she would be a better person now — no more sodas, candy, or ice cream, more workouts, less mind-numbing TV. She would get her act together, and then she'd know what to do. She supposed that in some ways, Renata had contributed to her current predicament. If not for the child, Christy would have kept her eye on business *and* on Michael. Without her, maybe none of this would have happened. And yet now, Christy couldn't imagine her life without Renata playing a central role — this lovely, smart, funny little person who introduced her to a side of herself that she'd never known. After training her butt off since she was twelve, then working it off since she was twenty-six, eating junk and languishing about like a couch potato was a revelation. Thanks to Renata, Christy had tasted the Zen of wasting time. But more than that, Renata cared about the real Christy. Her public glory and recent defeat meant nothing to her. No matter how things turned out with Michael, she knew Renata would stick by her.

When the twinkling dawn skyline of the city appeared over Shea Stadium, Christy realized how nervous she was. She didn't know if her arrival home signaled the beginning of the end or some kind of new beginning.

Christy paid the cabdriver, then rolled her suitcase into the lobby. The doorman was nowhere to be found. She asked the concierge to hold her bag while she ran to the deli on Lexington to pick up a quart of milk. A few minutes later, she was prowling the aisles, loading up on cookies, candy, dough-nuts—no form of sugar was too low for this attack. After pay-ing for it, she looked at the pile and thought, I have *got* to get something healthy, so she threw down a quarter for an apple. Running outside, she ripped open bags and started shoving the goodies down her throat. Then she stopped. I *cannot* do this, she thought. I promised myself I wouldn't. She ditched what was left in the trash, then bit into the apple, and told herself it was delicious. Christy shook her head sadly. I have a long way to go before enlightenment, she thought.

The apartment was dark and quiet when Christy made her way into the living room. Renata must still be sleeping, she thought, disappointed. Ali's backpack was in the middle of the entry hall, and her jacket and fur boots were on the floor. Christy kicked them to the side. On the bridge table, four stacks of mail were waiting to be opened. She sunk into the living room couch and sat in silence. A note was taped to the frame of the Frank Stella that hung over the fireplace. That was the first piece of art Michael and I bought together, Christy remem-bered. She walked over to it and ripped it off:

Christy, I'm at the Harvard Club if you need me. Michael

That's it? I'm at the Harvard Club? What does that mean? Have you moved out? Aren't we going to talk? First you cheat on me. Then you leave it up to me to make the next move, she thought angrily. And what about Ali? Am I supposed to take care of her? When she'd meditated about her marriage at Dharmadhan, it all seemed like a bad dream. Now, in her empty apartment, it was real. Damn him for Galit. What was he thinking?

She went back to the couch and lay down, taking stock of her losses. Let's see, her marriage, her business, her money, Katherine, Maria. At least she had Renata.

"Christy?"

She sat up. Renata was standing at the foot of the sofa.

Christy smiled. She was happy and relieved to see her. "Hey, come here. I really missed you," she said.

Renata stared at her.

"What?" Christy asked.

Tears started down her face. The words wouldn't come.

"*What?*" she asked again.

"M . . . M . . . Mrs. De Mille. She . . . she d-died."

"Oh my God, when? Here, come, sit, tell me what happened."

Renata collapsed onto the couch, sobbing. Christy put her arm around the child and held her as she cried. "You poor thing. First Maria, now Mrs. De Mille." Renata's tears were soaking the front of Christy's shirt.

"It ha-happened two d-days ago. Nectar and I were coming home from school and there was an ambulance. They were taking her out. She had an oxygen mask on her f-face."

"That must have frightened you," Christy said.

"No, I wasn't afraid. But I knew it was her because Nurse Ratched was right behind all those doctors. Mrs. De Mille saw me and waved for me to come over. She looked *so scared*." Renata began sobbing again and could hardly catch her breath.

"I'm sure she *was* scared," Christy said, remembering when she saw Maria in much the same condition. She hugged Renata until the girl could speak again.

"She pulled her mask down and said 'Mr. Koodles.' I told her not to worry. I'd take care of him for the rest of his life."

"Good for you."

"But then Nurse Ratched told me I was in the way and to move. Mrs. De Mille told Nurse Ratched, 'fuck off.' Then she looked at me and said, 'Pardon my Fre-french.' " Renata started wailing again.

Christy rocked her like a baby while she cried.

"Those were her last w-words," Renata managed to say.

"I'm so sorry, sweetheart. I know how much you loved her. Is Mr. Koodles doing okay?" Christy asked.

Renata nodded. Christy handed her a Kleenex. She blew her nose.

"You want breakfast?" Renata suggested weakly.

"I don't think so. But let me sit with you while you eat some, okay?"

Renata nodded and they trudged into the kitchen together.

A few minutes later, Ali poked her head in. "Hey, why didn't you invite *me*?"

"You can join us if you want," Christy said, hoping her reluctance didn't show.

Ali grabbed a bowl and pulled up a chair. "What's the matter with you, Monkey Wart?" she asked Renata, while pouring herself some Cocoa Puffs.

"I'm still upset about Mrs. De Mille," she said, bursting into tears again. Ali frowned, then walked over to Renata and hugged her. "It's gonna be okay, really, it is."

After breakfast, Christy, Renata, and Ali all crawled into

Christy's king-size bed, Renata exhausted from emotion, Ali from pigging out. The girls fell asleep in a cuddle that lasted until noon. As brokenhearted as Christy was about Michael, she felt a comfortable happiness in being back home with Renata and even horrid Ali.

Christy Hayes—New and Improved— Take Two

The next day, Christy walked her grieving daughter to school. Taking Mrs. Smart aside, she let her know what a terrible loss the child had suffered. The teacher promised to call Christy if Renata needed her. Damned if Mrs. Smart didn't squeeze her hand, letting Christy know that she was now finally making the cut as a parent.

Christy's cell phone rang as she strolled home. She answered quickly, hoping it was Michael. It was Jerome Fudderman. She sat down on the bench in front of a pastry shop to take the call.

"Exciting news, Christy. I have a spokesperson opportunity that will put you back on the map."

"Really, and what would I be hawking?"

"Hawking? Nothing. I'm talking first class all the way, just like you, kid, heh-heh-heh."

"Okay, Jerome, what is it?"

"The Olympic Foundation wants to raise a hundred million dollars to be used to sponsor promising athletes. They'll fund living expenses so our top competitors can train full time for the Games. They want to give you a chair on the foundation's board."

"That sounds interesting."

"Interesting? It's fucking fantastic! It's one of those honorary positions, the kind they only give to classy broads like Audrey Hepburn and Angelina Jolie. It's high status, not too much work. But they also want to talk to you about starting a mentoring program for young athletes. You know, matching past winners with the kids coming up the ranks. That might take more time."

"That sounds like something I'd like to do. I would have loved to have an experienced athlete to guide me when I was competing."

"There's a fee, of course, but I told them you'd probably want to donate the money back to the foundation."

"I wish . . . Jerome. I may need it."

"Really? Well, it's yours if you want it. You're back, baby!"

"Thanks to *you*, Jerome. You're a genius," she said weakly.

"I can't argue with you on that. So, you'll take the meeting with the foundation president?"

"Of course." Christy realized this would be a much better use of her time than going to power-girl salons, attending charity luncheons, or taking orders from Brownie. In fact, this possibility made her feel like she might actually have a life again.

Who's That Knocking at My Door?

When Christy got home, she noticed an old Volkswagen van parked right out front, in the loading zone. It was dirty, orange and beat-up, like Scooby-Doo's van. You sure don't see many of those anymore, she thought. Walking inside, she spied a man holding a tiny white goat, a dark-skinned lady who was quite a bit older than Christy, and a twentyish woman holding an Apple PowerBook and the hand of a five-year-old girl, all standing across from the concierge desk. Wow, Christy thought, what's happening to our building? Beat-up cars in front, a goat in the lobby? What's next?

"Thank goodness you're home, Mrs. Hayes. These people are here to see you," Tony said.

"But I don't know them," she said.

"They're asking for you."

"Who *are* they?" she whispered.

"Renata's family. From Mexico."

"What? Renata doesn't have family."

"Tell *them* that."

Christy walked over to the motley family to introduce herself. "*Hola, me llamo* Christy Hayes."

"Hello," the old man said in a Mexican accent. "I'm Jorge Ruiz, Maria Ruiz's brother. This is our big sister, Maria, her daughter, Maria, and her daughter's child, Maria."

This cannot be good, Christy thought. What she said instead was "I've never met one family with so many Marias."

"It's a tradition for us. Can we go upstairs, Mrs. Hayes? We need to talk."

"Of course."

As they got into the elevator, Tony called out, "Tell them they have to move their van! And no goats in the elevator."

"Don't let them ticket the car, Tony. We'll move it in half an hour." Hopefully with Renata's family inside and on their way back to Mexico, she thought. "And since when aren't goats allowed upstairs?" Christy shouted back to him.

"How did you find me?" Christy asked as the elevator doors closed.

"We saw you on TV," Jorge answered.

"Señor Robert Beck," Old-Maria said, "on satellite."

Great, she thought. Not only did my *Robert Beck* appearance humiliate me for all eternity, it brought the whole Ruiz family to my doorstep. What do they want from me? Money?

"So, how can I help you?" she asked when they stepped inside the apartment.

"We've come to take Renata back to Mexico with us," Jorge said.

"*What?* No, that's impossible. Maria, *my* Maria that is, she asked me to take care of Renata. I promised I'd raise her."

"Can we have something to eat? Young-Mother-Maria said. "I'm *famélico*."

"Of course. Oh, shoot. I let my cook go. There's not much in the fridge. Do you like Chinese?"

Young-Mother-Maria shrugged. "I like eggrolls."

"Give me a minute." Christy called Eve on the intercom and asked her to order from Duck River. "Now, where were we?"

"We've come to take Renata back," Jorge said.

"Yes, right. Of course. But she was entrusted to my care. Maria appointed me her guardian. I've already started adoption proceedings. And she's thriving in school. You wouldn't want to disrupt her when she's doing so well," Christy pleaded.

"Yes, but her mother left instructions in her will that *we* should raise her if Maria couldn't. And we're her flesh and blood. It's all right here." Jorge pulled some papers out of a raggedy leather briefcase. "See." He handed Christy some kind of legal document that appeared to be a Last Will and Testament. She skimmed it. Assuming this was really written by Renata's mother, her wishes *were* that Renata go with Jorge and Old-Maria if her grandmother couldn't raise her. This is certainly going to complicate Renata's adoption case, Christy thought glumly.

Mr. Koodles wandered into the living room and spotted the baby goat, who was chewing Christy's dracaena plant. He hissed at the animal. The goat kept eating.

"Has Renata ever met you?" Christy asked.

"Yes. Well, no. Maria's daughter, Maria, brought her to visit when she was just born, but we live in a tiny town outside of Monterrey. Maria never brought her back."

"You mean *my* Maria's daughter?"

"Yes."

Christy was having trouble keeping track. She wondered how Renata had been spared the family name. "Ahhh, so you live in a small village. What do you do there?"

"I'm a carpenter," Jorge said. "Maria"—he gestured to

Old-Maria—"has a goat farm, a hundred acres. She exports goat cheese to the finest restaurants and gourmet stores in the world. You can order from her website, YouGoatGirl-dot-net. Maria is the webmaster," he added, gesturing toward Young-Mother-Maria.

Christy laughed and said to Old-Maria, "Cute name. Not what I'd expect, just having met you. Tell me, are the schools good in your town?"

"The local school ends at eighth grade," Old-Maria said. "There's a Catholic school about twenty miles away that goes through high school. But it doesn't matter. We'll need Renata to help with the goats."

"Ah, I see. How many goats are there?"

"Eighty," Old-Maria said proudly. "Eighty-one counting this baby."

"That's impressive," Christy said. She really meant it. "I didn't know they let you bring goats across the border."

"They don't," Jorge explained. "We snuck this *cabrito* in. Our little Maria wouldn't leave home without him. Do you know where we can get goat's milk near here?"

"There's a gourmet market nearby called Eli's. They'll probably have it, but it'll cost you."

"That's one of my accounts," Old-Maria said. "Their cheese and goat's milk come from our farm."

Christy smiled. "That's lucky. Maybe you can negotiate a discount," she said. "How often does he need to be fed? Should we walk him?"

"We give him a bottle twice a day. The rest of the time, he grazes outside. Can we tie him to a tree in your backyard?" Jorge asked.

"This is Manhattan, Jorge. We don't have a yard," she said.

The conversation was interrupted by the interesting

sound of goat retching. Before anyone could get the animal to a dry floor, he threw up the dracaena plant on the new Persian rug.

Cynthia, who had been spying from the kitchen, came running to the rescue with a roll of paper towels.

"Let's put him in the laundry room. He'll be more comfortable there," Christy said. She wondered if the goat could be trained to use Mr. Koodles' litter box.

Christy took Jorge and the goat to the laundry room. The doorbell rang, and Eve shouted that she'd answer it. When they returned from the laundry room, Eve was setting up a Chinese buffet at the table.

"Come, everyone. Let's eat," Christy said.

"I'll bring water," Eve offered.

Everyone except Christy helped themselves to the food. She was sick to her stomach. How could she possibly send Renata back with these relatives she didn't even know, to work on a goat farm no less? What about her education?

"Jorge, Maria, is there any way you would consider leaving Renata here? She's doing so well. I would make it worth your while."

Jorge looked offended. "Do you think we're here for money? What do you take us for? We're here for the child. This is a family obligation."

"Right. But I'm happy to take on the obligation. I know Renata, and I love her. Plus, I can offer her so much more than what she'd have in Mexico."

"Joo Americans think it's all about money, don' joo?" Old-Maria said. She emphasized the point by spitting into her moo shu pork. Then she stormed out of the room.

As soon as Old-Maria was out of earshot, Jorge sidled up

close to Christy. "If we *were* to take money for the child, how much are we talking about?"

Christy was about to answer when Old-Maria returned in a snit. "As soon as Renata comes home from school, we leave."

Christy was desperate. "*Please!* Don't take Renata from me. She's all I have."

Old-Maria looked around the apartment. "Joo have a lot more than Renata. Joo live in a palace."

"Tell you what," Christy said. "This doesn't have to be re-solved today. Why don't you stay with us for a while? We could use the company. The couches in the living room are comfortable for sleeping. And Renata has a sofa bed in her room. I know she would love to meet you. In fact, she'll be home from school in a few hours. Let's just start with that, shall we?"

Jorge and Old-Maria looked at each other. Old-Maria shook her head, but Jorge said, "Okay, we'll stay."

"I'm *not* walking that *cabrito* in this *ciudad grande*," Old-Maria said, wagging her finger in Jorge's face.

"Fine," Jorge said. "Renata will walk the goat. She needs to learn how to take care of him, anyway."

Lord give me strength, Christy prayed.

෨

DEAR DIARY,
   MY WHOLE FAMILY AND THEIR GOAT CAME TO NEW YORK TO CLAIM ME. THEY WANT ME TO GO HOME WITH THEM AND BE A GOAT HERDER. WHO DO THESE PEOPLE THINK I AM-HEIDY? ALL THE GIRLS IN THE FAMILY ARE NAMED MARIA AND THAT IS JUST WEIRD. GRANDMA WANTED ME TO GET AN EDUCATION

AND NOT TO TAKE CARE OF GOATS. I'M VERY WORRIED THAT
CHRISTY WILL SEND ME BACK WITH THEM NOW THAT SHE AND
MICHAEL BROKE UP. LAST NIGHT, CHRISTY HAD A MEETING
WITH MY MEXICO FAMILY IN THE LIBRARY. I SPIED FROM THE
CLOSET AS USUAL. EVERYONE AGREED THAT I CAN FINISH THE
SCHOOL YEAR. MY RELATIVES ARE STAYING WITH CHRISTY
UNTIL THE TERM ENDS. BUT WHAT HAPPENS AFTER? I NEED TO
TALK TO MRS. DE MILLE ABOUT THIS BUT SHE'S DEAD. THE
PEOPLE I LOVE ARE DROPPING LIKE LICE.

    YOUR CURSED FRIEND,
    RENATA HAYES

∽

It only took a few days for Christy to get used to having Renata's family in the apartment. If she wasn't so worried about their taking the child, she would have enjoyed the company more. When Old-Maria wasn't calling on her local goat-cheese accounts, she took over kitchen duties. And she was a fabulous cook. Young-Mother-Maria cleaned circles around Cynthia and, on top of that, managed the YouGoatGirl website. Cynthia finally quit out of embarrassment. Nectar took care of Little-Maria, Renata, and Ali, taking the older girls to school, accompanying Little-Maria to the art, gymnastics, and music classes she found for her. Jorge was redoing all the cabinets in the kitchen and building a new dining room table. Christy mastered the family's European washer-dryer and took responsibility for everyone's laundry. Renata did the dishes. Ali (reluctantly) watered what was left of the dracaena plant. Between Renata, Ali, Jorge, the three Marias, Mr. Koodles, the baby goat, housework, school, the goat farm, and carpentry projects, Christy had a little less time to miss Michael.

Ali and Renata put on their bathing suits, got into the tub, and gave the goat his first bath. Christy, Renata, and Little-Maria walked the animal, which Renata had named Princess Anastasia in honor of Mrs. De Mille (even though it was a boy goat). They tried taking it to the Central Park dog run, but it caused such a stir that a park ranger threatened to write a ticket. Still, Christy was pretty sure the goat was becoming housebroken.

Michael Doesn't Live
Here Anymore

*C*hristy had just come in from a run when the buzzer sounded.

"Miss Kilborn's here to see you," Tony said.

"Who?"

There was mumbling on the other end of the intercom as Tony conferred with the visitor. "Miss Katherine Kilborn."

"Send her up," Christy said. *I suppose.*

Soon, the doorbell rang. Why hadn't she told Tony to turn her away? Instead, she was standing there frozen with the intercom phone in her hand. "I'll get it," Christy said, shooing Jorge. She looked through the peephole and caught a distorted view of Katherine—forehead enlarged, no chin, minuscule body. It was her best angle, Christy thought, opening the door. Sure enough, there Katherine stood, all decked out in a checkered Chanel suit and Prada heels, carrying her Gucci bag. The bitch was as stunning as ever. Seeing Katherine filled Christy with a sense of loss. For some reason, she felt the old tug of her former girlfriend and confidante. She remembered the day *Vanity Fair* had photographed them modeling fall executive fashions. They were both so proud of having their picture in that magazine. Then she flashed on that last board meeting, the one she had relived hundreds of times. How could she possibly think of missing this Judas?

Christy stood at the door and said nothing. Katherine's eyes misted up, and she burst into tears. She stepped forward and embraced her. "We *need* you back."

Christy waited for Katherine to stop blubbering.

Katherine composed herself and reached for Christy's hand. "How *are* you, Christy?"

"I'm great. Everything's hunky-dory." She would never tell her about Michael. Christy knew she'd act all concerned but would be secretly delighted. "What about you?"

"Christy, it has been *so* hard for me since you left. I hate being at the company without you as my partner. More than anything, I hate that we aren't friends anymore. Everyone misses you at Baby G. I'm here to ask you to come back."

Christy's jaw dropped in disbelief. "You have *got* to be kidding."

"No, I'm not. The place is a mess without you."

"But that *Journal* article said business was soaring. You've made all those amazing changes and turned around what *I* wasn't capable of leading."

"You know how it is with the media. We had to put our best foot forward for the good of the company."

"Yeah, while you smeared me."

Katherine looked down. "I'm sorry about that. And also about what I did to you at the board meeting. It's just . . . I was so sick of living in your shadow. You probably can't understand that because you've never *been* anyone's second banana. I just wanted to be in charge for once. But it's lonely at the top. That's a cliché, I know, but it's true. If I can't run Baby G with you, I don't want to run it anymore."

"So let me guess: the business is in some kind of trouble, and you want me back so I can take the heat."

"No, don't be ridiculous. Times aren't easy. But they never are, are they? The company needs your guidance and leadership."

"And what does the board say?"

"They want you back, too. Especially Niles Raines."

"Katherine, you've set me up as a complete loser in the press. News that I was coming back would start a selling frenzy."

"I'm sure Rick can handle the press, spin the story into a positive. At least tell me you'll *think* about it?"

"In what capacity would I come back?" Christy asked. "Special projects?"

"No. Of course not. It would be the same as before. You'd be number one; I'd be number two."

"Wow. That's big of you," Christy said. *Too big.*

"That's how *much* I want you back," Katherine said urgently.

Christy looked at her watch. "Listen, I gotta go. Sorry. Not interested." With that she shut the door in Katherine's face and looked through the peephole to watch her leave. As soon as Katherine disappeared into the elevator, Christy leaned back against the door and started breathing again. If Katherine had stayed one more minute, Christy knew she might have been sucked into believing that she really cared. That girl was poison. Christy walked to the library to tell Michael that she had finally put her past behind her. Then she remembered he didn't live there anymore.

෩

To: <u>Michaeldrummond@aol.com</u>
Fr: <u>Galit@TFJ.com</u>
Michael, we need to talk ASAP. I met with your ex-CFO today, Andy Chapman. He gave me an earful. Says Drummond Enterprises is in serious trouble. Provided documentation that you have pledged assets you don't own to back up your credit lines. Says Drummond Enterprises is a house of cards. If any of the loans are called, the whole company will topple. If I put this in your biography or write an article about it for the Journal, it would be disastrous. But as a responsible reporter, how can I ignore it? Meet me for drinks at the Sherry Netherland, 6 p.m. It's private there. Galit

An Uneasy Truce

Christy walked up the red-carpeted stairs of the Harvard Club carrying a garment bag. Dead white men stared down at her from portrait after portrait. She walked quietly upstairs to Michael's door and stopped, listening for Galit's voice. Only Michael was talking, most likely on a call. She could just make out a few words: *Galit . . . mortgaged . . . renegotiate*. Finally, when all was quiet, she knocked.

"Coming," he said.

Michael opened the door and smiled.

Christy's stomach did a flip. Logically, she knew she was furious with him. So why did her heart melt at the sight of him? Play it cool, she told herself. "Can I come in?"

Michael opened the door for her.

"I brought you some clothes," she said. "I figured you were trying to make do with one suit." Taking one look at his crumpled appearance, she knew she was right.

"Thanks," Michael said. "It's so great to see you."

As he hung everything in the tiny closet, Christy looked around. The room was old, dank, and in need of renovation. There were two single beds, a color TV, a small desk and dresser, a green plaid chair with stuffing coming out, and water stains on the ceiling. "Why are you staying *here*?"

She knew he could afford the presidential suite at the Plaza Athénée.

"This is where all Harvard men go when they separate from their wives."

"Ah, I see. Tradition."

"I guess," he said. "It is pretty small, now that you mention it."

"Yeah, it is. You're not looking too good, Michael. Is anything wrong?"

Michael looked at Christy like she had two heads.

"Oh right. Us."

"You look good, though," he said. "I guess you're managing."

"Yep, I'm running again—six miles a day. I decided to train for the New York City Marathon. Plus, Jerome got me this amazing deal with the Olympic Foundation. I'm gonna help raise an endowment to support our athletes."

"That's exciting. Congratulations." Michael looked devastated. He seemed to be barely functioning. She felt a moment of triumph.

"Not only that, they want me to start a mentoring program for new Olympians. You know, match past competitors and medal winners with young contenders coming down the pike. Isn't that a good idea?"

"It sounds like a great project."

"Oh, and Katherine asked me to come back to Baby G in the number-one position."

Michael looked surprised. "Are you considering it?"

Christy would sooner become one of Brownie's minions than go back to work with Katherine, but she wasn't about to tell Michael that. "Depending on what happens with us, I may need a job."

Michael cringed. "Just be careful. Don't let her suck you in again, Christy. She's already caused you a lifetime of pain."

"Yes, there's a lot of that going around." She paused. "Are you coming to see Ali tonight?"

"Yeah. I'm sorry I haven't been by yet. I've been looking for an apartment so I can get her out of your hair."

"She's not a bother, really. But you need to spend some time with her. Last night, she asked me if I'd help her get birth-control pills."

"*What?* I hope you told her no." Michael stood and began pacing on the tiny patch of carpet between the end of the bed and the bathroom door.

"No, I told her she should talk to you. If she's sexually active, you'd better get her on birth control."

"But she's only sixteen," Michael said, still pacing. "I can't condone that kind of behavior."

"I suppose you can lock her in her room until she's twenty-one. Or you can talk to her. Maybe you can help her see that she's not ready to have sex."

"Right. That's what I'll do. I'll stop by tonight. Girls need to have involved fathers. Ali has to know she can depend on me."

"And what about Renata? You don't think *she* depends on you? You don't think *she* needs an involved father?"

"Christy, we agreed. You're the one who wanted her."

Christy groaned. "You're some piece of work, Michael. You once told me that if you couldn't live with Ali, you couldn't live with someone else's child. Remember? Well, now we have Ali. So why can't you let Renata into your heart? She's a great kid. And truth be told, you need her as much as she needs you." Christy walked over to the door and opened it. "I'll see you."

"Wait," Michael said. "It's *you* I need. I miss you so much. Do you miss me?"

"I'm too angry to miss you," she said. That wasn't true. Christy missed him like crazy. But too many issues were unresolved. She wasn't about to admit her true feelings. Still, she wanted to give him something without giving him ground. "Listen, Renata's graduation is coming up a week from Friday. Will you come? It would mean a lot to her," she said.

"Sure, just have Eve call my office with the details." Michael brightened a little.

"Her family showed up," Christy said.

"Whose family?"

"Renata's."

"She's got family? Well, that's wonderful. She can go with them. You and I can be together again the way we used to be." Michael took Christy's hands in his. "Ali can live with us. Suzanna's already stipulated to my having permanent custody. You'll have a *real* daughter. What do you think?"

"What do I think? I think you haven't listened to a word I've said. You want to throw Renata out for Ali? Your daughter for mine? Let's get something straight, Michael. I already have a real daughter. And I'm going to do everything I can to keep Renata with *me*. So if we *do* get back together, and that's a huge *if* right now, she's part of the package."

Michael stood silent, thinking.

"I guess we'll see you at graduation?" Christy said.

"Of course."

Christy left. It was all very civilized. And sad.

∽

To: <u>Michaeldrummond@aol.com</u>
Fr: <u>Galit@TFJ.com</u>
Michael, what say we take the jet to Argentina next Friday for a long weekend of spring skiing? I know an amazing place— Cerro Castor. We can ski Cerro Krund. It's some of the most beautiful terrain in the world. You free? Galit

To: <u>Galit@TFJ.com</u>
Fr: <u>Michaeldrummond@aol.com</u>
Galit, I have to go to Christy's kid's graduation. Give me a rain check? Michael

To: <u>Michaeldrummond@aol.com</u>
Fr: <u>Galit@TFJ.com</u>
I'm finding it harder and harder to stay quiet about your company's financial problems. Ben is losing patience with all the time I'm spending on your book. He's asking for some interim articles on Drummond Enterprises. What if I write about the loans that are secured by mortgaged collateral, but I list the steps you're taking to rectify the problem? Galit

To: <u>Galit@TFJ.com</u>
Fr: <u>Michaeldrummond@aol.com</u>
Galit, I can't go to Argentina over the weekend, but can go for the next three days. You free now? We can talk about your interim article on the way over. Michael

∽

Michael was terrified.

Once Upon a Goat

The fifth-grade graduation was held in the Astor ballroom on the top floor of the Colby mansion. The palatial room featured travertine panels, crystal chandeliers, and enormous windows that overlooked Park Avenue. The space was so spectacular that the school booked it on weekends for weddings. The money went to the PTA. Brownie told everyone that renting the room was *her* idea, but it was really Patty Fitch's. Brownie took credit for all the best ideas.

Today, the space was decorated with magnificent flower arrangements of yellow and white. The two front rows were set with twenty-four chairs where the young graduates sat in their white gowns with their yellow-rose wrist corsages. The head of the lower school, the headmistress, Brownie, and LaShaun Mason were seated at the dais, which was set up on the side of the stage, across from the podium. As chairwoman of the graduation exercises, Christy was on the dais, too.

Andrea walked up to the stage and motioned Christy over. "Christy, did you ask Jorge if he'd be willing to build us four walls of library shelves?"

"I did. He said he'd be delighted."

"Brilliant! I love what he's done with your kitchen. Tell

him I'll pay twenty thousand plus expenses. That's what my old carpenter bid on the job. But he's so unreliable."

"I'm sure Jorge will think that's fair," Christy said. *Fair!* That was probably more than he made in a year in Mexico. Christy couldn't wait to tell him. Even Old-Maria's business was booming now that she was in New York and could call on her customers personally. Every evening she'd e-mail her daily orders back to Federico, the plant manager, who would ship fresh goat cheese to the finest restaurants and gourmet shops in the city. Christy desperately hoped that the lure of the American dream would keep Jorge and the three Marias from leaving. She already had a lawyer working on securing the proper immigration papers, just in case they decided to stay.

She glanced over Andrea's head, looking for Michael. Nectar and Ali were sitting toward the back with Renata's Mexican family. Princess Anastasia was on the chair next to Little-Maria, who had tucked the goat into her play stroller and snuck him in. Christy was sure the kid would get busted. They were so serious about rules at Colby.

"Have you seen Michael?" Christy asked Andrea.

"Yeah, there he is," she said, pointing to the very back row. "He asked me to give you this." She handed Christy a note, which she promptly opened.

Can I take you, Ali, Renata, and her family out for a graduation lunch? Michael

Christy looked up, caught Michael's eye, and smiled, pointing to the note, nodding her head.

He gave her a wave. God, he looks haggard, Christy thought sadly. Not the invincible man I married.

Christy told Andrea she'd better get going. She was the mistress of ceremonies, and they were about to start. All the women at the dais were miked, and the parents would have to endure speeches from every one of them before their girls would get their fifth-grade diplomas.

"Thank you, Mrs. Greer," Christy said after the headmistress had given her speech. "Now I'd like to introduce the woman you've all been waiting to hear from. I could spend an hour regaling you with the many awards and accolades this amazing woman has earned, from Olympic gold medals, to number-one rankings on the WTA Tour to championships at Wimbledon, Australia, France, and the U.S. Open. But let's not get bogged down in the details. Everyone knows her as one of the most accomplished tennis players in the world. Here today, speaking in honor of the fifth-grade Colby graduates, I present to you . . . LaShaun Mason.

The girls applauded enthusiastically and then gave LaShaun a spontaneous standing ovation.

When the girls sat back down, LaShaun spoke. "Thank you, fifth-grade Colby graduates, Christy Hayes, and Brownie Rich for having me here today. As I look at all of you sitting in this beautiful room, in your lovely dresses, having been given every advantage life has to offer, I envy you. But I also worry for your futures. Why, you ask? Why worry about what will become of young women who come from the best families, who live in the most magnificent homes, who study at the top private school in Manhattan? I worry for you because, perhaps, you have been given too much too soon.

"When I was your age, my family was living in a drug- and gang-infested section of Detroit. I practiced my tennis on public courts in a neighborhood where drive-by shootings were common. I was striving for something better. By the time I was eleven years old, as many of you are today, I'd been play-ing tennis for six years. And I believed with all my heart that the game was my family's ticket to a better life. I was hungry, and that hunger fueled my drive to become the winning player that I eventually became.

"For years and years, my father pushed me. He insisted that I become the best that I could possibly be. I was the great hope for my family. It was an awesome responsibility to have. Can you imagine what it would be like, at your age, to know that *your* success was your family's only chance for a better life? I took my obligation to heart. I knew there was no one to rescue us if I failed. It was win and live the good life, or lose and stay in one of the most dangerous communities in America. If it hadn't felt like life or death, I don't know if I would have been driven to succeed the way I was.

"As you sit here today, about to move on to the next level of your education, I want you to consider what you are doing today toward creating a winning future for yourself and your family. It is not too early for you to begin to think about where your talents and passions lie. It is not too early for you to begin training to become the best you can be, whatever your dream. I urge you not to be complacent just because there's no one depending on you and your success. You, the privileged daughters of Colby, must create for yourselves that hunger that was so real for me. And when you do, there is nothing you cannot accomplish. Thank you."

The girls applauded. Soon the whole room was giving LaShaun another standing ovation. What a relief! Christy thought. She was a success. "Thank you, LaShaun, for that *very* inspirational commencement address. And now, ladies and gentlemen, we're going to take a five-minute stretch break. When we come back, we'll hear from our PTA president, Mrs. Brownie Rich, and then our lower-school head, Miss Trudy Becker, will present the diplomas."

Everyone stood up and stretched. Brownie and her minions left to go to the bathroom. Michael started to approach Christy, who was chugging down a bottle of Evian. Before he reached her, she mouthed "bathroom" and pointed to the ladies' room. The break was short. They could visit after.

Christy made it to the restroom just as Brownie's two minions were leaving. Brownie was stepping out of the stall.

"Oh, Brownie, I'm glad I caught you," she started. "What did you think about . . ."

"YOU!"

"Me?"

"*YOU!* You *ruined* our fifth-grade graduation. *RUINED* it!"

"I did? Gee, I thought it was going well," Christy said.

"Are you *crazy*? How could you bring that . . . that ghetto girl here? How dare she criticize our little girls because their parents can afford to give them everything they want? Who does she think she is?"

"Well, to begin with, she's one of the most accomplished athletes on earth. Everything she got, she earned herself. I thought her message was perfect. Anyway, you knew I was bringing her in to speak. You approved it."

"Yes, but I *never* approved that speech. How could you not get me the text ahead of time? What were you thinking? That girl is . . . is . . . *common*. She talked about *drugs*! and . . . and gangs, and drive-by *shootings*! Our daughters are too young and innocent to have their minds polluted by such trash. No amount of therapy will ever heal this trauma."

"*Trauma*? What are you talking about? Our girls *need* to learn about the real world. That was her point. LaShaun

Mason succeeded in spite of *and because of* her circumstances. She was warning our daughters not to let their privileges lull them into complacency."

"There are hundreds of athletes you could have brought in to speak. But *nooooo, you* had to bring us a lowlife from some slum!"

"But she has *so* much to teach our daughters . . ."

"You are naïve, aren't you? This isn't about our *daughters*. It's about our *donors*. And I guarantee that you offended every one of them. You made *me* look bad to the donors, Christy. That's unforgivable. It's clear to me that you aren't cut from Colby cloth. You'll never go *anywhere* with the PTA. Your career with us is *over!*"

Christy started giggling. She couldn't help it.

"Don't *you* laugh at me, Christy Hayes."

She laughed harder. She laughed so hard that she cried. "Oh, gosh, I'm sorry," she said, wiping tears from her eyes. "It's just that, wow, I can't believe I actually cared so much about *making* it in the Colby PTA. When did I lose my way?"

"What are you talking about? Lose your way? There's *nothing* more important than leading a community of parents in support of your children's school."

"Lead? You don't *lead*, Brownie. You *terrorize*. What you do has *nothing* to do with supporting your children's school. It's all about manipulating the other parents to make *you* feel important. *Your* PTA should be called the Pain, Torture, and Agony Association. No one can say what they think. Working mothers are excluded. Everyone's afraid they'll screw up and you'll blackball them. Well, guess what, sister-girlfriend? For me, the reign of terror is over. I quit. You can stick the PTA up your gold-plated ass. And now, I'm going to go watch my little girl graduate."

Christy walked out of the bathroom. Brownie followed her. "You can't quit," she yelled. "I'm *firing* you."

"You do that, Brownie. See if I care." Christy opened the door to the ballroom. The room was so quiet, you could hear a goat fart. All mouths were agape as everyone watched Brownie and Christy walk in. No one moved. Then Michael rose to his feet. He started clapping. Andrea joined him. Fran Rich stood up and applauded. Brownie's minions were whistling and yelling "Whoo-hoo!" Soon the whole room was cheering. Christy blinked in disbelief. Then she realized that their mikes were on. Her argument with Brownie had been broadcast over the PA system. LaShaun Mason was standing up and cheering. Christy started laughing and applauding, too.

Brownie finally tuned in to what had happened. She looked around anxiously. Then she marched up to the podium and held her hands up to stop the noise.

"People, *peeeee*-ple!" she shouted. "Let's have some quiet, *please*. Today's focus should be on our daughters and *nothing* else."

The crowd began to boo. Mothers started hurling insults at Brownie. "You're through, Brownie." "Go home, Brown Nose." "You're common, Brown Cow."

The headmistress, Mrs. Greer, appeared onstage. "Why don't you sit down, Bronwen? It's time to present the diplomas."

"Yes, but as *head* of the PTA, it's my *duty* to shake every girl's hand."

"Give it a rest, Brown Nose," she said, shooing her off the stage.

Brownie walked away, shell-shocked. She pushed Princess Anastasia off the chair and took the only empty seat in the ballroom, right next to Little-Maria. As Brownie sat in the cheap seats watching Stephanie get her diploma, the baby goat that had been so unceremoniously shooed aside pooped on Brownie's favorite khaki slingback shoes.

Damn, Christy thought, watching Brownie run out of the room kicking goat shit off her shoes, I guess Princess Anastasia isn't housebroken after all.

I Come Bearing Gifts

ichael took everyone to lunch after graduation. Little-Maria insisted on bringing the goat, but the Four Seasons insisted right back that they had a "no farm animal in the dining room" policy. Since Michael was such a good customer, they assigned someone to guard Princess Anastasia in the alley so he wouldn't be stolen. Christy didn't think there was much danger of that.

"I'd like to propose a toast to Renata," Michael said, after drinks had been served. "Congratulations on your promotion to middle school. We're all very proud of you." Glasses were clinked all around in Renata's honor.

Christy's stomach dropped. She prayed this wasn't the end of Renata's education. How could her family not see that staying here would be better for her?

Renata blushed. "I just wish Grandma and Mrs. De Mille were here."

"Oh, they're looking down on you right now," Nectar said. " 'Vex not his ghost: O, let her pass!' That's Shakespeare. Don't you feel their spirits?"

"Yeah, I think so," Renata said, looking around, unconvinced.

Christy stood up and raised her glass. "And I want to propose a toast to Ali, who is now back in her father's life. I'm thrilled for both of you."

"Yay!" Renata said. "Now we can all live together like one big happy family." Renata looked at Michael hopefully. Michael eyed Renata's family suspiciously. Old-Maria stared longingly at Renata. Christy wondered what she saw when she looked at her—Renata or an extra farmhand. There was an uncomfortable silence that Michael finally broke.

"Here, Renata," he said, handing her a small black velvet box that could only hold a ring. "This is for you."

"Thanks," she said, popping it open. Her eyes lit up when she saw what was inside. "Wow, I love it."

"If you love it so much, why don't you marry it?" Ali said.

"Ali, stop being a smart aleck," Michael said.

"Let me see what you got," Christy said, peeking into Renata's box. There was a small gold ring, with a yellow diamond surrounded by five white diamonds. "It looks like a sunflower."

"What about me, Daddy? Didja get me one, too?" Ali asked.

"Did you graduate today?" Michael asked.

"No."

"There's your answer."

Ali made a pouty face.

Christy was impressed. It was the first time she'd heard Michael say no to his daughter.

"Thank you, Michael," Renata said, giving him a hug. More progress, Christy thought, his being sweet to the kid. Renata walked around the table, showing the ring to Nectar, Jorge, Old-Maria, and Young-Mother-Maria. She even stuck it in front of Little-Maria, who couldn't have cared less. Ali asked if she could borrow it. Renata said no. Ali called her "period face." Michael told Ali not to call her sister a period face on her graduation day. Her *sister*, Christy thought. Now, there's a first.

André, the waiter, came by and told everyone about the specials. They ordered. Old-Maria and Young-Mother-Maria whispered and pointed at a celebrity they recognized sitting at the corner table right behind them.

"Christy," Michael said quietly, "I have something for you, too."

"Oh?"

He pulled a velvet box out of his pocket and set it in front of her. Another gift from Sonny's, their favorite jewelry store in Denver.

She opened it and was blinded by a fifteen-carat pink diamond. "Wow, that's quite a ring. It's huge. But *why*? Why are you giving me this?"

"I feel terrible about what happened," Michael said. "I'm sorry, and I'm hoping you'll forgive me someday."

Christy wasn't sure what to do. Michael had presented her with the classic guilty-rich-husband oversized rock. Should she keep it? she wondered. If she and Michael did manage to get back together, it would be a nice ring to wear. And if they didn't, it could pay the rent for quite some time. She put it on her right ring finger and admired the way it sparkled.

"Wow! Did you just get that?" Renata asked. "It's way bigger than mine."

"Wanna trade?" Christy teased.

"Yeah!" Renata said, and started to take her ring off.

"Just kidding," Christy said.

Old-Maria, Young-Mother-Maria, and Jorge all ogled the ring, then spoke rapidly to one another in Spanish the way they did when they didn't want Christy to know what they were saying. The only two words she recognized were "Kobe Bryant."

"Thank you, Michael. I don't know what to say," Christy said.

"Just say—"

At that moment, several waiters appeared with their food, keeping Michael from finishing his thought.

"That was *so* funny, what happened at your graduation," Ali said.

"Which part?" Michael asked. "The argument Christy and Brownie had in the bathroom? When the headmistress wouldn't let Brownie hand out diplomas? Or when the goat pooped on Brownie's shoe?"

"The goat-shit part," Ali said. "That was awesome."

"Child, don't say 'shit.'" Nectar whispered. "You were raised better than that."

"No, I wasn't, and anyway, you just said it."

Nectar gave her a scary look.

"Sorry," Ali muttered.

"No, no, you know what I think the best part was?" Renata said, grinning. "The *best* part was after the graduation, when all the girls in my class told me what a cool mom I had. I think they like me now."

Christy gave Renata a broad smile.

"I liked the argument part. You were *brilliant*, Christy," Michael said. "I'm so proud of you for standing up to that PTA Nazi."

Christy blushed. She wondered why Michael was being so nice to her. Did he want to get back together? Was he finished with Galit? Was he willing to help her fight for Renata? Would he be a father to her child? If they got back together, could she ever trust him again? Should she act friendly or aloof? This was all new territory for Christy. For a fleeting moment, she missed having her old best friend Katherine to give her advice.

∽

DEAR DIARY,

TODAY WAS THE BIGGEST, MOST MAJOR, INCREDIBLY IMPOR-
TANT DAY OF MY LIFE. FIRST, MICHAEL GAVE ME A PRICELESS
SIX CARROT SUNFLOWER DIAMOND RING. SECOND, THE GIRLS
IN MY CLASS LIKE ME NOW BECAUSE CHRISTY TOLD OFF MRS.
RICH THE BICH (EXCUSE MY FRENCH). THIRD AND MOST HUGE OF
ALL, I GRADUATED FROM FIFTH GRADE WHICH MEANS I'M A
WOMAN NOW. IF ONLY GRANDMA COULD HAVE BEEN THERE.
SHE WOULD HAVE BEEN SO PROUD. OF COURSE, IF GRANDMA
WERE HERE, I NEVER WOULD HAVE GRADUATED FROM COLBY.
THAT IS SO DEEP IT GIVES ME A HEADACHE.

I HAVE STARTLING ATHLETIC NEWS TO REPORT! LAST
WEEK WE HAD THE PRESIDENTIAL FITNESS TEST AT SCHOOL.
I DIDN'T DO GOOD ON THE SIT-UPS BUT I HAD THE BEST TIME
IN MY CLASS ON THE MILE RUN—5 MINUTES AND 51 SECONDS!
CHRISTY SAYS I HAVE NATURAL TALENT AND SHE WANTS TO
KEEP TRAINING ME. I'VE DECIDED TO BE AN OLYMPIC CHAM-
PION WHEN I GROW UP. THE ONLY FLY IN THE UNDERPANTS IS
THAT MY BLOOD FAMILY WANTS TO TAKE ME BACK TO MEX-
ICO TO BE A GOAT HERDER. THIS IS NOT IN ANY WAY, SHAPE,
OR FARM WHAT GRANDMA WOULD HAVE DESIRED. AND WHAT
ABOUT MY OLYMPIC ASPERATIONS? AM I TO FLUSH THEM
AWAY FOREVER IN THE TOILET OF BROKEN DREAMS? I MUST
TRY TO STAY CALM AND THINK. THERE HAS TO BE A WAY TO
STOP THIS RUNAWAY TRAIN.

YOUR NERVOUS FRIEND,
R. E. HAYES

Fatal Attraction

To: Michaeldrummond@aol.com
Fr: Galit@TFJ.com
Where were you yesterday? I called several times. Your assistant refused to tell me where to find you. Obviously she didn't
give you the message or you would have called me back. I've
written a piece you'll want to see. If you come over tonight, I'll
give you a peek at the article and maybe something else. Galit

To: Galit@TFJ.com
Fr: Michaeldrummond@aol.com
Galit, hard to refuse such an invitation. Sorry about my assistant.
She can be so protective. Michael

Making Up Is Hard to Do

*C*hristy dashed over to the Harvard Club, which was a few blocks from the John Barrett Salon. Why put this off any longer?

She walked into the lobby and dialed his room number on the house phone. A woman answered. Her stomach sank. "Who is this?" Christy asked.

"Who is this?"

"This is Christy, Michael's *wife*. Is he there?"

"You must have the wrong room. There's no Michael here."

"But he was there last week."

"Well, he's not here now," she said, hanging up without so much as "good-bye."

Christy walked to the front desk. "Excuse me, but is Michael Drummond still registered?"

The man behind typed something into his computer. "He checked out three days ago."

"Did he leave a forwarding address?"

"Afraid not."

"Thanks anyway," she said. Christy walked outside and tried Michael's cell, but there was no answer. She called Mary Ann, his assistant.

"Christy, give me a minute to call him. I need to make sure I can tell you where he is," she said, clearly uncomfortable.

"What are you talking about? Of course you can. I'm his wife."

"Look, Christy. He told me not to give anyone his new address without asking him. I could get fired."

"Well, if you don't tell me where he is, you can bet your ass that you *will* get fired." Christy was seething.

"Christy, just hold tight," Mary Ann said. "Let me call him. If he says I can tell you, I will."

This wasn't going well. Michael's disappearing act and his assistant's overprotectiveness was pissing Christy off. I should go home, she thought. Then her cell phone rang. It was Michael.

"Where are you?" Christy asked.

"I'm at the Pierre. I moved. Sorry, I should have called as soon as I left the club. It happened suddenly."

"Why all the secrecy? Are you hiding from your creditors?" she asked.

"You don't want to know."

"Okay, fine, whatever," Christy said. "I was hoping we could talk. Can you meet me?"

"Of course. I can be at Harry Cipriani's in five minutes."

Ten minutes later, Christy walked into Cipriani's. Michael was already at the bar drinking a beer. He'd ordered a martini for Christy.

"Hi, there," he said, standing up and pulling out a barstool. "You look great."

"Thanks." Christy knew she looked good. Her hair had just been styled. Her athlete's figure was back. And she'd turned the corner in more important ways.

"Listen," she said, as he said "Beegee" at the same time.

"You first," they both said.

"No, you," they both said. They smiled at each other.

"Fine. I'll go first," Christy said, taking a big sip of her drink. "Michael, I'm obviously not the woman you married anymore. You married a trophy wife. I'm anything but that now. I gained weight. I stopped dressing up for you. I didn't pay attention to you the way I used to. I was so busy with that ridiculous PTA that I gave up traveling with you. I'm sorry. Maybe I had a hand in driving you to Galit. I don't know. But I'm here to say that I'd like us to see if we can work things out."

Michael took Christy's hand. "Beegee, I want that, too. I never cared if you were a CEO. I mean, if it was important to you, I wanted you to have it. What I mean is . . . oh, hell. I just want back the girl I married. And I take full responsibility for what happened with Galit. She's been after me for some time. I thought I could resist her and still get the book done. I was wrong. I was weak."

Maybe we can put our marriage back together again, she thought. Christy pulled out her cell phone and handed it to Michael. "Call Galit. Tell her it's over. Tell her you aren't going to cooperate on the book anymore and you won't see her again."

Michael held the phone in his hand. He hesitated. "I can't just call her like that," he began.

"What do you mean, you can't? Then forget it." Christy stood, downed the rest of her martini, and stormed out the door.

Michael ran after her and grabbed her arm.

"Let go. You're hurting me," she said.

"Christy, come back. There's something I have to tell you. Please just give me a chance and listen."

She looked at him dubiously, and finally said, "Fine."

They sat back down at the bar. Michael was silent for an uncomfortably long minute. She could tell the news would not be good.

"Do you remember when we bought Anipix Studios?" he asked.

"Sure. California, animated films."

"Yep," he said. "Well, it started with that. Andy Chapman, my CFO, led the due-diligence team. But they weren't very diligent. There were significant liabilities, starting with massive debts that weren't booked. He didn't want me to find out that he'd screwed up, so he pledged assets from some of my other companies to pay back the loans. But the idiot pledged mortgaged property. Things we didn't own. Later, our bond rating was lowered, and some of the loans were called. Andy pledged mortgaged equipment and real estate to cover those. He double- and triple-pledged assets and then lied about all of it. One of his direct reports blew the whistle on him. Of course I fired him as soon as I found out what he'd done. Now I'm working like hell to clean up the mess."

Christy was stunned. Michael seemed too omnipotent to allow his company to get into this kind of trouble. He always gave the impression of having everything under control. Now his business and reputation were at risk. "How long has this been going on?" she asked. "Why didn't you *tell* me?"

Michael ran his hands through his hair a few times until he'd achieved that Nick Nolte mug-shot look. "A few months. You were so distracted that I kept it to myself. The thing is, Galit tracked Andy down and interviewed him for the book. He told her everything. Of course, he didn't take responsibility for *causing* the problem. He gave her all the documentation just to hurt us. He thinks he was screwed when we fired him. Ever since, she's been threatening to write an article for the *Journal* exposing the whole thing. Anytime I try to brush her off, she lets it slip that her management is pressuring her for the story. If I call her and tell her I'm back with you, the piece will be in the paper tomorrow. I'm sure she's already written it."

"Jesus, Michael. How could you get yourself into such a mess? *You*, of all people?" How could her fearless protector have screwed up so royally? She wasn't sure how she felt about *this* Michael.

He shook his scruffy head. "I keep asking myself the same thing."

Christy realized she would sort her feelings out later. Right now, she had to help him. "How far away are you from cleaning this up?"

"Some of our banks know; some don't. We've leveled with our biggest lenders, and we're negotiating new terms."

"You need to level with *everyone*. Convince them that they can't afford to call the loans. Make them your partners. Put a plan together to get out of this hole."

"We have a plan. I just haven't shown it to everyone."

"Well, I think you'd better reveal it sooner rather than later. You don't want it revealed for you."

"I'm so glad to have you in my corner again," Michael said, pulling her toward him, holding her. "You have no idea how lonely I was."

It was strange for Christy to see Michael so vulnerable. He'd always been the powerful one. Until now, she'd counted on him to make her feel safe. Whenever she'd been in trouble, he'd supported her no matter what the charge. His love was there for her, even when she was weak, even when she had been accused of the worst things. Now the tables were turned, and Michael was no longer a paragon. For the first time, she saw that he needed her strength the way she needed his. Could she be there for him? "Call Galit," Christy said. "Tell her you want to see her this afternoon."

Galit Shows Her Hand

our hours later, Galit was buzzed up to their apartment. Jorge, the family carpenter and situational butler, answered the door. He laid Galit's jacket on the chair in the entryway instead of hanging it up. Without that one faux pas and the fact that a baby goat was tailing him, he might have pulled off the butler act. He walked Galit into the library, where Christy was waiting.

"Christy?" Galit said, looking around. "Where's Michael?"

"Michael's not here. This is between you and me. Sit down."

Galit took a seat, acting nonchalant. "Fine."

Jorge walked in to serve a Mexican high tea. That is, chips, guacamole, and tea. He poured two cups and left the room.

"Okay, Galit, tell me what you want from Michael."

"What are you talking about?"

"You know exactly what I'm talking about. You've been threatening to expose his financial problems to the business community. If you do that before he has a chance to renegotiate with his banks, the consequences would be devastating."

"You have a nice home, Christy," she said, looking around. "I'd like a home like this."

"I'm sure your apartment is very nice," Christy said.

"Yes, but it's not like *this*. Do you know how hard it is to make ends meet on a reporter's salary?"

"No, I don't."

"It's tough. By this point in my life, I would have expected to hook up with a CEO who would marry me and take care of me in style. Like Michael takes care of you. But no such luck."

Galit looked forlorn, and for a moment Christy felt sorry for her. Apparently Galit had never realized that her "don't fuck with me or I'll cut your dick off" attitude wasn't much of a turn-on. "Well, I'm sorry you haven't met the right guy yet" was all Christy could say.

"My life would have been so much easier with assistants, stylists, chefs, drivers, masseurs, maids—all the things you have."

"I don't have a stylist, Galit," Christy said.

"Obviously," she said, looking Christy over. "I was hoping Michael would find me enticing enough to leave you."

Whoa! All that time Christy had been envious of Galit's beauty, brains, and sophistication, and Galit was jealous of *her*. She laughed out loud. "Galit, you have no idea what it takes to entice a man like Michael."

"Then why don't you tell me?"

"Sorry, I don't give lessons in husband stealing. You'll have to figure that out on your own. Can I offer you some chips? Guacamole?"

Galit took a blue corn chip and dipped it in the chunky green dip. "Did you make this? I heard that you'd given up everything to become Suzy Homemaker."

"Galit, just tell me what you want." Christy was losing her patience.

"Okay. I want a million dollars. Give me that, and I won't

publish the article. If you don't, the story runs in Friday's edition. In fact, it's already written."

Christy swallowed hard. A million dollars. "Okay," she said evenly. "That's going to take a few days to pull together."

Galit rolled her eyes. "Don't bullshit me, Christy. Michael can get that kind of money with the snap of his fingers. I want it in bearer bonds. By Thursday."

"*Thursday?* That's two days." She thought about it for a moment. "Okay, fine. Come back Thursday at five. You'll have your money."

As Galit left, Christy heard her lay into Jorge. Apparently, Princess Anastasia had licked her on her way out. "Get that thing away from me!" she screamed in Christy's direction. "Who ever heard of a pet goat?" she muttered. Then she slammed the door.

Christy sat on the couch thinking about what to do next. There was a rustling sound in the closet. Mice? Bats? *Naah.* Quietly, Christy tiptoed over and yanked the door open. There was Renata on the ground, holding a glass to her ear where the bottom of the door had just been.

"What in God's name are you doing in there?" she asked.

Renata looked up and smiled weakly. "Ummm . . . I was looking for my contact lens?"

Christy reached down and pulled the girl up by the arm. "You don't wear contacts. Try again."

"Okay, okay. Don't get mad. Just listen to what I have to say."

"It had better be good."

❧

When Galit arrived on Thursday afternoon, Michael was with Christy.

Jorge escorted her into the library once again.

"Hello, Galit," Christy said politely, before realizing that she really didn't need to treat their blackmailer so civilly.

"Christy, Michael," Galit acknowledged coldly.

"Here," Christy said, handing her a duffel bag. Galit unzipped it and started counting stacks of bearer bonds.

"It's all there," Michael said.

"I'm sure it is," she said, still counting.

"What assurances do we have that you won't demand more money later?" Michael asked.

"None," she said, looking at him with those icy blue eyes of hers.

He walked over and got in her face. "Listen, Galit, you can do this to us once, but not twice. We don't ever want to see your ass again."

"You seemed to like my ass just fine in Aspen," Galit said.

Christy recoiled. Galit was one nasty piece of work.

"There's one more thing," Galit said, peering around Michael at Christy. "I want that ring you're wearing."

"Are you nuts? That's Christy's. You can't have it. In fact, fuck it." Michael grabbed the bag from Galit. "Get out. You're not getting anything."

Galit stood up and walked to the door. "That's too bad, Michael. Look for the story tomorrow, front page, center column."

"*Wait*," Christy said, taking off the ring. "Here. Take it. Give her the money, Michael."

Michael's face was red and his jaw was clenched, but he handed her the bag.

Galit left in a hurry. Jorge politely opened the front door for her. She didn't acknowledge him or the fact that Princess Anastasia had chewed a cantaloupe-size hole in her Burberry trench coat. Jorge had personally seen to that.

Renata the Hero

After Galit left, Christy and Michael heard a scuffling sound from the hall. They ran to check on the noise.

At the elevator, two tall, burly men had the blackmailer in handcuffs. The look of utter disbelief on her face was priceless.

"Renata," Christy called, "bring the clock from the library."

"We're going to have to take the bonds with us, Mrs. Drummond," one of the cops said.

"She's got my wife's ring, too," Michael said. "The cash wasn't enough."

One cop started oinking at her. The other said, "You have the right to remain silent . . ."

Renata came running down the hall, a clock radio in her hand.

"We nanny-cammed the whole thing," Christy said, handing the hidden camera to the cop reading Galit her rights. As they stepped into the elevator, Galit maintained a defiant expression even as both officers held their noses up and snorted loudly right in her face.

"And I heard the whole crime go down from my *secret hiding place*," Renata said.

Michael looked at Christy, confused. "Renata knew about this?"

"Honey, the sting was her idea," Christy said, "not mine."

"How did she even know?" Michael asked.

"Well, when I met with Galit the other day, before you and I decided what to do, Renata was hiding in the closet."

"What possessed you to do *that*?" Michael asked Renata.

"Christy told me that Galit was threatening to tell a big secret of yours. And secrets are my specialty. They're what I'm known for. Christy said it would be bad if people found out, so she was gonna meet with Galit to talk her out of it. I decided to spy to see if I could help."

"How could you tell Renata something so personal?" Michael asked.

"We tell each other a lot of things these days, don't we?" Renata nodded.

"Anyway," Christy continued, "she was hiding in the closet during my first meeting with Galit. Which you will *never* do again, is that clear?"

"Yeah, I promise," Renata said. Her secret hiding place was blown, but it was for a good cause.

"After Galit left, I caught her. But she had a good idea—to tape the next meeting. She thought we should get the police involved. So I suggested it to you."

"*And* the *Financial Journal*," Renata added. "Don't forget that I told you to call them. Something just like this happened on *Diff'rent Strokes*. Arnold saved Mr. Drummond just like I helped save you." Or was it Buffy who saved Uncle Bill? She wasn't sure.

"I don't know what to say," Michael said. He looked at Renata, *really* looked at her. "You and I have a lot of catching up to do, Renata."

"Don't toy with me, Michael," Renata said.

"I'm not. I mean it. I do."

Renata's eyes teared up, and she bit her lip. She took Michael's hand in hers and squeezed. "In that case, it's time you started calling me Freckles."

Christy and Michael looked at each other. "Why?" Michael asked.

"I just think it's important for a father to have a pet name for his daughter, that's all."

Christy smiled at the two of them. Then she turned to Michael. "While you were meeting with the banks yesterday and Renata was at school, the detectives came over to show me how to work the wire, and I remembered the nanny-cam that was hidden in the clock radio. Katherine gave it to me when Nectar first came to work for us."

"You *spied* on Nectar?" Renata said. "How *could* you?"

"Well excuse *me*, Little Miss Snoop. Look who's talking!"

"Oh, yeah. But still, you should have trusted her."

"I did. I never used the thing. But we tested it, and it worked perfectly. So the police didn't have to wire me."

"That would have been so much cooler," Renata said, disappointed. "Big Pussy wore a wire on *The Sopranos* before he got iced."

"When were you watching *The Sopranos*?" Christy asked.

"Ali has the first five seasons on DVD," Renata said. "There's nudity on that show. And cursing," she added with a measure of pride.

"I know. And that's why you're *forbidden* to watch it again. Is that clear?"

"Awwww . . ."

"Anyway," Christy continued, "Renata's been our silent partner in this operation all along. She even went with me to the *Journal* yesterday when I told them what was about to happen."

"Boy, did they have a spaz attack," Renata said.

Michael turned to her. "Renata, I want to thank you. You are one clever kid, you know that?"

"Yeah, I know," she said. "And it's Freckles to you."

Can This Marriage Be Saved?

*T*he jet began its graceful descent over the Mediterranean. The sun was almost gone, and Christy could see the evening lights sparkling by the shoreline. Michael wanted to surprise her, so she still didn't know where they were going. She felt glamorous in a way she hadn't for months, being whisked away in their plane to a beautiful seaside getaway. When they landed, the pilot came on over the speaker. "Welcome to Saint-Tropez." No wonder Michael had allowed her to pack only three outfits: a bikini, a summer dress, and running clothes.

As their driver sped along a curvy seaside road with tiny villages on each side, Christy let out a long sigh. She and Michael had been through so much together since their wedding—an unexpected child, who made Christy break a promise to him; the crash of her career and her ego; Michael's fling, which broke his most important promise to Christy; another unexpected child—and then a threat to everything he had built. Christy wondered if the damage could be repaired. She didn't think they could go back, but maybe they could go forward. As though he was reading her thoughts, Michael moved closer and put his arm around her.

They pulled down a steep driveway to a small house with purple bougainvillea covering every wall. Michael got out and motioned for Christy to wait. Then he lifted her up and carried her over the threshold, to the delight of a plump, white-haired woman Christy assumed was the housekeeper. Inside was cozy and elegant, with an exquisite antique stained-glass window. The house was perched on the edge of a cliff, and as Christy walked to the back, she could see the clear blue-green of the sea swooshing against the rocks.

Michael put his arms around Christy, as he had so many times. She stiffened involuntarily. He pulled back. Christy turned around. "I'm sorry, Michael, I'm just not there yet."

"I was such an idiot, Beeg, not to see what Galit was doing. And not to understand what you were going through. All I saw was that you were turning into *her*. It all seemed to be starting over."

Suzanna, of course. Christy shuddered.

"Then, when I felt like I could lose everything and you helped me through that, I realized how much I'd failed you. I'm sorry."

And it could happen again, Christy knew, once he was back on top of the world. Could she really ever again rest in his arms and feel safe? At least she had Renata, who accepted her just as she was.

Christy knew he wanted to kiss her, to make love to her again, so she changed the subject. "Let's go eat. We don't have to figure this out tonight."

They dined at the top of the Old Village, a collection of stone buildings dating back six centuries. On the way, they passed the communal bread oven used in the medieval village and watched the sun set over the Mediterranean from the ancient wall. Then they sat at a table in a small restaurant, with candles and a fifty-year-old bottle of wine, and the French waiter remarked on what a beautiful couple they made.

Later, their driver took them down the hill on winding roads into the town, which at eleven P.M. was just heating up. They stopped at a small club Michael had heard about, Cinq a Cinq. It was filled with tanned couples and sophisticated European beauties with big breasts and tiny miniskirts who were hoping to catch wealthy beaux, just as Christy had done without really trying.

The music beckoned them to the floor. They began with a slow dance. She felt his heat as she moved to the music and then to him. She didn't want to give in. But her body wanted Michael's, and she languidly ground into him. She was afraid to put herself back in a position to be hurt again, and yet she was starting to feel swept away. It was as though she was with a stranger, a hot, disheveled, sexy stranger, far from home, and she wanted him until she forgot everything.

She was breathing harder and harder. "Michael, let's go," she whispered. He grabbed her hand, and they pushed through the growing crowd. He led Christy around a corner into a narrow dark street, with only a stray dog about, and pushed her up against the warm Provençal stone wall. He kissed her deeply and she met him full-on. Christy was almost dizzy with desire, needing him. He slid her silk dress up her smooth thighs, and lifted her up until she could wrap her legs around him. She savored every sensation, the brush of the hairs on his arm against her leg, the sweat running down his face, his smell. He seemed to have more power over her than ever before, and she welcomed him into her body. "Michael, I love you," she said afterward. He gently lowered her and then held her like he never wanted to lose her again.

That night she slept twined around his warmth, trying to burrow deeper and closer. She couldn't believe how much she had missed this.

The next twenty-four hours passed in a blur of sensual gifts. It felt as if they were the only two people in the world. Swimming naked in the cool water, lying on the velvet warmth of the stone, making love over and over. What was this? she wondered—something she hadn't really felt the first time around with him. Surrender. Knowing she belonged to him, no matter what. Christy realized she could not leave this man. She would just have to learn to live with the fact that he could hurt her again.

And then they were on the tarmac. They slept the whole way over the Atlantic. Christy woke up once and just watched him, his crazy hair and his smile lines, looking like a trusting child in sleep.

Steven met them at Teterboro with the Mercedes, and soon they were driving home in the hour before dawn. Christy lay across the seat as Michael stroked her hair. "I can't wait to get back to life as it was," he said.

"Me, too," Christy said, and she meant it.

"So, you'll help me raise Ali?" Michael asked.

"I will," Christy said.

"Good. Do you think your midwestern values can possibly trump the sense of entitlement Suzanna instilled in her?"

"I think so," Christy said dreamily.

"God, I hope," Michael said. "I *need* you for that. I want to do the right thing by Ali, but I'm not sure how."

Christy smiled. "Will you be a father to Renata?"

"Absolutely," he said. "Just as long as her family vamooses back to Mexico."

Christy sat up. "No, Michael. They have to stay."

"Would it be so bad, Christy, you and me and two daughters? Isn't that enough?"

"Don't you realize if they go they'll take Renata with them and turn her into a goatherd? And even if they were somehow willing to let her stay with us, she *needs* to be around her own family. Can't you see how fast she'll lose her Mexican identity living on Fifth Avenue?"

"She can visit them in the summer."

"Yes, but what about me? I don't want them to go. Michael, I never had a big family. I love having Jorge and the Marias around. Just give them a chance. Please?"

"Christy, we can't have the entire Ruiz family and their goat living with us. Get real. They go, and we'll do everything to get custody of Renata."

"No, Michael." She had let her guard down, and now he was going to impose his will when it came to Renata and her family. I never should have let him near me again, she thought. A man like this, a Master of the Universe, can never be trusted to take my needs into account. What was I thinking? She asked Steven to pull over.

"No, Steven, *don't* pull over. Christy, you *can't* get out here, it's five in the morning. We're in Harlem."

"Steven, pull over now," Christy said. She didn't give a damn *where* they were. She was angrier than she could remember being, angry at herself for thinking things could be different. Steven wasn't sure which boss to obey, but Christy must have been more convincing because he pulled over and let her out. Michael was pissed off now, too. He slammed the door after her and drove off.

Christy walked along Lenox Avenue, watching Harlem wake up. Then she found herself moving faster, finally starting to calm down with the decades-old comfort of running.

She hit Central Park just as it was getting light, and she ran along its outer edge until she hit Seventy-eighth Street and turned toward home.

Christy had absolutely no idea what she should do. Or what she would do.

Mrs. De Mille's Legacy

Michael was sitting in his chair in the living room when she walked in the door. He was holding a letter. "Christy," he called to her. "Come here."

She walked over to him, maintaining an emotional distance. "What is it?"

"Take a look at this."

She sat on the sofa and unfolded it. It was from the law firm of Pizzarello, Knowles, and Levy.

Re: Estate of Anna De Mille

Dear Mrs. Drummond,

We have tried unsuccessfully to contact you over the last week. It is our understanding that you are the legal guardian of the minor Renata Ruiz. We represented Mrs. Anna De Mille prior to her recent passing. Please be informed that Mrs. De Mille has left the bulk of her estate to Renata Ruiz. The estimated value of the inheritance is yet to be determined. It includes Mrs. De Mille's Manhattan apartment and an oceanfront home in Palm Beach, Florida. The remaining assets are in securi-

ties, silverware, jewelry, loose diamonds, and three
Fabergé Imperial eggs. The will specifies that Ms.
Ruiz not be told that she is the owner of these assets until she has reached the age of twenty-five
years. I would appreciate it if you would contact
me at the telephone number listed above so that
we can commence the execution of Mrs. De
Mille's will.

Sincerely,

Lara Nisonoff

P.S. There is also a Testamentary Trust on behalf of
Mr. Koodles, Mrs. De Mille's cat. Renata Ruiz has
been named the Executor of that Trust. I will explain more when we talk.

Christy looked at Michael. He was smiling. "You know
what this means, don't you?"

"No, what?"

"It means that Renata can live downstairs in Mrs. De
Mille's old apartment with her relatives and that goddamn
goat. Thank you, Lord! How did you know?" Michael actually danced a jig. He was *that* happy. She couldn't help but
smile at him. Okay, she had to admit it. Things were looking
up.

You Can't Go Home Again

The elevator opened to Baby G's tenth-floor offices. Christy's feet had barely touched the hardwood floor when the receptionist jumped out of her seat and ran over to hug her old boss.

"How *are* you? Oh my God, it's *so* great to see you. We've missed you *so* much. Are you coming back? Please say you're coming back," she begged.

Christy just smiled and walked toward her meeting. She looked around at the headquarters that used to be her second home. It felt like she'd never worked there.

"Christy, how *are* you? You look wonderful!" Lisa said, as she walked into the reception area. "Staying home really agrees with you."

"You think?" Christy said, smiling. She had dreamed of this moment so many times, of being welcomed back by her people. She drank it in.

As she strolled through the sea of desks in the communal workspace, Christy could barely make it to the boardroom. Almost every employee came over to greet her and give her a hug, show her wedding or baby pictures, let her know how much she was missed.

Christy reached out to open the boardroom door, but it

opened on its own. Niles stood there to greet her. He started to shake her hand and then threw his arms around her instead. The one person in this room she could trust. Dick Bender was next. Had he no shame? When Karl Lehmann came at her, she held her arms out to keep him at bay. "Enough, guys." As she took the closest empty seat at the large oval table, she remembered picking it out with Katherine at an antiques store on Twelfth Street. She looked around slowly, eye to eye with each man in the room. Katherine was not there. These were the men who had screwed her. It was clear that today, for reasons she didn't understand, she held the cards. She was going to take her time bringing them relief of any kind.

Niles broke the quiet in the room. "Christy, I know I speak for every board member when I say that we are so glad to see you sitting here. We asked you to meet with us today because we realize we made a big mistake five months ago, and we want to make it right." It wasn't quite as satisfying as it would have been coming from one of the six scumbags who'd ditched her, but it was pretty damn good. As if her reaction was felt, Dick Bender took the baton.

"Christy, we've learned that the sex scandal attributed to you was in fact true"—she started in her chair—"but it was true about someone other than you." Christy nodded her head, as if to say, Yeah, I told you.

Karl looked at Christy sheepishly. He had been completely seduced by Katherine. "The company is in a bind. There's a scandal brewing with our new operations in India. We don't know if the news will be leaked or not, but we're sitting on a time bomb. We know that if we fire Katherine without bringing you back, it will signal big trouble at the company. Two CEOs gone in six months—not a good story. The stock will tank. The company may not recover."

Rami Shah seconded the plea. This seemed well choreo-graphed to Christy. The worst offenders were each personally making the case to her. Eating their percentage of the humble pie chart.

"If I were to come back, what would happen to Kather-ine?" Christy was playing her poker face, not letting them read anything into her question.

Warren Heider spoke. "We'll put her on special projects, until this blows over, and then fire her quietly a year from now. We would have had to let her go anyway. You were right about her all along." Christy heard nothing after *special projects*. She was busy doing little victory dances in her head. Now that she had partaken of the sweet nectar of revenge, she had to figure out what to do. Her baby was in jeopardy, all the people she cared about, present company excluded.

"Gentlemen, I'm sorry to hear that the company we all worked so hard to build is in trouble, and I'm gratified that your confidence in me has been restored. I'll get back to you very soon with my decision." Short and sweet felt like her best bet. She needed to get out of this room and think things through. She rose, and they all rose with her. She cracked up at that, and so did they. It was hard to miss the ludicrousness that is the daily fare of capitalism. *General Hospital* had nothing on Baby G. Christy slipped out the door, catching a last glance at seven faces trying to look dignified in their moment of need.

Christy walked down the broad, open hallway toward her old office. The door was open, and she peeked inside. It had been completely redecorated. Everything was upgraded. The wool carpet had been replaced with silk Persian rugs. Instead of Christy's Office Depot furniture, the room was filled with marvelous antiques that must have cost Baby G a fortune.

Behind a sleek Art Deco maplewood writing desk, Katherine stood to greet her. "What do you think of the new furniture?" she asked.

Christy kept her reservations to herself. "Impressive."

"We got it at Sotheby's. It's from David Rockefeller's estate. He died, you know."

"So I heard."

"Well," Katherine said, looking into Christy's eyes, "have you thought about the board's offer? Are you and I going to have a second act?" Her expression was conspiratorial. The Christy she knew would never be able to resist saving her labor of love. Katherine seemed oblivious to the fact that her own neck was on the chopping block.

Christy walked over to the antique desk. "No, I don't think so. I appreciate the gesture. I do. But it's funny. I love my new life. I don't care about being famous anymore. I don't need to conquer the world."

"Christy, please, take more time to think about this. Reconsider. For me." Katherine bit her lip, and her face took on a nervous blotchy glow.

"What is it? Is there something you aren't telling me?"

She shook her head. "I can't."

"Of course you can," Christy said in that sister-voice she used to use with Katherine. "You've always been able to tell me anything."

Katherine took a deep breath. She gazed out the window for a moment before speaking. Turning back to Christy, she said, "Well, I did something. Something I shouldn't have, something that, when it comes out, could get me fired, or sued, or, I don't know, maybe sent to jail."

Christy bit her cheek to keep from screaming, YES! There is a God. Instead, she kept her face sober and said, "Katherine, tell me *everything*."

Katherine began to pace. "We moved our operations to India to cut costs. You don't have to pay people shit there. That's what makes it so attractive. Anyway, there was this fire at the factory a couple of weeks ago. An exit door had been blocked by machinery we had just brought in. There was only one other way out, and eight workers were killed trying to escape."

"Katherine, that's terrible. Those poor people."

"Well, yes, that, too. But the real victim here is Baby G. So far, we've been able to keep our involvement under wraps in America. But that meddling reporter, Galit Portal, got wind of it. She wrote an article. Then she held us up for a million dollars to kill the story. I thought that was the end of it. But now she's in some kind of trouble over taking bribes. The *Financial Journal*'s about to run a big exposé on its own reporter. They're disclosing everything about the accident in India and how I paid to keep it out of the paper. Our stock price will tank."

Christy's jaw just about hit the floor. "*What?* You actually paid Galit to hush up the story?"

"Yes."

"Does the board know?" Christy asked. She couldn't believe they would agree to anything that sordid.

"No, and I was hoping you could talk to them for me. Apparently Galit got caught blackmailing someone else. They arrested her. The news is going to hit the paper any day."

Oh my God, Christy thought. Wait'll Katherine finds out she was hoist by her own nanny-cam. She shook her head in wonder. The universe works in such strange and perfect ways. "Gosh, that's a shame, Katherine. But you know what? This isn't my problem to solve. It's yours." Christy felt a surreal sense of indifference to a place she had given twelve years of her life. She turned and walked out of her old office, down the hall, toward the front door.

Katherine ran out and cut her off. "*What?* You're choosing to be a *housewife?*" She said it as though no lower form of life existed on Earth. "You'd abandon the company you started, the company that *needs* you, to be a *housewife?*"

Young men and women in their twenties, dressed in stylish black and bold colors, stopped in their coffee treks, their errands, their trips to the restroom. Suddenly the room was still. The employees, who seconds ago had been buzzing with activity, grew silent. All eyes were on Katherine and Christy.

"Better a housewife than a sl—"

"Christy, please," Katherine interrupted. "I'm begging you. Baby G is *your* baby. You don't want to see it in trouble." Katherine was unsure of the outcome now, less strident, realizing that this conversation shouldn't be happening here, in front of everyone.

"Katherine, didn't you tell me once that you're as tough as they come? That no matter how bad the news, you could turn it around and come out smelling like a rose? Well, now's your chance."

"I don't remember," Katherine said. "But if I said that, I was wrong. I can't turn this around. I don't know how. I need your help. You always know how to make things right. Please."

Christy saw two futures open up before her. Since the day she left, she had fantasized about coming back to Baby G. She imagined a hero's welcome, the restoration of her good name as she carried her company into the next phase of unimaginable greatness. And here it was, being laid in her lap. Not only was it being offered, they actually needed her to save the day.

Or, a whole different future awaited her at home—being Michael's wife, Renata and Ali's mother.

Christy noticed Allison, one of her protégés, about ten feet away. Christy had taught her how to do killer presentations. The day before Christy left, Allison had landed an important new retailing partnership. Dan, next to her, had come from an old media company, and he'd flourished in the go-getter atmosphere of Baby G. Chloe, the redhead behind Dan, was a refugee from Morgan Stanley. Christy remembered Chloe's first day. She had shown Christy her blue toenail polish and said, "I couldn't have worn this there. Thank you so much." Then she had gone on to create several successful relationships with key analysts. There was Lizzy, the girl Christy had found making out with the Ivy League summer intern and forgiven with some motherly advice. Her eyes traveled from face to face in the dead silence. A shared ten P.M. pizza here, a companion on the endless road show there. Christy looked at the stunned employees, all witnesses to Katherine's meltdown. She hoped they wouldn't lose their jobs over her screwup. But it was too late to save the day, much as she would like to be Xena one more time. She had made new commitments now. They were waiting for her at home. This time, she realized, she really *was* leaving to spend more time with her family.

Christy faced the impromptu gathering. Everyone was crowding in to hear the decision that could shape their futures. "It is because of all of *you* that Baby G is what it is. You've given so much to this dream of mine, and I know you'll carry it forward. I know you'll find your way. It's up to all of you now."

To Katherine, she whispered, "Don't let the door hit you in the ass on the way out." She walked through the small crowd, shaking hands and hugging those she knew well. They all wanted a moment with her. Then they broke into applause for the woman who would always be Baby G to them.

Leaving the office for the last time, Christy felt tremendous sadness—until she got as far as the exit. Then she bounded down the stairs, all twelve stories to the lobby, toward that other future she held so clearly in her mind's eye.

Katherine's Karma

"ichael, can you pass the eggs?" Christy asked, looking up from the paper.

"Here. Do you want hot sauce?" he offered.

"I got it," Renata said, pushing the bottle Christy's way.

Little-Maria spilled her chocolate milk. Ali rolled her eyes.

"Ali, could you get some paper towels?" Michael asked.

Ali sighed at the imposition, but did what her father said.

"Who wants coffee?" Old-Maria asked.

"I'll take some," Christy said.

"I think she needs to go back to a sippy cup," Michael said.

"Who?" Renata asked.

"Little-Maria. She keeps spilling her drinks," Michael said.

"No, she's too old for a sippy cup," Nectar said. " 'Happy in this, she is not yet so old, but she may learn.' "

"Let me guess. Shakespeare?" Michael said.

"Why sir," Nectar replied, "how did you know?"

Whoa! A headline on the front page of the *Journal* caught Christy's eye: JOURNAL REPORTER ACCUSED OF EXTORTION. "Oh my gosh, you guys, the Galit story hit the paper," she said. "Listen." She read it aloud to a rapt audience:

It has been learned that a staff reporter for the *Journal* demanded payment to keep potentially damaging stories out of the news. In at least seven separate incidents that have been uncovered to date, Galit Portal extorted millions of dollars from companies anxious to hide bad news from the public. The actions of this reporter represent a betrayal of the trust that was granted to her by this paper. For that, we are profoundly sorry.

In a unique theory, Attorney General Graham Edwards alleges that by fraudulently withholding damaging information, Ms. Portal caused stock prices to be held at artificially high levels. Should stock prices for the companies involved in the scandal drop when the information Ms. Portal attempted to hide comes to light, Attorney General Edwards will hold Ms. Portal criminally liable for any losses suffered by the public as a result of her intentional failure to disclose.

Companies that paid Ms. Portal up to two million dollars to hide damaging stories include Verber Industries, Mutual Resources, Baby G Sports, American National Radio, Time Out Technologies, Worldwide Press, and Preston Oceanics. Ms. Portal's alleged crimes were brought to light when Christy Hayes, wife of media mogul Michael Drummond and former CEO of Baby G Sports, told authorities that Ms. Portal was attempting to extort money and jewels from her husband in exchange for keeping certain information out of the paper. In a sting operation that took place in Drummond's home, Ms. Hayes taped Galit Portal making her demands using the family's nanny-cam.

Attorney General Edwards announced plans to bring the CEOs of every involved company to justice for paying off a reporter with the intent of lying to and deceiving the American public. "We intend to prosecute these executives to the full extent of the law," he says.

"*Whoa.* Katherine's in enough trouble as it is. She's getting fired. And you know the shareholders will sue. Now Graham Edwards wants her in jail, too," Michael said, shaking his head.

"Wait, there's more," Christy said.

Ms. Portal offered this comment: 'I am innocent of all charges and I look forward to having my day in court when I can fight to clear my name. I simply held off on filing stories I was investigating until my assistant could fact-check everything. I can't understand why Mr. Edwards is attempting to criminalize my efforts to comply with the high standards of journalistic integrity set by the Ethics in Media Association. I am certain that I will soon be exonerated of these ridiculous charges.

"I guess you feel terrible for Galit and Katherine, don't you?" Michael said.

"Truthfully?"

"No, I want you to lie."

"Daddy, my adviser wants to see you and Christy today after school," Ali said.

"What did you do?" Michael asked.

"Why do you always assume *I* did something wrong?" Ali said indignantly. "I feel like I'm living in a police state."

"She took pictures of boys changing their clothes in the locker room with her camera phone," Renata said.

"You snitch," Ali said, pulling out her chair.

Renata jumped up and ran upstairs with Ali close behind.

"It's nice to see them act like real siblings," Christy said. "Don't you think?"

Michael smiled. "Oh yeah, warms my heart. C'mon, let's get to the bottom of this."

Everyone forgot about Galit and Katherine.

It's a Family Affair

One year later . . .

"Fre-e-e-eckles! Ma-riiiia! Ma-riiiia! Ma-riiiia! Jorge! Aa-lee! Come upstairs. Dinner's ready." Michael yelled down the grand staircase that had just been constructed to combine Christy's apartment with Renata's. Tonight, Old-Maria had cooked goat cheese lasagna for the family. It was one of Renata's favorite dishes, even though it was healthy.

Christy was on the phone with Jerome, recalling the latest family drama—one of the girls was suspended for showing up at school yesterday smelling of alcohol. They said they would kick her out next time.

"So which one was it?" Jerome asked.

"I'm not saying. Anyway, it doesn't matter."

"It's that little infidel whose name rhymes with 'valley,' isn't it?"

Christy sighed. "What do *you* think? Anyway, the thing is, I need to resign from the Olympic board. I'll keep doing the mentoring program, but it's obvious I need to pay more attention at home."

"But Christy, the board is the visible position. If you drop out, in six months no one'll remember who you are. My advice is to give up the mentoring. No one cares about that."

Christy scrolled through the plan she had developed for supporting new Olympians. "I care. And anyway, I don't need to be in the limelight anymore." She hoped this was true, feeling a slight twinge of her old ambition. "I have to make my family work, Jerome. Please don't tempt me . . ." Christy rubbed her pregnant belly absentmindedly, sadly letting go of the last thread of glamour that represented her old life.

Jerome hesitated before speaking. "Kiddo, if I had the chance to have something real like you and Michael do, I'd probably do the same."

"Jerome Fudderman? Putting love before money? Am I hearing things?" Christy said in jest.

"You're right. I'm a heartless fuck. Always have been, always will be. Heh-heh-heh."

Christy laughed before saying good-bye, but she was touched. Maybe all the hard-bitten New Yorkers she knew really did want what she had been lucky enough to find. You would certainly never know it by watching them operate. She closed her PowerBook and set it next to the pillow. Mr. Koodles sidled over and curled up like a ball on top of the warm computer. Can I do this? she thought. Be a real mom, from the beginning? I'm already white-knuckling it through Ali's teenage years . . . Renata's manageable, at least so far . . . but a baby, too?

Christy's thoughts were interrupted by the sound of footsteps bounding up the stairs, except for six-year-old Maria, who took each step backward while sitting on her butt, thoroughly mussing up her brand-new Colby uniform.

"Lord have mercy, child," Nectar said. "You're going to ruin your pretty dress. Stand and come upstairs properly, like a lady."

When everyone was situated, Ali said grace. This was Old-Maria's idea. She felt they needed to instill moral values in the children. Christy couldn't agree more.

"Mmm, yummy, this smells so good," Renata said. "Is this the recipe you're selling at Eli's?"

"Yes, except I added extra garlic and shiitake mushrooms," Old-Maria said.

"Next time add even more vegetables, Maria," Michael said. "Christy's eating for two."

Christy looked down in time to see a little elbow or knee gliding across the inside of her stomach. "The baby's having a party in there tonight," she said.

Michael immediately put his hand on Christy's belly and felt, as did Renata. She squealed with delight each time the baby moved.

"Be careful with your drink," Christy said to Renata. Everyone was sitting around her bed and eating from dinner trays. They'd been dining that way for the last month, ever since the doctor ordered Christy off her feet. "Are your rooms clean?" she asked the girls.

"Mine is," Renata said.

"Mine is, too," Ali added.

"No, it's not," Renata tattled.

"Climb out of my butt, Big Mouth," Ali said to her sister.

"Ali," Michael said, "what did we say you were grounded for? Four weeks? Well make that five. We've all had it up to here with your language."

Ali gasped in outrage. "Christy, why did you marry him? Why?"

Christy ignored the remark. "Michael's going downstairs to inspect after dinner. No one gets allowance unless her room is clean."

Ali stood up and excused herself. "I need to go check on something in my room."

Christy smiled. That kid is something else, she thought. But she's better than she used to be . . . if you didn't count yesterday's incident. Maybe when the baby comes, it'll hit her that she's not the center of the universe. "Can you pass the salt?"

"No salt for you, Christy. Remember what the doctor said," Michael said.

"Right."

"Did you hear about Stephanie Rich?" Renata said. "She ran away with that rapper guy."

"Yeah, I heard. Brownie must be beside herself," Christy said, clucking her tongue. She wasn't fond of Brownie, but no mother should have to endure her twelve-year-old running away with a fifteen-year-old rapper, even one with five gold records and four gold teeth.

"Don't even *think* about going on a date," Michael said to Renata.

"Boys gross me out," she assured him.

"Good," he said.

"Too bad Brownie's Golden Latchkey Foundation couldn't have saved Stephanie. They tried, you know." Christy said.

"That is *so* sad," Jorge said.

"Say, Jorge, when'll the crib be ready? We don't have much time," Michael asked, patting Christy's tummy.

"Soon, Mr. Drummond, I promise. I just hired two men to help me with all the projects I'm getting. *¡Caramba!* I can hardly keep up with those Colby parents and their cabinets."

"Jorge, you do great work. What can I tell you? Word gets around. Say, is everyone finished?" Christy asked.

"I'll do it," Young-Mother-Maria said. She started picking up the dishes.

"I think I may need to incorporate soon," Jorge said to no one in particular.

"Did you see the *Journal* yesterday?" Michael asked.

"No, why?"

"There was a follow-up on Galit and the companies that were involved in her blackmailing scheme."

"Did you save it for me? I *have* to read it," Christy said.

"It's at the office. I'll bring it home tomorrow. It said that even though Galit has to serve ten years, she signed a book deal with Random House, and Miramax bought the movie rights to her life story," he said.

"Doesn't that figure?" Christy said. "She practically brought down seven companies and comes out smelling like a rose. Oh, oh, quick, someone grab a towel."

Little-Maria had spilled her milk all over the bed. Old-Maria ran to the bathroom to grab a towel to wipe it up. "Sorry, sorry," the child said, with tears in her eyes.

"That's okay, sweetheart," Christy said, touching her cheek. "Happens to everyone."

"The attorney general says Galit can't keep the money. He considers it the spoils of her crime. She'll have to fight him for it."

"Good! Did they say anything about the securities case against Katherine?"

"Trial starts after the new year."

"That's rough. Alex must be crushed," Christy said.

"No, Alex is doing good," Renata said. "She was just elected president of the student council. Her dad's marrying Emily Osgood's mom."

"That's news. It must be hot off the press," Christy said.

Renata shrugged. "Who wants ice cream?"

"We don't have any, honey," Christy said.

"Don't worry. We do. I'll run down and get it." She raced out the door.

Michael took Christy's hand and squeezed it. "So, will you be okay while I go out?" he asked, putting on his jacket.

"Sure. Where are you going?" Christy asked.

"Beegee, how can you forget? Tuesday's my night to walk the goat."

He kissed her good-bye.

Wife in the Fast Lane

INTRODUCTION

Former Olympic track star Christy Hayes has created a successful sneaker company from the ground up. Apart from being athletic, she's smart, beautiful, and married to a dashing entrepreneur. But when her beloved housekeeper dies and leaves behind her eleven-year-old granddaughter to raise, Christy soon learns the price to be paid for having it all. Though she's far from the mothering type, she tries her best to help the shy young girl acclimate to her new home by becoming like those fabulous city moms she runs into in Barney's or Bergdorf's. She begins by throwing herself headfirst into the treacherous waters of New York City private schools. All the while, trouble is looming on the horizon for her company. Can this two-time Olympic gold-medal winner strike a balance between her hectic career and chaotic home life? Will she create a life for herself that is true (or truer) to the person she really is?

Questions & Topics for Discussion

1. Former Olympian Christy Hayes has turned her athletic expertise into corporate success. In what ways is she a good role model? In what ways could she improve?

2. At their cabin in Aspen, Michael tells Christy "There's *no way* we can take a child, not with our responsibilities and lifestyle. You promised me, Christy. This is the only thing I really asked you for." Is this the real reason Michael keeps his distance from Renata?

3. Although Christy had decided not to have children of her own, she is Renata's godmother, and she decides to adopt her. Why do you think Christy changed her mind? Did she make the right decision? What are the biggest challenges these two face? How did the fact that Christy lost her mother at such a young age affect her ability to mother Renata?

4. If you were in Christy's position, would you have done the same thing? What would you have done differently?

5. Do you think attending a private school like Colby will affect Renata in a positive or negative way?

6. Loving nanny Nectar Freedom tells Christy about the rule of two: "Love, career, children, pick two." Do you agree with her? Is it possible for today's women to have all three? What impediments stand in the way?

7. What do you think of Michael and Christy's relationship? Did you believe him when he denied the alleged affair with Galit?

8. Why do you think Katherine, after years of friendship with Christy, decides to covertly work against her and have her removed as the head of Baby G.?

9. Why is it important to Christy to impress Brownie Rich? Does everyone have a Brownie in his/her life? Do you think Katherine, Galit, and Brownie got their just deserts?

10. What was your first reaction when Renata's relatives arrived from Mexico? Why do you think Renata bonds with Mrs. De Mille?

11. What do Christy and Renata have in common? How does Renata's reading *Harriet the Spy* ultimately help Christy?

12. Did Christy make the right decision by not returning to Baby G.? Why or why not?

13. Were you surprised to discover that Christy is pregnant at the end of the book? How do you think this newly merged family will fare?

14. What factors make someone a "wife in the fast lane"? Do you consider yourself to be one? If yes, do you find this role rewarding?

15. In the past, the "conversation" was about whether or not women could do it all. Could they find balance? Is it time to reframe the question and ask ourselves how can we create lives that are true (or truer) to ourselves? We're so busy living complex lives, but are we fulfilling to do lists or are we doing things that are deeply meaningful to us, things we're passionate about? Is there something you are passionate about that is getting short shrift in your busy life? What would you change if you could? What is stopping you?

A Conversation with Karen Quinn

What inspired you to write *Wife in the Fast Lane*?

I heard an expert on one of the morning shows say that women today can have it all, just not at the same time. You hear that a lot. In my own case, I have a husband, two kids, a career, a home, two cats, and myself to pay attention to. There is nothing I would give up. So I'm doing my best to have it all, and I'm doing it at the same time, and so are my friends. I wanted to write a story about a very accomplished woman struggling with these issues.

So many of your characters have interesting names—Nectar Freedom, Brownie Rich, Galit Portal. Any symbolism behind them?

The names are symbolic, but I didn't realize that when I made them up.

When beginning a novel, do you know the end before you start or do you just write and go where the story leads you?

I usually outline the beginning. I know what I want the story to be about, who the protagonist is, and how I'll get to the central conflict. After that, I go where the story leads me. I never know the ending until I get there.

Christy struggles with raising Renata, running a company, and being a good wife to Michael. How is her plight similar to most of today's modern women? Do you find yourself wearing many hats in your own life?

The only difference between Christy and most other women is that she has more help. On the other hand, she has demands the rest of us don't have, like the requirement for endless personal maintenance and an extensive and chic wardrobe. I'd choose going to my son's Little League game over going shopping or getting my legs waxed any day. Seriously, I do wear many hats and I struggle with finding balance daily. Every woman I know does. I feel lucky in that I'm passionate about the important things in my life. I work hard, but it doesn't feel like it's a sacrifice. It's the details that drive me crazy—errands, bill paying, checkbook balancing, that sort of thing. And computers that crash—don't get me started on that.

Your last novel, *The Ivy Chronicles*, was optioned for film, with Catherine Zeta-Jones slated to star. If *Wife in the Fast Lane* were a film, whom would you cast as Christy?

Sandra Bullock or Julianne Moore would be wonderful.

You have much corporate experience behind you, first as a lawyer, then as an advertising executive, and later you had your own private school admissions business called Smart City Kids. How did you get started in that field? What made you decide to start writing?

One thing just led to another. After I was downsized at American Express, I decided to start Smart City Kids because getting my own children into school in Manhattan had been so painful. I thought, if I can make this easier for other people, there might be an opportunity. After I couldn't take the school admissions business for one more season (you can't imagine the stress!), I realized that I had so many funny stories to tell from the experience that I should try to write a book about it. I had no idea if I could, but I gave it a whirl since writing was a secret fantasy of mine.

Do you have any fun, real-life stories to share about the lengths parents went to for their child to be accepted at a prestigious school?

I have so many. There was once a father who hired an acting coach to work with his four-year-old because he thought his son's personality was so "blah." He hoped acting lessons would help the kid sparkle for his interviews. There was a mother who insisted that I keep tutoring her son on his colors even though the child had fallen asleep in the middle of the lesson. She said, "he'll get it subliminally." There was a little girl who stopped me from tutoring her for her kindergarten admissions test. She said, "Can't you see I'm only four?"

Do you subscribe to Nectar's rule of two?

I believe if you're trying to maintain a loving relationship, raise children, and build a career at the same time, you probably won't be as successful with each as you would be if you were only trying to do two of these things. But that hasn't stopped me from going for all three.

What message would you like readers to take away from *Wife in the Fast Lane*?

Christy ended the book having made choices to put her energy into the things and people she cared most deeply about. As women living in the fast lane, it's crucial for us to stop, reflect, and make sure that our efforts are going toward our life's passions, whatever they are.

Any plans to revisit the characters from *The Ivy Chronicles* or *Wife in the Fast Lane* in future books? What are you working on next?

Both Ivy and Christy have completed the journeys they set out to make. But I sometimes imagine new adventures I could take them on. It would be fun to write a book with Renata as the central character, or Faith (from *The Ivy Chronicles*). I'm working on another book with a strong female protagonist right now. She's getting into all kinds of trouble.

Enhance Your Book Club

1. Christy Hayes, a former Olympic athlete, started her own sneaker company and watched it grow into a hugely successful corporation. For your meeting, why not research other female athletes and see how many turned their athletic success into thriving businesses. *Sports Illustrated's* website is a great place to start: http://sportsillustrated.cnn.com/.

2. If your book club meets for dinner, assign a character to each member and have them bring a dish that their character would make or enjoy. For example, Renata was a fan of her grandmother's casserole and was proficient using Shake 'n Bake. Christy was more into healthy Asian foods, and Brownie would no doubt be a fan of haute cuisine.

3. Learn more about the author Karen Quinn by visiting her official site, www.karenquinn.net/.

Are you living in the fast lane?

Tell us about it for a chance to win cool prizes!

Enter Karen Quinn's *Wife in the Fast Lane* contest or view entries from other readers and vote for your favorite. This is *your* chance to express your own fast-lane truth in whatever media you do it best—video, essay, or a quick one-liner. Visit www.wifeinthefastlane.com **for a full set of rules. No purchase necessary.*** Details are at the site!

*Void where prohibited or otherwise restricted by law. Open to legal residents of the United States (except Puerto Rico), Canada (except Quebec), age 18 or over as of March 15, 2007. Contest begins March 15, 2007 and ends May 15, 2007.
Sponsor: Karen Quinn

Praise for *Wife in the Fast Lane*

"Karen Quinn does it again! *Wife in the Fast Lane* is funny, entertaining, sweet, and smart. Every woman who has ever had to juggle kids, work, and marriage (or even two of the three!) will relate to its wise and witty voice."
— Leslie Schnur, author of *The Dog Walker*

"*Wife in the Fast Lane* is a hysterical journey up and down both corporate and romantic chutes and ladders—and a delicious, tart, juicy, slice of Big Apple life."
— Jill Kargman, author of *Momzillas* and
coauthor of *The Right Address*

Praise for *The Ivy Chronicles*

"[A] ferociously funny tale."
— *Us Weekly*

"Entertaining . . . picks up where *The Nanny Diaries* left off."
— *New York Post*

"Hilarious."
— *Child* magazine

"A guilty pleasure worth indulging."
— *Booklist*

"Tales of Manhattan's elite trying to get their tots into private schools is sure to make you smirk condescendingly. . . . *The Ivy Chronicles* delivers."
— *Boston Herald*

"If you think you may be a neurotic parent, read this and feel sane."
— Allison Pearson, author of *I Don't Know How She Does It*